AN UNHOLY TRINITY
Vol. I

C. Bailey-Bacchus
Terry Grimwood
Vanessa Hawkins

A HellBound Books Publishing LLC Book
Houston TX

HellBound Books Publishing

A HellBound Books LLC Publication

www.hellboundbookspublishing.com

Printed in the United States of America

Foreword

Well, here we are, dear reader, and may we wish you the very warmest of welcomes to this, the first of our *An Unholy Trinity* series.

It is always a nerve-wracking occasion for any publisher, the trying out of a brand-new concept – but, just the very fact that you are reading this, means that our experiment to bring outstanding talent to the great reading public has been a resounding success!

To bring together three such exceptional authors, in novella form, in a single book, is a brave move to be sure, especially so when our aim is to showcase this intrepid trio to as wide an audience as is possible. We just know that you will fall in love with them, as their stories are phenomenal, their words engaging and ultimately spine-chilling!

We are confident that you will enjoy this new concept of ours, and hope that you tell all of your fellow lovers of horror and all things dark And, please be sure to not only look out for more volumes of *An Unholy Trinity,* but to check beneath your bed before you go to sleep…

…because you never do know, do you?

HellBound Books Publishing 2018

Introducing the Trinity...

THE REMNANT
By
C. Bailey-Bacchus

Dedication:

For my husband Garry, who believed I could.
For my mother Dianne, who said I would.
For my friend Tom, who made sure I did.

PROLOGUE

A burning pain radiated across Bianca's chest. Her hand rushed to the source. It was her mother's necklace. Her breath quickened at the thought her mother's hatred was burning her through it. She tore it from her neck and looked at it through her windswept hair. It had been handed from mother to daughter for at least four generations. Except, it hadn't been handed to Bianca. Like most things she owned, she had simply taken it.

She climbed to the top of a large boulder and stared out at the heaving expanse of water. *Disgusting thief, give it back!* Hearing her mother's words made Bianca's stomach lurch. She was only trying the necklace on. But, as usual, her mother had assumed the worse.

Angry tears blurred the pearl droplet as she rolled it between her fingers. She wiped her eyes to see it one last time. Then leant forward and watched a colourless wave sweep across the pebbles. As it broke into a churning white spray below, she let the necklace slip from her fingers. "You want it? Go and get it," she whispered.

Bianca detested everything. This town, her school, but most of all, her mother. A ripple of frustration coursed through her. Not even the tepid air created by clouds swallowing the sun could cool her temper. As the beach dimmed, Bianca was sure the darkness within her was seeping into the world and steering the elements.

It was certainly powerful enough. It had started as a voice—for when she couldn't muster one—the moments when her anger and fear overwhelmed her. But it had become something else. Something stronger. It had manifested itself in the pit of her stomach. And as she lost sight of the necklace, the darkness retched and contorted within, begging for release. She took a deep breath in a vain attempt to subdue it.

Bianca urged herself to take solace in the fact she would be sixteen next year. She pictured herself leaving it all behind without a backwards glance. *Should I just go now?* She craned her neck towards the top of the precipice. There, she was sure to be released from the stagnancy of the trap created by the cove. Given that fleeing into the sea wasn't an option, there was only one way out of the cove. The zigzagging steps carved into the rock face.

"Bianca, please get down from there," Mrs. Stanton called.

Bianca's frustration bloomed into anger. It wasn't incited by her teacher's words, but by the glare Mrs. Stanton gave her as she crawled down. It was the way Mrs. Stanton always looked at her. As though Bianca was some foul thing stuck to the bottom of her shoe.

"Right. Gather around," Mrs. Stanton ushered the class towards her. "Has everyone measured how long it took their float to travel ten metres?"

"I have!" Cara waved her hand in the air.

Bloody suck up! That hand spent so much time in the air. Surely, it would be easier to leave it there.

"Yes, Miss." The class groaned in unison.

"And when we collate our data, we will have a good idea of the beach's… what?"

Cara was bouncing up and down. Mrs. Stanton pointed to her.

"Longshore drift," Cara said.

Bianca moved towards her best friend, Grace. "I can't stand that Cara," she whispered.

Grace nodded. "She was slagging you off earlier. Called you a chav."

"What?" Bianca's fury shifted to Cara. She winced at the little half-moons her nails had left in her palm. *How dare she?* Cara's rich parents didn't make her better than Bianca.

"Bianca, seeing as you have so much to say, perhaps you would like to answer Mrs. Stanton's question." Mr Hardy's words focused everyone's attention on Bianca. "What were some of the obstacles that the experiment faced today?" he added, knowing that she hadn't heard the question.

"I don't know," Bianca said.

"Duh! You were just sitting on one," Cara scoffed.

The class erupted into laughter. It wasn't funny. But that did nothing to ease the sting of having her inadequacies publicly exposed. Bianca stifled an outburst.

"Are you okay?" Grace asked when Mrs. Stanton continued.

"Yes," Bianca said flatly. She didn't need the pity. It made the darkness writhe.

"Right, are there any questions before we go?" Mr Hardy said.

Cara opened her mouth, and Bianca instinctively

knew this would delay their departure. The darkness leapt, and Bianca's scowl caught Cara's eye. For all her intelligence and self-entitled swagger, Cara faltered. Encouraged by her success, Bianca raised a finger to her mouth. Cara clamped her mouth shut. The forming tears went some way to pacify the darkness. But it wanted more — full restitution for Bianca's humiliation.

Grace's slow smile excited Bianca and told her she wasn't alone in her hatred. Nor was she alone in feeling that weakness should be punished. Bianca nodded in response, a silent agreement that there was work to be done.

Mrs. Stanton moved forward. "Follow Mr Hardy," she said.

As they did so, Grace brushed Bianca's arm. "What are you going to do about Cara?" she asked.

"Teach her a lesson, I'll scare the shit out of her," Bianca said.

The thought of terrifying Cara added to Bianca's excitement. Though she keenly anticipated the moment, she didn't know if it would be enough. She tried to make sense of her messy thoughts. Because she was well off, Cara seemed to think she could call her a chav. In fact, she had probably not wanted for anything her life. Not like Bianca, who had never owned a thing of worth.

Then there was the fact she was a teacher's pet. Always answering questions, getting awards, and new shoes. *You're jealous!* The darkness had proffered an opinion without permission. *Could it be that?* Could all this hatred stem from the fact Cara's life was the antithesis of defeat and waste that was Bianca's? *No, she's a spoilt little girl, who needs to understand life in the real world isn't like that!* The darkness responded.

"What a big baby!" Grace laughed. "She was about to cry when you told her to shut up."

"But look at her now. I want to slap that smug grin

off her face!" Bianca said.

"We'll have to get her away from them first."

Grace was right. Bianca had to find a way to separate Cara from their teachers. She hurried on, alert for an opportunity, spurred by the fact they were fast running out of pebble-strewn beach in which to catch her. Then, as though Bianca had been made a conciliatory offering, a fight broke out behind them.

"Boys, stop that!" Mrs. Stanton and Mr Hardy rushed passed Bianca.

In a move so swift that Cara couldn't anticipate it, Bianca dragged her behind a boulder. There was no room left for error and no time for Cara to scream. No lioness, hungry for flesh, could have been more efficient. But now, with Cara pinned to the ground and her pleading muffled, Bianca was afraid.

You are doing the right thing, the darkness soothed. *There is nothing to fear*. Events had been set in motion. Bianca must eradicate her own weakness. This was no time for compassion. There was a lesson to be taught.

Cara's stifled yelps rose and fell between Bianca's fingers, then rose and fell again. They fell into sync with the ebb and flow of the roaring sea. The natural elements were colluding with Bianca, giving her cover, and soon her reservations faded.

As the encroaching tide built, so did her excitement. She took in short, sharp breaths. The sea and her exhilaration reached their crescendo, and, as the wave impacted with the rock, Bianca lifted Cara's head and let it crash to the ground. For a few peaceful moments, Cara fell silent before her sobs were again fighting against Bianca's hands.

"Shut up, you dumb bitch! Oh, you think you're so good, don't you?" Bianca said.

Bianca squeezed Cara's face, and the beach brightened. A sign that she was on the right path. She turned to Grace. But there was no slow smile, no smile at all. She saw Grace's attention was elsewhere. She focused the red syrup dripping from her fingers. *Is she bleeding?* Bianca had not seen Grace cut herself. Then in the confusion, Bianca felt a trickle slick her own fingers. It was Cara's blood.

"What on Earth do you think you're doing?" Mrs. Stanton shouted.

Then the clouds seemed to engulf the sun again, and the colour seeped from the beach. The sea pitched, this time without the desire to peak again.

Bianca stood. There was nothing to say as Mrs. Stanton pushed her aside to attend to Cara.

Bianca was suffused with sound, a voice, its provenance within. *You are a useless waste of space.* Her mother's words were bitter and icy. Bianca had gone too far. It was then, she knew something was coming to an end, she just didn't know what.

The ability to understand what was happening was beyond her, so she didn't try. She stood still. As Grace rose, her eyes never left her hands. *Why isn't it the silence worrying her?*

Bianca had no time to reason. People were gathering. She saw nothing of their faces, felt none of their concern. Their faces blurred, and they jittered in a way that made her head ache.

"Where is Mr Hardy?" Mrs. Stanton said.

"He's near the top with the rest of the class," someone behind said.

"All of you follow him up. Tell him what happened. Slowly, stick to the side in singles file and be careful," Mrs. Stanton said.

Then, in the commotion, the sound of pebbles mashing together at her feet made Bianca's heart thud. It was Cara swaying and stumbling upwards. Her dull eyes rolled, and a whimper passed her lips. Mrs. Stanton propped Cara up and led her forward.

Expecting to see flayed skin and bone, Bianca felt confused disappointment when there was only glistening blood binding Cara's hair.

"Are you okay?" Mrs. Stanton said, with a gentle tone Bianca had never heard before. She brushed away the hair to get a better look at Cara's wound. "It's just a little cut, it's not bleeding too badly, but I'll bandage it. She turned to Bianca and Grace. "You two. Start making your way up,"

Bianca made no attempt to move. The cove was no longer oppressive. She felt safe within its walls.

"Did you hear me?" Mrs. Stanton demanded.

Though she tenderly bandaged, the kindness in her voice was gone. Her nose flared, and her cheeks reddened. The darkness stirred. *You're fucked now!* It giggled. Bianca turned away. Grace was already making her way towards the cliff. *When did she go? And the others? Where were the blurred faces?* She looked up to see the last of her classmates reach the cliff top.

"Bianca! Do you hear me?" Mrs. Stanton guided Cara forward.

Bianca limply followed. "Yeah."

The events were expected, the reaction was not. She was carrying out a service. She was not the only one who despised Cara and her superiority. Who wouldn't agree she ought to be brought down a peg or two?

The disdain was unexpected. She had anticipated her teacher's reverence. A knowing nod, thanks for silencing the tormenting questions. She had expected an apology from Cara. Validation that she was right.

Bianca should be adored for her actions instead of being loathed for them. But there were no thanks. No praise for a job well done.

She strained to hear the conspiring whispers ahead.

"She's crazy, I didn't do anything," Cara whispered

to Mrs. Stanton.

Bianca heard enough over the crashing waves to rouse the darkness. Any feeling of regret dissipated. As she watched Cara's over-the-top frailty, the darkness stretched and flexed its muscles for the onslaught. Her only regret now would be not to act.

Bianca battled against her gritted teeth. "I'm going to beat the shit out of you."

"Don't you dare!" Mrs. Stanton said. "I don't want to hear another word from you. Walk in front. "

Yet another look of disgust from Mrs. Stanton forced the darkness and its rot to Bianca's mouth. "Fuck off!"

"I beg your pardon?" The colour drained from Mrs. Stanton's face.

Bianca and had no time to attend to questions. She stared at Cara's widening smile. "You don't actually think you've won, do you?" she said. But Cara seemed to find confidence rather than fear.

Bianca had crossed a line from which she could not return. Suspension definitely, perhaps even expulsion, but it all equated to the same thing. Bianca had nothing to lose. The darkness crouched in preparation for the strike. "You haven't won!"

Mrs. Stanton stepped towards her. "Bianca, this isn't a game, you—"

"Fuck off!" The darkness struck. "I swear to God I'll…" Words with enough venom failed her.

"Enough!" Mrs. Stanton said.

Bianca ignored her. "What's wrong, Cara? Too scared to talk? Do you need your precious Miss to speak for you?"

"Stop…" Cara began.

"Stop." Bianca mimicked her whine. "Stop or what?"

Mrs. Stanton huffed. "Right, if you say just one more threatening word, you'll be in very serious trouble. I'll be forced to call the police."

Bianca turned to Cara. Her voice broke under the weight of her unmitigated rage. "I'll make you pay."

Inside, somewhere deep, she relinquished control to the darkness. It moved forward from its prison. Then it clenched her fists and bared her teeth. Rabid and ready, Bianca lunged forward, pushed Mrs. Stanton to the ground and turned to Cara. "Run."

"Bianca…please—"

"Run!"

No further encouragement was required. Cara's skittish steps across the pebbles excited Bianca into pursuit. Cara, despite her injuries, was more adept at crossing them than Bianca. She was already metres ahead and negotiating the first step. Fueled by the darkness, Bianca pressed on.

Cara rounded the first turn, and as she ran above, Bianca jumped. Her fingers grazed Cara's shoe, the near miss sent spasms of both excitement and rage within her. The darkness had Cara's scent. The delicate fragrance of feebleness and atrophy goaded it on.

At the next turn, Cara struggled, her legs were failing her. Bianca's own thighs were beginning to throb in protest. But the darkness had a will far greater than hers and did not allow her to slow. When Cara stumbled at the last turn, Bianca threw herself forward and clasped onto her ankle. They fell to the ground with a sickening thud. Bianca couldn't stand. Her feet could not gain traction against the loose scree.

An explosion of pain blistered her skull. She instinctively let go of Cara to clutch her head. *Oh God! What happened? Did she kick me? Did that stupid bitch actually muster the gall to fight back?*

Nauseated by her momentary lapse of judgement, Bianca's stomach ached to expel its contents. The reverberating pain brought her to the verge of unconsciousness. She heard her mother's voice again, recorded in high fidelity, available for playback without request. *Can't you do anything right?*

Her heart beat the last ticks of a time bomb. It exploded in a brilliant flash of violent, uncontrollable anger. She surged like the roaring tide below. In the disorder, she registered the urgent footsteps ahead had stopped.

Grace blocked Cara's path. Fear glued Grace's eyes wide and kept her feet still.

Better that than running. Bianca's stomach heaved, unaccustomed to the limits she had pushed herself. But her convulsing muscles were grateful for respite.

"Mr Hardy!" Cara shouted into the void for help. Her voice was barely audible over the discordant sounds of the sea and screeching gulls.

"Grab her!" Bianca said.

Grace sprung to life as though grateful for instruction. She pulled Cara's arms behind her, and like the simpering idiot she was, Cara sobbed, and her knees buckled.

Bianca, or rather the darkness within her, was the mistress of events again. She moved forward. Much like a swan, she was serene above the surface and raging beneath it.

"Please!" Cara begged. "Why are you doing this to me?"

Bianca smiled. *Is she trying to appeal to my better nature? Surely, she should know I don't have one!* This product of excess and indulgence was a quivering mass of flesh. *Why doesn't she see what she is?* A moment of realisation! No one had told her. Not even her mother. Not in the way that Bianca's had told her daughter anyway. The inarticulacy coating her tongue melted away.

"Because you walk around here like you're better than everyone, but you're not, and it's time you learnt that!"

"I don't..."

Self-righteous satisfaction swelled, and as Bianca crept on, Cara's pleading cries gave the sensation potency. *She will finally understand!* Bianca's hand snapped back and landed an instructive lesson against Cara's cheek.

Elation coursed through Bianca's veins. She broke into uncontrolled laughter as Cara winced and wheezed in pain. Nothing—not even her stinging hand—could diminish her boundless joy.

Then, amid the tumultuous cries, Mrs. Stanton appeared, heaving for air, her face crimson from exhaustion and, Bianca supposed, anger.

Grace, despite not receiving instruction to do so, let go of Cara. She fell to the ground but just as quickly found her feet again. Mrs. Stanton took advantage of the distraction to assert her dominance.

"Everyone move slowly up these stairs now!"

The world went black. Bianca screeched into the emptiness. There was the sensation that her hands were fighting, no, squeezing for her life. The images came slowly as the desperation quickened. Her body stiffened, and it was only then she realised what she was grasping onto. Mrs. Stanton's face was near purple. Her blue eyes faded into a sea of white, and her neck throbbed beneath Bianca fingers.

The world fell on its side. Bianca let go, and all thought was eclipsed by searing pain. There was a vacuous pause before she was able to follow events.

Cara had pushed them to the ground and was now crouched beside Mrs. Stanton in an attempt to soothe her rasping breaths.

Bianca looked to Grace for help. Terror had swallowed everything but Grace's ability to blink.

"John," Mrs. Stanton pleaded. She stumbled to her

feet and clutched her throat. "You arrogant little pig, you'll leave with the police." All sense of professionalism had left her. With the pretence discarded, the monster beneath was callous and cold. Mrs. Stanton's shadow loomed over her with a hunger that devoured Bianca's anger.

Bianca looked to the darkness, but it was despairing, lost in hesitation. She finally understood what was coming to an end. It was her life as she knew it. She closed her eyes and yearned for a precious moment of silence to think. There were so many hateful voices. Some echoed through the cove, some vibrated from within.

Enough! An eruption of frustration propelled Bianca's legs forward. A frightful shriek lacerated her ear drums. *Is that me? Is it the darkness?*

Silence. Her eyes opened to the empty grey sky. Mrs. Stanton was gone.

She forced herself up on her elbows. Furious scrambling drew her attention away from her aching head.

"What have you done?" Grace shrieked as she ran to edge.

On some level, though she didn't give the thought time to form, she knew what she had done. Could there really be any question? She looked again to the darkness, but it had abandoned her, its rotten deceit left her mind racing.

Though Bianca rushed towards them, time seem to slow. The air was viscous, and every movement was as arduous as wading through water. Grace and Cara were sobbing at the edge, no doubt, too afraid to look down. When she reached them, they took in the wretched sight together.

At first sight, Mrs. Stanton was gently sprawled across the ground as though she had fallen into a deep slumber. Then maroon seeped across her ivory shirt, and she saw that Mrs. Stanton was not gently sprawled. She was angular—broken and contorted. And Bianca knew that it wasn't sleep that had come over her, it was death.

Bianca stood. And finding its footing again, so did the darkness. She took a clump of Cara's hair and pulled. "She slipped whilst we walked. If you say otherwise, Grace and I will say you're lying. Won't we, Grace?" she said.

ONE

Oh, I'm dreading this," Grace said as Elliot started the car. This party was not going to be fun. She couldn't abide Elliot's brother, his dull colleagues, or his wittering girlfriend for that matter.

"We have to go. My little brother only turns thirty once." He tilted his head towards her. "I promise we won't stay late. We've got to prepare for the exhibition in the morning."

"He and his friends are just so boring. All they do is talk about work."

"I love those crazy stories. Max told me about this guy they arrested last week. He was running through a supermarket naked!"

She smiled, and though the smile didn't reach her eyes, he didn't notice. "I don't know. There's something about being around them that makes me feel awkward."

"Darling, do you have a criminal past that you haven't informed me of?" he said with mock surprise.

Her laugh was too loud and hollow to maintain. "Of course not! I just meant they're judgmental. I worry about saying the wrong thing."

"Max loves you. What could you possibly say wrong?" he said, turning to face her fully and brushing the hair from her cheek.

"I don't know. I'm just being silly."

Much like his brother, Elliot had the ability to bore beneath the surface and see a person's emotional core. In that moment, as he cast his eyes over her, she felt him trying to reach the place where she kept her most despicable secrets. He would not reach it though. She had buried them so deep, not even her own subconscious could find them all.

He relented. "It will be fun. Okay?"

"Okay."

"Let's go, radio on or off?"

***

The party was still at the starting line. Grace hated this part, where well-dressed strangers observed each other. Hoping to catch the eye of another with a thirst for more than alcohol — awkward conversation.

Heads twitched towards them as they walked into the hallway. Though she recognised many of them, there was no spark of recognition in response. It appeared their memories of previous parties had been erased, most likely by the time the ensuing hangovers had cleared.

"We'll stick together." Elliot smiled.

But she was too lost in awkwardness to find comfort in his words. Every limb was aching to run. As the thought crossed her mind, she found herself in the embrace of Alice, Max's girlfriend.

Alice peered down to assess her. Grace's victory curls, vintage tea dress, and scarlet lips would fall into

Alice's 'Rockabilly Chic' category. But from Alice's disingenuous smile every time she said it, Grace assumed she meant 'Old-fashioned Chic'. The thought that not all women were concerned with 'this season's must have' seemed to escape Alice.

"You look nice." Alice's unconvincing tone categorised Grace as Old-fashioned Chic. "I'm so glad you came. You can save me from the dull work conversations." Her dreamy drawl suggested she had enjoyed a glass, or two, of wine before the guests had arrived.

Grace stepped back and took her in. Alice looked stunning. Her red dress clung to her statuesque curves, while waves of brunette hair fell gently at her cheek. But there was no need to comment, Grace was certain she was aware of her own beauty, and if not, the men (including Elliot) salivating at her side were informing her.

"How are you?" Grace said.

"Brilliant!" Max appeared from nowhere and staggered to hug them. He had also clearly imbibed a glass or two.

"Happy Birthday, Bro! Here." Elliot struggled from his brother's embrace to hand him his present.

"Thanks!"

"I'll take that." Alice whipped away his gift. "Cake and then presents."

"I'm not a child, Alice," he said, too late. She was already making her way to the dining room.

"How is work?" Elliot said.

Grace's temper frayed. He hadn't even waited for her to unfasten her coat before initiating what would likely be a tirade about restrictive policing policies.

"Tough." Max turned to Grace. "Have you heard about the missing girl in Shoreton?"

The thought of having to discuss that abhorrent place,

and the horror that it bought with it, sickened her. "Yes, I saw it on the news."

"Only five years old." He shook his head. "We might be drafted in to help with the search, that beach she went missing from, isn't that where your teacher had that accident—"

"No talking about work!" Alice reappeared and held her hands out for their coats. However, the relief her interruption brought was short-lived. Alice turned her attention to Elliot and Max. "You two go and get us drinks."

"Okay." Elliot dutifully followed Max, shrugging with shame as Grace's glare screamed, *so much for sticking together*.

"Oh! There is someone I want you to meet." Alice said.

Grace internalised her exasperation. "Who?" Her mind created images of brunette Barbie's blonde counterpart. An evening talking about marketing trends and nail polish shades —oh joy!

"A new friend from work. She just said she's also from Shoreton. You might know her."

Grace hoped sincerely that she didn't. The constant reminders of that hellhole were becoming all too frequent. She was beginning to believe that she had offended some perverse higher power who, in response, was orchestrating events around Shoreton as punishment.

But Alice had no time for procrastination. She had taken Grace's hand. The insistent pulling towards the living room put Grace in mind of Alice's namesake. A petulant child best suited to play in her imaginary wonderland.

"There she is." Alice pointed obtusely towards the twenty or so guests. "Cara!"

Grace stopped dead. *It can't be.* But as the woman,

hunched in defeat, politely excused her way through the huddle, Grace's heart missed its rhythm. There was no doubt that the podgy frame squeezed into a black dress belonged to Cara Porter.

"Grace?" Cara seemed to shrink further into her crooked shape. She too had been caught unaware.

"Oh great, you do know each other," Alice said.

"Yes—" Cara started.

"Yes," Grace interrupted. "We were in the same year at school, but we didn't really know each other." She fought to hide her mortification. "How are you?"

Cara's cheeks flushed. "Fine. How are you?"

"Fine."

"Is everything okay?" Alice said as she looked from one to the other. Beneath the beauty and scatter-brained chattering, she was far shrewder than Grace had given her credit for.

"Of course," Grace said. Though, even she had to admit, not convincingly. "I'm just going to check on where Elliot is with the drinks."

"I'll go. I need to hang up your coats anyway. You two catch up," Alice said.

The crowd parted and allowed Alice to go before Grace could object. She stared into the empty space that Alice had occupied. Internally cursing Elliot for insisting she come and praying that when she finally turned back around, Cara had sloped back to the huddle in the corner.

No such luck. Cara was waiting close, as if keen to converse. Though sixteen years had passed since she had last seen Cara, the blank expression with jittery eye contact had not changed a bit. Cara would not dare bring up the past. Grace steeled herself. She would only need to engage in the merest of pleasantries before Alice would permit her to leave Cara.

"So, you also work in marketing?" Grace said.

"Oh no. I'm the accountant."

"You always were clever." Grace's smile was so weak, her lips didn't even part. "Are you married?"

"No, I'm single." Cara exhaled her long held breath and smiled. "How about you? What do you do?"

"My husband and I own the art gallery in town. He's the art aficionado, and I run the business side of things."

"Oh," Cara said, awkwardly ending the conversation.

Grace surreptitiously watched the group chatting in the corner, and, for what would be the first, and certainly the last time, she yearned to be with them. As she was about to excuse herself, Cara cleared her throat.

"Grace…" Every movement, from the straightening of her glasses and the cupping of her arm, was carried out with a jarring inelegance. Grace realised she had made a gross underestimation and with that surrendered to despair.

"Don't," Grace said.

Unheeded, Cara cleared her throat again. "With Shoreton being in the news, I've been thinking a lot about what happened, then seeing you here —"

"Is nothing more than a coincidence," Grace finished the sentence on Cara's behalf.

"We shouldn't have lied," Cara said suddenly, and, as it had been the case more often than not, tears began to well in her eyes.

"But we did!" Grace lowered her voice. "I don't spend time thinking about it anymore. It gets you nowhere. Nothing we do or say will change what happened." Grace gave her a hushing glare, but she didn't abide by it.

"A murderer walked free," Cara whispered.

"Do you ever see Bianca?"

"No."

"Me either. That psycho is probably in prison right now."

"But Mrs. Stanton's family deserves the truth."

"They would have mourned her loss and moved on. This will only open old wounds. Besides, even if someone was prepared to listen, there is no evidence. It's just our word against hers. Think about our own lives and families, what this could do to them."

"But—"

"But nothing, Cara! We agreed to keep our silence, and that's what we'll do!"

The others finally returned in deep fits of laughter. Elliot gave her a glass of red wine and a flirty wink. Once again, he seemed too self-involved to notice that she had not returned the customary smile.

"So, this is your old school friend?" Elliot said.

"Yes, this is Cara. Cara, this is my husband, Elliot."

"Alice tells me you're new to town," he said.

Cara forced a smile. "Yes, I've been here two weeks. I moved for the job."

"Well, Alice and Max can't make it, but we're hosting a party tomorrow to celebrate a new exhibition by this brilliant Spanish artist. We insist you come, don't we, Grace?"

"Yes, you must," Grace said. It was the last thing she wanted, but Elliot had boxed her into a corner. "I'm just going to pop outside for a bit of fresh air."

"Are you alright?" Elliott said worriedly.

"Yes, just a little hot." But Grace didn't go outside. She went to the kitchen, downing her wine on the way, and poured herself a large whisky.

This confrontation with the past had been inevitable. She had expected it at some point but just hadn't been able to prepare for it. Her mind raced at a savage pace as she tried to keep the memories repressed.

Grace had forgotten the last time she had even thought about Cara, or the day itself for that matter. Time heals all wounds. But the passing minutes had ripped hers open. It gaped and tore with every moment. It oozed and bled into everything. No kind word, or hand holding, or promise of silence was a tourniquet fit to staunch it.

Something must be done. But what? Cara would be motivated by the worst thing of all, righteous indignation. There would be no logical argument to dissuade her. She took a sip of whiskey. Her bitter tongue soured its sweetness, and suddenly she was overcome by the need to cry.

At least I'm ahead of it. Had Cara decided to spill her rotten guts without her knowledge, she would be facing questions by the police now. There was still time to dissuade her. She would try to do that now, and if she couldn't—her stomach churned as the loathsome thought came to her —she could deny all knowledge and paint Cara as an attention-seeking liar.

What would everyone say if they knew the truth? They would no longer see Grace, just the fifteen-year-old girl she once was. She had played that day over countless times. *Why didn't I stop Bianca? Why didn't I let Cara reach Mr Hardy? Fear!* And as she thought about it, that same deep fear began to course through her.

How could she explain her silence as anything other than an attempt to keep her involvement secret? That her reputation and future meant more to her than ensuring a murderer went to prison. *I could still go to prison.* Obstructing the course of justice was a crime, and that would probably be one of a myriad of charges. *Elliot would never trust me again.*

She looked to the amber liquid — a medicinal elixir. But the medicine didn't work. As the whiskey left its trail of warmth, her memory languished in violent blood red tides.

TWO

Guilt eases through stages, much like grief, until any wrongdoing is cleansed.

Any attempt at denial is quickly quashed. Having had blood literally on your hands will do that.

But being a victim of circumstance incites a welcome anger. It perpetually justifies and motivates. But even anger can only beat its fists for so long, before thoughts of the task ahead are tiring to the point of despair.

Surely, there is someone up there who is prepared to bargain and take away the despair.

Agitation and sleeping problems are just two of the pieces that form a jigsaw of depression. When the puzzle is complete and seen in its harrowing entirety, some are afforded a gift of sorts.

Acceptance. It happens with the sudden and striking realisation that the past cannot be changed.

With that, Bianca set her focus on motherhood to rectify her mistakes.

***

Cara worked to tease her hair into something close to presentable. She had been surprised to receive email confirmation of Grace's invitation this morning. *This isn't a practical joke, is it? Will I find myself doused in pig's blood?* She shook off the thought. *Alice would not have only given her my email address but forced her to send it too.*

Without question, her approach had been rash. The sudden sight of Grace after all those years had not permitted her time to filter her thoughts. Perhaps Grace felt guilt about her part in it all. That was forgivable, if she had changed her mind and was finished with the lies. Despite Grace's objections to the contrary, their meeting was not a coincidence. Grace could not fight fate.

Mrs. Stanton's brutal end seldom left Cara's thoughts. In hindsight, she hadn't even tried to dismiss them. *How can I forsake the woman who had given her life to protect me?* No, she did not deserve to break free of the melancholy, so she treasured it, kept it close.

Cara deeply regretted the lie. *Mrs. Stanton fell by accident.* Those five words were a weed-like lie she should have rooted out. Left unattended, the weed had grown strong and invaded every part of her life. Yet, she regretted more the pain thrust upon Mrs. Stanton's parents. At the funeral, having insisted she attend, it seemed to Cara they would never get over their grief. Not even the tributes, or talk of their daughter's wonderful attributes, could soothe them.

There would be questions, no doubt. Especially for Grace. Hopefully, people would understand the torturous power they had surrendered to. Bianca Baker—the thought of her still sent Cara's stomach into violent spasms. But she was no longer that weak girl. She had built strength of her own and now felt an unquenchable need to correct her error. If she were able to satisfy that need, it would surely result in a confrontation. The thought of having to see Bianca again, even if it was only in a court room, started the spasms again.

In the sixteen years and nine months since Mrs. Stanton had died, she had created countless scenarios to put an end to it all. At first, her imagination sugar-coated them.

She'll be saggy and aged beyond her years. She'll gladly throw herself on the mercy of the court. Then fall to her knees and beg for my forgiveness.

There was little time to enjoy that thought, all too soon Cara's subconscious urged for realism.

Bianca will stand tall with her head held high. She'll speak with her condescending lilt and manipulate with her complacent smile. She'll make me look like a delusional psycho.

As that scenario played out to Bianca's malicious cackle, Cara's burgeoning tears were absolute proof she needed Grace. No matter how many times she pictured Bianca in a weakened state, she knew deep down it wouldn't be the case. Bianca would make counter-accusations, and only one thing, the testimony of Bianca's former friend, whose brother-in-law was also a police officer, would have them take her seriously.

Enough with the self-pity. It wasn't seeing Grace again that had prompted her need to tell the truth. Nor was it the crime scene constantly flashing across the television because of the missing girl. This had been a long time coming. She wiped away the mascara that had run and then smoothed her creased blouse. The doleful exterior gave way to confidence. She may be rash, but stupid she was not. Grace's invitation meant she was open to conversation. Cara would take advantage of that.

She packed her handbag and when she looked up, saw her tears had become a smile. A smile she had lost years ago. She would no longer think about when she lost it. She would focus on keeping it.

***

Cara detested parking in the multi-storey car park, particularly at night. But there was no other safe option in the centre of town. As she locked the car, Cara tried to convince herself everything was okay. She had planned what she was going to say and rehearsed it repeatedly. But as she ran through it once more, she sighed. The words seemed hollow and trite.

Exhausted to tears, she wiped her eyes and walked towards the staircase. Cara's resonating footsteps quickened as she realised that she was alone amongst the cars. Her hand rested on the chrome hand pad but stopped shy of pushing the door.

Beyond the thick slab of wood leading to the staircase, there was a rumble.

The rumble wasn't tempestuous, not like the cacophony caused by the waves thrashing against those jagged rocks at Shoreton's shoreline. This rumble was like distant thunder, the warning of an encroaching storm. Loud enough that it caused Cara's fingers to momentarily hover, but too quiet for her to be sure that she'd heard anything at all.

She gently pushed the door and looked beyond the small crack. It gave just enough leeway for her to see the fluorescent orange glow of the empty stairwell. She pushed it further and convinced herself that with the absence of a source, that rumble had been in her head.

As she took tentative steps inside, the light flickered

with a static hiss, her fluttering heart urged her to turn and reach for the door, but her movements were too slow, her fingers grazed the door as it swung to a reverberating close.

Cara choked. The urine-scented air made her throat close, and her lungs clung to her breath in protest. Heat flared across her face as she became aware she was trapped in a concrete box. She fumbled at the door, suddenly unable to comprehend whether she should push or pull. She spun on her heels, desperate to find a way out as the sickly orange beams flashed across the oppressive walls.

Then the light stopped flickering.

She steeled herself. The exit was just one floor below, and it was silly to feel fear because an old strip light was faulty. But she did feel fear. The sort of fear conjured by ghost stories before bedtime. The kind of fear created when you anticipate the end of the story.

Cara edged to the top of stairs, careful to take hold of the banister should the light falter again. She stumbled down the first stretch of stairs and rounded the corner to the next. Then stopped suddenly as though her concrete surroundings had absorbed her and turned her to stone.

Something caught her eye on the landing below. She struggled to define it. A thick black liquid, like motor oil, was slathered across the grey concrete. Her knees unlocked, and she stumbled backwards. Upon closer inspection, the mass had form. More like a huddle of clothes with matted hair. Perhaps it was a sleeping vagrant? She looked yearningly at the exit beside it. Then something caught her eye, a near imperceptible judder in her peripheral vision.

Despite her quickening heartbeat, she paused to take a closer look. It occurred to her that someone could have fallen, because of that flickering light, and may need help.

"Hello?" She had intended that her voice be clear and authoritative, but instead it was muffled and meek.

She bent forward to investigate, but there was no sound or movement in response. The light above fizzled and dimmed. Sensing that it might flicker again—or worse yet, fail completely, Cara turned back to get help.

A pitiful whimper stopped her. She ventured a few steps further than she had before. "Hello! Are you alright?"

This time, she received a reaction. The huddled mass writhed its way into the space beneath the staircase. Dread pinned her to the wall. "Do you need help?" It momentarily crossed her mind that she was the one in need of help.

Carefully, Cara began to slide up the stairs. Her eyes never wavered from the landing. Her back never left the wall.

Seized by the urge to run, she turned and immediately fell against the stairs with a nauseating thud. For a moment, between heartbeats, nothing happened. Then pain radiated across Cara's left leg. Her stomach churned as spots of blood developed in her trouser at the knee.

In the disorientation of it all, Cara cast her eyes once again to the landing below and wrinkled her nose, uncertain as to whether she had seen anything more than a shadow.

Though feeling more than a little sorry for herself, she tried to stand and quickly realised why she had tripped. Her right trouser leg was snagged on the metal tread of the step. She tugged at her trouser, but the splinter would not release her. Too tired to bend down and save her already blood-stained trousers, she took a deep breath and with a swift kick tore herself free.

Cara looked up and released a throat-scorching scream.

In an instant, she took in the horrid sight. The mass was no longer hiding. It was a woman sheathed in black. The first thing that registered in Cara's mind was the woman's skin. It was like cracked porcelain, pallid and etched with otherworldly green veins. Not a woman, but a creature. Its black eyes sat deep and heavy within dark circles. It moved closer. Its eyes darted over Cara like a surveying hawk. As it squared up to her, Cara felt a spark of recognition, but it couldn't be. *Mrs. Stanton?*

There was something of the woman she once knew there. It was the line of her nose, or perhaps it was the angle of her chin. This thing was not the woman, but a remnant of her. Something left over when Emma Stanton moved from this world to the next. Terror shackled Cara to the wall as the creature approached. The scent of rotting meat made her stomach wretch. Her heart thumped, and her breath quickened, but the only movement Cara could make was to turn away and shut her eyes. She broke down into hefty sobs as the creature's icy breath stung her cheek.

"I will tell the truth," Cara cried.

The creature's laboured exhalation was the only response.

A cold, emotionless thought entered Cara's mind, as though it had been whispered on the creature's breath. *I'm going to die.* In that moment Cara could do little else but agree. She resigned herself to that terrible fact, and her body braced itself.

"I'm so sorry," she whimpered. She buried her head into the rough concrete. The icy breath grew closer and closer. Cara fell into its rhythm. Ice… nothing…ice… nothing… she anticipated the ice, but it didn't come.

Cara finally allowed her eyes to open and peered up and down the empty stairwell. She slid to the stair before relief became panic, and she reached for the banister to pull herself up. The light hissed again, and somehow, she knew it signaled the creature's presence.

Cara mustered all her strength to hobble down the last few steps and speed through the door. Her eyes struggled to adjust to the white glow of the streetlight, but in anticipation of the creature they never left the open door. Not even when her flailing legs bought her crashing to the ground.

****

The torment of planning the exhibition had paid off. The catering had arrived on time. The champagne was flowing. The area's best and brightest art connoisseurs were in attendance. Their arrogance made Grace smile. Each attempt by one to surpass another's expertise drove sales upward.

"Isn't that your friend?"

Grace followed Elliot's eye line to the door. Startled murmurs rose above the chatter as the crowd seemed to recoil in disgust.

Cara moved through them like a crazed woman. Her eyes were puffy with tears, her clothes bloodied and torn. As Cara came careening towards her, Grace was seized with a powerless anger.

"What happened?" Grace asked her.

"We have to tell the truth." Cara huffed. "Mrs. Stanton's death wasn't an accident!"

Grace felt the first of what would surely be an onslaught of accusatory glares. "What is she talking about?" Elliot said.

"I…I don't know," Grace said.

Cara's mouth gaped. "Please, Grace! You know that Bianca killed her, we have to tell the truth."

There her sentence hung. The truth: wrapped in the ravings of what appeared to be a lunatic. Grace's cheeks were aflame.

"I'm sorry, sweetie. I have no idea what you're talking about. Sit down… did you fall? Hit your head?" Grace said.

THREE

Cara avoided Grace's eye. Grace always seemed so confused when she looked at her. As if it were a constant surprise that someone so pathetic had not been put out of their misery. It was always visible. Even beneath the mock concern she was exhibiting.

"Elliot, will you put some ice in a bag and get Cara a glass of water?" Grace waited for his departure before leaning towards Cara. "Not another word."

Cara's despair begun anew. Again, her actions were rash, and, had she not been blindsided by panic, she would have considered her approach. She felt like a fool. If there was any doubt that she wasn't, it was abolished by the disapproving crowd that had gathered at her side. The smiles plastered over disgust and conspiratorial whispers caused her to hang her head and shrink from their scrutiny. Had she been capable of leaving, she would have. But there was security to be had amongst the connivers.

So much vagueness in her pounding head, until she closed her eyes, for then she saw the creature in glorious Technicolor. The creature was real, not even the scornful crowd could dissuade her. But as she nursed the golf ball sized lump expanding on her knee, she began to question herself. *How could it have been real? It's finally happened.* The past, that she had so consciously buried, had unconsciously driven her to madness. With that thought she began to sob and then shrank from Grace's half-hearted caress of her shoulder.

With the self-recrimination done, Cara turned her attention to Grace's cowardice. She was only thinking about herself. That was why she refused to leave Cara's side. *She doesn't care. She's just worried I'll tell them everything.* Cara's skin was hot in a flash. She moved her feet to make her last stand. But the rest of her body wouldn't comply. *They'll laugh, call me crazy.*

It all came so easy to Grace. Cara looked up at her as she instructed a waitress to keep the drinks flowing. Grace looked like a Hollywood movie star. Long waves of raven hair fell against her flawless caramel skin. Cara looked at her ruined trousers and bet herself that Grace's long black gown cost more than her entire wardrobe.

It was obvious the lie had not affected Grace's life at all, for it included wealth, security and a handsome husband. Cara's long held belief that Grace had been under Bianca's control was wrong. She was just as vicious and callous as her friend. But what made Grace worse was she chose to be like that.

"Do you think you can drive?" Grace said.

Cara took this as her cue to leave. But Elliot would have none of it. He had returned with ice and insisted Cara rest in his office until he could take her home. Cara was sure she saw a look of umbrage cross Grace's face when he insisted that she attend to their guests. But as

Cara looked back to verify, it had become concern.

***

Grace had fallen into a state of intense awareness, a state in which every utterance, every drink that she held to lips conveyed, with a little whisper, that Cara was about to ruin her life. She circled the gathering with a counterfeit smile to placate their guests. But eventually her worries over what Cara was saying lead her to she and Elliot's private washroom.

It was the only place remotely close to silent. Grace found herself washing her hands over and over again. Uttering profanities, she was finally able to convince herself that her hands were clean. As she dried them, she pressed her head against the cool tiles, desperate to feel something outside of herself.

The air grew stagnant, too thick to inhale. She choked as she moved to escape it, but as her fingers neared the lock, the light faltered. She shook her head, dizzied by the intermittent presence of light, and nauseated by the hiss it brought with it. Upon finding the lock, her fingers floundered, unable to muster the coordination or strength to turn it.

The light failed. Grace blinked in the darkness, momentarily unsure if it was the light, or in fact her eyes had ceased to work. She turned to the window, and, as the silver-blue moonlight seeped into the room, she repeatedly flicked the light switch, to no avail.

The hair on her arms rose, as the stagnant air grew icy. That feeling was gone in moments as the white heat of desperation burned throughout her. Her fingers, already panging with defeat, seemed to grow fatigued by each attempt to turn the lock.

What was that? Movement in the corner stilled her endeavour. Long shadows crept across the floor like a cluster of spiders. Grace huddled against the wall as though it could protect her. Her mind raced to save her dignity before chastising herself. *Surely, only a child is frightened of shadows.*

She searched at the window for their source. An old weather-stripped tree oscillated in the wind. She returned to the shadows on the floor, finding their source was not as reassuring as she had hoped.

The tree's silhouetted branches held her attention. Goaded by the wind, they lurched back and forth like a metronome. And inevitably, its shadow echoed the movement at her feet. But now, the shadow seemed less spiderlike and more like long, reaching arms. Her knees quivered, and her mouth dried. The shadow's limbs crept forward one by one, in juddering succession. *Go!* Her body would not comply with her pleading. Instead, she followed the shadow that darkened every crevice of the tiles as it approached. It stopped. Just two tiles away from her feet. Then it retreated backward in a large, sweeping motion.

Like a hunting wolf with its prey in sight, the shadow prowled silently towards Grace again. Her legs would not submit to her control. A hungry and cruel terror devoured her. She clung to her breath as though it might be her last. She focused on the tile the shadow had reached before it retreated last time. *It won't pass that.*

Against her better judgement, her eyes left the tile and moved to the jittering mass of black. This time, it seemed like an insatiable creature. It came on its hands and knees. The edges like gnarling fingers, clawing their way forward. It reached the tile that signaled the point of no return. Time seemed to slow, and the shadow lingered for a moment. Then it inched forward.

The harsh timbre of the wind coursed through the room like a symphony chasing its crescendo. "Please!" Grace begged her legs to move. But like the Shadow, they were perfectly still. She did the only thing she could and looked to the window. The tree was upright, no longer in the grip of the wind. But its shadow remained frozen in its downward arch.

Finally, her limbs relented. One foot stumbled towards the door. The other one moved to join it, but the shadow lurched forward. It twisted itself like a noose around Grace's ankle. A weak yelp of disbelief passed her lips. Then it pulled. Grace tumbled so quickly, there was no sensation of falling. She crumpled and writhed against the floor in an effort to break free. Her finger tips bruised as they tried to find traction. But the shadow's grasp was as cold as steel against her skin and just as strong.

"Let go!" Grace didn't know to whom or what she pleaded, but she did so for her life.

"Do what you should have." The voice seemingly rose from nowhere. Had she given birth to it? She couldn't be sure. "Do what you should have." The voice croaked and heaved. Her face numbed. Grace's eyes flickered like a child fighting sleep.

Black silence. The panic and fear left her. *Am I dead? Is this what it's like to die? You are forsaken in the darkness, forgotten and alone.* Unease pricked at the base of her spine. Though somewhat distant, there was a sound. At first, she thought it was the voice. *Do what I should have?* But there was no time to ponder. This sound was different. Its ebb and flow familiar. She fell under the power and pacification of the rumbling sea. But within that, there was something else— an echo — of urgent cries and hurried footsteps. It was the soundtrack of a long-forgotten nightmare.

Then, so slowly that she wasn't sure at first, a pinprick of light pierced the black. And as the solitary distant star began to expand, the sound diminished. She was staring up at a glistening ball. The bulb above emitted light as though it had never stopped. She instantly recoiled. Her hand flailed at her ankle as though the noose remained, but the light had chased all the shadows away.

She staggered up and found the lock. It finally relented, and the door swung open.

"Damn it," she sobbed.

***

Cara's limbs ached with fatigue. Her mind was losing the battle with regret, but she would not let it. Not tonight. Letting it win was like letting Grace win, and that could not happen.

As she floundered to sit upright, her hands slipped against the papers on the desk, and she winced. The small slit on her thumb released a trickle of blood. Unconsciously, she placed it in her mouth and looked to the offending page.   Soft green eyes peeked through blonde curls. Cara picked up the newspaper *Little Magda Ford still missing.*

A shadow crossed the page, and she was suddenly aware that Elliot had returned with fresh ice. She put down the paper and pressed the soothing bag against her knee.

"What you said…" Elliot had started a sentence he couldn't finish.

"It's true," Cara replied, trying to prevent the words from instigating her tears again.

"I don't understand," Elliot said. He directed the words to her but was staring at the door, no doubt worried about Grace making an appearance.

"Grace and her friend Bianca used to… bully me." Her shame-filled answer was greeted with skepticism.

His brow furrowed, and his mouth formed soundless words. "I know Grace can be willful, but she's not a bully."

Willful? The word was an affront. To categorise what Grace had done as mere stubbornness ignited outrage. "Oh. You… you just… have no idea." Having spent years quelling it, Cara did not express her anger well. He had no time to react as every detail of Emma Stanton's death etched on her memory spilled from her lips.

Elliot became unsteady. He clung to the desk as it guided him to the chair opposite. "What did Grace say when Bianca threatened you?" he said. "She agreed to say you were lying if you told the truth?"

"She is saying that I'm lying, you just heard her!" she said, only mildly aware that she was playing the role of the deranged maniac as cast by Grace

There was no response forthcoming, and as the anger dissipated, she felt anxious.

"This thing you saw in the car park," he said, clearly attempting to show her the ridiculous element of the plot, "it was the ghost of your teacher?"

There was no time to respond. The door flew open, and Grace crossed the threshold. Her serene façade crumbled before them.

"Were you just in the washroom?" Grace said. Her tone was strange, simultaneously resolute and weak.

It took a moment for Cara to realise that the question had been directed to her. "No," she said.

"Are you alright?" Elliot asked her. But his words didn't reach Grace.

"You were, weren't you?" The words sounded more like pleading than a question. "No, I was alone, the door was locked," she muttered. "It is you though!" Her brow smoothed as she reached her conclusion. "You are dredging up the past. It's making my mind…" She stopped abruptly.

"You saw her, didn't you?" All residue of pain left Cara as she stood.

"No," Grace whispered, shaking her head. "No!" she said more forcefully, perhaps trying to convince herself too. "The light stopped working." Confusion swept across her face. "I'm just tired, it freaked me out."

"What on Earth is going on?" Elliot said.

There was no reply. Cara took this cue to move around the desk and towards Grace. Grace immediately looked to her feet, preventing any accidental eye contact.

"I should go," Cara said simply, and this time no one tried to stop her. As she pulled the door in behind her, she heard a whisper.

"What did she say?"

"Nothing," Elliot said as the handle clicked up.

Cara smiled. For once, there was someone who didn't explicitly trust Grace.

***

Grace rolled onto her back. There was no choice but to relent. Sleep was not even remotely imminent. Her mind was playing tricks—that was all there was to that. But she struggled to convince her subconscious of this fact. What she had seen and heard brought about a fear that would not allow her to rest, let alone sleep.

Then, there was Elliot, quiet and distant, like he was locked within himself. Worse, it was by choice. He was locking her out, rather than locking himself in. In the dimness, his dark auburn hair seemed black. She focused on it, trying to work out what he knew, despite his assurances otherwise. Grace knew that Cara had told him something.

As if her mind had called out to his, waking him from his easy sleep, he shuffled and cleared his throat. "Grace," he croaked.

"Yes."

"If there is any truth to this, you should tell Max everything." His sleepiness made the statement sound mundane. It was anything but.

"What?"

But he said nothing more. Grace suspected he knew she had heard him. She stared at the back of his head again, a void in the gloom, still and waiting. Her muscles flexed with apprehension.

"What did Cara tell you?"

"Everything."

"Everything?"

"It was an odd thing. It didn't occur to me until now." He rolled over to face her, and she cowered as the glint of his eyes fell upon her. Not quite glinting — possibly glaring. "Her story was so detailed, with nuances that rang true about you. What have you ever said? No more than a sentence about your teacher falling in an accident. I thought perhaps you had been traumatised and couldn't talk about it."

Grace could no longer bear the secrecy afforded him by the darkness. She rose up and switched on the lamp.

He didn't flinch. His eyes needed no time to adjust to the light. "But tonight, I heard true trauma." The sentence had been spoken, not as the relaying of a story, but as an accusation.

"Well, until you tell me what she said, I can't defend myself. But if it is anything other than Mrs. Stanton's death was an accident, none of it was true," she said with a finality that signaled it was the end of the conversation.

Grace now craved the secrecy of darkness for herself. She switched off the light, lay flat, and pulled the covers up in one fell swoop. He didn't believe her. Of that, she had no doubt. Instead he had soaked up every whining word from Cara. *But she told him the truth.* She quietened her objections. *That's not the point.* She was his wife, and he had not even considered that she was telling the truth.

How could he possibly think telling Max would be a good idea? Did he wish to see her languishing in prison? *What good could come of it?* Surely, it would be the end of the gallery. Who would trust their livelihood with a deceiver?

Now he lay beside her. No longer breathing the slow breaths of sleep. "Is it true she was pushed?" he asked.

"No, it was an accident," her voice crackled as she fought the tears of frustration.

"Why is Cara saying this?"

"I don't know." Only a half lie; she truly didn't know why, after all these years, she was saying this. "How could you believe I would do that? Why would I invite her tonight if I thought she was planning to say this? What must everyone think?"

He wrapped an arm around her and nuzzled her neck. "Okay," he whispered unconvincingly. Then, "You know a few of them thought it was part of the installation." She felt him smile against her neck. "The detail of her story though, if it isn't true, the madness required to dream that up..." Words appeared to fail him. "Maybe you should stay away from her."

"It is made up, and I intend to stay away," she said.

"How are you feeling?"

"What?" she said, confused.

"After what happened in the washroom. Actually, what did happen?"

"I told you, the light flickered, and it freaked me out," she said with faux sleepiness.

"Okay," he said, even less convincingly than the last time. "Get some rest."

Elliot's grip loosened, and as he drifted off; he rolled over, taking all the warmth with him. Cara would not be so easily swayed. Grace began to wonder if she would she tell Alice everything. In fact, why hadn't she already? *She needs me.* She knew it, and now Grace knew it.   Cara's story was too easily dismissed otherwise.

Grace scoffed at Cara's ineptitude, and then herself for not seeing it sooner. Well, she could be just as insistent with the protection of the lie. In those early days, when she had been excused from school for the remaining month before the summer break, she had learned to do so. The constant worry of her parents, doctor and counselor had spurred her to. They believed that her abject sorrow was hiding something deeper, so she worked hard to prove otherwise.

There is nothing I can do to change it. That had been her mantra. Repeating it had not only given her strength but added truth to the lie. The repeating thought calmed her, and even now took away the worry and desolation. Whatever it took to maintain the lie, she would do it without question.

How can I stop Cara from confessing? It had been easier then. Back when everyone saw Grace as Bianca's sidekick. Bianca herself had believed it was the case, but it wasn't, not really. Bianca was a loaded gun, and all Grace had to do was point her in the right direction. Then with the hand of friendship, pull Bianca aside and whisper puerile conspiracies originating from those that had upset Grace. With the trigger pulled, the bullet flew, and Bianca would demolish everything and anyone in her path.

Something unpleasant rose from her stomach. *Is that what I did the day Mrs. Stanton died? Pointed the gun at Cara?*   More than once her name had made the selection. But she couldn't (or wouldn't) remember if it had that day. She put it aside. *There is nothing I can do to change it.*

She focused on now and realised that there would be

only be one thing that could stop Cara from taking this further. Bianca Baker. Grace snuggled against Elliot, and once again able to sap up his warmth, the thought of losing it forever was reason enough to point her gun.

FOUR

A piercing ring rose in the darkness. Bianca's eyes blinked open, dry and unfocused. As she rolled over on the bed, her stomach convulsed and expelled a flow of burning bile. It rose, reaching her breast, then scorched its way back down.

The room developed in full colour like a hazy Polaroid from the grey. She searched for the source of the sound. There was no movement in the room, aside from the clumsy dance of dust motes in the shard of light that defied the curtains. She was drawn to the source on her bedside table by ear, not eye. It was her phone. She rejected the unknown caller.

With stiff hands, she reached to the floor and clasped at the bottle. It slipped from her grasp. She lunged for it again, more forcefully than she had intended, and painfully crashed to the floor. She sat up and caught her hideous image in the full-length mirror.

Her limbs shook partly with dehydration, partly with

disgust, as she raised her hand to the hair that had become matted. Sunken eyes stared at her through sallowness, lifeless and unrecognisable. Crumbling under the scrutiny of her own gaze, she turned away from the mirror. *I need a drink.*

Her fingers rifled across the litter of empty cigarette and food packets until they felt cold glass. Her thirst was left unquenched by the paltry drop of bargain vodka that fell to her tongue. The bottle dropped into her lap, and for a moment she sat in the detritus, still and without purpose; or at least no purpose she could determine.

These moments were the worst—that sorrowful moment between one drink and the next. But she took solace in the fact they never lasted long. And with that, her mind euphorically recalled dulled senses and subdued thoughts.

Things had not changed. Not as she hoped. Her euphoria was poisoned by the thought. No matter how much she devoted herself to motherhood, it did nothing to make things right. Perhaps naming her daughter Emma was the problem.

At the time, it had seemed the proper recompense. She had replaced the Emma she had taken, effectively redressing the balance. But instead, her daughter was a constant reminder of that moment she had succumbed to the darkness and lost herself.

On unsteady feet, she reached for the pair of jeans huddled on the floor. Without care for cleanliness, she pulled them on, opened the door and then listened outside Emma's room. There was no sound. Convinced her daughter was still in the reverie of her dreams, she went to the bathroom.

The flush of the toilet thundered against her ears. Hands shaking, Bianca clung to the sink to steady herself. The bile rose again, more slowly this time, and she swallowed great gulps of air to settle it. A splash of cold water to the face helped return her to even keel. Then, she rifled through her pockets in the vain hope she would find funds for her much-needed remedy.

"Shit." Her pockets came up empty. A sharp prickle crossed her forehead. Sobriety was near, that prickle was the hangover coiling like a serpent in preparation to strike.

The cycle began again. The pity and dejection of the hangover fed the darkness. It forced her barriers down with a torrent of images. She saw hair bound by blood, pure white bone penetrating skin. But worse of all, she saw someone else's blood trickle along her own fingers. Overwhelmed by the flow, her thoughts turned to the macabre. She hobbled from regret for taking Emma Stanton's life to those of ending it all. Until all sorrows were drowned by the first intoxicant she was able to happen upon.

Didn't I take a purse yesterday? The memory hid behind frosted glass. As she pressed for the picture to clear, it was a feeling rather than an image that came forth — exuberance. The aspiration of the vodka haze, where those who had mouldered in hopelessness might find some semblance of consolation. Quickly the exuberance dissolved into frustration.

At the till, she had come up short, eyes had rolled, and noses were upturned. Snapshots flickered with pockets of sound. There was an attempt to barter, what had been her bargaining chip? The frustration became humiliation— she had offered herself.

She touched the place on her arm where the hand of coercion had rested.

'Rip-off merchant,' she shouted as she was forced out. Then she was lost in obscurity for a moment. Blurred faces and singing birds. A woman so laden with bursting shopping bags, she hadn't noticed that she had missed her handbag. Bianca had watched her purse fall to the ground. There had been no recourse other than to take what she needed.

With the promise of further funds, it became easy to put aside thoughts of how she had attained them. Her vigour renewed, she rushed back to her room.

On the floor, no doubt where the purse was hidden, she turned over dropped clothes and refuse. As she began to worry that her dreams and drunken memories had merged, she found it. A waft of leather rose as she rushed to open it and pull out three crisp twenty-pound notes. She took one, enough to feed Emma, and yes, enough to cure what ailed her.

She replaced the other notes and put the purse into her bedside cabinet. *She who hides her spoils away, has spoils for drink another day.* She smiled. Ordinarily, wit was not her strength.

Bianca would be back before Emma woke. She would return better able to deal with the world and make her a proper cooked breakfast. She pushed the note into her pocket and picked up her phone. A rare thing, the flashing light signalled the arrival of a voicemail message. Unsure of whether she had enough credit to hear it, she tried anyway.

"Bianca, it's Grace Peters, ah … Grace Reed. I got your number from your sister… I don't know how to tell you this, so I'm just going to say it. Cara intends to tell the police the truth about Mrs. Stanton's death. Call me back."

Bianca had always scoffed when people said they felt numb after some horrific incident. They should feel something — scared, sad, distressed, disgusted, or depressed. But now she understood that when those intense emotions came in quick succession — when they don't abate and each new one compounds itself with the others, you just don't have the capacity feel anything anymore. You feel numb.

She had not been foolish enough to think it wouldn't happen. No, there had been no naive belief that she had gotten away with murder.

It didn't matter that she hadn't meant to kill Mrs. Stanton, that it was in fact the darkness committing the act. Her mind was mother to the darkness. It had been in its infancy then. A toddler, unable to control its tantrum, it had kicked out in frustration.

Having reached adulthood, Bianca had better control of it. But it was still there, a rampant surge beneath the surface. Bianca was engulfed in its riptide, and it had twisted and turned her with a battering force, until she could not even discern which way was up.

She may not have been imprisoned physically, but she was in a prison of her own construct. Bianca had been locked in a singular moment, until her mind had been devoured by insanity, turning to alcohol and drugs to mute the recollection of memories. She had considered it her sentence, far worse than prison, and perhaps it was.

Bianca had imagined that incarceration would bring relief; no need to look over her shoulder, no need to worry. She welcomed the prospect of mercy from her suffering. For the years and months that separated the day of Mrs. Stanton's death to this had certainly never given her that.

Perhaps release would come from handing herself in. The darkness heard that thought. It woke from its slumber. A bitter laugh rose from within. *What about Emma?* It was right. *What would happen to her?* Bianca knew better than anyone what being neglected by your mother did to a girl. She imagined a growing darkness within her daughter.

Her heart began a dreadful beat, harder and harder it thumped, until it was reverberating in her ears. She looked down, half expecting to see each beat. Should she achieve escape, she had nothing to fund a new life with. Alone, she might survive. But forcing Emma to depart again from the world she knew, without funds to provide for new identities, would condemn her to a life of absolute poverty.

This life was meagre, but there was no profit from living it without Emma. She was an anchor for Bianca's sanity. Emma provided the grounding for her to become something of worth.

She would have to fight.

Bianca returned to Emma's door and slowly opened it. She crept into the dimness to watch her daughter sleep. Emma began to fuss and frown. She muttered incoherently. Bianca knelt beside her and gently stroked her forehead.

"It's alright, sweetheart, Mummy's here," she whispered.

With every rhythmic caress, Bianca seemed to take her elsewhere, to a place of safety and quiet, where eventually she lost her rising consciousness to sleep. Emma's frown relaxed, and she was soon breathing softly again.

Bianca took the small rag doll from the shelf and neatly arranged her red woollen hair. She knew they were old fashioned, but the little doll reminded her of the only one that she had ever owned. Bianca slipped it beneath Emma's arm, and she snuggled into to the doll. Bianca watched her little princess for a moment more to make sure she was alright, then left.

She could not run with her daughter, nor could she leave her behind. She steeled herself for the fight. The darkness laughed again. It was savagery, it was relentless, and it was all she needed. When she finally released it, the darkness would demolish Cara and the past.

FIVE

Grace switched off the car engine and arranged the bouquet of white daisies. They effused the scent of summer but brought none of its warmth. Today, they seemed apt. She had a vague memory that daisies represented friendship. But as she thought about it, perhaps it was a fresh start. With them she would give the appearance of the former, and hope for the latter.

When Cara said she lived near the harbour, Grace had pictured her in one of those Victorian terraces, scurrying around the warren of tiny interlocking rooms. She never would have guessed that Cara lived in a leafy Avenue with sparsely laid out semi-detached houses set back from the road by large gardens.

Is this the right address? She double-checked the text message Cara had sent. Twenty Camberwell Avenue. *This is the place. Who knew small business accounting paid so well?* She looked up to the scarlet front door that clashed with the mid-blue garage door. She cringed. *So garish!* It didn't compare to the three-story detached splendour that was Grace's house. She took a deep breath and got out of the car.

As she neared the tree-lined path to number twenty, her pace slowed. A raucous wind coursed through the trees, and those rust coloured leaves that were able to resist it filled the silence like a rustling choir. Unheeded, she ignored their whispered warnings and reached Cara's door.

The doorbell rang. Grace's mouth dried. *This is a bad idea.* As she was about to retreat, the door swung open.

"Hi Grace. Come in." Cara's face blossomed with joy at the sight of the flowers. "Are those for me?"

As Grace crossed the threshold, she implemented her scheme. It was going to be easier than she thought. Cara had one of those old-fashioned locks with a snib button. She would just have to push it up unseen, and the door could be closed without the lock engaging.

"Yes." She forced the bouquet into Cara's hands to obscure her view of the lock. "An apology. I should have been more understanding." Grace raised her voice to cover the clink as she forced the snib up. "For the way I handled things." She pushed the door in and hoped it would keep the façade of closure.

Grace was sliding into regret. She was breathing so hastily, she was sure that Cara had noticed. But she hadn't. Instead, she smiled widely and pointed Grace towards the living room. "Do you want a coffee?"

Grace hesitated. She glanced at her watch. *Ten to four.* Coffee would kill some time. "Yes, please."

Cara gave her a friendly smile and headed to the kitchen.

That smile made Grace's heart sink. She remained in the hallway. Once Cara was out of view, she went back to the front door. Her fingers rested on the snib. She almost released lock. But her desperation to stop Cara from going to the police betrayed her. She left the snib up and scuttled into the living room.

The room was as mismatched as Cara's navy blouse and bottle-green trousers. The garish pink wallpaper clashed with the blue carpet, and not one item of furniture belonged with another. Grace sat on the burgundy sofa and reassured herself the whole mess would be over soon.

Cara returned with the coffee. She gave Grace a jittery smile that flashed her uneven teeth.

Clearly uncomfortable with painful silences, Cara began naming the biscuits as she placed the plate on the table. Ordinarily, Grace would tire quickly of this wittering. However, she had already decided to keep the conversation light.

The plot had required her to surround herself with stone, and she couldn't allow her empathy towards Cara erode it. Talk of biscuits, the weather, and the traffic would suffice. Grace checked her watch, just mere minutes to wait.

"After I came rampaging into the gallery, I didn't think you would come." Cara said.

You mean after you spilled your guts to my husband. Grace quelled the urge to bring that up. "Well, you were right. We need to talk." Grace picked up the coffee and took a sip. "I love this blend. I adore strong coffee," she said, trying to steer the conversation to the trivial. It worked.

"Oh, I picked it up when I was in Rome." Cara launched into a detailed account of the coffee shop where she had purchased it.

Grace smiled spuriously as Cara talked about intricacies of the blend. She concluded that time had slowed. She glanced at the mantelpiece clock as it ticked towards four. *Finally!* Grace counted every shrill peal of the bell. One—her smiled waned. Two—her mouth dried. Three—her knees began to quiver. Four—she held her breath.

Nothing happened. *Has the plan changed?* Grace exhaled. It was too soon to worry. She was quickly proved right.

"Did you feel that?" Cara asked as she wiggled her fingers in the air, her expression was a mesh of confusion and concern. "There's a cold draft."

It's finally happening. Elephantine footsteps boomed from behind the closed door.

"Hello!" Bianca flung the door open. "Now, how could you have a Shoreton High School reunion without me?" She tripped over her feet towards the coffee table. "Shall I help myself to biscuits?"

After their phone call, Grace had worried Bianca would turn up inebriated. But her state was much worse than she could have imagined. The woman looked like she had been dragged through a hedge backwards. Her hair had been pulled into a messy bun on top of her head. Her baby pink jogging bottoms were pockmarked with cigarette burns and stains, whilst the rest of her was drowning in an oversized black puffer jacket. The only thing worse than her clothes was the smell she brought with her: A mingling of stale cigarettes, alcohol, and vomit.

"You're drunk." Grace said.

"Nope! Just really, really hungover."

Cara recoiled. She instinctively turned to her betrayer. "Grace. You called her?"

"You're so hell-bent on confessing, Cara. Not only do you want to go to the police, you told my husband everything. It isn't fair. This doesn't just affect you," Grace said.

"No, it doesn't, does it?" Bianca's fingers waggled over the biscuits whilst she made her selection.

Cara nervously scratched her forearm. "What did you

expect, Grace? That you'd call Bianca and she'd bully me into submission? I saw Mrs. Stanton in that stairwell. I saw her! This has to end now."

"You saw her in the stairwell?" Bianca turned to Grace. "What the hell is she talking about?" She selected a custard cream and shoved it into her mouth.

"Later," Grace whispered.

Cara stood and walked to the door. "Get out." Her voice broke under the weight of fear.

Pitying Cara's meekness, Grace stood too. "We need to talk about this properly. Sit down, Bianca," Grace said firmly.

As Bianca brushed past Grace, she caught her self-satisfied smile. Bianca chose the seat opposite Cara's. Grace waited for Cara to follow her gesture to sit and then sat on the sofa between them.

The room cooled, but the sensation was no longer like a draft. It was more like a cloud had obscured the sun, absorbing its beams and leaving Grace yearning for its warmth. She had suspected there was cruelty to this plot, and, as she met Cara's watery eyes, her suspicions were confirmed.

Grace steeled herself for the battle and knew, without doubt, that Bianca would bring her victory. But at what cost? There would be no mercy. Grace would have to dismiss her compassion, her morals, and offer indifference. The victory would be a Pyrrhic one. There was a price to pay for an easy life.

"I don't want this, I want you to go," Cara said with a little more force.

Neither woman obeyed. Grace turned to her gun, Bianca was aimed. Grace winced in anticipation of the bang.

"I didn't mean to kick her. I regret every moment of that day," Bianca said.

Grace's eyes strayed momentarily to Cara, whose

eyebrows rose skeptically. Grace felt her own face slacken. She had no idea how to react. This was the last thing she had expected.

"It really was an accident. I have played that moment over and over again. My eyes were closed, and I was trying to think, but there was just so much noise. I just kicked out in frustration... I am so sorry for what happened," Bianca said.

"Then you'll go to the police?" Cara asked.

"No," Bianca said.

Grace swallowed deeply, for a moment she had worried there truly had been a change of plan.

"I thought about it many times, but I have a daughter, and no one to take care of her. I don't want her to suffer because of me," Bianca said.

"Sympathy for the Devil," Cara said, her trembling hands betrayed the boldness of her statement. But that was the only sign of weakness. She sat straight-backed and looked Bianca directly in the eye.

Grace shuffled uncomfortably. *What is she thinking?* A breathless silence settled. She prayed this was the moment Bianca ejected the defeated attitude in a blinding explosion.

"I understand..." Bianca began, "but for the sake of my daughter, I have to ask you not to go to the police."

"Ask me?" Cara said. Her eyes took on the gentle sheen of confusion.

"Yes," Bianca said flatly. "I am asking you."

"What is this actually about?" Cara said to Grace, her obstinate tone finally vocalising her disbelief.

"We all have something to lose if we confess, and nothing to gain," Grace said.

Cara's trembling stopped. "Nothing to gain? What about justice?" Cara ventured. Her eyes shifted to Bianca.

"What about it?" Bianca said.

"What about it?" Cara said incredulously. Her face was pallid and glossy, like she had succumbed to the flu. Her eyes portrayed the disgust that her gaping mouth could not convey. She cupped her hands around her mouth as though terrified she might regret any words that escaped.

"Yeah. What about it?" Bianca said again, with anger reminiscent of the fifteen-year-old girl they feared.

"This isn't going to get us anywhere," Grace said.

"You're right," Cara said as she stood, "I think you should both leave."

"Cara," Grace pleaded, "we need to talk about this." Behind her, she heard the chair heave as Bianca lifted her weight from it.

This isn't working. She just won't listen. Grace had to think of a way to get them to agree to continue their silence.

She looked to Bianca, who simply put her hands into her coat pocket.

"I urge you to reconsider." Her tone was one of hateful promise.

Cara pointed to the hallway. "Leave." She turned to look at them. If the firmness of her tone wasn't confirmation of her resolution, her glare was unequivocal proof.

Somehow their roles had been reversed. Grace felt herself wilting and then relenting to Cara. She walked towards the door, pausing to speak. But anticipating this, Cara raised her hand.

"I'm sorry. I've made my decision," Cara said.

Grace shook her head and crossed the threshold to the hallway.

"I'm sorry that you feel that way," Bianca said.

An unbroken, coarse wheeze ended the conversation. Grace turned before she had time to think better of it. Over Bianca's shoulder, she could only see Cara's wild, motionless eyes. *Oh god! She's punched her!* Bianca pulled back her arm and made another three sharp blows to Cara's side.

"Bianca!" Grace shouted.

Cara was released. She doddered back against the honey pine door, then painted a streak of red down it as she slunk to the floor.

It was only then that Grace saw the thick blood oozing down the shaft of the knife in Bianca's hand. It pooled at the end of the glistening steel until the oversaturated tip shed droplets. Grace covered her ears for fear of the sound when they exploded on the ground.

"What have you done?" she said, rushing to her knees to cover Cara's spurting wounds.

"Déjà vu," Bianca muttered ineptly.

It only took the span of Cara's laboured exhalation, before she had pushed Grace's hand aside and reached for the handle above her. Roaring with pain, she pulled herself up. For one grave moment, no one moved. Then Cara pounced toward Bianca with a primal rage.

She clawed where her hands landed on Bianca face. The act was thoughtless but not fruitless, for her sheer force slammed Bianca's head against the wall. Grace pulled her legs up to avoid Bianca's crashing body. Cara clung from one stair baluster to the next towards the front door. Her first attempt to open it failed. Her fingers barely grazed the lock as she swayed.

Bianca moved swiftly, she was on her feet, knife in hand, and upon Cara in one sweeping move. She took a clump of Cara's hair and swung her around to face Grace. "I gave her a chance." She pulled Cara's head back and exposed her throbbing neck.

"Let her go," Grace begged.

Bianca held the knife up high for Cara to see and then plunged it into her neck and drew it across her throat. The wound opened like a widening smile, then gurgled and spewed its gore and blood onto Cara's front. Cara faded. Bianca staggered under Cara's growing flaccidity. She let her body crash to the floor.

Too late to benefit her, Grace shut her eyes. A powerful shriek tore through her head, rendering her incapable of rational thought.

"Be quiet! I need to think," Bianca shouted.

Grace fell silent but not on command. She had no more energy to lend to the scream.

"You've got blood on your hands," Bianca said matter-of-factly.

"You did this!" Grace said, sickened by her gall.

"No, you really have blood on your hands."

Grace looked down and realised that it was the drying blood making her fingers stiff. She retched at the sight as she scrambled into the kitchen, unable to process anything beyond her next action. Grace turned on the tap and doused her hands in washing up liquid. Then watched the pink effervescence circle the drain. She stepped back as Bianca approached.

Bianca was methodical. First, she rinsed the knife, and then her hands. She took the tea towel hanging on the side and wiped both dry, then placed the knife in its slot on the block. She dabbed the blood stains on her coat. "Good job it's black," she muttered to herself.

Completely entranced by Bianca's serenity, Grace followed her as she wiped down the door handles. They went to the hallway. Grace's sapped power of thought began to return. She avoided looking down at the pooling blood. Instead, she opted to duck behind Bianca into the living room.

Bianca set about wiping the coffee cups. "Did you touch anything else in here?"

Grace shook her head.

"You've got blood on your jumper. Put your coat on," Bianca said.

Grace picked her coat up from the side of the sofa. She could not coordinate her quivering fingers to do up the zip.

After a groan of exasperation, Bianca seized the bottom of Grace's coat and with steady hands brought the ends together.

Grace walked to the hallway as she pulled the zip up the rest of the way. She looked to Bianca to open the door. The will power required to stop herself from looking down to Cara drained the dregs of her resilience. Her head dropped. Every muscle involuntarily contracted, and her stomach moaned as she met Cara's startled glassy eyes.

There was a crash from the living room. She stepped carefully over the blood, more concerned about igniting Bianca's fury than getting it on her shoes. As she rounded the corner, Bianca was standing beside the upturned coffee table, amongst the shards of the broken clock. She threw Cara's handbag over her shoulder.

"What are you doing?" Grace said.

Bianca searched the room as though trying to ascertain the source of the voice.

"We have to go!" Grace said.

Suddenly, Bianca flickered to life. "I'm making it look like she'd disturbed robbers," she said.

There was no time to decide whether she admired or despised Bianca's fortitude. A croak from the hallway unbridled the terror Grace had so arduously fought. She spun to meet Bianca's wide eyes. "She's not dead..." Grace whispered. But as the words left her lips, she knew that couldn't be true.

They were skittish deer, with ears pricked in the quietude and eyes fixed on the small gap in the doorway. Grace's muscles were poised to run.

A cackle soared and then broke, soared and then broke again, with a melody like a bitter nursery rhyme.

The doorway darkened as a long shadow crept through the open inches. Grace staggered backwards behind Bianca. The door slowly creaked open. The shadow loomed forward. Then it stopped.

"Cara?" Bianca's voice had an inflection of uncertainty.

As Grace tried to decipher its form, the silhouette thickened, and then fluctuated in the gloom.

"No, not Cara," the voice rattled. It was a grating, hoarse voice. Like the rambling caw of a crow.

Grace was able to discern one thing. The voice had origins devoid of humanity. She looked to Bianca, expecting her to forge forward on the attack. But whatever motivated her violence had deserted her. She was little more than a petrified husk.

"Who is it?" Grace ventured, on the verge of hysteria. Adrenaline surged as she huddled against Bianca's arm.

The room rapidly cooled. The acrid smell of decay stung the back of Grace's throat. She peered through the rolling vapour caused by her quick breaths to the murky doorway.

"You know," the ragged voice said.

She did. But Grace daren't verify the statement. A sudden riot of sounds suffused her. Every heartbeat was an echoing thunderclap in her head. Every swallow unleashed a raging river down her throat. But the one that terrified her, the harsh scrape of lacquer from wood, besieged her from the hallway. It made a resounding declaration of approach, tearing and ripping toward them, and then it stopped.

From behind the glazed timber doorframe, a long, bony finger curled. Its iridescent skin gleamed, devoid of flesh and blood. The red raw stump at the end clamped the frame, and then another rotten digit arched behind it.

Grace's tenuous hold on reality slipped from her

grasp. She howled and pleaded for a third not to come. But the unwanted third and dreaded fourth fingers emerged together. The surge in momentum seemingly provoked by Grace's beseeching cries for mercy.

When her lungs could no longer power her pleas, Grace's bellows were eclipsed. Bianca's hollering reverberated through the room as she rushed towards the door. It groaned under the burden of her force as it swung. But a force much greater reacted. The door flung open, throwing Bianca back.

She ploughed into Grace, bringing them both crashing to the ground. Grace's head cracked against the floor. White brilliance erupted. Her senses drowned in the drift. Momentary numbness gave way to searing pain. She was acutely aware that she was writhing in agony on her back but only mildly aware of how she had gotten there.

Someone was screaming. She opened her eyes. Bianca was clawing and pushing at the wall behind them as though it should relent and let her through.

Timidly, Grace rose up on her elbows. Her head felt heavy. She fought its backward loll to face the source of Bianca's fear. In the doorway, there was movement. A flexion of the fingers brought forward a deepening gloom and then the louring wraith.

It paused in the threshold. As though to savour the horror it incited. Its rotting head inched forward, and Grace saw the form was not an *it*, but a she. The nose. The almond shaped eyes. There was no question; this monstrous being had once been Emma Stanton.

A mantle of black undulated around her with the fluidity of water. The woman underneath, with ashen green skin and black eyes, divided her bleeding lips to flaunt her familiar smile.

There was no ambiguity to the smile. Syrupy saliva seeped down her chin in anticipation of satisfying a savage hunger. Her jaw fell loose, and the saliva dropped in protracted strings to floor. Nor was there any ambiguity over what would sate her craving. Her eyes rolled like inky marbles and centred on Bianca.

"Are … are you the darkness?" Bianca asked.

"I am not your darkness," the creature crackled.

Grace could only claim enough control of her body to sit up, and as she did so there were fingers clenching her arms. It was Bianca, her face contorted in horror, all rationality devoured. Her grip defied Grace's attempts to escape it.

The creatures jaw dislodged again. "Murderer, thief,"

"What?" Bianca said.

When Grace looked up again, she met the creature's eyes.

"Do what you should have," the creature said.

Grace let out a pleading cry, but no one answered it. Losing her sanity and therefore her disbelief, "I don't know what that means!" she screamed.

A mouldering finger pointed towards Grace. "Do what you should have," the creature repeated.

The monster moved her eyes to Bianca. Grace felt Bianca cower against her in response. They had nowhere to go.

The creature came closer, and though Grace was transfixed, she forced herself to her haunches. She pushed Bianca aside before taking her elbow and wrenching them both up. Bianca stumbled against her as they came face to face with the revenant. But Grace's plan ended there. The hesitation gave the creature time to sweep forward. Bianca was the target, and she reeled backwards and fell to the ground.

Looking for defence, Bianca's flailing arms tore at the air. But as the creature came upon her, she stopped and cupped her hands to her mouth. Tears were forced from her eyes. The creature hung inches above her. Its long fingers extended to Bianca's temples. Bianca opened her mouth to scream, but no sound came.

When Grace could no longer swallow the depravity, her eyes closed.

"Help me—" Bianca's plea was weak.

Grace opened her eyes and saw only the empty doorway. With little concern for the melee on the ground, a cruel panic propelled her forwards. There was no resistance from the creature as she moved. She sprinted past Cara to the front door and flung it open.

As she reached the other side of the road, Grace saw their tormenter was not in pursuit. Her head swivelled desperately, seeking a saviour. The street was empty, there was no help forthcoming. *Oh Cara!* Grace didn't vocalise her cry. But as she thought of Cara, her eyes fell to where she lay in the open doorway. "I'm so sorry."

It had been an error to contact Bianca, a very grave error that had cost Cara her life.

SIX

Grace drove on autopilot. The realisation came when she pulled into the garage with little memory of how she'd gotten there. It took three attempts to coordinate her tremulous fingers to press the button on the garage's remote control. After waiting for what felt like an eon for the door to defend her against the world. She was submerged in darkness and slumped, sobbing against the steering wheel.

A cacophony of whispers jostled for attention.

She prayed that the voices originated from children playing in the road. *Let it be that!* The fanciful wish was quickly dispelled. The whispers were rising. Words were now distinguishable, and worse, they were familiar. She heard Cara summoning her. 'It's time. Come Grace.' But to where, she didn't know.

The coward in her spoke up. *Just open the door. Drive away and don't look back!* The thought made her chest tight. She daren't exhale for fear that her lungs had no power to inhale again. Grace summoned what wits she still possessed and ran from the car. The whispers chased her. More and more voices came forth. *Do what you should have.*

Grace closed the hallway door behind her. Silence. She pressed herself against the door as though it could prevent the whispers from finding her. But in truth, it propped her up as her knees buckled. She had unleashed this unending horror. She would never reach anything close to the sensation of contentment again. She would be dogged by self-hatred and sickness for her remaining days. *Calm down!*

The murky hallway offered no solace. When she viewed the house two Julys ago, the entrance was drenched in natural light, but no one told her that for nearly six months of the year, the sun's path didn't include passing by its windows. Accordingly, the house no longer provided a warm welcome. She crossed the bleak hallway to the staircase.

Grace's stomach heaved as she moved towards the bathroom. She dropped to her knees just as the vomit burned her tongue. She covered her mouth, to stop the barrage from defeating her, but nothing could stop the violent flow. She wiped her mouth. *Oh God!* Cara's blood stained her sleeve. Revolted, she wrenched the jumper off.

Annoyingly, Elliot always left the shower on a high setting. But for once she was grateful. The hot water scalded and sterilised her. The pain felt good. But when the second cycle of scrubbing ended, the heat made her giddy.

Her eyes became hyper-focussed. The water reflected a vivid rainbow of colours. Blood—all the droplets, were suddenly deep red. Grace shrieked. Her knees lost their strength and brought her body crashing down. The pain shocked her, but not as much as the now colourless water pooling around her. Driven to the point of nausea, she forced herself upwards. The tiles seemed to flex beneath her feet. She miscalculated the distance, and her heel crashed to floor. Shaken, she switched off the water and slipped on her bathrobe.

Grace inspected every item of clothing for traces of blood before putting it in the laundry basket. Her jumper was the only item splattered with evidence of her misdeeds. It had to be disposed of. She couldn't bear to touch it again. She ventured downstairs, retrieved a plastic bag from the kitchen, and a large whisky from the dining room. After scooping the jumper into the bag, she went to the bedroom.

The room felt cool after the shower. Goosebumps flecked her skin. She switched on the light and went to the window. Her stomach flipped. For countless days, Grace had watched the world from this window. And now, after all that had happened, it remained unchanged. *How can that be?* The room she stood in was filled with despair but out there, the world was settling into its Sunday routine. Claire, over the road, was unpacking the shopping from the car. The noisy little boy from two doors down was riding his bike at speed along the pavement.

She knew, with absolutely certainty, she had fallen out of sync with that world. She closed the curtains and drained the whisky glass. "There is nothing I can do to change it," she murmured to herself. There was no time for regret. She had to find some semblance of function. Elliot would be home soon and expecting dinner.

Grace got dressed and forced herself to confront her image in the mirror. Her skin had taken a yellow hue. She pinched her cheeks, but the redness had no staying power, they were sallow in seconds. Grace dusted her face with bronzer. She looked marginally better but still sickly. Elliot would not be convinced that she was anything but anguished. She would have to legitimise the paleness and masquerade as ill.

'Grace.' The whispers restarted their torment with her name. Soon there were innumerable voices, mutterings of anger, professions of hate, cries and pleas, snippets of confessions, all baying for her attention.

Sickened, she shut her eyes and clamped her hands to her ears. "Stop!" As her lips formed what felt like her desperate last word, the torture ceased. Grace wallowed in the abrupt dark silence. There was no bereavement for the loss of hearing and sight. She relished the emptiness, but all good things must come to an end.

Voices spoke in the quietude. Not whispers, but a tangible conversation. Grace tried to fall deeper into the nothingness. But the chatter had taken hold and was dragging her away. She opened her eyes. The television had somehow switched itself on.

But that was just the beginning. "Oh God!" This was a new level of cruelty. White crests charged from the grey water towards the pebble beach. It invoked savage memories that led Grace to the brink of hopelessness.

Shoreton Beach!

Grace's mind regressed. She saw herself desperately grappling against loose shale. Then she tumbled in the air, uncontrolled and flailing. A sickening eternity passed in the span of a second. In the terror, there was time for the realisation that this was the end. Advancing ground–pain–nothing.

"Oh God!" Grace was swift. She leapt across to Elliot's bedside, scooped up the remote control, and switched off the television. *I can't take any more of this!* With the bag containing her jumper in hand, she managed to pull down the handle and open the door, but not wide enough.

A beseeching cry. So close to the one that echoed in her head, she stopped mid-exhalation.

"Magda, I love you more than anything. Daddy will be looking for you with the police every day until I find you." The man sobbed.

Grace turned. Images of the craggy black outcrops rolled across the screen.

"Sixteen years ago, a teacher tragically fell—"

"No! No! No!" Grace grabbed the remote control, aimed it at the television and switched it off. She dashed the remote control on the bed and sprinted from the room.

A shadow lurched from the bathroom. Having lost all hope for her sanity, she addressed it, "What do you want from me?"

"Tell the truth," the voice growled.

Its words reverberated in her head. *Tell the truth.* Had her heart not pumped abject terror through her veins, she would have laughed.

"The truth? What good will that do?"

No answer came.

"No doubt you dealt with Bianca."

A rumbling cackle was the retort.

"Well, then! Nothing will bring any of you back. I buried the guilt before, and I'll do it again."

The shadow purred.

SEVEN

They (whoever they are) say a criminal always returns to the scene of crime. Grace knew this, and yet she found herself pulling up beside Cara's house under the pretence of fixing her make-up. Three days without word of Cara and Bianca's untimely demise had brought on a greedy compulsion to find out why and necessitated a detour on the way to work.

As she held up her compact to her face, her eyes shifted to the front door. But there was no police tape. No busy crime scene investigators. The front door was closed and showed no sign of the horror that had unfolded behind it.

Closing her compact, she was confronted by an elderly woman in the window of the house next to Cara's. Under her scrutinising gaze, Grace made an ill-thought-out half-wave, which only served to make the woman lean forward and inspect her more intently. Grace's thoughts collided. *Did she see me on Sunday? Is she taking note of my license plate number?* Panicked, Grace got out of the car and headed down Cara's path to appear as nothing more than a friend paying her a visit.

Her heart thumped in sync with her urgent footsteps, but when she reached the door, the thudding reached a deafening level. Not knowing what do, she kept up the pretence and knocked on the door.

Her eyes drifted to the letterbox and her mind to what lay beyond. Her curiosity piqued to an incurable level. Her throat constricted to the point that she could no longer swallow. She lifted the flap.

The view was clear from the doormat to the kitchen door. Clear in more ways than one, there were no gory streaks along the doors, no bloodied Cara in a pool of claret.

"Hello."

Startled, Grace yelped.

"Sorry dear, I didn't mean to scare you," the elderly neighbour said. "Are you a friend of whatsit?"

"Cara...yes," Grace said.

"Cara." She nodded, and suddenly the question seemed like it had been a test of Grace's friendship.

"I saw her leave on Sunday night. My grandson was taking me home on Sunday after dinner. He's so—"

"Did you say you saw Cara leave?" Grace asked.

The woman turned up her wrinkled nose. She didn't care much for the interruption. "Yes, she sped past us, making an awful din. She was in such a hurry, she didn't even close the garage door. Luckily, my grandson was there. Otherwise, it'd be open now."

If the woman had continued to speak, Grace didn't hear her. On the verge of passing out, she abandoned the doorstep.

***

A string of hoarse coughs answered the phone call. Followed by a deep breath. "Hello."

"Hi Cara, it's Alice. I was just calling to see how you are. Sue said you were off sick."

"I'm still not well." Her voice was little more than mouse squeaks.

"You sound awful, have you seen a doctor?"

"Yeah. It's tonsillitis."

"You poor thing, do you need anything? I can pop over and bring you some soup."

"I'm in Shoreton."

"Shoreton?"

"Got signed off. I'm visiting my mum."

"That's lovely. Is she looking after you?"

"Yes."

"I can barely hear you, does it hurt to speak?"

"Yes."

"Well, I'll leave you to it. I hope you feel better soon, and if you do need anything, don't hesitate to call."

"Thanks, bye."

"Bye."

***

The rain presented its own exhibition. Though weak, the afternoon light reflected a waterfall of droplets across the gallery floor.

It was always quiet on stormy days. But Grace was grateful for it. There was no way she could pass herself off as anything but traumatised.

Grace went back to her dusting. She traced her finger along the amber crocuses. She had kept the painting on the gallery floor, not because she liked it, but because five years ago Elliot had wagered that they would sell it easily. She smiled to herself. It served as a reminder of her husband's endless hope.

It had struck her as odd the artist would paint such vivid flowers against a snowy mountain scene. She had been certain the focus of the painting was the Elizabethan black and white cottage with its finely painted thatched roof. The little huddles of crocuses were surely just there to bring colour. But now she saw something else. Those little brightly coloured flowers defying the snow existed because they had evolved to be resilient.

That was what Grace had done too—evolved. Her evolution had culminated in her being so resilient that she could experience true horror and carry on. That was until today.

There is nothing I can do to change it. The words were so ingrained now. The odd slip had her shake her head and utter the words out loud.

The mantra had worked to an extent. It had lightened this, the bleakness of moments. Which started with her memories regressing to the day her class had gone to Shoreton Beach and ending with Cara's dying breath.

Had it even happened? A myriad of unanswerable questions pulsed through her mind. *Did I miss something?* Each time she replayed the images from beyond the letterbox, Cara was not there. Nor was there a trace of blood. *Did Bianca survive?* Surely, if she had, she would have called Grace. *Had Mrs. Stanton cleaned up her mess?* The shadow that slipped from the bathroom confirmed that Bianca had been dealt with. *Did I make it up?* There was no way. Not even on her darkest day could she invent the brutal acts that lead to Cara's death.

The memories rose quickly. She clamped her eyes shut as though it could stop the blood seeping from Cara's wounds. *There is nothing I can do to change it.*

Much like the heavy rainstorm outside, the mantra

washed away the images. She slipped into an exquisite moment of stillness. But those images were relentless, and if her mantra was the rain, then they were the worms that writhed to the surface in defiance.

The clang of the bell at the door made her turn. A sodden timewaster came in from the street. He'd given the gallery the merest of glances and flashed a weak smile before turning to watch the street from the window. He was almost certainly looking for a place to escape the rain. He would have to find somewhere else. It was already twelve o'clock, and Elliot was due back from his meeting any moment. Desperate to go home, Grace planned to continue her sham illness. She needed to polish the performance, not offer sanctuary from the rain to strangers. She plastered on a smile.

As her heels came clacking behind him, he turned to face her.

"Are you looking for anything in particular?" Grace asked.

"No, I'm just browsing," he said and began a meandering slow walk around the plinths. He was not going to be turned out so easily.

Grace's patience was failing quickly. She left the painting and picked up the duster. Across the room, she heard the clunk of knuckle against stone. *What is he doing?* She moved as quickly as her pretence of nonchalance would allow and began to dust the plinth next to the marble lion sculpture he had been fingering. She sensed the unease her presence caused.

His hands rushed to his pockets as he edged away. He'd left fingerprints, grubby ones, on the lion's paw. She diligently rubbed them away. The bell rang again, signaling his exit. *Thank God!*

"Grace."

She spun on her heels, he hadn't left. She trotted to the front of the gallery and was surprised to see the man enter the greengrocers across the street.

"Grace."

The voice was coming from the back office. "Elliot?" The door was ajar, but the lights were still off. There was no sound from the dimness. As she reached for the light switch, something shifted in the dense silhouettes.

"Elliot? This isn't —" The dreadful dance of flowing black cloth prevented her from forming the last word. She peered into the dark opening. Before her eyes could adjust, the creature was at it and licking its putrid lips with a slug-like tongue.

"No... you killed her... you've had your revenge... it's over," Grace pleaded.

Its mouth widened, and a long, low groan of pleasure rumbled from its throat.

"Not over."

"What do you want from me?"

"Do what you should have." It lurched forward, and Grace staggered backwards. Its hand reached towards Grace's tear-stained cheek.

"No…please!" Grace sobbed as she collapsed.

"Grace? What's going on?"

Grace half turned away from the office. Then stood and rushed into Elliot's open arms, glancing back only to confirm that the creature had gone. He lifted her chin until she met his searching eyes. He wiped her cheeks with his fingers.

"Who were you talking to?" he said, lowering his head to the dark office.

"I thought I heard something." She clung to him as he tried to move towards the office.

"I'm just going to switch on the light," he said with a complacent grin. He strode to the doorway and flipped the switch.

Grace flinched in preparation of the creature's fury.

"There's no one in here," he said.

She followed him into the office. Her creased brow and pallid complexion greeted her in the mirror. Despite her attempts to mask the week's events, the disguise was deficient. She yearned to go home, crawl beneath the covers, and seek solace in thoughtless sleep. But it probably wouldn't be forthcoming. It had not been since Sunday.

Elliot pulled her close and kissed her forehead. "Are you okay?"

The gesture gave pause to the horrid show, and she welcomed the distraction, but it only lasted for a moment.

"Is all this upset to do with Cara?" His words were said with thoughtless rapidity.

She moved from his embrace and sat behind the desk.

"It's just you've been acting strangely since we saw her."

"Strangely?" she said. *Is there no end to this?*

"Yes…worried…depressed, even," he replied and perched on the desk to face her.

She grew warm as she felt that burrowing gaze of his eyes scan her face. Reading her concern, he brushed her cheek. "You can tell me anything." He assured her. "No matter what's happened, I'm on your side."

She diverted her eyes from his.

"I know you. I think there is more to this," he said.

"Enough, Elliot," she said.

"Enough?" His tone was that of a man losing his patience.

A burst of frustration coursed through Grace. "Yes!" Almost immediately, it dissipated. She calmed herself. "I really don't feel well."

He stood and started to walk away, then stopped and turned back. "Please talk to me."

She looked down to her hands. The blood was gone, but they were still stained. It overwhelmed her. And for a moment, she considered confessing. But the time for that had passed. Now, she had committed a greater crime.

There is nothing I can do to change it.

"I know," she whispered.

Everything that had happened, everything she had done, swelled up in her mind. If she hadn't been so fearful of losing the life she had crafted with Elliot, she wouldn't have contacted Bianca, and in turn Cara would not be dead. *I don't deserve Elliot.* His kind heart would be broken by the foul blackness that resided in hers.

"I know your teacher's death wasn't an accident."

"You know that?"

"Yes, you said Cara is lying… but too much of it rings true. Did that girl push her?"

"What girl?"

He couldn't be dissuaded with obtuse responses. "You know… Bianca?"

Grace balked when he said Bianca's name, a move that did not go unnoticed.

"That's it, isn't it? Bianca."

"Yes," she said. She reached out and took his hand. As always, he was warmer than her. She brought it to her chin. There was something in his earthy scent that always soothed her. She breathed it in, but now it brought no relief. Almost as if, with his distrust, came a relinquishing of his love.

"I know you're worried. But we can talk to Max. He won't let anything bad happen. You were just a kid. I doubt there will even be charges."

There might not even be charges? Her pulse pounded in her ears at the thought. Cara was right, they should have just gone to the police. She thought of the creature. *Do what you should have. Tell the truth.* It was obvious what it wanted. Tears pricked her eyes.

Now, a confession would implicate her in Cara's

death. *Or would it?* She paused and then started at the beginning.

From Elliot's point of view, she had been exposed, and that was what filled her with worry. If she were to admit Mrs. Stanton's death wasn't an accident, the police would want to speak to Cara. If they found her missing, or dead, they wouldn't accuse Grace.

Why would I confess after killing her? Then, if they didn't come to the correct conclusion, she could offer a theory. Perhaps Cara had also contacted Bianca, and upon hearing her plans to confess, Bianca had silenced her.

She moved his hand to her mouth and brought her lips together in a faint kiss. Abandoning the last of her scruples, she looked into Elliot's eyes, those soft, patient, all seeing eyes.

He gave her an encouraging half smile.

If there was one thing this life had taught her, it was the intricacies of a lie. She would have to construct it carefully. A fine lie wasn't splurged, it was spread, one thin layer at a time.

"I've made so many mistakes…but you're right. Cara was telling the truth," she said.

Let that be the end of it. Let the ghost finally be laid to rest.

***

Too gluttonous for absolution to allow fear to prohibit her, Grace stepped into the living room. Max wasted no time in answering his brother's call, she sat opposite him on the sofa beside Elliott. She steeled herself for his accusatory onslaught. Surely, Max would proceed in that manner. She was a monster. No better than Bianca, perhaps worse even. She closed her eyes. Now was not the time for self-pity, she had a story of half-truths to tell.

"Sorry, I don't have long, I'll have to leave in an hour for my shift," Max told her. His face was full of concern, genuinely so.

She nodded her reply.

"I'm not here in an official capacity, we're just going to talk." He sat opposite her. He forced an unfamiliar half smile.

"I want to make this official," she said.

"Max just wants to hear what you know," Elliot said, trying to calm her growing agitation. "Then you can make a statement at the police station."

Elliot sat beside her and cupped her hand in his. Then he turned to Max.

"Grace, why don't you start?" Max said. He settled back into the chair. His face was expressionless, but his eyes locked onto hers.

Her practiced words abandoned her. They were flitting around her mind, the beginning, middle and end — blurring and merging — twisting and turning. She closed her eyes and took a deep breath. *The beginning, focus on the beginning.* Her eyes sprung open.

"Bianca was a bully. I was her friend, but only to escape her wrath."

From there, Grace's tongue easily weaved its tapestry of horror. She looked from brother to brother, expecting to see scepticism. What she saw was quite the opposite. Elliot's face was flushed with concern. His doe-eyes full of warmth. Max looked similarly concerned. But he guarded his feelings better than his brother.

"I am so sorry, Grace, the stress of keeping that secret, it must have been awful." Max shook his head.

Grace made a half nod.

"Where does Bianca live?"

"Bianca? I ... don't... I haven't spoken to her in years. She might still be in Shoreton, I think," Grace said.

"With the missing girl, the Shoreton Constabulary is swamped. I want to have as much information as possible before I approach them. I'll speak to Cara first," he said.

"Okay," Grace said. *Good luck with that!*

"I'll ask Alice to let me know when she's back," Max said.

"Back?" Grace said.

"Yes, Alice spoke to her yesterday. She's ill and visiting her mother in Shoreton." His eyes widened. "You don't think that's the real reason she's gone back, to see Bianca?"

"I…don't … don't know." Grace's mind was distracted by her twitching stomach. *Alice had spoken to Cara yesterday?*

"I had better get off. I'll call Cara when I get to the office. I'll be in touch, but call me if you need anything." He gently kissed her cheek.

"I'll walk you out," Elliot said to Max. "Grace, you just relax, I'll make some tea. He smiled as he closed the door behind him.

Grace tried to steady her trembling hands. *Cara's not dead? Oh God! What's happening to me?*

The fruit of suppressing her guilt was a ripening madness.

EIGHT

aralysed, Bianca shut her eyes. But there was no escape within. Mrs. Stanton was in her mind too, invoking memories that came with such pain; she was pushed to the edge of hopelessness.

She felt the agony of her mother's belt strike her back; felt the sting of humiliation at Cara's behest. The torment didn't end there. Every trauma, every point of hurt rushed her at once. But then she saw Emma, her Emma, and the pain abated as each of their days together passed by her.

Then there was nothing.

Her eyes opened to the ceiling. No longer in the grip of the monster, the room was flooded with light. She stood. *Grace?* Bianca looked to floor where she had fallen. No Grace. *Did Mrs. Stanton take her?*

Beyond the window, Bianca saw Grace scuttle away to her car. *Bitch!*

She ran from the living room. The hallway was warm

and bright, but it did nothing to soothe her fear. Bianca's searching eyes rested on Cara. Her blood pooled like red wings at her back.

She was startled by a sound from the living room. That horrid scratching made its approach again. Bianca inhaled sharply. The noise unleashed panic. She rushed to the open front door. But as she reached out to the light, it slammed shut.

Bianca released her held breath and addressed the monster. "What do you want?" she said, unsure as to whether Mrs. Stanton herself knew the answer after letting her live. The scraping stopped, and Bianca turned back and awaited the response. When none came, she took a step away from the door. "What do you want?"

"Come."

The monster had underestimated the darkness within Bianca, *that thing is impotent! The worst it can do is bring pain, but this life is pain,* it cooed. Bianca was unconvinced. She raised a hand to the wall to steady herself, then to guide her forward.

Something black flowed from the living room door, a spectacle that brought icy air. Bianca stumbled, light-headed and confused by the cold.

There was little humanity left in the monster. But the face, though hollow and decayed, was undoubtedly Mrs. Stanton. A corruption of her, anyway. The gleaming black eyes were still, and the extending fingers were devoid of flesh. The rancid stench turned Bianca's stomach.

But as she looked at it, Bianca wondered what Mrs. Stanton had done to become this. Perhaps her assumptions had been correct. Mrs. Stanton's angelic exterior hid a demon's innards.

Bianca imagined Mrs. Stanton had spent years in a hellish prison, plotting against her. If that were the case, what a shame this was. She had been reduced to a stinking, powerless monster.

Bianca's pity liberated her from her fear. The dizziness subsided, and she stood straight. "Well?" she said.

The monster's bloody lips curled into a snarl. "Take the girl home."

Bianca looked at Cara. "Take her home? Why —"

When she turned back, the monster had vanished. Mrs. Stanton seemed like a diver who found this world in the depths of her own. She was only able to keep herself submerged for a moment, speak a few words, before being forced to resurface for air.

Bianca's mind shifted from one thought to another. *Doesn't she hate me for killing her?* She was to take Cara home. *Why?* Each thought was a hexagonal cell in a hive of uncertainty.

She watched the space Mrs. Stanton had occupied. Refusing to blink, for fear that she might miss her return.

But when she could no longer see for forming tears, she retreated to the living room and sat on the sofa. Mrs. Stanton's plan, whatever it may be, was far more elaborate than Bianca thought. Perhaps she understood her death was an accident.

Only then did Bianca realise that Mrs. Stanton must possess some other-worldly insight. The conclusions formed rapidly. She had seen the truth about Cara. The pain was communication. A way to convey understanding of what Bianca had been through. That is why she had been shown Emma, her darling daughter, her salvation, her motivation.

Her mind ticked on until she laughed at her stupidity. She was being asked to act on Mrs. Stanton's behalf. She was her sword. It was not for her to reason why. So, if Mrs. Stanton wanted her to take Cara home, then that was what Bianca would do.

She stood and took a deep breath; the restorative air made her lungs new. She rocked back and forth on her heels. The task was an onerous one, there was so much to do, she would have to be organised.

Cleaning was certainly not one of Bianca's strong suits. But she had never approached it with such vigour. She went to the kitchen, fetched the rubber gloves from behind the sink, and then began pilfering the cupboards for supplies.

She laid the goods on the floor, disinfectant, wood polish, duster, dustpan and brush, parcel tape, bin bags and thankfully a vacuum cleaner. The kitchen was so well stocked, she could not help but think Cara had anticipated this.

Half an hour later, every part of the broken clock had been disposed of. The space it had left on the mantel, filled by adjusting the surrounding photo frames. The now spotless carpet had been vacuumed twice. The table had been righted and every smudge buffered away. Every trace of blood on the door had been removed with disinfectant.

Bianca took the cups and plate of biscuits, the remaining sign of their presence in the room, to the kitchen. There, the biscuits were returned to the jar. The cups and plate were washed, dried, and put away. She surreptitiously looked to the hallway and the biggest mess. From the window, she was pleased to see the sun had set, and it seemed to her that once again the elements were conspiring with her.

As she went back into the hall, she sighed. She had dreaded having to package Cara for the journey, but it wasn't the nightmare she had expected. Once she forced Cara's head into the bin bag, avoiding the dry tongue protruding from Cara's lips and glassy eyes that refused to close, the task was made easy. She pulled the bag down to Cara's midriff and taped it in place, and then manipulated and taped her legs into another bag. She stood to admire her work. No fowl for the oven could be trussed up tighter.

Outside, a moonless night had closed in. Soon Cara's neighbours would be settling in for the evening. Bianca had watched and waited for their curtains to be drawn, and when they were, she waited until there were no silhouettes stirring behind them.

The air was steeped with a chill that promised ice. She moved quickly to drag Cara from the back door to the small door at the back of the garage. She took the top end of the package and strained to push it upwards. Cara had not looked this heavy. She took a breath, then heaved her top half into the boot. The job was made easy when she lifted the bottom of it. Cara toppled into the boot. The suspension creaked under the weight. *Tell me about it!*

Back inside, she continued to toil. There was still blood on the floor, a congealed mess, with a meaty smell that made her stomach growl. On her haunches, with paper towels in hand, she scraped every visible drop and then disinfected the area.

The last thing to do was clean Cara's bloody handprints from the balustrade. As Bianca finished the last one, she picked up Cara's handbag and stopped. She had the urge to go upstairs. She wasn't sure why she went up and regretted doing so.

The air was unusually stale and heavy. It was like the house had fallen into a period of mourning at the loss of its owner. In the dimness, she saw the door to Cara's bedroom was ajar. Light from the street lamp gave the inside an orange glow. Bianca headed in, her mind inevitably focusing on profit, led her straight to the dressing table.

She opened Cara's jewelry box, a small ballerina sprang up and began a continuous pirouette. The tinkling music was familiar, but she couldn't quite place the tune. Within was a knot of tangled costume jewelry. Just one piece seemed to be of worth. She picked the gold chain from the mass, and her heart leapt.

Dangling at the bottom was a pearl droplet. Close to but not quite the same as the one she had discarded in the sea. A replacement for Emma, she thought. She put it back in the box and checked her watch. She had lost track of time, it was nearly six, and Emma would be waiting. She put the box into Cara's handbag.

Bianca made her final checks, washed her gloved hands and put the refuse bag in the boot. She opened the garage door and pulled out. *Shit!* Her timing was off. Bright lights turned the corner. It was too late to turn back. She pulled up her hood. As she sped past the oncoming car, a convulsive gasp rose from her throat, almost a giggle, but more like the start of inconsolable tears.

***

As Bianca drove past the harbour, the blurred shop fronts roused a faded memory of the last day they were all together, or rather, alive together.

They were on the coach, making their way to the beach. She and Grace were talking to Cara. Her memory had softened events. Bullying Cara was a much better description.

Grace screeched with laughter as Bianca taunted Cara. *How can you be so fat and still have no boobs?* They reveled in Cara's attempts to wipe away her tears unseen. What Bianca enjoyed most was her silent suffering. But Mrs. Stanton had a sixth sense for trouble. She didn't know what was going on but told them to behave. Bianca had not listened. Cara was her vessel, and she enjoyed pouring her hatred into her.

Still, there was no time to dwell on the past.

The place where it all started was a perfect resting place for Cara. Bianca assumed she was right as she turned into the cove's car park and found it empty. Bianca left the key in the ignition and got out of the car.

They were both home. Bianca removed the rubber gloves and pushed them into Cara's handbag before swinging it over her shoulder. "Bye, Cara."

***

The first sign of the approaching storm was not drizzling rain. It started by making mountains out of the waves. The salt -gilded air emitted as they crashed against the rocks made Bianca's eyes sting. For as long as she could remember, she had felt an affinity with storms. The flashes of lightning were as quick as her rage and her tone as menacing as the rolling thunder.

She had decided in the passing days that she should probably dispose of Cara's phone. She pulled it from her pocket. *One new message.*

"Hello, Cara. It's Max, Alice's boyfriend. I know this is out of the blue, but Grace approached me, in my capacity as a police officer… and well, she told me everything that happened on the day your teacher died. I understand that you want to speak to the police too. Call me when you get this message."

Damn that Grace! She couldn't bear to deal with her own problems, so she had exploited Bianca to do her dirty work. Then, when Bianca needed her, not only had she abandoned her, she had run to the police. *Sly bitch!* She had clearly made no mention of Cara's murder. *Of course not! She's implicated in that!*

The thought made her anger swell.

But Grace had no idea of the duty assigned to Bianca. She smiled to herself. She would have her revenge. She would make Grace feel the rejection she had inflicted on her.

Bianca waited for a great spray of white at the base of the cliff before relinquishing the phone to the sea. She took the long way home so she could watch the storm come in. It gave her time to think.

When will I get my next task? Not that she needed instruction. Grace was a glaringly obvious problem she needed to resolve.

No longer able to carry the burden, the clouds shed large droplets. Bianca held her hand to catch one. When finally she did, she dipped her hand so that it ran down her palm until it was absorbed. Then she set about devising how she would dispose of Grace as easily.

NINE

The rain had been heavy all night. The residual water droplets absorbed the golden light from the morning sun. The glowing beads seem to hold Emma's attention as Bianca brushed her hair.

Sleep had never come easily to Emma. But with every passing day, she seemed to be beleaguered by a sadness that made her restless.

Emma yawned. "When is Daddy coming?"

Bianca should have guessed he was the source of Emma's malaise. "Soon," she said. *Never,* she thought.

It seemed that it was Bianca's thought and not her words that reached the girl. Her delicate features pouted as her hope dissolved into despair.

Perhaps she should just tell Emma the truth. If he had any idea where they were, he'd hurt them. Bianca's atrocities paled in comparison to those he had committed. He was a thief and a liar.

But as Bianca looked into Emma's eyes, she couldn't

bring herself to say it. It was an apparent contradiction. Despite being a thief and a murderer, she knew that she could never be that cruel.

She pulled Emma into her lap. "I've got a surprise for you!" She placed Cara's jewelry box into Emma's hands. "Open it."

Emma gasped with joy as the little ballerina started her dance. "I love it. She's got a pink tutu like me!"

"She does." Bianca gently kissed her cheek. "There's more. Look inside."

Emma's smile grew wider as she pulled out the necklace. "Can I wear it now?"

"Of course." Bianca undid the clasp and placed the necklace around her neck and switched the television on.

Emma rolled the pearl droplet between her fingers as she intently watched the little cartoon pig dancing. Her gasps and giggles at the pig's antics grew louder. Then she jumped up and began to dance too.

Bianca knew she must do everything she could to keep her daughter safe.

"We have a big day ahead of us," Bianca said.

***

A pair of Herring Gulls were squabbling at the step of the back door. Their presence this far inland heralded a storm out at sea. But Grace didn't care for the news they brought. She found the sound maddening. She opened the door and shooed them away.

The silence gave her a moment to think. This is the first time that she'd had the house to herself since her confession, and she intended to use it wisely. Despite all evidence to the contrary, Grace needed to prove to herself that she had witnessed Cara's murder.

She had hidden it beneath the baseboard of one of the kitchen cabinets. Grace pulled the pans from the bottom shelf in one clamorous move. Then forced the base upwards. There it was. The plastic bag that contained her blood speckled jumper. She had no desire to keep it, just to hide it until she could conceal it in the bin on collection day. Self-revulsion would not permit her to lift it, just to uncurl its opening and see the darkened spots of Cara's blood.

Its presence did nothing to ease her concerns over the loss of her sanity. Indisputably, it went some way to confirm she was insane. She caught the reflection of an unrecognisable eye in the pot lid at her side, it contained no more humanity than the creature's glossy black ones and cast a greater light on her part in Cara's death.

She tried to steady her trembling hands. She had no doubt what was happening. The phone call from a dead woman, a call supposedly originating from the town her murderer lives in. Then there was Cara's neighbour witnessing her driving away. Bianca was not dead. She was posing as Cara and tying up loose ends. That was why things were not over.

She stood and unconsciously started pacing. Her thoughts were like knotted strands. She picked at it until one thread came loose. *What was Bianca's plan?* She was up to something. Grace was sure of that. Whatever it was, she had not contacted Grace. *What does that mean? Should I call her?* No, she would already be in trouble for the call she had made before Cara's death. Another would really implicate her. She steadied herself on the table.

As her thoughts moved to what Bianca's plan might entail, a strange sensation pricked the hairs on the back of her neck. Someone was watching her. She instinctively looked to the hallway door. But it was still closed.

Still, the feeling remained. She searched the kitchen. There were too many places the light never reached. She looked from the pantry to the gloomy utility room. As she resolved that she was alone, there was movement. A silhouette crept across the table towards her fingers. Grace reeled backwards and opened the door to the hallway. She stopped. Though she desperately wanted to turn, she denied the urge.

"You should have just killed her," she said.

There was no cawing response. When she finally had the courage to turn and face the shadow, it had gone. Every sense in her body went on high alert. Grace started toward the table. She felt the presence stalk from behind.

"Grace?" Elliot said.

"Jesus!" She flinched into an uncontrolled stumble.

"Sorry. I didn't mean to scare you," he said.

"I didn't hear you come in." Grace fought her shaking limbs, to rush to the floor beside the open cupboard. "We have so many pots that aren't really used. I thought I'd put some away." She adjusted the base into its slot. "I wasn't expecting you home. Who's looking after the gallery?" She daren't look up; for fear that the guilt was etched on her face.

"I closed up and put the note on the door to call the gallery's number. It's diverted to my mobile. I don't expect anyone will call though. Weekdays are always quiet. I wanted to spend the day with you."

"There was no need, I'm fine."

He looked to the scattered pans at her feet and then to the empty cabinet. "I thought I saw something under the base?"

"No, I was just cleaning it." She closed the cupboard door.

Elliot held out a hand, and she took it and stood. He took her by the waist and pulled her close.

"I thought I'd come home and look after you," he whispered as he nuzzled her neck.

"Look after me?" she said. "Why?"

"I don't know, I thought that after everything that happened yesterday, you might want some company. Hey! Seeing as our cookware is on the floor, we can eat out."

"No," she said hotly. Offended that he thought her a child, incapable of looking after herself, she slipped from his embrace. Forcing all emotion from her voice, she busied herself by putting a pot in the dishwasher. "I've started cleaning now. I'd rather finish it. You can go out if you like."

"Oh, come on, it's been a tough week, it will be fun."

She felt her temperature rise again. Her blood was close to the boiling point. She couldn't commit to listening to him. She had to take control of herself. *There is nothing I can do to change it.*

"Grace, are you listening?"

His angry plea was directed to her, but his gaze was drifting to the kitchen cabinet. He looked like a naughty child with his sights on chocolate, waiting — but only just — for his mother to leave the room. At the first opportunity, she knew he would lift the base of that cabinet.

She needed to get him out of the kitchen, but no rational reason to lead him out came to her. Other than the obvious one. She placed her hands on his shoulders.

"I really don't feel up to going out," she said softly and stepped closer to him. "I'd rather stay in."

"If that's what you want," he said sulkily.

"It is." She locked his eyes with a look that only he, her love, could read. She gently traced her finger from his shoulder to his hand. Then wrapped her fingers around his.

He swallowed deeply and made no attempt to resist her touch. He searched her eyes, seemingly for permission to act. "I thought you had cleaning to do?"

"The dishwasher will be a while," she said and raised her free hand to his face and pulled him towards her.

Permission granted. He leaned into her. His lips went from nibbling her ear to kissing her cheek and finally to her lips.

Grace stepped back from his embrace. Then undid and pushed her jeans passed her thighs until they dropped to the floor. As she walked to the hallway, she removed her T-shirt and threw it towards him. She turned at the door and momentarily enjoyed his hungry eyes scanning her body. "Are you coming?" she said.

She enticed him away from the kitchen with a sprint up the stairs. He chased her. His rumbling steps behind incited excitement.

He caught her at the bedroom door, and as he worked his fingers into her bra from behind, she realised that she had never needed his loving caress as much as she did now. "I love you," she said as she led him to the bed.

"I love you too," he said, bringing his lips to hers. His kisses moved down to her chest as he removed her bra, and then down to her waist as his fingers deftly pulled down her underwear.

Every nerve ending was sparked into elation. So much so that she only became aware that he had undressed when his love and lust bought them together as one. She raised her hand to his face and basked in the warmth of his chestnut eyes. When she could no longer stand the building ecstasy, her eyes flickered shut. Brilliant flashes of colour danced in front of her eyelids.

As the sound of his breathing quickened, she opened her eyes to see that his irises had been submerged by blue opacity. The sight incited a scream that went unheeded. Unable to move beneath Elliot's weight, she closed her eyes again. It wasn't a light show that played across her lids. This time, she saw Cara's blue-white glassy eyes staring back. She screamed again.

Elliot's moans increased. And as his euphoria climaxed, he finally untangled himself from Grace.

She opened her eyes and stared up at the ceiling through a blur of tears.

"It sounded like you really enjoyed that," he said breathlessly.

She turned, and so grateful to meet his chestnut eyes, she shed a single tear that rolled across the bridge of her nose and fell to the pillow.

"What's wrong?" Elliot's eyes were wide with alarm.

"Nothing." She was too heartsick to face his gaze. She snuggled against his shoulder.

"Tears of joy?"

She breathed in his woody scent. "Something like that."

He traced the line of her tear with his finger. "I really do love you," he mumbled drowsily and then pulled her into his arms. Her head settled on his chest until his breathing slowed.

Grace listened to his heartbeat slow, and when she was sure he had been overcome by sleep, she dressed and went back downstairs.

Her T-shirt lay crumpled at the kitchen door. Grace picked it up and brought it to her chin. Dark spots formed where the warm tears landed. She brought it to her mouth to stifle her sobs.

Light-headed, she collapsed to her knees. *Is death always going to be with me?* She feared it would linger in her peripheral. Waiting and watching for the perfect moment to take her. Then she thought of Elliot, sleeping the sleep of the contented. *Will death always lie between us?*

Instantly, she was overwhelmed by self-revulsion. She had given herself in the seediest of pursuits, a pleasurable distraction, and had paid the price.

What have I done? What am I doing? Each of her

despicable actions marched in front of her in a parade of selfishness. It felt like the room was collapsing in on her. She couldn't breathe. *Put an end to it, do it now.*

Grace crawled to the empty cupboard and opened the door.

"No!" There was no need to lift the base. It was wedged upwards and leaning against the side. She pulled it out and threw it to the side. Then she scoured the bottom as though had eyes had chosen to deceive her. "No!" They hadn't. The bag was gone. "It can't — "

The deafening thud against Grace's temple instantly separated her from any semblance of control over her body. She slumped forwards. A half-formed thought about numbness was quickly quashed as her vision swam into blackness.

TEN

As her rising consciousness reached its culmination, Grace woke rejuvenated. The feeling was fleeting. A hammering ache saturated her skull. The clash of peace and pain turned her stomach. She raised her hand to her head. Her other senses were returning. The musky scent of leather came first. Then a window filled with perfect grey. Her reaching hand met a wall of black. *A glove box, wasn't I at home?* She lifted her head. There was a pink travel mug in the console, her mug. This was her car. *Where am I?*

She pulled herself upright and faced a mottled grey blur of sky and sea. *Oh god! No!* From the passenger window, she saw tarmac meeting the undulating curve of the cliff top.

Movement! A person! No, two people were walking in the distance towards a bench on the path. Grace clawed at the handle by her side. But her hands straggled behind her mind's readiness to open the door.

"Hi, Grace."

Grace's limbs were too heavy to be startled into movement. She rolled her head to the side.

A familiar smile beamed at her from the back seat. "You bumped your head and fell asleep." The little girl fought against her seat belt to sit forward. "Mummy said when you wake up, she's got something to show you over there."

Grace followed the little girl's finger. *Fuck!* Bianca was emptying Grace's plastic bag into the boot of a car a few spaces away. *My jumper!* She ducked down.

"Shall I get her?" the girl said.

"No!" Grace smothered her tone and smiled through the gap between the seats. "I'm still a bit sleepy."

Grace stared at the little girl. *I know her.* She clung to the thought through her ascending panic, so powerful now that her heart seemed ready to burst from her chest.

The little girl was still speaking, her chocolate coloured curls sprouted from beneath her woollen hat as she gestured animatedly.

But Grace could no longer hear the words. *Shouldn't she be blonde?* Her mind was ticking on—gathering pace—putting together the evidence. *Oh god!* "It's you," she said. "You're Magda Ford."

"When my Mummy came back from heaven, she said I'm s'posed to be Emma."

For the first time, Grace truly understood the depth of Bianca's madness. "She isn't your Mummy."

"Yes, she went to heaven when I was a baby. But she came back because she missed me."

Grace reached between the seats and took the little girl's hand. "Darling, when people go to heaven, they don't come back. They can't come back—even if they want to. If they could, they would come straight back."

Magda's brow furrowed, and then amid the confusion she shook off her doubt. "No. Because when Daddy comes back from his trip, he's going to pick me and

Mummy up so we can go home."

"Your Daddy isn't on a trip. He's been looking for you everywhere. So have the police."

Magda's cheeks flushed as her face crumpled into sobs. "Am I in trouble?"

"No darling, don't cry." Grace urged, "You haven't done anything wrong. The police are helping your daddy. They want to take you home."

"I don't understand," Magda cried.

Grace glanced to the other car. Bianca was consumed with tugging at something in the boot of the car. She pulled the lever and let her seat fall backwards until she was almost beside Magda. "I know it's confusing. But you want to see your daddy, don't you?"

Magda nodded.

"She's pretending to be your mummy." Grace undid Magda's seatbelt. "She's not a nice lady,"

"She is sort of. But sometimes she shouts a lot and falls over and swears. And she leaves me alone. And she made my hair brown like hers. We always have chips. I'm not s'posed to have chips."

"You see, mummies aren't supposed to do those things," Grace said, taking her hand again. "I bet your daddy would tell you that isn't your mummy."

Magda squeezed Grace's hand in desperation for whatever sliver of protection she could give. "I think…I think we should get Daddy." She choked back her tears.

Grace commended the child's bravery. She felt nowhere close to it. Fear had snaked itself around her chest and was squeezing the air from her lungs. There were only moments to convince the girl of Bianca's lies. She gently unlatched the back door above her head. She almost forced it open to shout to the people at the bench. They were too far away to hear her, but Bianca definitely would.

Grace pulled up the seat to give Magda a clear path.

"Do you see the people over there? They're sitting on the bench. I want you to run to them. Tell them your name. Tell them to call the police and get them to bring your daddy."

Magda climbed up and squinted through the window. "It's too far. I'm scared."

"Don't worry, I'm going to go and distract her. When you see me talking to her, I want you to slide across to this door. It's already open. All you have to do is push it. Then I want you run as fast as you can to those people." Grace hoped the child was not overwhelmed by the flurry of instructions.

Magda looked to Bianca, who was pulling her scarf up to cover her mouth and nose. "But what if she chases me?"

"She won't. When I'm over there, I'll be able to stop her. Those people will get your daddy, okay?"

"Okay."

Grace opened the door and stepped out. A glacial squall dried her throat. She was scarcely able to swallow.

"Grace!" Bianca called.

Her stomach twitched. She turned to look at the people. Freedom was in her sights. They weren't that far away.

"Do you think they can help?" Bianca said before drawing breath. "Help! Help me!" she shouted.

Grace looked to the bench. Shouts spewed from her own lips, a story of murder and kidnap, a futile plea. The wind and sea were too loud. Her saviours remained unmoved.

"It doesn't seem like they can hear us, does it?" Bianca said.

For a moment, Grace considered running, but she quickly dismissed the plan. Magda was looking up at her with a world's worth of hope. A fierce desire to save her came over Grace. *That is why Mrs. Stanton came back!* The realisation struck her with the force of a twenty ton weight. This was not about what happened sixteen years ago, it was about now. It was about saving Magda.

"I wouldn't rush to call for help. You might want to see what I have here," Bianca said.

Grace smiled reassuringly at Magda. Then moved towards Bianca with an impotence she had only ever experienced in her nightmares. Nightmares, when she was mercilessly hunted by untold assailants, powerless to stop herself careening into a darkening tunnel. Though never, not even in that dark place, had she ever envisioned that she would walk toward Bianca Baker to save a child.

Grace held the back of her throbbing head. "What did you do to me?"

Bianca laughed. "Hit you on the head with your broom handle. But never mind that." She took a step backwards. "Surprise!" The contents of the boot were presented like the climax of some seemingly impossible illusion.

Grace's surprise was entwined in shredded black plastic. "Oh God!" Cara's head lay crooked on her shoulder. Her eyes bulged from plum coloured skin, and her swollen tongue protruded from her mouth.

The fetid stench filled Grace's mouth and nose. She turned away, nauseated. Her thoughts raced to find words the equal of her disgust. There were none. "Why?"

"Why, what?" Bianca said.

Grace aspired to lucidity. The questions formed in quick succession. "All of it! Why did you kill Cara? Why would you do this to her? Why did you bring me here?" She drew breath, and her oxygen deprived brained reeled.

Dismissing her questions as though they were mere

frivolity, Bianca scoffed, "You were always so fucking nosy." Then seemingly overcome by the stench herself, she closed the car boot. "There is this thing inside me, I call it the darkness." She paused as though searching the deepest recesses of her mind. "Well, it's not really a thing. It's me. I know it's me. It's the anger and hatred I can't control. Sometimes it's a voice in my head. It tells me things, takes me over."

She really is insane! Grace longed to turn and see Magda at the bench summoning help. But she couldn't. The slightest twitch of her eye over her shoulder would draw Bianca's attention.

The erratic thoughts continued to babble from Bianca. "It's what made me kick out at Mrs. Stanton." Her voice was hardly a whisper. "What made me do that." She pointed to the closed car boot.

The intolerable rambling rendered Grace's thoughts to tatters. She was circling the rim of her sanity. "Why did you drag me here?"

"She's on my side, you know?"

"Who is?"

"Mrs. Stanton."

Grace struggled to keep a flimsy hold on the scream forming in her throat. If she were to lose her grip, it would ruin her.

"She told me to take Cara home." Her lip curled upwards. "That day when you left me behind," she snarled.

Grace's head begged her to run. But it would only serve her up to Bianca's flaring rage.

"You see, she didn't come back to kill me. She's seen you and Cara for what you are. That's why you're here. You see, after killing Cara, you wanted to get rid of her body and your jumper that is stained with her blood." Bianca tapped the lid of the boot.

"What are you talking about?"

Ignoring the question, Bianca continued. "It was all too much for you. So, you started the car and…." Her hand swooped forward. "You drove over the edge."

"I was scared. I wasn't thinking when I left you there. I was sure she was going to kill you."

"You're just like Cara. You think I'm a piece of shit. That's why you thought she'd kill me, right?"

"No, I'm not saying that."

"I always knew that you were using me to fight your battles. When we were kids, I thought if I did it, it would earn me your friendship and your loyalty. But it never did. Did it?"

Where were those people? Please let the police be on their way. Grace was confident that they were near and would soon bring an end to the insanity. Hope soared. She just needed to keep Bianca talking. "That's not true."

"Oh! But it is. When you called me, was it to save me from going to prison? No, it was so you could protect your reputation. Keep up that posh lifestyle."

"Bianca—"

"Save your breath. I've had an enough of your bullshit. I just want what Mrs. Stanton wants. An end to this. With the two of you gone, Emma and I can—" Bianca's eyes skated past Grace. Her face fell slack. Bewilderment darted across it, followed quickly by alarm. Then, a misshaped yelp as she bolted.

Grace's heart plummeted. Magda had only just started her escape. She was only metres away.

As Bianca passed Grace, she snatched at her. But her grip was easily avoided with a sideways step. Grace reached for her again, and this time her fingers caught hold of Bianca's sleeve.

Bianca pushed her aside and launched into a sprint far superior to Magda's, and Grace followed.

"Emma!" Bianca screamed.

Magda turned. The expression on her face was a mingle of dread and confusion. Her hesitation allowed Bianca to catch up to her.

Bianca clamped onto Magda's collar. In her haste to part them, Grace lunged. She brought all three colliding with the ground. Grace's hands moved like pincers, seizing cloth, flesh and hair as she climbed over Bianca. When she forced her fingers into Bianca's shoulder, Bianca squealed and twisted her head. Her face taut, she seethed, all reason devoured. Still, her grip did not slacken from the necklace around Magda's neck.

Grace reached up above her head and hooked the necklace with two fingers. She wrenched against Bianca's grip. The chain snapped. Bianca growled as Grace let go of the necklace and pushed Magda away from them.

"Run!"

Overcome with fear, Magda's eyelids retracted, revealing the whites of her eyes. Her muscles had succumbed to paralysis, suspended in terror, she only had the capacity to watch the horror unfold.

"Run! Get your daddy!"

Daddy, the magic word, sent Magda into motion. She clambered to her feet and began to run.

"No!" Bianca screamed.

Grace raised a balled fist, but her assault was haltered by Bianca's hand at her throat. "Bi—" Her plea was neutralised by a second hand squeezing her neck. *I can't breathe!*

Bianca hauled her to the side. Grace momentarily lost her hold on the light. When her eyes flickered open again, Bianca was on top of her. Grace's heart drummed erratically. Tears were forced from her eyes, mucus from her nose. In a last, desperate act, Grace ploughed her fingernails into her face. Bianca was unfazed by the small furrows of bleeding flesh in her cheek.

Elliot! His chiseled features appeared from nowhere. He cracked a wide smile that made his cheeks dimple and little wrinkles cluster at the outer corners of his eyes. *Oh!* Those tender brown eyes. She let go of Bianca and held on to his warmth.

114

ELEVEN

Bianca felt the palpitating sinews of Grace's neck go flaccid. She let her head fall to the ground. Then traced the imprint of the pear droplet in Grace's skin. She hadn't noticed the necklace was still entwined around her fingers as she squeezed.

The darkness scattered. Yet, there was no remorse, not even a fleeting pinch of regret. She was becoming something else. Something soothed by the touch of Grace's hot, clammy, pulseless neck.

It was incontrovertible. Those years denying the darkness were a mistake. As one, they had eradicated all threats of the past and reset the world so Bianca could start anew. The sensation she felt, looking at Grace's lifeless body, was freedom.

Bianca rolled Grace towards Cara's car. She kept her movements quiet, for fear that she might draw attention to herself. Then opened the back door and got in. She took Grace under the arms and pulled her in. Bianca caught her reflection in the mirror. It showed bleeding welts erupting on her flushed cheek. She ripped apart her hair bun and pulled the knotted strands to cover her wounds. She climbed over Grace and locked the door behind her.

Bianca was so concentrated on clearing up her mess, she'd almost forgotten about Emma. She started running. Emma had already reached her destination. Bianca saw that the people were a man and a woman. The woman crouched to Emma's eye level with a phone to her ear. What was Emma telling her? More to the point, would they believe her?

"There you are!" Bianca said as soothingly as her heaving chest would allow. "I was so worried. You shouldn't run away from Mummy," she cooed.

Emma said nothing. She buried her face into the woman's side and clung to her sleeve.

Bianca addressed her audience. "You've been so kind." She smiled so widely, it made the scratches on her cheeks hurt. "Emma gets herself so excited. She just runs off without a second thought." She reached to take Emma's hand. "Thank you for stopping her—"

"Don't even try it." The man stood between Bianca and his wife. "That child's face has been splashed all over the news for weeks. We know exactly who she is. We're on the phone to the police."

"No, you're wrong," Bianca said.

Her common sense told her to remain calm. The darkness defied the judgement. It wanted to take Emma and run. She sidestepped him.

But he was quick. He moved to pick Bianca up but underestimated her weight. Instead, she was flung down onto the cold, wet ground.

Bianca stumbled to her feet. "Give me back my daughter!"

The man took her by the elbows. She struggled

against his hold.

"Just stop! The police are on their way, they said they'll be five minutes," the woman shouted. She returned to her call. "Yes, please hurry. There is a woman claiming to be her mother."

"No, she is my daughter!" Bianca swallowed her rising anger. "Emma, darling, we have to go."

"Grace said we should get Daddy," Emma said.

"Grace has gone home, sweetheart. Whatever she told you…she was just joking…look." She fought against the man's grip to let the pearl droplet hang from her fingers. "You dropped your necklace…come on, we need go."

"Tom." The woman the woman pointed to her phone. "They've just told this lady that her father is with the police. They're searching further up the coastline." She bent to Emma. "Don't worry, sweetheart, your dad will be here soon."

"No, she is my daughter!"

The man's grip tightened around Bianca's arms. "If that's the case, the police will quickly clear this up. In the meantime, why don't you sit?" He pushed Bianca to the bench. "What did you do over there?" He was looking towards the car park. "I saw you crouched between those cars, but I didn't see your friend leave."

Bianca felt something convulse in her stomach. The darkness was clawing at her bowels. *They will take her from you forever.*

"Fuck off!"

"Anna, take Magda up to the road and wait for the police," the man said, pushing Bianca's shoulders into the bench.

"No!" Bianca screamed. "Emma, Emma, sweetheart, tell them. You're mine. Your Daddy lied to you. I didn't die…look at me, baby."

Emma didn't turn. She allowed herself to be led away

by the woman.

"She's my daughter. Let me go!"

The darkness seized control. Its only intention was murder. Each kick and clawing hand were intended to kill. Only the inaccuracy of its savagery kept the man on his feet. That was until a particularly vicious kick caught his crotch. His eyes gashed wide open in pain. He staggered back and dropped to the ground.

Bianca stood. "Emma!" Her calls were drowned out by the shrill wail of sirens slicing the wind. The flashes of red and blue brought her close to fainting. Stumbling back from the sound, her foot tripped over a heaving mass on the ground. She plummeted. It wasn't the cold and wet ground she fell to, however, but a fevered, writhing body.

"You bitch!" the man screamed. Taking a fistful of hair, he wrenched with all his strength.

She bellowed. Her scalp came unsewn. Released, she rolled away from him to see a clump of her hair tangled in his fingers. She pushed herself upwards to flee, but there was nowhere to go.

A scream came from her throat, but at her lips, it was halted. Emma was running to her father. *Shouting, so much shouting.* Not only were there police officers swarming in the car park, scores more were heading towards her.

There was only one way to go. The sea called to her, and she complied. The avalanche of angry voices followed her across the metres to the cliff's edge. As her feet halted at the edge, loose scree cascaded over the edge. She shuffled from side to side. Movement and heavy breath suffused her head. It was as though she were a shark. Stillness would cause her to drown.

I have to get out of here. The rush of hope was quickly subdued. Bianca heard them coming after her and turned to find a man standing less than five metres away from her.

Everything, from his sparse smattering of white hair to his ill-fitting navy suit and worn leather shoes, screamed television detective. His expression was calm and his eyes ineffectual. Beyond his outstretched arms was Emma.

Bianca fixed her eyes on her, hoping against hope that she would unbury her head from her father's neck. Just for a moment, so that she could see her cherubic face.

"You shouldn't have taken her from me, James. She is mine. Things could have been so different," Bianca said.

"Oh God! Stephanie?" James held his hand on Emma's head so that she wouldn't turn.

The police officer turned to James. "This is Stephanie? The surrogate we couldn't trace?"

For a moment, James's expression was confused. "Yes, that's her." He looked to Bianca. "I'm sorry, I need to take my daughter home."

"James, wait. You can have the money back. Let me see her. Please, James! Just one more time." Bianca pleaded. Only a tuft of curls was visible over his shoulder as he walked away.

The police officer shuffled forward. "No, wait. I need time to think."

"Stephanie—" he said.

"Bianca! My name is Bianca."

"My name is DCI Pope... Kevin. Just take a breath and give me your hand."

"Don't come any closer!"

He stopped. "Okay, just stay calm. You gave them a fake name?"

"I didn't want them to look into my background. But you see, he admitted she is mine. Bring her back to me!"

"I heard him. Why don't you step away from the

edge and we'll talk about it?" He ambled forward.

"Don't come any closer…or I'll…or I'll jump." *Talk about it?* She knew he was placating her.

She turned and stared into the endless grey. Her knees buckled as she started to sway in sync with the dizzying pitch and peak of each wave before it crashed against the rocks below. The dangling pearl swung like a pendulum in the wind. She held out her hand and let it go.

"One…two…three…four." The necklace had fallen from sight before it hit the water. All was lost. She would have to follow it and hope for nothing, other than an end as quick as Mrs. Stanton's. "There has to be another way," Bianca whispered. *No, no other way, too much has happened, you've done too much.* The darkness responded.

She inched forward, to her place at the edge. Her heart leapt as her feet skidded over the stones. She leaned forward.

As she teetered at the edge, desperate voices chugged along the cliff top like a locomotive. She looked to the car park, certain she was the source of concern. But they did not look outwardly, there were no upturned faces, their focus was on the car. On Cara and Grace. *Even now, at the end, I don't matter.*

The rage of the darkness exploded. She clenched her jaw to prevent herself from sobbing. Suddenly, there was little remorse for the pain she had caused. She was glad for it now, as whether it wanted to or not, the world would remember Bianca Baker.

"Fuck it!" She ambled forth. *Do it!* the darkness said.

"Bianca."

She turned to see Mrs. Stanton slipping from behind the DCI Pope.

Hope swelled. "Help me! They have my daughter… get her back for me."

"No." Mrs. Stanton was different. Before she had seemed like something trying to come forward, now she seemed like something that had been left behind. Her form was more corporeal. Her cloak was whipped by the same wind as Bianca's hair. Her feet made audible steps on the ground.

"Please."

"I told you to take her home."

The smell of rotten meat came on the wind. "I did... she's..." Bianca turned to Cara's resting place in the car park.

"She's? Who are you talking to?" DCI Pope said gently.

Bianca pointed to Mrs. Stanton.

DCI Pope followed her finger. "There is no one there."

But Mrs. Stanton was there. The expression on her face was familiar. But this time, it didn't incite the darkness. No, even the darkness understood why Mrs. Stanton regarded her as something unpleasant to be scraped off the bottom of her shoe.

"You never meant Cara, did you? You were never on my side."

"No."

"She is my daughter...you... you are a monster!" In one last act of defiance, Bianca spat in its face. The monster dropped its heavy head. The black pustules in place of her eyes rested on Bianca.

Then it laughed. "I will take pleasure in this." Mrs. Stanton took hold of Bianca.

"Don't!" DCI Pope shouted.

"I can't help it. She is making me," Bianca said.

"There is no one there." He rushed towards Bianca. A hair's breadth away from Mrs. Stanton, the momentum carrying him seemed to crash against an invisible wall. The air huffed from his lungs. He collapsed backwards, barely conscious.

"This ends here." Mrs. Stanton's palm closed around Bianca's shoulders and turned her to face the sea.

Just one more step was required. The turbulent waves emitted great white sprays of water. The sea was growing more violent. Bianca's heart began to thud.

"Wait. I've changed my mind…I don't want to…wait!" She searched for the darkness. But it was no help, it was crying in the deepest recesses of her mind.

"It is time." Mrs. Stanton wrapped her arms to Bianca and stepped forward.

Bianca screamed bloody murder until a rush of air choked her. The monster's mantle was an undulating cocoon. Snippets of sky penetrated the blackness, threatening to swallow her whole. Time moved differently. Slower. She grasped at the endless grey and let loose a scream of defiance. Mrs. Stanton released her.

A thunderous shockwave tore through her. Skin ripped. Bone splintered. The pain was a beast that devoured her entrails. Thankfully, paralysis came in furious pursuit to chase it away.

A shadow loomed. Bianca's eyes rolled up to meet Mrs. Stanton's. The blackness of her eyes was fading into grey and then to white, from which cornflower blue irises developed. A golden line, like smouldering embers, singed away the green from her skin, revealing soft ivory tones. The folds of her hood fell back, and russet hair tumbled to her shoulder. "The girl is safe."

"Wh-What is hap—" Bianca choked. Plucking her vocal cords had sent a dribble of blood from her throat into her lungs.

"The end," Mrs. Stanton said.

"She is… is mine."

"You would have ruined her." The words incited her cloak into a frenzy, as though it had been snatched up by a violent tempest. The undulating swathes parted, emitting a yellow blaze from beneath.

Bianca closed her eyes and rejoiced in the warmth of the last rays of a summer 's day. All too soon it was gone. Her eyes drifted open. The absence of warmth left her cheeks stinging. The vestiges of her lifeblood were draining. But she smiled in anticipation of the sunset, the place of glory that would soon welcome her.

Bianca's end followed quickly. But not the one she hoped for. What came was a rampant starving blackness. Raging forward to the sound of the incoming tide. She looked to the light and did the only thing she could. Breathe. Her ever-decreasing gulps of air did nothing to keep her safe from the desolation. *Please, God...* The plea went unfinished and unanswered into the abyss.

END

C. Bailey-Bacchus is a devotee of dark fiction. Born in the U.K to Vincentian parents, her love of all things horror started with cautionary tales of Caribbean creatures that plagued poorly behaved children.

She started writing in her teens after reading Clive Barker's Hellbound Heart, a book that incited a genuine fear of her own damp room.

In her endeavor to recreate that heart-pounding terror in her work, she delves deep into her personal fears to express the horror that might linger at the periphery of a mundane existence.

Bibliography
C. Bailey Bacchus. "The Blister." *Graveyard Girls*, edited by Gerri R Gray, HellBound Books Publishing LLC, 2018

Link:
Facebook: https://en-gb.facebook.com/c.baileybacchus/

ENÛMA ELIŠ
(When on High)
by
Terry Grimwood

DEDICATION

Matthew and Millie - two gifts from Heaven
Acknowledgements - HellBound Books for believing
in this story

NOTES

ENÛMA ELIŠ is the name of the Babylonian creation myth. The words can be roughly translated as "When on High", the opening phrase of the myth. The gods and monsters, and the "Tablets of Destiny", which feature in this story have all been taken from that creation mythos, stirred into a vat filled with artistic license by the author and spread liberally over the pages that follow.

"The Place" found within this tale was first explored in Terry Grimwood's novella, *The Places Between* (Pendragon). However, *Enûma Eliš* is a stand-alone story and not a sequel.

Contents

PROLOGUE

*T*ime slows for Corporal Luke Harris. Every moment, every image, smell and sound, is suddenly vivid beyond normal sense as the metal flank of the Vector troop carrier bulges inwards. Right there, it is, between the shoulders of the camouflage-and-Kevlar-anonymous Kapoor and Whitman. They don't seem to notice, even when the bulge glows cherry red then boils to molten orange. And still, everything continues as normal; the melded scents of dust-and-sweat and long-extinguished cigarettes, the clank and shudder of the carrier as it bounces over the unkempt road, the way each of the five infantrymen crammed into the vehicle sway and jerk and the webbing and wires of its radio equipment swing back and forth with every bump.

The bulge stretches. The metal pulls apart. And now Whitman half turns to see what is happening. The wound in the metal becomes a hole, its edges blackened and ragged. And through the gap comes a fury of flame.

Luke sees Whitman's head dissolve into a brief scatter of blood, brain and scorched flesh. He sees

Kapoor hurled sideways, but not far in the cramped space. His body snaps into an unnatural sideways fold, like the closing of a hinge. Luke feels the heat then, and the beginning of the shockwave, and throws himself forward, onto the steel floor, to grovel amidst the dusty boots and discarded ration wrappers. There is noise, loud and violent beyond comprehension. It is a physical blow, it bends his eardrums inward and rips away his breath. He can see the noise, white and all consuming. It rises towards a crescendo.

And stops.

Replaced by silence, overlaid by a ringing that ricochets around his head and greys the whole world.

The violence hasn't stopped though. The Vector's interior has become a tornado of flame, smoke and debris. Luke is pummelled and burned and then picked up and slammed against the rear door, which flies away, to bounce into the distance along the desolate road to Basra.

Luke, too, bounces and rolls. Rocks and stones punch into his already bruised, scorched and bleeding flesh.

Then there is stillness, except for the ringing of course.

And the stink of smoke and burning metal, all mingled with the perfume of roasting meat.

When he is finally able to lift his head, Luke sees that the Vector is on its side, licked by flames. The Spartan escort vehicle is also burning, though still upright on its tracks. Luke glimpses someone clambering free. The figure stumbles away then goes down, jerked into a brief dance then flung aside and motionless.

Wrong.

That little jig the soldier performed. Wrong -

Something patters into the ground, a few inches from his boots. He can't hear them but sees little spouts of rock splinters and dust. He freezes, shakes his head,

*trying to clear it of the ringing. More tiny puffs of dust
are stitched into the earth close by.*

*Bullets, yes. That's what they do when they hit the
ground -*

Christ, bullets. Someone is shooting at him.

*Luke throws himself into a desperate worm-like
slither towards the edge of the road. There is no pain
now, only fear, panic, that bloody noise in his head.
Bullets are hot, and they bring hammer blows of agony
and ruin. Then death, if he is lucky. If not, the attackers
will come, and fuck knows what they will do to him when
they find him.*

*He tenses, then launches himself at the nearest rock.
A moment, exposed, a target, waiting for the impact, the
pain, the darkness. He hits the rock and swings himself
round and down into its shadow. He sees more bullet
strikes, tearing at the dirt and the scrubby vegetation
nearby. Carefully, carefully, he slides round until he can
see the road. There is a rocky slope on the opposite side,
about twenty metres back. The landscape beyond is
bleak and hot. He glances behind him, desolation, rocks.
The Euphrates sparkles in the distance.*

*He returns his attention to the slope opposite and
sees figures closing in on the burning vehicles. One of
them carries a rocket launcher. They wear no uniforms
other than the local dress, knee-length, loose fitting
shirts, waistcoats and baggy trousers. Three of them are
heading towards his hiding place, bearded, rugged men.
Luke has no weapon. He's hurt.*

He's fucking dead.

*He slumps back, sits against the rock and covers his
face with his hands as the ringing becomes a roar and
the world slides away into Hell.*

Then someone shouts for help.

CHAPTER ONE: STRANGER ON THE SHORE

There was something on the beach. It looked like a bundle of clothes, dumped onto the surf line.

Spray slapped at Luke Harris's face as he walked across the shingle towards the object. The sea reached for him but was wrenched back. It hissed and roared as if frustrated and grew angrier with each attempt. The grey water was whipped into foam, blown into a salty mist from the wave tops by the brutal east wind. A bank of dense, heavy cloud hung over the horizon and threatened to quench the last, hopeful vestiges of the morning's pale winter sun.

Luke pulled his gloved hands from the pockets of his parka so he could run, because he was sure he could see hair, a leg and, perhaps, an outstretched arm.

He didn't want this. He didn't want drama or crisis. He wanted to be left alone.

But he couldn't walk away.

It was a woman.

For a moment, shocked, Luke simply stood and

stared down at her. The old paralysis was back, his breathing shallow and fast. Warning signs. He needed to concentrate on the problem at hand. Get help.

A woman then, probably dead, here at his feet. Drenched from her time in the lethally cold water. Her coat was open and splayed about her, the fur-edged hood, half on, half off. Under the coat she wore a dress, which clung, wet-tight, to her body. Her face was ashen, her eyes hidden behind bruise-coloured lids. Her mouth was slightly open and drawn back into a grimace.

Do something...

Luke forced himself to crouch down. Swallowing hard against his stress-dry mouth, he reached towards her. The skin of her face was clammy and ice cold. His fingertips moved to her neck.

There was a pulse.

Thready, barely perceptible.

Pulse. Heartbeat. She was alive.

If he had his phone on him, he could call an ambulance, but he seldom carried the thing on these walks. These moments of solitude were important to him. The phone was an intrusion, an unwanted gateway through which others could interfere with his life.

No longer thinking, Luke scooped the woman into his arms and carried her off the beach and across the coastal road to his bungalow. Behind him, the waves raged and hissed, the predator robbed of its prey. A startling shock of desire stabbed through him as he held the sodden bundle close to himself. What the hell was wrong with him? The woman was probably dying, and here he was getting a hard-on.

Once inside, he carried the woman to the single bedroom. She shivered, her teeth chattered. He knew he should get her out of her wet clothes, but he couldn't do that, not to an unconscious woman. So he cocooned her by pulling up the two sides of the duvet and wrapping them about her, coat and all. Then he grabbed her dank, ice-cold hand and held it tight, trying to work out what to do.

Her eyes opened.

She screamed.

"No," Luke jumped away, startled. "I'm not going to hurt you, it's okay, please."

She thrashed on the bed and struggled with the duvet. Panicked by her cries, Luke grabbed her arms, the action instinctive. It made her struggles worse.

"Let me go. You let me go." She had an accent. She was crying.

Luke snapped at her. "I'm not going to fucking hurt you!" He forced himself to calm down and released her arms. He stepped back, waved towards the door. "Go, if you want to." He spoke as gently as he could, but his voice still sounded gruff in his own ears. "You're not a prisoner." He waited. She calmed, pulled the duvet more tightly about herself and stared at him. Her eyes were pale blue and wide with fear.

"It's cold out there," Luke said. "You've been in the sea. You're probably suffering from exposure."

Still no answer.

"I found you on the beach. Do you understand?"

A nod, the slightest of movement of her head.

"Look, I should call an ambulance." If he could find his bloody phone. "You need to go to the hospital -"

"No!" Her panic was back. "No hospital..."

"Okay, okay."

Shit. He wanted her out of here, he didn't know how to deal with this.

The woman managed to sit up.

"A doctor, then," Luke said.

She shook her head. "I have to go."

"You can't, you shouldn't...." Luke sighed. He offered his name.

She appeared to consider this for a moment, then said, "I am Crina."

"Okay, Crina. Why won't you let me get you to a hospital? No one is going to hurt you."

"I shouldn't be here. Not allowed."

Ah. The truth. "You mean you're in Britain illegally. Hey, it's all right, I won't tell anyone." And he wouldn't. Because he owed the powers-that-be fuck all, after what he'd been through in Iraq. "What happened to you?"

A pause. Then, "I was on ship, yes? To England."

"A ferry? Container ship?"

"No. Small boat for fishes."

"A fishing boat?"

"Yes, fishing boat."

So it was back to old-fashioned smuggling; small boats and deserted coastlines, only this time it was people. Not whisky and tobacco.

"I'm to be model."

"A model." Luke sighed. "I don't think there are any modeling jobs here for you, Crina."

She smiled sadly, and for a moment a more knowing, disconcertingly arch version of Crina looked at him through that smile. "I know, is no model. Is prostitute. That's why I jump in the sea."

"Christ, it's the middle of winter. You jumped into the North Sea in January. You must have been desperate."

"Yes, scared. Bad pimps on the boat. They rape my friend." A moment, her face changed. "Something in the sea...something came to me." She shook her head, frightened. "Strong, tries to take me..."

"You're safe now," Luke said and held her hand again, an unconscious action.

"No, is still here."

"What's still here?"

"Still here. In...in me. Need..." She lay back, eyes closed as if exhausted. She muttered something else. The word sounded like "Priest."

"What you need are dry clothes. I'll lend you some of mine. Then I'll make coffee."

She nodded.

Glad of something to do, Luke went to the airing cupboard, which was in the hallway. He was supposed to go to work soon; general handyman and gardener. He was in the middle of redecorating the nearby town's museum, giving the place its winter freshen-up. They would have to wait. They owed him anyway. He was, after all, the man who had brought them their current prize exhibit. He found a sweater, tee-shirt and tracksuit bottoms, then returned to the bedroom.

Something was wrong. Crina was shivering again, violently.

"Crina?"

Her jaws clenched, and her eyes rolled up to the whites. Spittle flew from between her lips. Then her body stiffened, her feet drummed the mattress and kicked the duvet open. Her neck arched back, the veins bulged. A *nnnnnnnaaaawwwww* sound was forced from between her teeth.

"Please, Crina, stop!"

He knew it was useless to shout at her. He needed help. His phone. He raged through the bungalow, throwing aside cushions and paperwork. There, in the kitchen odds-and-sods drawer. He switched it on. Battery low, but enough. He stabbed at the number he wanted, heard a ringing tone. Please let her be there, Christ, let her be there -

"Doctor Hannah Makebo."

"Hannah, I need you here, now."

"Luke? Is that you?"

"Yes, yes, Hannah, please come to the bungalow, it's

urgent."

"I'm about to start my surgery -"

"Someone's dying here."

"Dying? What are you talking -"

"I found...she's having convulsions...fuck it, Hannah, I need you here!"

"All right, stay calm. I'll see what I can -"

He hung up. Crina's convulsions grew worse.

*

This morning, the big East Anglian sky was a glorious winter blue. The sun was bright and the town quiet, because Eastlee was in hibernation, its holiday season a long way off. Not a bad thing, in Hannah's opinion. There was room to breathe in the winter, and space to walk. She could own the beach and the coastal footpaths. She could think.

Right now, however, there seemed little space for thinking. As she drove to Luke's bungalow, all thought seemed soured by something she recognised but did not want to name.

Jealousy, green-eyed and poisonous.

Was that why she had abandoned the health centre only half an hour before surgery was due to start? Jealousy? Because if it was, she should turn around and go back. Now.

She ought to do that anyway. The waiting room would be full. All hands needed, as Doctor Kerslake, the senior partner, would say. Call-outs like this were for emergencies only. This was not an emergency. She could have told Luke to call an ambulance.

But it was his voice; the fear, its brittleness. She had come to recognise the signs. "She's having convulsions." That's what he said over the phone. *She.*

For God's sake, it could be his sister, his niece, a

neighbour. And what business was it of hers anyway? They were not an item (oh, how she hated that term). He could see any woman he wanted. He was free.

But you're jealous...

Doctor Hannah Makebo knew that her colleagues at the health centre were unhappy at the way she was, in their opinion, at Luke Harris's beck and call. She didn't see it that way. The man fought for his country, and his country, it seemed, had turned its back on him.

And while he was out fighting for his country, something terrible had happened to him.

He never spoke about it. He wouldn't seek help, and she couldn't force him. But the truth of it was there, in his eyes, in the haggard, bleak landscape of his face, and in the act that had brought him staggering into the centre late one evening six months ago, his wrists hacked and bleeding.

She should have called an ambulance. But she knew full well that, once the bleeding stopped, he would have been transferred to a psychiatric hospital. And Hannah sensed, even on that first, terrible meeting, that such a place would destroy him.

Stitches and bandages had healed the flesh wounds. They were not deep, a sure sign that the attempt had been the ubiquitous cry-for-help, rather than a genuine attempt at suicide. He was an ex-soldier for God's sake, someone who knew how to kill, himself as well as his enemies.

There were other wounds, of course. And those *were* deep.

Bleeding staunched, he had sat in her consulting room, broke down and wept like a child. Hannah held his hand and waited. When it was over, he looked up and said, "Thanks."

"Can you tell me why you did this?" she asked.

He shook his head.

"Will you do it again?"

"No. It was bloody stupid. I don't know what…" He straightened and drew his hand away from hers. Hannah was shocked by her disappointment at losing this small but powerful contact. She had only just met the man, for God's sake, and she certainly didn't believe in such nonsense as love at first sight.

"I was in the army," he said. "Iraq."

That was all he said. That was all he needed to say.

"Look, if you need someone…if you feel like this again. Call me, okay?"

Unprofessional, unwise. Dangerous, even. It also felt …right. And wasn't compassion a prerequisite of practising medicine?

The other Hannah Makebo, the one born and raised in the dust-dried heat and brutal poverty of a South African mining township, the world-weary and cynical Hannah Makebo, was not convinced.

Compassion? Hah! You know exactly *why it feels right.*

The bungalow was a small, isolated dwelling on the edge of the town. It had been built just after the war, the trailblazer for a new, cheap estate to help ease the housing shortage, but the money had run out. As a result, this was the only one completed.

Hannah liked it here. Not too far from civilisation (barely two miles), but far enough.

The door opened after the first press of the bell.

Luke was haggard, pale. "Thank Christ," he breathed.

The moment she stepped inside, Hannah heard the wet hiss of breath drawn and expelled through gritted teeth. The sound came from deeper within the bungalow.

"The bedroom," Luke said. "I didn't know where else to put her. What the hell was I thinking? I should have called an ambulance."

Hannah barged past him. She didn't hesitate, because she was afraid and needed to crush her fear with action. She didn't understand her fear. It was a cold thing, a foreboding, strong enough to make her baulk at entering the bedroom.

You got it bad, girl. Can't even look at this woman of his.

No, it wasn't that. This was different, this was fear of shadows.

She saw the woman.

Her body was arched like a bow, the back of her head and her heels the only parts of her that touched the mattress. She drooled from between her clenched teeth. Her face was sheened with sweat, her hair lank with it.

Her eyes were rolled up to the whites.

Hannah took a step towards her.

The woman's hisses turned to a keening sound. It grew louder until it tore open her mouth and became a howl. The convulsion stopped. The woman's jaws snapped shut, and she dropped onto the bed, apparently unconscious.

Flinching, nervous, Hannah forced herself to place her hand on the woman's forehead. She was hot, feverish. Hannah felt her glands -

Something moved...

Hannah recoiled, unsure of what she had seen. She moved slowly back to the bed. The woman's filthy, damp coat was open, her sea-soiled dress tight across her abdomen. Hannah saw the beginnings of swelling.

She sensed Luke behind her and spoke without turning around.

"She's pregnant."

"Christ."

It moved again.

Hannah started. There should be no kicks or outward

signs of life at this stage.

But it wasn't a kick.

Hannah's gorge rose. The movement had been insect-like, as if something had scuttled across the inside of the woman's flesh. She stared at the gently rounded shape of the woman's abdomen. What she had seen was impossible. And loathsome.

She needed to palpitate. She didn't want to, but it was her job.

The woman woke. Her eyes were wide and frightened. "Where Luke? Don't touch me!"

"It's okay," Hannah said. Her voice was shaky, hoarse. She tried again. "I'm a doctor. Luke called me."

"Leave me alone. I don't need doctor."

"Yes, you do, Crina," Luke said.

Crina? Hearing Luke speak her name brought yet another little spear of irrational hurt. "You've were in the sea for God knows how long, you're unwell." He glanced at

Hannah, then said, "And you're pregnant."

"In the sea?" Hannah said. "What are you talking about? What happened to you, Crina?"

Luke spoke before the woman could answer. "She was washed up on the beach. She fell overboard from a boat."

Crina sat up. Her face was flushed. "Go away, Doctor. Fuck off. You fuck off, yes?"

She made to get out of bed and then collapsed back and began to cry.

"Crina," Hannah said gently. "Crina, please listen to me."

A nod. Her eyes were closed, tears squeezed from between her eyelids.

"You have to go to hospital."

"No, not hospital."

"You must go to the hospital for your child -" had

that thing been a child? "- if not for yourself. Do you understand me?" Hannah glanced towards Crina's belly again. Nothing moved.

"I understand you. But not hospital."

Hannah turned to look at Luke. He leaned against the doorframe, arms folded, head down. She caught his eye, and he looked up. "I need to talk to you," Hannah said. "In private."

He led the way into the kitchen. He stood by the window. Beyond him, Hannah could see the coast road, the beach and the breakers. Clouds hung heavy over the horizon.

"What happened?" Hannah asked. "Who is she? I mean *who*?" The hardness in her voice made Hannah feel like a jealous wife. She needed to stop this.

Luke shrugged. "I found her lying on the beach this morning. She was unconscious. I thought she needed to be in the warm, before anything else, so I brought her back here. She didn't want me to call an ambulance. I shouldn't have listened to her. She's scared because she's here illegally. She was being trafficked, smuggled in on a fishing boat. That's what she claims anyway. She was either thrown overboard, or she tried to escape." He looked away, then back at Hannah, and this time his stare was level, steady. "I had to help her. It felt right."

A lot of things felt right, it seemed.

"I understand," Hannah said. "But she can't stay here. She had a major seizure. If it happens again, she could stroke, have a heart attack. And she could well miscarriage. She has to go to a hospital."

"I'll talk to her -"

"No, Luke. You look terrible, you need to make coffee and relax for a moment. Plus, you're emotionally involved -"

"What?"

"I don't mean you've fallen in love with her." Had

he? "I mean, she's become linked to your…your troubles."

"I'll put the kettle on."

"Good." Hannah smiled and touched his face. The action was un-self-conscious and natural. Embarrassed, she withdrew her hand quickly and hurried back to the bedroom.

Crina appeared to be asleep. Her breathing was steady, her body relaxed. Hannah crossed to the bed. The woman was still flushed and feverish. She needed to be changed out of her damp clothes, not something Hannah wanted to attempt, and certainly not appropriate for Luke to be involved with, if, that is, she was the stranger to him he claimed her to be. Hannah moved in close to examine her abdomen. She laid her hands on the swelling, over Crina's clothes -

Movement.

Fast. There was an impression of legs, pressed against the inner surface of Crina's skin. These were far from the usual twitches and reflexive kicks and shifting of a foetus.

There. Another. There were at least two of the things in there.

Parasites? Something that had entered her body while she was in the sea?

Hannah removed her hand. She felt sick. She would need to sit down for a moment before making her next move, which would be to contact the hospital the moment she got back to her car, with or without Crina's, or even Luke's, consent. Hannah made to straighten up and leave.

Crina's hand lashed out, grabbed a fistful of Hannah's hair and yanked her down towards the bed. Hannah was too shocked to cry out or react. Her face was only a few inches from Crina's. The woman's lids fluttered, then opened. Her eyes were once more rolled up to the whites.

"Do not call the fucking hospital, you bitch." Her voice was gritty, deep, but still female. There was no accent. Her breath was scalding, and it stank of rot. "You can't have the soldier. He'll never cum between your legs, you hag. Do not interfere, you vile little sow, or I will rip the life from his chest."

The stench and the sheer, raw hatred closed about her. Hannah managed a strangled moan of assent. She wanted to cry, beg, plead with this thing to let her go and not hurt her. The woman's grip was brutally tight. It felt as if she was ripping the hair from Hannah's scalp.

Crina exhaled, and there was darkness in her breath. Then she threw Hannah away from her with such violence that she fell backwards, lost balance and slammed against the floor. She lay there, an ungainly tangle of limbs and coat, winded, shocked. She clawed for breath, then, once she had succeeded in gulping a mouthful of stale air, twisted over onto her hands and knees and scrambled to her feet. She lurched for the door and out into the hallway. She looked back. Crina was once more peacefully asleep.

Shaking, cold, Hannah headed for the front door.

"I made you a coffee," Luke called out from the kitchen.

"It's okay, I've just had an urgent call from the centre. I'm sorry."

"What about Crina?"

She's sleeping, I…I'll talk to you later. Okay?"

Luke emerged from the kitchen. "Hannah, you look terrible."

"I've got to go. I really must."

She couldn't look at him. She couldn't talk anymore. She had to get out of the bungalow.

*

Luke didn't want her gone. He stood in the hallway and felt the old fear come back.

He glanced towards the bedroom. The door was open. He could hear Crina, breathing

heavily, possibly crying. He should go to her, but he couldn't, not at that moment. He turned round and went back into the kitchen. He sat down at the table and waited for the coffee to cool.

It was obvious why life was better when Hannah was here. He liked her. It was as simple as that. He wanted her, and it didn't take a psychic to see that the feeling was mutual. But to take The Step would be unfair to Hannah. He was complicated, unstable, the single-minded career soldier whose own structures had been blown apart just as effectively as that Vector troop carrier. He was not to be trusted. He was a coward, an animal that ran when the carnivores were near.

Also, he could not subject himself to the complications of emotional drama. The welds barely held as it was –

Work.

Christ, he hadn't called the museum yet. He couldn't afford to piss off the council -

Ah, he'd phone later.

So, back to the problem at hand. Hannah was right about this current crisis. He should phone the hospital. He had done his duty, saved the woman from death by exposure. Time to hand her over to people who would know what to do. They would probably send her home, but even that was better than dying, surely. Fighting his guilt, which whispered to him that, for Crina, going home might *not* be better than dying, he glanced around for the phone. The bloody elusive phone. Not in here.

He sipped the coffee, then got up and made his way into the small, comfortably shabby sitting room. He hunted under the cushions on the worn leather sofa, under the books on the coffee table, under the sofa itself.

There, on the bookshelf. He snatched it up and stabbed in three nines.

There was no signal.

Just a roar of static. The noise brought a rush of claustrophobia, which was ridiculous. The front door wasn't locked, his battered old Land Rover was outside, the roads were clear. He tried again. Nothing, mush, dead. Done. The sound filled his head, the roar of blood, the ringing of blast-hammered eardrums…

…he recognises the voice. Greene, the private sitting next to him when the rocket hit. And who now sounds as if he's in agony and very fucking scared. Luke sees the fighters stop and look around. They're looking for Greene. And they're not about to give him first aid.

Luke ducks back behind the rock. He breathes hard. His ears still ring from the explosion. There's nothing he can do. He's unarmed.

A shout. Not Greene this time. The fighters. He looks up and sees them moving quickly to the right. The air is heavy with the stink of burning fuel. The smoke from the stricken vehicles fogs Luke's vision. He needs to cough, but he can't. They'll hear it.

Greene's cries turn to screams.

Luke twists around and scuttles away, belly on the scrubby, sandy ground, exposed now but praying, begging the God he had ignored for most of his life to keep him invisible. To keep their attention on Greene.

Two rocks ahead, shade between them. No, not rocks, manmade, ruins. He glances back. The fighters have gone, no doubt preoccupied with their bloody work. The screams are no longer human.

Luke runs.

He runs with everything he has, powers towards the

ruins.

Another shout. A shot. He hears the bullet. Close, but it misses him. Then he plunges into the gap between the pillars.

And stumbles to a halt, because he is no longer in the desert.

He is no longer in Iraq. Perhaps he is no longer in the world.

"Luke?"

Crina sounded frightened. She watched him come through the door to the bedroom. She held the duvet over herself. Luke saw that her clothes, all her clothes, were piled on the floor by the bed.

"I found you some things," Luke said awkwardly. He nodded towards the sweater and track suit bottoms he had fished out of the cupboard earlier. They were folded on the wicker chair by the wardrobe. He crossed the room and picked them up.

"I'm scared," Crina said. "That doctor, she tell police?"

"I asked her not to." An evasive answer, but the only one he could think of. He was not going to lie.

"She won't listen," Crina said.

You're right about that, Luke decided. He sat down on the edge of the bed. "How do you feel?"

"Tired and weak. I'm hot, but I shiver all time."

"You've a baby to look after," Luke said. "You have to think of that. It's not just you anymore, Crina."

She nodded. The action and her expression were childlike.

"There is something wrong…with baby."

Luke could barely hear her. Her voice was hoarse, small and terrified.

"And me. Something is in me. Is not a child. Is…" She looked away, crying quietly. Luke put the clothes down on the bed and took her hand, and it was hot and tremulous and felt good in his own.

"You like her? The doctor?" Crina asked.

Luke was startled by the sudden change of direction. He shrugged. "She's a good doctor."

"You do like her." Crina smiled mischievously, and there was something mildly lascivious in that smile, something that held a promise.

"You can't stay here," Luke said. "I can't...I don't know how to look after you."

Crina nodded again, once more childlike, though different now. What looked up at him from her large, pale blue eyes was far from innocent.

Luke realised that he was still holding her hand and that he was bending down to kiss her.

He straightened abruptly and got to his feet. He released her hand, and there was a snap like an electric arc. He took a step away from the bed. "Do...do you want a drink? Coffee, tea?"

"Black tea," she said, and her smile was more tease than regret. "Much of sugar, yes?"

CHAPTER TWO: GODS AND DEMONS

You don't look so good, Hannah," said Nina, the locum. The concern in Nina's voice was in direct contrast to the chilly stare Hannah had received from the receptionists when she had returned to the health centre.

"Tired," Hannah said and tried to get past Nina and to her consulting room. She felt Nina's hand on her arm.

"It looks like more than tiredness to me. You should go home."

Nina had only been at the centre for a week. She was an enigma. She seldom spoke of her life outside her work. She was, Hannah decided, Mediterranean, but whether Greek or Italian, she couldn't tell. Her hair was black and lush, her eyes dark, and filled with sharp intelligence. Hannah liked her a great deal.

Right now, however, all she wanted was to be left alone to get on with her work. Her head ached, her eyes stung. She tried to forget the last image she had of Crina. Her threat, that strange exhalation.

"If you feel unwell, let me know," Nina said. "I will take your list."

"Thanks," Hannah said and meant it.

She glanced around the small, neat consulting room, wanting someone else in here with her, even if it was a patient. The room seemed full of threat. A closed-in box of unease.

God, that was so stupid.

Her headache intensified, each hammer blow perfectly synched with her heartbeat. Her skin felt sore. She was nauseous.

The first patient arrived. It was an elderly man who introduced himself as Gregory Allen. He told her in a thin, quavery voice that he had seen blood in his…uh…you know…*pee*, several times over the last month. He had thought little of it but felt that perhaps he should mention it. Probably nothing, but, you know, can't be too careful, eh?

The patient left with a referral to the local hospital's oncology unit. Hannah pressed her fingertips to her temples and felt the steady pulse of her veins. Her mouth was dry. The light hurt. She swallowed another wave of nausea and pressed the call button.

Allen was replaced by a thin young woman who claimed to be suffering from sys-tie-iss and wanted some annybotics, the same what the other doctor gave her.

"I'd like to examine you," Hannah said.

"What for?" the woman said.

"Any recurring condition should be investigated."

"Can't I just have the annybotics?"

"Not until I'm satisfied that there isn't a more serious underlying condition."

"There ain't."

So, you're the bloody doctor now, are you?

The woman complied, however, and lay down on the

couch. Hannah pulled on a pair of disposable gloves and moved in for her examination. Nausea again, stronger this time. She paused to let it pass. She had to go home. She took a look at the patient. No, it wasn't sys-tie-iss.

"I'm sorry," she said. "I think you have a sexually transmitted disease."

"A whah?"

"Possibly gonorrhoea."

"Piss off." The woman sat up, face contorted with anger. "You don't know what you're fucking talking about."

Hannah stepped back and watched as the woman gathered herself together, picked up her bag and headed for the door. "I want to see my normal doctor." Her voice turned acidic. "You know, someone what knows what they're doing."

Hannah should have told her that it was her prerogative and that she was sorry that she, the patient, was unhappy with the diagnosis. Instead, she nursed her weakness and headache and resisted the urge to tell her to go to hell.

The door slammed. Alone, Hannah slumped into her chair. She was hot, cold, the room shimmered in front of her eyes. It was no use. She had to go home.

Worse still was the darkness that crept in from the edges of her vision.

*

Halfway home, Hannah rammed on the brakes, flung open the car door and leaned out to vomit onto the road. Mouth sour, stomach cramped, she slumped back in the driver's seat and waited to catch her breath. She was frightened. There had been blood in the vomit.

Darkness once more tainted the edges of her vision. She saw things; fibrous writhing, like a mass of cotton-thin, black tendrils that reached across her line of sight.

She should go back to the centre. She needed proper medical care.

She needed an exorcist...

Door shut, foot down, home.

Which was a small terrace house on the western edge of the town. Once indoors, she all but crawled up the steep, narrow staircase, scrambling to her feet on the landing and barely making it in time to empty herself again, this time into the toilet.

More blood.

She slid to the floor and lay, foetus curled, trembling and groaning as her stomach cramped. She was dank with sweat. She burned. Her mouth tasted foul and dry, her tongue swollen.

The darkness slithered back, to obscure the periphery of her sight, waving like seaweed blown by the ebb and flow of the tide. She wanted to rip the stuff away, but she could barely move. Her joints were aflame, her skin raw.

Now there were voices, hidden in the rush and rustle of her blood. She couldn't hear what they were saying, only that their whispers were malicious and foul. The writhing darkness pressed into her skull. The tendrils brushed her cheeks, stabbed at her gritty, burning eyes, sought entrance through her lips, her nostrils. She shook her head feebly. The movement turned the world to a shuddering blur.

The voices grew louder, their babble unintelligible but scornful, threatening.

She sobbed. Waited.

Her bag. She forced herself to lift her head. There, her handbag. Her phone.

Slowly, painfully she reached towards it. She felt the soft leather, tried to curl her fingers about the strap, but they were too stiff. She closed her eyes against the harsh glare of the bathroom lamp, and when she opened them again, the world was a glimpse of light through the mesh of tendrils that covered her face.

She plucked at them weakly. They twisted and tangled about her fingers, and she understood that they were growing from her own skin.

Fever dream, she decided, the thought a dim flicker in the encroaching black.

The bathroom floor was hard and uncompromising. Every point of contact painful. She closed her eyes and hugged herself and waited. There was fear, somewhere deep inside. It was a dark thing that spun and howled.

She was at the bottom of the sea. The water was cold, yet she was burning. All about her the seaweed waved. She tried to fight her way through it, but it was too dense. She was tangled.

Drowning –

She opened her eyes. Blind.

She clawed at her face and felt the tendrils. She felt the floor under her, the side of the bath. Things slithered up her nose, prised themselves into her mouth. She tasted them, and they were foul.

She gagged, shivered and beat at the stuff and clawed at it, but she was too ill. Too weak. She curled herself more tightly. She saw her mother and her father. Kind, smiling, but broken by the hardship of their lives. She saw their lips form her name, but she couldn't get to them and couldn't speak because her own mouth was filled with the seaweed. They waved, their movements slowed by the weight of the water. They turned and trudged into the green fog, their feet kicking up clouds of silt. Hannah tried to follow, but the seaweed had her, bound her tight as her lungs burst and she sucked in freezing, salt-tanged ocean.

*

The Bell Hotel overlooked the seafront on what was described, somewhat ambitiously, as Eastlee's promenade. The promenade was short. There was little there but a wrought iron bench, faux Victorian street lamps and the beach itself. The Bell was winter quiet. Its scant, out-of-season guest list consisted mainly of people working away from home and the odd romantics at weekends. It was a place of faded (and fading) glory. Grand in its way but expensive to maintain in the fashion to which it had once been accustomed.

The concierge that evening was Alison Palmer. She was twenty-seven, too tall (in her own opinion), with long, non-descript (also in her own opinion) light brown hair, and about to get married. To Nathan. It was four pm, and she was also bored. There had been no new guests today. She had been standing then sitting then standing then tidying then sitting at the reception desk since two in the afternoon. It was almost unbearable. But it was a job. She and Nathan needed the money. They were buying a house, one of the two-bedroom semis on the new estate on the edge of the town.

One and half months, and she would become Alison Beck. She would lose her name.

Inactivity was not good for her. It allowed her to think, and, inevitably, she thought a lot about her impending marriage and tried to work out why it was wrong.

Nathan was a decent enough man. He was kind to her. He had a good job, he managed a hardware shop in town. He had a sense of humour, and, although she didn't really understand it, his mates seemed to. In fact, they seemed to have little else other than their sense of humour.

Nathan was…

She shrugged, mentally at least.

He was *right* for her. Her mum and dad adored Nathan. Her friends loved him. Well, almost all her friends. Laura didn't like him. And that was why Alison was wracked with doubt. She trusted Laura. She understood Laura, and Laura understood her.

She daren't tell her about her doubts because she was sure that Laura would advise her to stop the wedding. Stopping a wedding was like stopping a train. It *would* stop, but it would be bloody.

Laura was blunt like that; forthright, clear thinking, decisive.

There was a short burst of sea noise, a gust of cold air, then the main doors swung shut. The visitor, a middle-aged man, paused a moment before he set off towards the desk. He wore a suit under a dark, expensive looking coat. He also wore an old-fashioned hat Alison knew to be a trilby. He carried no suitcase or overnight bag, which meant that he was unlikely to be a potential guest. As he approached, he removed the hat. The action, like his clothes and his general demeanour, was redolent with polite charm.

He was familiar, something about his hair, which was dark, grey-peppered and wavy. He was about fifty, square jawed, determined, yet there was kindness in his face. He reminded Alison of a film star, an old one from the black-and-white films her granddad had loved. There was one about a gang of ex-soldiers, brought together to rob a bank by a charming criminal mastermind, and another about a ship, a war film…the star of those films had been someone called Hawkins, that was it, Jack Hawkins. And that was who this man looked like.

He smiled.

Alison swallowed nervously. "Good afternoon," she said. "How can I help you?" Her voice sounded false in her own ears. Her brightness and good manners fake.

"I'd like a room, please." God, he even sounded like

Jack Hawkins. "A single room."

"Of course." Alison turned to the computer and rattled buttons. "Yes, no problem. Sea view? It doesn't cost extra this time of year."

"Thank you."

Alison passed him a booking form. "How would you like to pay?"

"Card."

Wrong. A man like that should produce a leather wallet and place a neat wad of white fivers on the desk. He should then produce a cigarette case and offer her a smoke before lighting up himself.

She gave him the price. "How many nights would you like to stay?"

"Let's say four for now."

"Okay. You can always extend your stay." She passed a registration form to him and indicated where he should sign.

"Thank you," the man said and handed over the card.

Alison started as her fingers closed over its smooth surface. She had expected it to be plastic. Instead, it was warm and yielded a little, like flesh. It also vibrated between her fingertips. When she looked down at it, she saw no bank logo or corporate colour scheme. The card was blank white.

She slid it into the reader, waiting for it to be rejected. But after a moment's thought, the machine told her that the card had been accepted and printed out a receipt.

Meanwhile, the man had written his name on the form. "Detective Inspector Murdoch." No forename, just his title and surname.

"Oh, you're a police man," Alison said unnecessarily and was immediately annoyed with herself. She was behaving like an idiot.

"Yes," he said, with no trace of sarcasm. "It would

seem that way, wouldn't it?"

"Do you have a car? You can't park it on the street, I'm afraid, but we have a special deal with the car park just a few yards down the road."

"No car," he said.

He looked at her, and she saw that the smile had faded, though not the kindness. That seemed ingrained into the lines on his life-worn features. "Don't," he said.

"I…I'm sorry?"

"Your doubts are justified."

"My doubts? What do you mean?" She knew what he meant, of course she did. It was just too ridiculous to accept.

"Nathan isn't the right one for you. There's someone else."

"How do you know? What…"

He reached out, and his hand covered hers. It was warm, and there was strength in his touch. "There's a reason you don't want to marry Nathan. Your friend, Laura, she knows, because she's…" The smile became kindly. "There is no sin in it, Alison, no shame. It's quite natural, right, for you. And for her."

God, this was too strange and frightening.

Too…*true*.

She looked up at his eyes, met his stare, and saw great age, something ancient. She was frightened by the authority the man carried, but not as a personal threat. She knew that Detective Inspector Murdoch was not going to hurt her in any way.

"Do what's right for you," he said and released her hand. "Do you mind if I smoke?"

Indoors? In here? In this enlightened, nicotine-hating age?

"No problem," she said and was both appalled and delighted by her rebellion. No, the feeling was more than delight, it was wild, like delirium. Do what you like. I don't care. *I really don't care.*

And yes, out came the gold-coloured cigarette case, and there were the coffin nails, all neat behind a tightly-stretched, elasticated band.

"Cigarette?" Murdoch offered.

Of course not. She didn't smoke –

"Thanks." She took one. As did he. He produced a lighter, held it out to her. She dipped the cigarette's tip into the flickering, uncertain flame, then breathed in. She expected to cough and splutter. The smoke rolled into her mouth, down her throat. It was clear, mint-edged, sweet.

Cigarette clenched expertly between the first two fingers of her left hand, Alison finished the booking and handed over the key. "Second floor," she said. "Room 240."

"Thank you," he said, smiled, then moved away towards the lift.

As the lift doors closed, Alison sat down and began to cry. She knew that when she regained control of herself, she would phone Nathan. Time to stop the train. The tears were tears of relief.

But there was grief in them as well, grief and a guilt she had thought long-hidden.

*

"Hannah? Hannah?"

The voice drifted into the warm, green darkness, which was now broken by great spokes of light.

"Hannah!"

The voice was loud this time. It boomed through the water and wrenched her upwards. Suddenly, she needed to swim, to claw her way to the surface, where there was air, where she could breathe.

Jesus, how she needed to breathe.

Panicked now, she clawed at the water, pushed against its unthinkable weight. Her lungs burned. The pulse of her heart drummed through her head.

She felt herself yanked back. There was pain. She looked down to see her legs tangled in the seaweed. Only they were not plants. They were tentacles; thorny and vicious, wrapped tight about her legs. They tore into her flesh and stained the sea with a billowing cloud of her own blood.

She tried to scream.

Bloodied water filled her mouth. She gagged and choked. She thrashed and twisted and slowly, agonisingly, dragged her legs clear. She felt her flesh part to the bone. The pain was immense. The pain had to be endured, or she would die.

Her cries broke free. She coughed and gagged and was convulsed by another wave of vomiting, but there was nothing left, only the brutal scouring ache of a dry heave. When it was done, she pushed herself up onto her hands and knees and felt the cold, bruising hardness of her bathroom floor.

Her arms shook, then gave way and collapsed onto the tiles and hugged herself and shivered. She tasted blood. The salt taste she had thought was the sea. Her mouth was full of blood. She gagged and spat it onto the floor. What the hell was wrong with her?

"Hannah, listen, you have to hold my hand."

There was someone in here with her. Hannah turned her head, looked up.

And saw Nina, her dark hair wild, her expression one of utter rage. She reached out and felt Nina's hand close about hers. Nina bent down and put her lips close to Hannah's left ear. Her grip tightened. She whispered. The words made no sense. The whispers grew louder, became a muttered litany, became a shout which deafened Hannah and made her flinch. Even sound was painful. Everything was painful. She wanted to be left alone. She wanted to sleep. To drift back into that warm, womb-like ocean and be gone.

The shout reverberated through Hannah and stretched into a roar of anger. The roar seemed to fill her, like heat that raced along her veins and nerves, like the tingle of electricity.

She needed to vomit again. No, not that. She was too weak. It would kill her.

The need rose like a wave. She was hot, cold. She shivered so hard, her teeth clattered and her joints stiffened into near immobility. The convulsion lifted her from the floor and wrenched its way into her throat. She groaned, and it was as if her throat had been pulled apart. Then her mouth was filled with moving things, and with a last gagging cry her whole body was thrust forward and the mass expelled violently from her mouth.

She screamed, the sound more croak than cry. The mass, the lump, was formed of worms. A writhing mass of red-black things, even now twisting in on themselves and growing bigger. The mass bulged and spread across the floor and drove Hannah back in disgust. She slumped against the wall by the door. Too weak to stand. Trapped, waiting for the things to smother her.

Nina appeared. She stepped into the middle of the bathroom and stood on the edge of the restless sea of worms. The mass suddenly withdrew and surged upwards to form a grotesque, human-like shape. Its structures and landscapes were restless, oozing impossibilities.

It spoke, its voice filled with grit. "Bitch." Then it lashed out and Hannah saw Nina's head snapped around by the blow. She stumbled back, then recovered without falling and threw herself at the creature.

She thrust her hand into the thing's chest. It roared.

Its flesh seethed and flowed. Then collapsed, a brief waterfall of monstrous worms that puffed into a cloud of dust. The dust billowed outwards into the dank air of the tiny room and dissolved to nothing.

There was something clutched in Nina's fist. Something that dripped blood and pulsed. A heart. Nina opened her mouth, too wide, and crammed the still-beating organ down her own throat. Hannah saw her hand, then wrist and half her forearm disappear. She saw Nina swallow. The act was dreamlike, hallucinogenic.

Nina dropped to her knees, head bowed, panting for breath. A moment, then she grinned at Hannah through her exhaustion. "I need a drink," she said.

Nina sat on the edge of Hannah's bed. She nursed a glass of red, poured from the bottle she had found in one of the kitchen cupboards. She still wore her heavy black coat and looked frail and tired. The coat was clean, no trace of worm slime or the ichors that had dripped from the monster's heart. Her face was as it should be. No sign of that impossibly huge mouth.

Perhaps it really had been a hallucination.

No. It had been real. Impossible, but real.

Hannah lay back against the pillow. She was weak, but the shivering and nausea had gone.

"Thank you, Nina," she said. "I don't understand…what happened? Those…" She shook her head. "I think I was dying."

"Yes. You were." Nina regarded her carefully. "I need to know where you were infected."

Hannah hesitated, not because she felt her own story would be too outrageous for Nina to believe, but because she was not certain how much she should tell the woman (if woman she really was). "I want to know who you are," she said instead.

Nina smiled. "It isn't simple."

"Just tell me, please."

"You'll find the explanation outrageous."

"I don't care."

"All right. I don't have a name. For us, names are mere labels, descriptions, sounds. The Babylonians called me Nintinugga." She produced a wry smile. "I don't like it much. I think Nina is better."

"The Babylonians?"

"See? I warned you it would be outrageous."

"I've seen and heard a lot of outrageous things today. One more won't hurt me."

"I suppose not. The Babylonians understood us," Nina said. "They comprehended our true nature. But, still, they worshipped us as gods, as did everyone else on this world, in one form or another, but we have never deserved your adoration. We were formed in the furnace of the proto solar system, when the sun was freshly born and the planets a swirl of hot gas and matter. Creatures like us, vast, all-but omnipotent, can't live in harmony for long. We squabbled, fought. It was our power struggles that created your world. Earth and everything on it is the result of war, moulded from the corpses of the vanquished. The victors, the good guys as you call such as us, were mortally weakened by the conflict. So we retreated to The Place, which is the bloodstream and nerves of this world. What happens here affects the Place, and what happens there ripples outward into this place. Do you understand what I'm trying to tell you?"

"So, you're…a goddess?"

Nina chuckled. "Yes, I suppose I am. But gods, goddesses…we're limited, of little use. You, humanity, carry the spark. It's why you were created. We're weak and cannot survive long if we take flesh and leave The Place."

"Why are you here, if that's the case? To save me from that…thing?"

"The Babylonians called it Asakku. They believed it

to be a demon of disease. I was seen as a goddess of healing, which, in a way, I am." Nina shook her head. "But as to why I'm here, the greater purpose, I don't know. I was drawn out of The Place, with no warning. I found myself in this town, was forced to create this body. Something has happened, here in this face of the world." Her attention returned to Hannah. "What are you involved in? What have you done? Why would Assaku visit you?"

Again, Hannah hesitated, unsure.

"When you came back to the surgery this morning," Nina said. "After you had been to see Luke Harris, I knew something was very wrong. Is Luke part of this?"

"I don't know. I…"

Nina stood. She seemed harder now, colder even. "Tell me."

"There's a woman, Luke found her on the beach, half-drowned. I was going to call an ambulance. She's suffering from exposure, but she's also pregnant. I think she was trying to get into the country illegally. Her name's Crina, at least that's what she calls herself. She seemed like a frightened lost young woman one moment, then…"

"Then?"

"Someone else, as if she was possessed, only I don't believe in possession. She breathed on me, deliberately." The last sentence was out before Hannah could stop it. It sounded ridiculous. "Perhaps she had some sort of illness…"

An illness? Hadn't she seen the thing she had vomited up, out of her own mouth?

Nina returned to the bed and sat down. She reached out and placed her hand on Hannah's forehead. "You're feverish. You need to sleep." Her hand was warm, comforting. Motherly almost. And Hannah was once again a child, in the hovel they called a home, and her mother was there; calming her and keeping away the fever dreams.

"Whoever she is," Nina said, "Crina isn't a lost and desperate young innocent from Lithuania or Estonia. The real Crina should be dead. It's mid-winter. Something saved her. Not from any kindness. It needed a body, flesh. Most of us don't steal what isn't ours. We form a vehicle for ourselves. Whatever was in the sea couldn't do that."

Hannah closed her eyes, now too tired for this.

"Christ," Nina said suddenly, a strangely human exclamation. "I know who it is."

"What…" Words were heavy, hard to say, things that clogged Hannah's mouth.

"Sleep," Nina said softly. "You'll be safe. You're no longer a threat to her. I have to get to Luke."

No. Hannah told her. Don't leave me. I'm frightened.

She heard the door close. Then gave in and slept.

*

Luke, on the other hand, couldn't sleep.

He paced and drank beer. He was edgy, restless. The bungalow was a prison. Its doors unlocked, yet he couldn't leave.

Crina was quiet. Asleep, hopefully. He could check, of course. He could check and find that she wasn't asleep at all, but wide awake and naked under that duvet. She would whisper his name and reach out, and he would fall onto the bed and into the warmth of her. He shook his head and crossed to the kitchen window for the millionth time that evening. He looked out to see the first flakes of snow swirl across the light of the lone streetlamp. The snowflakes were like insects. The world had gone. He was alone in here, an island of light and shadow in an ocean of nothing…

...this isn't Iraq. This isn't anywhere he has ever been before. Yet, somehow, it's familiar. He feels as if he should know what this place is. He should turn around and go back, try to do something for Private Greene. But he can't. He has no weapon. It would be suicide.

Surely, Greene understands that.

So why doesn't he shut up? Why doesn't he shut-the-fuck-up?

Luke stumbles deeper into the place that isn't Iraq, no longer caring about how wrong the place is. He has to get away from here, as far away as possible, before they find him.

Greene's cries become an endless shriek.

Then stop. Suddenly.

Luke breaks into a run. He is in a long, seemingly endless passage. The walls are close, the ceiling arched high above him. There are windows, portholes set into the roof, through which blood-coloured light lances into the dark. He glances upwards. Red clouds can be seen through the windows. They boil and collapse with unnatural speed. Lighting slices through them, like pink-edged tree roots, ablaze with furious energy.

The walls and ceiling are decorated with murals, of struggle, war, and bloodshed. The combatants are not human but an array of fantastical, savage looking creatures. As he plunges deeper into the tunnel, Luke is sure he can hear the sounds of battle. He is sure that the murals are moving, the images writhing in mortal struggle around him.

The sounds grow louder, the clang of steel, screams and shouts, the grunt of effort and of pain, the groan and cries of the wounded.

Louder.

The red light is blood, pouring from the portholes

above him.

Things squirm and thrash in the stuff, which is filling the corridor now. In moments, the floor disappears and Luke wades, ankle-deep, through a fast running stream. He can't stay here. Hands clamped over his ears, he staggers back the way he came. A body falls from the wall into the deepening river of blood. There is a huge splash, which sprinkles the liquid into Luke's face.

He sobs as he runs. The fighters will be waiting for him. But he can't stay in here. Better to lose life than sanity.

He trips and falls. Crashing into the blood before he can stop himself. He wallows and struggles up into a sitting position. He reaches for his ankle. The pain is briefly excruciating but quickly eases to a dull throb. There's an obstacle in there.

He gropes for it and feels it. Sharp metal edges, heavy. Luke hauls it from the blood.

A piece of twisted, torn metal. Corroded. Rubbish.

No, it looks like a Kevlar vest. A breastplate, or the sorry remains of one. He sits in the blood and runs his hands over the object's surface. He feels a pattern engraved into the ancient metal. Without thinking, he struggles to his feet and resumes his journey. He carries the breastplate.

The battle rage is deafening now. The walls are alive with warring flesh. More and more bodies fall. The air is fogged with blood.

Luke sees a disc of bright, hot yellow up ahead. The exit. His death. He tries to prepare himself as it gets nearer.

He prays it will be quick.
He prays for forgiveness.

Now, he prayed for help, for Hannah to come. The snow fell harder. The sight of it made him cold. He could be warm though, he could be warm and safe. Luke closed his eyes and forced himself to stay where he was. Someone would come.

*

The first big flakes spiraled out of a dark, starless sky as Nina hurried to her car. To attempt this alone was a mistake. What had come into the world was powerful. It had summoned and re-formed the demon of disease. She could smell its stink in the snow-heavy air, could feel the strain in the fabric of the world. It could crush her as easily as she could crush a fistful of this snow.

But the thing had not shown its face yet, which meant that it was gathering strength and was, therefore, vulnerable.

Nina also sensed another presence. An ally. He or she was close by, which was reassuring, but they were not ready either. The transition from Place to world, from spirit to corporeal was exhausting. Whoever her ally was, he or she would, like the enemy, be feeding and growing. Nina knew that she ought to wait. But time was not on their side.

She opened the door and sat in the driver's seat, tired from her fight with the demon. She should wait, that was the wisest course. Instead, she started the car and set off towards the seafront. She didn't need an address for Luke's bungalow. She could already feel the corruption, the disease that festered there. She drove slowly, despite her own urgency. Visibility was lethally poor, the dark splintered with hypnotic swirls of white. She glimpsed pedestrians, straining against the wind as they made their way home from work. Nina wanted to shout at them to hurry and to stay indoors where they would be safe.

Oh yes, *safe*. A relative term. As if brick and glass

would protect them from whatever had burst through into the world.

The snow thickened on the road. Difficult to drive. These machines were awkward to control. Junction, traffic lights, the colours barely visible though the crusting of white that shrouded them. Green. The tyres ground against the snow, then the engine shrieked as grip was lost. The car weaved, steadied.

Light spilled from bars and shop windows but was muted by the piling snow. Children and teenagers were out. They laughed, slipped, threw snowballs.

Then it changed.

There were people running, towards her. The faces, glimpsed in the light of the car's headlamps, were contorted in fear. Nina rammed her foot onto the brake, and the car once more fishtailed, then stopped. More people, scurrying from…something.

Big. And fast.

It erupted from the snow-torn dark, a raging, thunderous shape. Nina watched it coming, hands tight about the steering wheel. Her body was immobile.

Move.

Move.

She scrabbled the door handle, then threw herself sideways and out onto the road. The impact was softened by the snow. As she rolled and scrambled to her feet, she heard the crash.

Glass, metal.

A roar.

She backed away as the Minotaur pushed itself from the wreck of the car. It saw her. She felt its mindless, animal gaze. She heard it snort, grunt. Then it exploded into motion.

There were screams, shouts of alarm. She was aware of people, frozen by curiosity, terror, by some instinct that made them want to see. There was no time to help anyone but herself. Nina danced aside. She skidded and staggered and all but fell on her face. The creature hurtled past to collide with another car, this one abandoned in the drift that hid the pavement. The car crumpled under the impact, its glass blew outwards, its whole structure folded and tore. The Minotaur wrenched itself back and round. It roared, and the sound was more lion than bull.

Its form was limned by the light from a shop window. Its body was vast, powerful, but human. It was covered in coarse fur that did nothing to hide its muscles and broad shoulders. Its head was that of a bull, its eyes red. Its horns were exaggerated, curved weapons, lowered now as it prepared to charge again.

Nina drew on what energies she had left. She turned and ran towards the nearest of the shops on the opposite side of the street. She saw mannequins in sweaters and heavy coats. Then she hit the glass, arm over her face, head down, like a bull herself.

The window shattered to dust. The mannequins fell back, ungainly in their frozen, poses. Nina careered through the wreckage and into the darkened interior of the shop. She blundered into a clothes rail and fell to the floor in a waterfall of spilled coats and jackets. She lay on her back, suddenly too weak to get up. She needed to return to the Place to feed. There was an entrance in the lane at the back of the shop. A million miles away.

She scrambled to her feet again and clambered over the counter just as the Minotaur crashed through the broken window. Nina watched it come in, clothes tangled about its horns. It stood, searching the darkness. Nina dropped down onto her haunches. She could hear its breath, a low growl. She could smell its animal musk.

The stock room door was behind her, only a few feet away. She crawled, slowly, painfully and curled herself against it. She would have to stand. She would have to move fast.

One…two…three -

She was up, heel of her hand slammed hard against the door just below the handle. The wood splintered, she smelled the odour of its brief burning. The door swung inwards, and she was through.

Behind her, the Minotaur broke the world apart with its howl of rage.

Nina blundered through the dark towards the fire door at the back. There was a short flight of steps. Her heart pounded, and her chest was almost too tight for her to breathe. She felt fissures tear open in her failing skin, she saw the glow of energies as they bled out of her beneath her clothes.

She reached the fire door and pressed all her weight onto the bar. It gave, and the door opened. An alarm shrieked as she stumbled outside. She felt the heat of the Minotaur's breath. She felt the weight of its presence bear down on her. She felt its speed and its violence.

Nina rushed into the cramped yard at the rear of the shop. The walls were six foot high. They were topped with razor wire. The gate was locked. All this she saw as she launched herself into the blinding snow. She hit the wall and scrambled upwards, gripping at the rough brickwork with her fingertips.

But her strength was almost gone. Her hands tore and bled light. There was pain, red and visceral as the body she had woven about herself began to disintegrate.

Then a greater, unimaginable agony as one of the Minotaur's horns was driven through her back and out through her belly. She screamed, briefly, the cry of a human, as she was wrenched back, then thrown into the snow at the Minotaur's cloven feet. The light was already fading as it ripped her open and trampled the bloodied remains of Nina the Locum.

As flesh and spirit parted, she heard the creature's roar of triumph.

She knew defeat.

Then nothing.

CHAPTER THREE: OFFSPRING

The sound of the telephone dragged Hannah awake. The thing trilled on and on until she had no choice but to answer it. She pushed back the duvet and sat up. Unsteady on her feet, she crossed the bedroom. The phone lay on the dressing table.

The call was from Luke.

"Hannah?" He sounded close to panic. The war hero, on the verge of breakdown. He spoke again, but his voice splintered to a digital staccato as the signal faded, then returned. "…nah? Christ, Hannah are…there?"

"Luke, it's okay. I'm here. The signal's terrible. Why don't we hang up and -"

"No, don't do that! The…" Again, his voice dissolved, re-formed. "…a dozen bloody times already. It's hanging on by a thread as it is."

"All right. All right. Just tell me what's wrong, quickly, before you break up again."

"The pregnancy...I don't know what's happening. Crina's in labour…"

"That isn't possible -"

"Her waters have broken, there's blood."

"All right, Luke, listen to me, call an ambulance -"

"I can't."

"What do you mean, you can't?"

"There's no sig…outside…town. Believe…I've been try…since this star…"

"I'm on my way over." Why was she shouting? Was she trying to yell across the gaps in the signal? She pressed on, hoping that Luke could still hear her. "There should be someone else there first, one of my colleagues, Nina. You have to trust her. She'll know what to do."

No answer. Just the blankness of a lost connection. And Nina obviously hadn't arrived yet. Should she be worried? Hannah had no idea how long she had been asleep. Nina could still be on the road.

Hannah tried a nine-nine-nine call. Nothing. She tried a direct call to the hospital. Nothing.

She gathered her clothes from the floor where she had left them before Nina had helped her into bed, changed her mind, then went to the wardrobe and selected the thickest, heaviest jumper she could find. She swapped skirt for jeans and boots. Then, dizzy and wracked with tremors, slumped back onto the bed. She wanted to lie down. She was too ill for this.

She struggled into her blouse, drowned herself in the sweater and battled with the jeans and boots. She pulled on her scarf and coat, zipped it to the neck, drew the hood over her head, then checked the time.

Almost eight pm. Which meant that she had been asleep for about four hours.

Why wasn't Nina at Luke's?

No time to worry about that now. She had to get there herself.

The snow was a shock.

The wind was almost gale-force. Hannah pulled her scarf over her mouth and struggled to her car, which was little more than a shape in the whiteness. She scooped snow from the windscreen as best she could, then opened the door. Snow blew into the car's interior. The engine, when it got it started, sounded oddly muffled.

She set off, careful, nervous. She had not seen snow until she came to this country, ten years before; as a bio-chemistry undergraduate at Warwick University.

The memory was suddenly potent. Her eyes welled.

The placement had been bought at a price, one that she had not really understood at the time. Yes, she had been aware of how hard life had been, both for her and her parents. Apartheid might have been dead and buried, but its demise hadn't made their existence any easier.

What she had not fully appreciated was the fact that her parents had worked their youth and health away to give their daughter a means to escape the life they had lived. Hannah was bright, exceptional. She deserved her chance, and they were determined she should have it.

For her mother it meant other people's laundry, mending clothes, nursing the sick and even laying out bodies. Anything to raise the money needed. For her father it meant extra shifts in the mine around which the township had been built. The amount of hours he spent down there broke every rule there was. But the company didn't care. Gold was dug, profits made and safety inspectors content with the bribes they received. Everyone was happy.

Ultimately, they gave their lives for her. Father first, two years after she graduated and entered medical school, stricken by silicosis. Mother, killed by a broken heart six months on. The death certificate called it breast cancer, but the fight had gone from her. Her daughter had escaped. Her husband had been taken from her. So, what else was there?

Only then, on that brutal, humid afternoon, beneath a cobalt-dark, rain swollen African sky, as her mother was laid to rest in the township's overcrowded cemetery, did Hannah finally understand the terrible engine of her success.

And her own ingratitude, blinded as she was by the dazzling world in which she found herself. There had been few letters home, even fewer visits -

Hannah's attention was snagged back to the present by the sight of police cars, parked along either side of the main street. Their lights cast an electric blue stroboscope over the scene and shattered it into visual confusion. As she drove, Hannah was startled to see smashed cars, a broken shopfront.

A police officer, bundled into a heavy coat beneath his Hi-Viz, stepped out to wave her down. Hannah stopped and opened the window.

"Do you mind telling me where you're going?" The officer was an anonymous shadow in the snow-streaked dark. His breath boiled from his mouth in puffs of steam. "If it isn't home, then I suggest you turn around and go there."

"I'm a doctor," Hannah said. "I need to get to a patient."

"Ah, okay. Well, be careful. The roads are lethal, and it's getting worse."

"What happened here?"

"Accident." He was lying. The answer was too quick, too certain. "You'd better go." He paused. "I'd like to give you an escort, but we're too stretched. Be careful, please."

"Can you at least call for an ambulance?"

"I'll try, but I can't promise anything, comms are patchy."

Hannah gave him Luke's address. The officer scribbled it down in his notebook, torch held between his teeth. He straightened. The conversation was over. Hannah started the car and drove on. The storm grew worse.

*

Luke didn't answer the door. It was unlocked, so Hannah went in. The place was in near darkness. She switched on the light and moved carefully across the hall.

"Luke, are you there?"

No answer. Hannah chose the kitchen. Another dark room, but a good guess. In the flicker of the fluorescent light, she saw Luke. He was sitting on the floor, legs bent, arms about his knees. He lifted his head slowly. Hannah was shocked by the bleakness of his face. His eyes seemed a little unfocused. She saw empty beer cans by his feet

Hannah crouched in front of him and touched his face. He covered her hand with his. "She's in the bedroom. She's stopped screaming. I think she's dead."

Hopefully.

Shocked at her callousness, Hannah stood and moved quickly to the bedroom.

The bedside light cast a soft red glow over the room.

The duvet was discarded, half on the floor, half tangled about Crina's feet. Crina herself was naked. She appeared to be asleep. The crumpled sheet on which she lay was stained and bloody, as were the insides of Crina's thighs. Everything was…wrong. The woman's belly was distended to inhuman proportions. Diagnoses ran through Hannah's head; fluid build-up, internal bleeding. Anything but labour. Labour was impossible. Evidence of the foetal activity Hannah had felt earlier was usually at 18 to 20 weeks, possibly 16, but Crina hadn't seemed big enough even for that.

If it had been a foetus, that is.

Hannah moved closer. Crina's eyes were closed, her breathing steady but fast. Her face was sheened in sweat, obvious even in this light.

Hannah became aware that Luke had entered the room behind her.

"How long has she been in labour?" Hannah asked.

Luke shook his head. "I don't know, the last few hours."

"We have to get help. There are police in the town. One us has to fetch them here."

Without waiting for a response, Hannah reached out, carefully, and touched Crina's belly. The skin was drum tight.

That movement, again.

She recoiled.

It was the same insect-like scuttling, stronger now, as if whatever parasites were inside her had grown. The parasite theory again. It was the only thing that explained this. Hannah felt weak and nauseous. She didn't want to get too close to Crina. She remembered the voice, the dark breath.

"We need to do something." She turned to face Luke. "Are you listening?"

He nodded.

"You have to go to the police, in the main street. Tell them to get a helicopter out, anything. Crina must get to a hospital, or she'll die."

"I've been drinking," Luke said.

"I know." Jesus, she was so angry with him, but anger was of no use here. "You'll have to take a chance, okay? I can't go. I have to stay here with her."

And that was the last thing she wanted. But she needed to be close by if something happened. Although, God knew what she could do if it did.

Luke nodded. "You're right. Okay."

Hannah grabbed his arms "Be careful. Please. Just get there safe, and come back in one piece. And for God's sake, bring help."

He kissed her. She responded, held him tight and drew in his warmth and never wanted to let go. But she had to. He stared at her for a moment, as if puzzled by what had just taken place, then smiled briefly and left. Hannah sat in the wicker chair by the bed and a few moments later heard Luke's Land Rover rattle into life. There was a wash of headlights, and he was gone.

Crina screamed.

*

The cold was a balm. Luke stood outside for a moment and let the storm enfold him. The icy air sliced through his clothes and flesh. He felt more alive now, his head clearer. He tramped the short distance to the Land Rover. It started the first time.

The army had trained him to drive in rough conditions, but this was the worst he'd encountered for a long time. The road was reduced to a narrow track that ran between two high walls of drifted snow. The blizzard hurtled out of the dark, like tracer. Luke sweated, despite the parka and thick arran-knit he wore.

He caught sight of another vehicle up ahead. Difficult to make out the details.

No, not there, nothing but the crazed patterns of spiraling white. He saw it again. It wasn't a lorry or van. He closed in and saw that it was an armoured car, a Scorpion escort vehicle. Did that mean the army was out? Luke accelerated. If he could catch up and flag the Scorpion down, they could get Crina to the hospital. A favour for an ex-soldier.

The whiteness grew more intense. Everything was snow and light.

Harsh, hot light.

The Land Rover bumped and rattled over a road that was cracked and rock strewn, sun-bleached cliff faces rose on both sides and bore down like tsunami, frozen in mid curl.

But where –

The Scorpion raced ahead. Luke pushed his right foot down, harder. The Land Rover accelerated. He saw the glint of water ahead. A river. The Euphrates.

Is -

This was dangerous. They shouldn't be on this road. Too many ambush points, too far off the main route. Again the Scorpion pulled away. Luke's foot pressed down. He had to catch up. Vulnerable on his own.

The –

Hard to see. The sun was low and too fucking bright.

Snow?

Sand and rock erupted from the ground directly in front of him. There was flame, smoke. A shockwave slammed through the Land Rover. Luke clung to the steering wheel as the vehicle reared and bucked and lunged towards the right hand cliff face.

The impact wrenched Luke forward, then back, in his seat. The world shuddered and tumbled about him. And was still.

Through the windscreen, he could see nothing but snow-encrusted bushes. Stark in the headlights. The front of the vehicle was slanted downwards, but, thankfully, the hedge had been dense enough to prevent a plunge into the ditch.

Christ, hallucinations. He was in a worse state than he had thought he was.

Shaken, Luke crunched the Land Rover into reverse and wrestled it back onto the road.

Only there was no road. Only snow. Deep and impassable.

He swung the vehicle around and headed back towards the bungalow, using his own tracks to keep him on the invisible road.

The world dissolved into white.

*

"Are you seriously going out?"

Murdoch stopped by the hotel's main entrance and turned to look at Alison. She was on her feet, worried for him. "The weather, it's awful," she finished.

"Thanks for your concern," Murdoch replied. "But duty calls."

"Can't it wait? It's terrible out there."

Murdoch smiled his slight, kindly smile. "I wish it could wait, but I'm afraid it can't. Don't worry about me. I'll be all right."

"Rather you than me. I'm sleeping here tonight once I go off duty. There are plenty of empty rooms."

"Wise decision, Alison."

There was a pause. Awkward as far as Alison was concerned. It was as if she had something to ask him and he was waiting for the question. But she had no words for it. "Well, don't stay out in that too long," she said. And wished she hadn't, because it sounded over-motherly in her own ears.

Murdoch's smile turned wry. "I'll try not to, but neither should you wait up."

The door opened, closed, and he was gone. His absence made the old building feel even emptier and colder than usual. Alison sat down. The reception, bar and restaurant were deserted. The few guests had all taken refuge in their rooms. She didn't blame them. She was beginning to feel uneasy herself. Though exactly why, she couldn't say.

*

Hannah sat on the wicker chair in the bungalow's bedroom. Crina was, once more, asleep. The fit of screaming had been brief but terrifying. Her face had been wrenched into an expression of raw dread. She had begged for mercy, for relief and then for death. All followed by an alarmingly sudden collapse. The duvet had fallen to the floor, and the girl was now exposed, pale and fragile. Hannah could not bring herself to replace the cover. She was transfixed by the grotesquely swollen belly, waiting for that horrible insectile scurrying.

Not for the first time since Luke had driven away, Hannah got to her feet and crossed to the window. The snow still fell, blown almost horizontal by the blizzard. She wondered if he had made it the town centre. She wondered at their kiss and if it meant what it felt as if it meant. The memory of it brought a small flare of pleasure. Endorphins, flooding the brain. God, so clinical. Sometimes there were disadvantages to being a doctor. Everything came down to chemicals. Despite his weakness and flaws, Luke represented strength to her. She wanted him back with her.

The doorbell sounded.

Nina, it had to be Nina.

Hannah glanced at Crina, then hurried through the bungalow. The bell sounded again. Hannah unlocked the door and opened it to the length of the chain. A middle-aged man looked back in. She saw a slice of his face, his coat, the brim of his hat.

"My name is Murdoch," he said. "Detective Inspector." He held up something that looked like a police ID.

Relieved, Hannah closed the door, slipped the chain, then opened it fully. Snow blew in. Hannah looked past the visitor, hoping that he had been brought here by

Luke. But Murdoch was alone.

The man stepped inside. He removed his hat as he did so. He seemed familiar somehow, a man out of his time. His coat, his trilby, his whole demeanour seemed anachronistic. His hair was wavy, salt and pepper, his features square, his eyes kind, yet capable of hardness. It was the look of a man who didn't suffer fools gladly.

"Is this your house?" he asked.

"No, the owner will be back in a while." She looked beyond him, at the driving snow, and added, "I hope."

"Are you alone?"

Bad question, and even worse to answer. Yes, made her vulnerable. No, brought Crina to his attention. And why not? He was a policeman, wasn't he? She had seen his ID.

He studied her, then spoke, voice assured but gentle. "It's all right, I'm not here to hurt you." He paused, then nodded. His expression turned deadly serious. "You're not alone, are you? Who else is here?"

"I...I can't..."

"I'll see for myself. You must stay where you are, please. No matter what happens or what you hear."

"Who are you?"

"I told you," he said, still gentle. "Detec -"

"No, I don't believe you. You're part of what's happening."

"And what *is* happening?" he asked.

"I don't know. I..."

"It needs to be stopped," Murdoch said.

"The Place...is that where you're from?"

He froze, spoke without turning around. "How do you know about The Place?"

"Nina told me. She's a doctor at our practice. She saved my life, and she said her name as Ninten..."

"Nintinugga?"

"Yes. Are you on her side?" Not just a bad question,

a dangerous one, because if he wasn't…

He turned to face her. "I am on your side, Hannah."

Hannah? She hadn't told him her name.

"Where is Nina?" Murdoch asked.

"She said she was coming here. That was hours ago."

"I'm afraid that means that something worse than the snow has stopped her."

Hannah remembered the demon Nina had fought. Did something worse mean another of those things or some other creature like it?

"What are you saying about Nina? Do you think she's been hurt?"

"I must deal with this problem first. Once it's done with, then I'll look for her." He nodded towards the bedroom. "Is your visitor in there?"

"What are you going to do? She's pregnant."

"She? Listen to me, the thing you have in this house is not a woman. It isn't human." As if on cue, Crina's voice rose in a wail of agony. Murdoch spun around, face hardened by determination, but Hannah saw, fear as well. "Don't follow me."

He strode away towards the bedroom.

He didn't make it.

Suddenly he was on fire. His skin translucent, as if there were flames buried under the flesh of his face and hands. His skin split to bleed flame. Sparks spiraled about and away from him. He opened his mouth to speak, but there was no sound, only light, a pulsing orange glow.

He grabbed at the walls for support, burning hands on wallpaper, feet on the carpet. Yet, nothing was singed or scorched. There had been no heat. There was no smell of roasting flesh and clothes. He stumbled back, and the fire died down. He doubled over, one hand against the frame of the kitchen door.

"Are you okay?" Hannah asked. The question

seemed puerile. "Did she do that?" The thought was terrifying.

"Yes. It was her." Murdoch sounded out of breath. He pushed himself from the door, grabbed a chair and sat down at the table. "She cannot be allowed to live."

Hannah sat opposite and tried to come to terms with his statement. Murdoch claimed that Crina was not human, something monstrous, and Hannah herself had seen things and experienced the darkness of that monster. But all she could see in her mind's eye at that moment was a woman, a human being, lying on the bed and in terrible pain. The thought of her death, her destruction, as Murdoch had called it, was too much to bear.

"Who are you?" she said again.

"Murdoch, Marduk, Yahweh, names don't matter."

"Yah…you mean God? You, you're God?"

"Something of a disappointment?"

Hannah stood, moved away from him. "You're lying." There was power here, authority and strength. But the man sitting at the table seemed as weak as Luke, and as vulnerable. "How can you be God?"

"What did Nina tell you? Did you listen?"

"She told me about The Place, and about how you created the world as a result of a war."

"With her, the creature in there. She's who I fought."

"Crina is the Devil?"

"Yes, another name for her. Like me, she has a lot of them. We should call this version of her Tiamat. That's what the Babylonians called her, she was their Goddess of Chaos. Their creation myth is the closest to what actually happened. That makes me Marduk, by the way. Do you mind if I smoke?"

Hannah found that she didn't. He produced a gold cigarette case from his coat and lit up. She noticed that his hands still glowed and trembled. Marduk took a deep drag, then exhaled. The smell was sweet, not like tobacco smoke at all.

"The world was made from Tiamat's body. I thought she had been destroyed, but something of her must have remained."

"Babylon, isn't that Iraq now?"

Marduk nodded. "Yes, it was centred around the Euphrates. There are Babylonian ruins in Baghdad, to match the ones you and your American friends created. There were more, but Saddam Hussein demolished some of those to build his summer palace."

Luke was in Iraq. Something happened to him there, something he had never spoken about.

"There's a connection?" Marduk said. "I can see it in your face."

"Shouldn't you know what it is? I thought God knew everything."

"Once, before our war. Not anymore. You humans are on your own, Hannah."

Crina shrieked again. The sound roared through the bungalow like a hurricane. Hannah put her hands over her ears, but the sound drilled its way in and felt as if it would crack her skull.

Marduk surged to his feet, and there was something oddly fluid in the movement. He rushed out into the passageway and towards the bedroom. Hannah followed him out but hung back by the kitchen door. The howling grew louder. And Marduk seemed to move in slow motion. His clothes split, and he once again bled flame. He groaned and staggered. He tried to press on, to drive his body towards the door. But the wounds grew bigger. Blue-white flames dripped onto the floor. Marduk cried out and fell against the wall. Hannah stumbled in his wake. By the time she reached him, he was a mass of flame, a burning man.

But again there was no heat, no smell.

Crina's screams were a debilitating hurricane of sound. Marduk lurched back down the passageway. As before, the flames decreased with distance and were gone when he reached the front door.

"I can't," he said. He seemed even weaker. "I have to feed." He opened the door. Icy air blasted in.

"Don't," Hannah shouted above the din of the gale and of Crina's cries. "There's food here. Murdoch, please stay -"

"I'm sorry," he said. "I'll come back." Then he stepped into the blizzard.

Hannah watched him go. She didn't shut the door but let the icy, wet air slap at her face. Murdoch was gone, Luke was gone. She was alone. With Crina.

She didn't have to be. Her own car was parked on the side of the road by the bungalow. Snow-smothered, all but invisible. Her keys were in her coat pocket. It would be a lethal drive, but it would get her away from here.

Crina's cries became a scream of pain. She screamed, and the scream was raw in its intensity. A cry of utter agony. Another scream, a shriek. No pretence. There couldn't be. Not for someone in that much pain.

Hannah pushed herself back inside and closed the door.

Crina lay across the mattress. Her head hung over the side of the bed. Her mouth was open. Her breathing was a frantic pant. Hannah moved slowly towards her. She saw movement. It was the skin of Crina's abdomen, which rippled and shuddered. Shapes pressed upwards. A face. Dear Jesus, a face, pressed against the skin. Then gone.

Crina screamed. There was a plea in the sound. She was a woman, a young woman, torn by whatever was trying to claw its way out of her.

Instinct made Hannah take Crina's shoulders and struggle her up onto the bed. Crina's mouth was locked wide, a never-ending howl of agony. Her face was wet with sweat. Hannah saw the blood seep from between her legs.

"Huh…huh…help me," Crina gasped. "Make it stop…"

She sounded genuinely terrified. Hannah fumbled in her bag for her mobile phone. Again, the signal was a scrambled mess of white noise. She swore and held Crina's hand.

"I'll do what I can," she said.

Crina nodded. No trace of guile or darkness. Hannah moved now to examine the woman. She should check the size of the cervix. Hannah hurried to the bathroom to wash her hands. Crina's screams of pain followed her. The wind battered at the walls. Luke was still not home. The image of the burning detective glowed bright in Hannah's mind.

She returned to the bedroom. Crina writhed in her agonies. Hannah moved in to begin her examination. She gently pushed her fingers into Crina's vagina. Which was slick with blood. She felt movement beyond. She tried to ignore it. There, the cervix. It was enlarged, startlingly, brutally wide.

Movement…

With a cry, Hannah wrenched her fingers free.

Bathroom, another wash, then back to Crina. She pulled the chair up beside the bed and held the woman's hand and wiped her forehead with a wetted towel. Her eyes were rolled to the whites. She moaned and muttered in her own language.

Hannah felt the illness wash over her again, a tremor. She was hot, cold. She had to hang on. She tried her phone again, the attempts becoming almost obsessive. Still no answer.

More blood.

And Crina's relentless screaming and cursing and

muttering.

Hannah prayed, though to who she didn't know. The night swirled into madness around her.

Then came the cry that drove Hannah back across the room. The sound was inhuman, too deep and throaty, too malevolent and ridden with hot agony. She shrank against the wall as Crina's body arched back.

And something emerged.

*

Luke found the coast road but had no idea how. Homing instinct, he supposed. He was exhausted. The drive back had been a relentless struggle against the snow and wind, and the scores of abandoned cars strewn across the road. He saw no one. It was as if the storm had emptied the world.

The lights of his bungalow appeared, he swung left up onto the layby and stopped behind Hannah's car, which was already half buried under the snow. Luke cut the engine and leaned forward to rest his forehead on the steering wheel rim. He swallowed dryly. Then he killed the lights, got out and stumbled through the dark to the bungalow's front door. Which was open.

Bad sign.

He went in, stood in the tiny hallway and listened. There was a sound. Then a scream. He ran for the bedroom, crashed in. And saw.

Hannah, on the floor, hunched against the wall, arms tight about herself. Her face was white, her eyes fixed on something far away.

Then Crina, on the bed, head flung back, eyes closed, and drool running from the corner of her mouth. Her hair was sweat-lank. Her skin was ashen. Her eyes were open in something that looked like ecstasy, but there seemed to be little or no awareness. Her legs were wide apart, and there was blood.

Luke crossed to Hannah and took her shoulders in his hands. She flinched and recoiled from his touch. She stared at him, shook her head, then frowned, as if trying to work out who he was.

"Hannah? Hannah! What's happened?"

She looked around wildly. "They're here…"

"What are?" Suddenly, she clawed at him and he gathered her to himself, and even in

the madness of the scream-wracked, blood-spattered bedroom, it felt good. He held her tight and forgot all of it. "Who are here?"

"Crina…"

Christ, she had given birth.

"Where is it?" Luke said. "Hannah, what happened to the baby?"

Hannah killed it…

The thought speared into his mind unbidden.

Hannah shook her head. "No, baby…God…"

Luke hauled her to her feet and, arm tight about her shoulders, led her out of the room. In the hallway, she broke free and turned on him. Her eyes were wild, her breathing almost as hard and shallow as Crina's. "They're not babies. They're…something else." She pointed at the bedroom. "There's one in there."

"What are you talking about?"

"Kill it." Hannah was urgent now, though her urgency was wide-eyed and feverish. "You have to kill it, now. Kill it, Luke."

Luke backed away, studied her for a moment longer, then returned to the bedroom. He was cold, his skin crawled. Christ, there was so much blood.

"Crina?" Luke said. "Crina, can you hear me? Are you okay?"

He moved towards the bed.

And saw it.

An incomprehensible shape on the floor. As he stared, he came to understand that it was a sac; translucent, wet and bloodied. Its surface stretched and distorted as something tried to tear itself free. He saw legs, black, almost metallic in their hard, chitinous smoothness. He saw a tail, segmented, a body, insect-like. Scorpion-like. He froze. He had seen his fair share of scorpions, even been stung by the black variety, but none of them had been the size of a rat.

The body thrashed and struggled and ripped through the last of the membrane. A final twist, and it was free, on its back, eight legs kicking and scrambling at air.

Where the hell had it come from?

You know where it came from.

No, impossible.

There was blood all over its birth sac.

There was blood everywhere.

Look at its head, look at it. Look at the fucking thing's head –

Luke took a step towards it, even though the ape in his survival brain was roaring at him to back away.

The scorpion didn't have a head. Growing out of the front of its thorax was a perfectly formed, miniature human torso. The torso was muscled-sculptured and topped with a vaguely human head. Its scalp was naked. Its eyes were formless and black. When it saw him, it hissed and its mouth opened to reveal rows of close-packed needle teeth.

It rushed at Luke's feet. He stumbled back, slammed against the wall and almost fell.

Then he crashed his foot down and felt the creature snap and crumble beneath his boot. Blood and other ichors squirted outwards. He stamped and yelled and swore and stamped until there was little but a bloody smear on the floor and he was panting for breath. And shaking as much as Hannah had been.

He stood by the wall, where he had found Hannah, and stared at Crina. She was sitting up now.

"Fuck you!" she shrieked, and her face was contorted in grief and rage. She made to get out of the bed but collapsed back onto the mattress in exhaustion. She sobbed and swore and snarled at him. "Murderer!"

"What was that thing?" Luke shouted back. "Crina. What was it?"

His shock broke into anger, and he was across the room, his hands on Crina's shoulders. They were thin and frail in his grip. "What the fuck was it? Tell me, what was it?"

She stared up at him and hissed. "My children." She gritted her teeth as another birth contraction shook her.

Her eyes rolled up the whites, and Luke felt something like an electric shock tear into his arms. It threw him back, and he fell onto his bottom. He scrambled to his feet, feeling sick now, scrambling at the wall to get to the door.

Child*ren*?

There were more of those bastard things? Is that what she meant?

Luke lurched out of the bedroom. Hannah was still in the hallway, staring at the bedroom door, then at him as he emerged.

"I killed it," he said.

She nodded. Some sanity seemed to have returned to her now. Replaced by a more ordinary fear.

"How many of them were there?"

She swallowed. Frowned. "Six...seven."

"Where are they, Hannah?"

"I don't know. In the bungalow somewhere."

"We have to kill them all."

She nodded. "Can't we...can't we just get out?"

"Then how do we bring ourselves to come back? We have to know they're all dead. Did you see where they went?"

"I was too scared. I couldn't move."

Luke steeled himself. "Come with me."

They went into the kitchen. There was a cupboard in there. Luke hesitated. He picked up a chair, wielded it as best he could, then opened the door. He stepped back. Tense.

Nothing. The cupboard was deep. He switched on the light. No sign of anything untoward. He kept the cupboard tidy. The vacuum cleaner was in there, and the broom and a couple of buckets, as well as a tool box. He pulled the broom free, then a Stanley knife and a torch.

He shone the torch around the darkest corners of the cupboard. No sign of any of those creatures. Hannah moved in beside him. She crouched down and drew out a hammer.

They looked at each other, nodded grimly, then shut the cupboard door.

"The bedroom first," Luke said.

He led the way back. His skin crawled, he glanced up and left and right, repeating the action until it became a tic. They reached the bedroom. Went in. Crina was still on the bed. She said nothing, made no move. Asleep then, or possibly unconscious.

"Under the bed?" Hannah said.

The bed was a pine type, legs, a gap underneath. Luke slowly lowered himself down onto his hands and knees. He aimed the torch into the space. Floorboards dust, fluff. Shadows.

"Cold," Crina said.

He started, heard Hannah's gasp of surprise.

"You're cold." Her voice, though deep and gravelled, was flawlessly English, haughtily amused, scornful even.

Luke withdrew himself and stood. Crina's head was turned towards him.

"Where are they?"

She shook her head. "You mean them harm," she said quietly.

"Tell us, you bitch," Hannah snarled at her, and Luke was shocked by her rage.

"Closer than you think, Hannah."

"Leave her," Luke said.

He moved towards the wardrobe. His mouth was dry, the broom was cumbersome in his hands. He wanted a gun. His skin prickled. It was hot in here, difficult to breathe. He closed his eyes against the sting of sweat. He wiped them with his arm and felt it tremble. He was crumbling towards panic. He couldn't do this.

He had to do this.

"Hannah?" he said.

"I'm here." She sounded scared but was trying to be brave.

Luke saw his fist curl about the handle of the fitted-wardrobe door.

Now.

He wrenched it open.

Clothes tumbled out, shredded wreckage of shirts and sweaters and jeans. The rail was splintered in two. Everything was covered in white. Snow? No, plaster.

Dust curled into his nostrils and his throat. He coughed. He shone the torch upwards. There was a hole in the ceiling, its edges made ragged by broken lathes.

They were up there, those filthy abominations were in the attic.

"Out!" he yelled. "Now!"

He stumbled back and spun around. He grabbed Hannah's hand and ran for the door.

Then they were in the hall. Hannah in jumper and jeans, no time to get her coat, him still in his parka. The Land Rover key was in his pocket.

There was a crash. Dust billowed from behind them.

Luke threw himself at the front door. He looked back as the lights went out. The beam of his torch beam revealed shattered lathes, torn wiring, slabs of horsehair plaster on the floor. Then he saw the first of them. It was the size of a Rottweiler, a confusion of arachnid legs and human torso, and that sting. Jesus, that sting…

Another of them dropped from the wrecked ceiling to land half on the first. There was a moment of struggle, of hiss and rage. Enough time for Luke to shove Hannah out into the snow and for him to follow.

He slammed the door shut behind himself, then, clutching Hannah's hand, ran for the Land Rover.

Glass broke, a window, something poured out onto the snow.

The Land Rover, unlocked. He had the door open. Hannah was in, scrambling across the seats. He was behind her. He clawed at the door, Hannah half in his lap, half on her seat, panting, almost mad with fear.

The thing came across the snow fast, so bloody fast. It launched itself at the vehicle.

Door shut, a fumble with the keys. The Land Rover rocked under the impact. Luke heard the scrape of the scorpion man's legs on the metalwork. The thing's head appeared at the window beside him. He cried out in shock. Hannah screamed. The Land Rover coughed into life.

A fist exploded through the window and slammed into Luke's right cheek. The blow stunned him, but he hung onto the steering wheel and rammed his foot hard down on the accelerator. Glass crunched under his heel, bit into his back and stung his face. The fist became a claw that raked flesh. More pain, the salt taste of blood. Then the Land Rover was skidding and wheel-spinning down the road and away into the darkness.

CHAPTER FOUR:
SAVIOURS FROM A CRUEL SEA

Alison was on her feet the moment Murdoch stumbled into the hotel's deserted reception area. She saw the wounds, the light that bled from them. She went to him, and he collapsed into her arms. He was heavy, solid, and she almost fell under the weight. His face was wrenched into an expression of pain.

"What happened to you?" Alison said breathlessly as she struggled towards the lift. "Never mind, come on, I'll get you to your room."

"Thank you," he whispered. "I am sorry, Alison. I am so sorry."

"You've nothing to be sorry about," she answered.

They made it to the lift. Once inside, he slumped against the wall and slid down to crouch in the corner. As the lift jerked into motion, Alison knelt beside him. He looked at her and smiled weakly.

"My advice," he said hoarsely, "is to get away from

this town."

"I don't understand."

"Things are happening, Alison, dark things."

She shook her head. "I'm staying here. You need help." And Laura. She was not going to leave without her.

The lift dinged, and its door opened. Alison helped Murdoch to his feet. He seemed to have regained a little of his strength. Once in his room, he collapsed onto the bed. Alison noticed that the window was open. The room was freezing cold. She closed the window, then filled the kettle and switched it on. When she turned back, she finally saw, consciously saw, the wounds, on his face and hands. The groans he uttered when he shifted position on the bed indicated that there were more injuries, hidden under his clothes.

"I need to be left alone," he said softly. "I have to feed."

"What food do you want? I'll make you -"

"Not that sort of food, please Alison, go. I'll be all right."

She nodded and made for the door. He called her name again. She stopped and looked around.

"I meant what I said. You have to leave this town."

"Why?" she asked. "You said that dark things were happening. Is that why you're hurt?"

"Just go, run. Take Laura with you."

Alison shook her head. "I can't just up and leave. I have family, friends, a job."

Murdoch smiled. "Who do I look like?"

Startled by the question, Alison said, "Jack Hawkins, the actor."

Murdoch nodded. "Why do I look like him, Alison? Of all the people I could have created as a vehicle for myself, why Jack Hawkins?"

"I...I don't know. I should go..."

"Look at me, think. Do ordinary people bleed light? How would a complete stranger know about your feelings for Laura? Do you really believe that I'm some old-fashioned Detective Inspector, paying for a bed at this hotel?"

No, of course she didn't.

"So, why Jack Hawkins?"

She shook her head. "I…I don't know." She did. She knew very well.

"Because he always played the dependable, no-nonsense type? Is that it, Alison? An attempt to win your trust?"

"Perhaps. I should to go." She went to the door. It wouldn't open. She tugged at it, frightened now.

"Why would someone of your generation have even heard of him? Whose favourite actor was he?"

She stopped, panic rising.

"Leave me alone, open the door, please."

"It's all right. I'm not here to judge you. Just tell me who loved Jack Hawkins."

"My granddad…"

Murdoch nodded. "Yes, he did. *The Cruel Sea*. That was his favourite film, wasn't it? You bought him the DVD, and you put it on that night, didn't you?"

Do it quick, sweetheart, don't worry. Just get on with it. I can't stand this anymore. It hurts too much. I'll watch the film. Jack on the bridge. You can always depend on Jack.

"No…" Alison wrenched at the door. "No, fuck you, no…"

A pillow, from the pile of spare ones in his illness-stinking flat. Alison turns towards the bed and the pain-wracked, skeletal figure it contains. I love you, Granddad.

I love you too, sweetheart…

"It's all right. Alison, you did the right thing. But you

need to see that. That's why you're here."

Here, why *she* was here, in her workplace?

She stood at the door, forehead against the wood. She tried not to cry.

"Room 240. When was a guest last given Room 240?"

She couldn't remember, never. Because there *was* no Room 240.

"Let me out -"

"You're still in the Bell, don't worry. But it's part of the hotel you've never been to before. It's an entrance, into The Place. No one goes there without a reason. For me, it's so that I can feed. For you..."

The door opened, and she was out into the passage. She stumbled towards the lift. The lights were dim, the place even shabbier than she remembered. Of course it was. Her sub-conscious had decided to believe that idiot in Room 240. She broke into a shambolic run.

Something bubbled out of the wall. Sticky, thick, it gibbered and chuckled, and the plaster seemed to dissolve and the wallpaper fray and crumble to ash. She heard the scrambling of feet. She felt a brush of cold air and the fast approach of something awful.

Alison careered through the fire doors and onto the stairs, down, towards Reception.

*

Crina was a fragment of awareness. She was surrounded by awful darkness, small, lost, screaming for help, though no one could hear her anymore. She was an insect impaled at the centre of a web, its threads driven into what remained of her body and bringing waves of white hot pain. And from a great distance, she felt the hot rush of haemorrhaged blood, she felt the tearing of flesh, the ruin of her body.

She was the parasite now, the invader, the infection. Something else had taken everything from her. It wanted to extinguish her, but she held on. She would always hold on.

Memories; they were the wreckage in the water, the flotsam she could cling to, but they were fading fast.

There had been a ship. Horrible as it was, the ship was an anchor in the shredded remnants of her mind. There had been the misery of sea sickness, made bearable by hope. A few hours, and she would be in England. They would treat her kindly there. She would be free. There would be a new life.

But first, now, there was the hold. Dark, stinking and never still. She was too weak to fight the stench of the place; rotting fish, vomit, the urine and faeces that festered in the bucket she and the other three girls had been given. The dim-lit hell hole shook constantly from the beat of waves and the relentless throb of the engines, which added their own diesel scent to the horror of the place.

A few hours, that was all.

A few short hours.

The hatch clanged open. There was no glimpse of daylight this time, only a slight lessening of the thick blackness, which meant that it was night. A figure appeared, Sczymon, the only one who had offered them a name, a false one no doubt, but a name nonetheless. So what was it this time; the muck they called food, coffee?

Crina heard the clatter of a missed step on the ladder that gave access to the hold, then a grunted curse. Sczymon's moment of clumsiness terrified her. It was redolent with a threat she couldn't name. He reached the bottom and stumbled towards them. A new smell forced its way through the fog of stench. Alcohol.

"Wake up, you whores," he growled. "Ready for fucking?"

"Please," Crina managed to say. Even talking made her queasy. "Sczymon, you are drunk, you should -"

He hit her, a blow across her face that was shocking in its violence. She was driven onto her side, where she lay, humiliated, shivering, unable to offer any more resistance. She felt his face, close to hers now. The melded perfumes of beer and whisky swamped all other smells.

"Shut up," he said quietly. "Learn some manners, you stupid little tart. Your nice English customers won't like it if you are rude to them, will they?"

Customers?

She had known all along. She had tried to convince herself that it wasn't so, that her new life would be a paradise of hard work and good clothes and friends and happiness. But that one word finally shattered any illusion she might have harboured.

She nodded. She didn't want to answer him, or to be weak, but he was close, and she could feel the violence of him. It was like a loaded gun, pressed against her temple, a moment away from destruction.

"Now, who to train first, eh?" He moved away. And Crina gave a silent plea to God that it would be one of the others.

God heard her.

And as the girl's cries were smothered by Sczymon's rough kisses, Crina's prayer became a plea for forgiveness.

She became aware that Sczymon's grunts of pleasure had become the snores of the unconscious drunkard. The girl sobbed quietly, still trapped under his body.

"I'm sorry," Crina whispered.

The hatch was still open.

Crina stared at the square of grey. The outside. A place that was not this stinking corner of Hell. She moved slowly, crawled, held her breath. If he woke, if he caught her…

Her hand closed about the bottom rung of the ladder. The feel of corroded metal under her palm brought back the memory of their descent into this place. The reassurances that it would only be for a few hours. That they had almost reached their new home.

She stood and felt vulnerable, huge. He had to wake. She was standing, there, for all to see –

Nothing.

She climbed.

Her arms shook from the effort. She was dizzy and weak. Movement had brought the sea sickness back, but she must not vomit, not yet. Sczymon would hear her.

Crina crawled out and onto the deck and lay, face down, on the hard metal. The air was as cold as a blade, but that was better than the stifling hell of the hold.

Death would be better than that place. And better than what was waiting for her only a few miles more across this dark, brutal strip of ocean.

Crina slithered across the deck to the rail. There was no moon. A scattering of stars was visible between the clouds. She stood, weakly, and this time she did vomit. Onto the deck, over her own feet. It didn't matter. Not now. Nothing mattered except getting off this ship.

She climbed onto the rail and leaned over. A freezing wind slapped at her, tore at her hair. She clung tightly. The was darkness below her was, an unspeakably savage nothingness. Her will crumbled.

She couldn't.

A light went on, blinding, white. There were shouts. She heard the words "Stupid whore!", then glimpsed two figures, scrambling over the obstacle course of deck equipment. They were animals, and they were going to tear her apart.

She threw herself outwards, and there was a moment of beautiful, beautiful freedom.

She hit the water, and the cold was like a thousand knives that sliced her open and tore out her lungs. She couldn't breathe as she was hurled upwards, then sucked downwards into the coldest of darks. She felt her body burn, as if on fire. She tried to cry out, but her mouth filled with icy, salt water. She couldn't move, she couldn't breathe, the pain was immense.

Crina, said the water. *Crina, it's all right. I'm here. Let me take you, let me hold you.*

The voice was almost too soft to hear. Crina gasped and let herself fall. The water turned warm, and as she sank, there was light, and when she opened her mouth she could breathe. The light shifted around her, beams of it pierced the water and danced through the shades of the rainbow. Heat enfolded her, and she curled, like a child, into the arms of the sea, and it crooned over her and stroked her hair, and as she drifted into the soft, red-edged darkness, she felt it slither into her, through her skin, her mouth. It flooded her with heat.

Then ice.

She tried to scream.

Then there was only the redness. She pushed at it, tried to keep it out. The soft voice turned hard, the coldness spread through her. Her fear was even greater than it had ever been on that boat.

The red darkness turned black.

When it parted, she was on this bed. A man leaned over her. She had screamed but understood that this man didn't want to hurt her. For a moment, for a few short hours, there was peace. Then the Other had come back.

*

Tiamat, now alone with her offspring, screamed a scream that thrummed through the very nerves of the world. She felt the push of something as it engaged.

Another contraction, a burning surge of pain. Tiamat forced Crina's near useless body up into a sitting position, legs apart. A last surge of agony and a bloody mass quivered between Crina's knees. Tiamat felt the thing ripple and stretch. She whispered its name as she watched it take form.

It unfurled huge black butterfly wings, wet with mucus. Its body was a twisted thing of bone and thin, thorn encrusted flesh. It had no mouth, only a proboscis coiled below its eyeless head and tipped with an organic needle of hyperdermic sharpness.

"Lamashtu," Tiamat whispered again.

It knew its purpose, fluttered its wings and rose above the bed, then threw itself out into the world through the window, which had already been broken by one of the scorpion men in its haste to pursue Luke and his doctor sow.

Now there remained only the child, curled inside her and growing fast.

*

The world closed in on them, nothing visible but the white swirl of the blizzard, no sound but the throaty roar of the Land Rover's engine, loud through the broken offside window. It was all right now that Hannah was with him. Her presence was warmth, a reassurance. With her beside him, the snow was snow. There was no hallucination, no landscape other than the madness of white-on-black painted across the windscreen.

"Where are we going?" Hannah said after a long silence. She was shivering. The vehicle's heater was no match for the icy air sucked in through the broken window. Luke had given her his coat, which she wrapped about herself like a blanket. "I can't go to my house. I'm too scared to go home. Crina knows where I live."

"There's a hotel, I do a lot of maintenance work for

them. We'll be safe there." It seemed right. The idea that they should go to the Bell had formed quickly after they had made their escape from the bungalow.

Hannah didn't answer, and Luke took that to mean that she was satisfied with the plan. Her hand rested on his thigh. The feel of her was good. He wanted to hold her and lose himself in her, but that would be later. Now he had to get them into the town and to the seafront in one piece.

There were no street lights. The power must have failed. It was hard to tell where they

were. He saw cars, parked or abandoned. Most were little more than mounds in the snow. There were no people in sight.

He glanced right and glimpsed the faint glow of the sea.

Now there were buildings, dark, hulking shapes, some with the merest flicker of light in their windows; candles, Luke assumed. He saw the iron railings of the promenade. The top of the railings at least, most of their height was buried in snow. Not much further.

Something loomed out of the blizzard. A figure, in the middle of the road.

Too big, too broad and bulky, too hulking and wrong.

Luke swore and swung the wheel to the right, just as the shape broke into a charge. Hannah was shouting. He couldn't hear what she was saying. He had to keep the Land Rover on the road, prevent it from burying its bonnet in a snow drift. At the same time, they had to get around that thing.

It was a Minotaur. A fucking Minotaur.

The creature slammed into the Land Rover, a glancing blow against the nearside door. Hannah cried out and threw herself against Luke. The glass of the door broke, there was a loud bang. The door caved inward.

Luke rammed his foot hard down. The wheels

thrashed at the snow, the engine howled, then the rubber bit and the vehicle staggered forward.

Where the hell was that creature?

"Are you okay, Hannah?"

"Yeah -"

The impact jarred through Luke's bones. Pain speared his back, and it felt as if his vertebrae had been ripped apart. The Land Rover lurched forwards and sideways, the offside shoved against the right-hand snow drift. He fought to regain control and a moment later saw the Minotaur running beside the vehicle. It swung around and once again rammed the nearside door. Metal twisted and tore. Luke wrenched the wheel back to the left, drove the vehicle into the creature, which stumbled sidewards. He raced away, then, still accelerating, spun the wheel.

"What are you doing? Luke, for God's sake."

The Land Rover pirouetted on the ice until its nose faced the way they had come. Luke snapped the steering wheel in the opposite direction. He stamped the accelerator again and fought the skid until the Land Rover was aimed directly at the Minotaur, which was already running towards them.

"Get down," he yelled above the engine noise. "Cover your head. Crash position."

Hannah didn't move, but Luke didn't have time to shout at her. He held on tight as the Land Rover wheel-spun into life. The tyres found traction. Luke slammed his right foot to the floor. He sensed, rather than saw Hannah curl forward, hands over her head.

The Minotaur became the world, a living battering ram that exploded out of the snow. Closer. Closer. Hannah, talked to herself. It sounded as if she was praying. Make it a good one, Luke told her silently as the thing hurtled towards him; vast and solid and mighty.

Luke jerked the steering wheel left and rammed his foot on the brake. The Land Rover swung into a broadside, and there was a violent, earth-tearing bang. The vehicle shook and bucked, then finished its maddened dance by driving itself into the seaward snow drift, nose facing the way they had just come.

In the headlight, Luke saw the Minotaur sprawled, face-down on the road, moving through, already raising its impossible bull head.

Luke opened the door and was out.

Hannah yelled at him to wait and not to be so bloody stupid.

He ignored her. The snow-splintered wind all but forced his eyes shut. He scrambled around to the rear of the Land Rover. The Minotaur was now, frighteningly, cut off from view. He opened the door and dragged out a petrol can and a gas bottle and blow torch. Then he turned and set off along the side of the vehicle, out into the cone of light from its headlamps and towards the Minotaur.

Out here, he was a small, fleshy, fragile thing. The Minotaur was vast and unbreakable. It was hurt though. The impact had stunned it, though Luke doubted that any bones were broken. It was a terrible mountain of brawn and muscle. Its horns were lethal spears. Luke broke into a jog, careful, afraid to fall, because that would be the end.

The Minotaur grunted, snorted and pushed itself up onto its hands and knees. It lifted its huge head to transfix its opponent with its hell-red eyes. Steam curled from its nostrils. It growled and bared its teeth, too sharp and long, not bovine at all.

Luke stopped. He was close enough. He dropped the gas bottle to the ground, twisted open the fuel can and darted forwards, swinging the can as he did so. So close, he could smell the creature's musky scent, could smell the sweat-pungent stink of explosive violence. The Minotaur grunted in, what sounded like, surprise as the fluid spattered over its head and shoulders. It pushed itself up onto one knee. Luke dropped the can and stumbled back. Keeping his attention fixed on the creature, he reached down and found the gas bottle.

He fumbled with the valve. His hands were cold, his fingers stiff and unresponsive. The Minotaur grunted again, and now it was getting to its feet. Luke heard a hiss, barely perceptible above the howl of the storm. The pistol-shaped lighter was attached to the gas bottle via a chain. He yanked it up towards the nozzle of the torch.

The Minotaur stood, wavering as if dizzy, then roared. The sound shattered Luke's self-control, and the torch fell from his hands. He was frozen, paralysed. The monster lowered its head, roared again.

A figure barged past, scooped up the torch, then crouched between Luke and the oncoming beast. Hannah, it was Hannah. She struggled with the lighter, the torch. She was tiny before the charging monster. There was a flash, a flare of light. A flame, maximum strength but so frail. Hannah stood, slowly, so bloody slowly. The gas bottle looked heavy in her left hand. She waited, a desperately courageous figure caught in the light. Luke cried out, desolate. The Minotaur was almost on her.

And then all sight of her was lost as the world erupted into flame.

*

Alison was drawn to the reception area's large windows by a flare of light. She peered into the dark and saw an unsteady glow. It looked as if something was on fire. The glow moved erratically for a few minutes, then faded, and there was only the snow. Riot and looting, broken out in sleepy Eastlee. Alison shook her head and chuckled ruefully. Who on Earth would want to be out there creating anarchy in this weather? It was strange though, incongruous, fire, in the middle of a blizzard. It added to her unease. Nothing was as it should be tonight.

She could hear the explosion of waves over the promenade, but she could see nothing beyond the closest shards of snow. The blizzard was hypnotic. It was terrible and beautiful. At least from in here.

It was past ten pm, and she should be going off-duty, but Rob, who was supposed to take the night shift, hadn't appeared, and she knew full well that he wasn't going to come in. Not that she blamed him. No one should be out there. He'd probably tried to call, but the phone wasn't working. There was no mobile phone signal either, which was unnerving. Like most people Alison knew, she lived by the phone, it was an extension of her*self*. Its failure left her desolate. She felt alone and vulnerable.

It was as if the world no longer existed outside the environs of the town.

Thank God Murdoch was here. She didn't know why his presence reassured her, they not had parted on the best of terms, but it did. He was up in his room, the non-existent Room 240, injured, and "feeding", whatever that meant.

But he was here. And that alone was enough to make Alison feel a little more secure.

That and the fact that she had locked the main doors. A grievous sin against the Bell's many rules. But who cared about rules tonight?

There were no people out there, no cars other than the snow-smothered vehicles parked along the promenade.

There were no people down here either. No one ate in the restaurant or drank at the bar. Everyone had gone to their rooms. There was a sense of siege about the place.

Suddenly frightened of the alien world outside, Alison turned away from the window and headed back towards the desk. She was tired, but she needed to stay on duty for at least another couple of hours. The lights buzzed and flickered, and their illumination was dim and dirty. Everywhere else seemed to have lost its power. From what little she could see of the town, it had looked to be in darkness. No lights. No electricity. So, why was there electricity in here, albeit dismal and uncertain?

Because it wasn't coming from the National Grid, that was why. It was coming from the Place Murdoch had told her about.

The wind rattled the windows. Alison wanted the night over. She wanted the snow gone so she could go to Laura and tell her how she felt and they could leave this miserable little town and see where the road took them.

Alison sat down behind the desk. Perhaps she should see if Murdoch was okay. Anything rather than stay down here.

She started and half-stood as someone beat at the main door.

Again, it sounded urgent, desperate. But Alison couldn't move. It might be anyone

out there. Any*thing*.

Again. Again. *Again.*

People, outside. Cold, frightened. Threatened, even. And she was just going to let them freeze to death? She stood and crossed the foyer carefully, arms wrapped about herself, prepared to see the terrible, the terrifying.

It was a man and woman. The man was the one pounding at the door, the woman

leaned against the wall, possibly hurt. The man wore no coat. God, no coat in this storm. Alison tore at the bolts, and the key and the door swung open. The couple stumbled in, snow crusted, the man supported the woman, who was wrapped in an overlarge parka, hood up.

It was only when they made it to the armchairs in the lounge area that Alison recognised the man. Luke Harris, who fixed their plumbing and electrical problems, who decorated their rooms and repaired what was broken.

The couple had brought a smell in with them, a scent of smoke and fire. Alison remembered the flare of light. Luke had been involved with that? Then the woman pushed down the hood of the parka, and Alison was even more startled to see that is was one of the local GPs, Dr Makebo.

Without comment or question, Alison went to the deserted bar to fetch some drinks; two whiskies, and a vodka for herself. When she returned, she sat down with them and they all drank in silence.

"Are you okay?" Alison said at last, the question mainly directed at Hannah Makebo, who nodded. She was, Alison noticed, shaking, and not entirely from the cold. There was a look in her eye, she had seen something bad.

"Why were you out there tonight?" *Together*, Alison wanted to add but held her peace. "What's happened?"

Hannah looked up. "Are the doors locked?" She sounded frightened.

"Yes. You're safe in here."

Hannah nodded, although she didn't seem convinced.

"What was that fire?" Alison asked. "Please tell me. I don't care how weird it is, I've seen some pretty weird things already tonight."

"We were attacked," Luke said. "And no, I don't really know who it was. I'm not sure I know what it was either." Luke regarded Alison intensely. "What have *you* seen?"

"The storm. And there's a guest..." She sighed. She

might as well say it. "There's a guest upstairs, in a room that doesn't exist."

"Who is he?" Hannah asked.

"He calls himself Detective Inspector -"

"Murdoch," Hannah finished for her.

"Yes, that's right. You know him? You've met him?"

"He came to Luke's bungalow."

"You never told me," Luke said. He didn't sound angry, just curious.

"There's a lot I haven't told you. I'm sorry. There wasn't time…"

"He said that there was something bad in the town," Alison said. "Is it at your house, Luke? Is that why Murdoch went there?"

"Yes," Hannah answered for him.

"It's my fault," Luke said. "All this shite. I'm to blame."

"No, Luke," Hannah said. "You had to help her -"

"I don't mean finding Crina on the beach. It's more than that. It's what happened in Iraq. I don't really understand, but…" He subsided, became lost in himself.

Alison saw Hannah reach across and take Luke's hand in both of her own. The act was tender, as was the look that passed between them. So *that's* why they were together. At least not everything about tonight was awful.

"We have to talk to Murdoch," Hannah said.

*

The Lamashtu returned through the broken bedroom window and folded itself on the bed, an ungainly black tangle of wings and claws. Its belly was bloated. It could hardly move. Tiamat cooed to it, and it struggled up the bed towards her. She held out her hand, and the creature came to her. She drew it to herself gently.

She petted it. The thing moaned, exhausted and replete. She saw fragments of glass embedded in its body. Windows broken, houses invaded, blood drunk.

Tiamat kissed the back of its head. Its flesh was dank and cold. It quivered in her hands. In one quick motion, she twisted it onto its back. It struggled, flapped its wings clawed feebly at the air. Tiamat surged forward and sank her teeth into its distended belly.

Its cargo of stolen blood poured into her mouth and down her throat, hot and rich. She drank until she could take no more. Then she cast the dried corpse aside.

The child stirred inside her, energised by its feast. Tiamat closed her eyes and let the rest of the Lamashtu's blood surge through the wreckage of the body she had stolen. The body began to change, wounds knitted, structures altered, melted and flowed and re-formed. Tissue re-grew, formed fibrous webs across wounds and the tears.

And somewhere, deep within the aching dark, Crina hid and waited. She was forgotten. She was sure of it. She was a spark of awareness, a splinter, a disturbing thought, a passing irritation. Of no concern.

*

Alison went in first. Luke leaned against the wall of the corridor outside Room 240 and waited. Hannah stood beside him, close, her hand on his arm. She told him everything that had happened; her illness, Murdoch's visit. When she had finished, Luke said, "In Iraq, there was an ambush."

"Luke, you don't have to -"

"I want to."

Hannah drew in close to him.

"Most of the lads died instantly. Two of us survived. Me and Private Greene. Good bloke, kind-hearted,

212

everybody's mate. I heard him, but I didn't try to help him. I was too fucking scared...."

...he walks as best he can through the deepening river of blood, towards the burning disc, that was the exit from the ruin. He is sure he is walking towards his death, but despite this, Luke clings to the ancient scrap of armour. He doesn't believe it will save him. It is simply important that he carries it. He is oblivious to the roar of the battle that rages around him on the walls and ceiling of the ruin. Of the bodies that fall into the blood.

He sees figures, at the entrance, indistinct brush-strokes of sun-distorted silhouette. He tenses, waits for the first shot.

The river is suddenly shallow, then he is walking on dry ground. He squints against the glare and stumbles out into the daylight. The heat slams into him like a wall. Dust swirls and scrapes at his face. He gasps for air. The roar grows loud. Men move in. He stands, wavering from shock and fatigue, but determined to die on his feet and not his knees or belly.

"Fuck me!" one of them shouts. "He's one of ours."

Luke blinks, sees British infantrymen emerge from the haze. The dust storm and the roar are from a helicopter, coming in to land a hundred or so metres away.

The nearest of the soldiers stops. "Christ, the poor fucker's covered in blood. Medic! Medic, get over here! Now!"

"...I was saved, but...I let them...I let them find Greene and kill him. I ran away. 'We never leave one of our own behind.' Well, I did."...

"It wasn't your fault. What could you have done except get yourself killed?"

"That breastplate, I should have left it where it was."

"Yes," Hannah said but not unkindly. "Because I think it's what brought all this…insanity here. But you weren't to know that, how could you have known?" She grabbed his hands. "Thousands of artifacts are taken from sites. Anyone who found it would have picked it up and brought it home with them." She hesitated. "Perhaps we should just throw it into the sea."

"Christ," Luke said and shook his head. "Listen to us. We actually believe in magic. The lunatics really have taken over the asylum."

*

"If you want me to give you forgiveness, Alison, I can't."

Murdoch was sitting up on the bed when Alison went into the room. It was the first thing he said, and it did little to thaw her anger or lessen her fear of him.

"I didn't come in for that," she managed to say.

"However, if you really are looking for forgiveness," it was as if Murdoch hadn't heard her, "this *is* where you'll find it, here, in The Place, although, you might not recognise it for what it is."

She didn't know how to reply.

"Alison."

"Yes?"

"Thank you, for being kind."

"And for not smothering you with a pillow?"

His eyes flared, and Alison recoiled. That ancient thing once again glared at her. And she was afraid. "Don't mock me with your self-hatred."

"I…I'm sorry."

He held out his hand. Alison hesitated, then took it. His terrible frown melted. He was Jack Hawkins again; offering her the wry smile he had once given the character of Detective Chief Inspector Gideon, protagonist in another of her granddad's favourite films. "I need to talk to all of you now, Alison."

240 was a modest double room; big windows, high ceiling, redolent with faded grandeur, and in need of fresh paint, carpet and curtain, but it was clean, functional, typical of the hotel. And for what Alison had described as non-existent, remarkably solid and real. There were smells, coffee, aftershave and hints of both Alison and Hannah's perfumes, all underlain by that musty scent found in old buildings.

Murdoch sat on the edge of bed. He looked familiar to Luke, an actor perhaps, though he couldn't come up with a name. Someone from the past. The man was in a bad way. He wore a white shirt, the tie pulled down, top button undone, and sleeves rolled away from his wrists. He looked tired, worn, and he was injured, his shirt torn, his flesh opened.

That wasn't the worst part, however, not for Luke. Murdoch bled light. It seeped and bubbled and dripped onto the bed and the floor, where it lay in momentary, shimmering puddles before it dissolved to nothing. Murdoch was, therefore, not human.

"Pleased to meet you, Luke," Murdoch said and held out his hand. His grip was firm and warm enough. His voice was deep, gruff, his accent correct. BBC English, wasn't that what they used to call it? "Sorry about my appearance. I encountered a friend of yours earlier, and we had a bit of a disagreement."

"Hannah says you're..." The name seemed too ridiculous to utter despite the impossibility of what leaked from the man's wounds. Despite everything else that had happened that day.

Murdoch smiled and nodded. "She's right. I am a god, God, the Highest of the High. But I'm not the God

I once was, nor should I be, my job was done once Tiamat was defeated and the world made. I shouldn't even exist, at least not in coalescent form. But needs must." He shifted position, groaned from obvious pain. "Every now and then, I wear flesh. It seldom ends well." He closed his eyes, as if gathering strength. "Alison?"

"Yes?"

Luke glanced towards Alison. She looked pale, her face tight with worry. Luke wondered what Murdoch was to her. Her concern was more like that of a daughter for her ailing father than that of hotel staff for a client.

"Coffee, please," Murdoch said. The gentleness of his voice heightened the sense of closeness between them. "For all of us."

Alison nodded, then abruptly swung away and got to work. It was the type of brusqueness that hid strong emotion. Hannah went to her. Luke heard a quiet offer of help.

"Never rely on a god, Luke," Murdoch said ruefully. "We always let you down. Right now this god is flesh, and flesh has its needs, caffeine for a start." He waved towards two faded armchairs arranged by the window. "Sit down before you fall down."

Luke did so.

"What did you bring home from Iraq, Luke?"

The suddenness of the question was unnerving.

"A…a fragment...some sort of breastplate. I gave it to the museum when I moved here."

"By accident?"

"What?"

"You chose this little town by accident?"

"I like it, I came here when I was a kid." Luke was irritated by Murdoch's questioning.

"Exactly where did you find the artifact?"

Luke glanced at the two women, who were busy around the kettle. Cups clattered. Hannah looked back at him. She nodded, the action so slight it was almost imperceptible, yet for Luke it was a powerful act of permission.

"There was an attack, I took cover in some ruins."

"Strange ruins?"

"Strange? I suppose so. Although, I've always believed that I was seeing things, hallucinating. The situation was…stressful."

"Do you still think it was a hallucination?"

"I don't know anymore. Not after today."

"It wasn't. Those ruins were in The Place."

"What?"

"You found an entrance into The Place. Which means that it was no accident you found the artifact. It's a catalyst. A means to draw and burst a boil."

"So, it brought that creature in my house; Crina, Tiamat, whoever the fuck she is." He was swearing at a god, at God. He needed to stop, but he was angry now. He hadn't asked for this shite. He wanted to be left alone.

"Tiamat, Lilith, Lucifer, Chaos, call her what you will." Murdoch seemed unperturbed by Luke's outburst. "Like me, she shouldn't exist." He was wracked by a fit of coughing. Each cough brought a fresh flow of light from his wounds. In a moment, Alison was there, her arm about his shoulder. He reached up, patted her hand. "It's all right. I need that coffee now."

"Why would she want it? It's a scrap of rusty metal."

"It is formed from what the Babylonians called the Tablets of Destiny. But that, of course like everything else, is misleading. The artifact was a weapon, which gave great power to Tiamat's 'husband', Kingu, and almost gave them a victory."

The drinks were handed around. The coffee was hot and black. Hannah sat down in the other armchair, next to Luke, Alison on the edge of the bed beside Murdoch.

"The breastplate acted as a focal point." Murdoch shook his head. "There was more of her remaining than I had thought." He chuckled ruefully. "I should have ground her up more finely before scattering her over the boiling surface of the newborn Earth. She was obviously strong enough to come back. It only needed a spark, a catalyst. If Luke hadn't found the breastplate, someone else would have done. But, like all boils, Tiamat needs to be drawn out into the open so that she can be destroyed." Murdoch turned his attention once more to Luke. "Why you, Luke? Why did The Place open up to you?"

"Because I'm a coward. I was running away. I left a friend to die."

"Luke…"

"It's all right, Hannah," Murdoch said. "And as to whether you are a coward, Luke, it's not for me to say."

"What do we need to do?" Luke asked. "Destroy that breastplate, take it back to the Place?"

"Break it. Tiamat mustn't get her hands on it. More importantly, Kingu, Anti-Christ, the Great Dragon, her…husband, son, lover, twin, whatever you conceive him to be, must not get *his* hands on it. What's happening out there, it will happen to the whole world if he does. Tiamat is merely the carrier, the womb for him. Kingu's the real threat."

Luke got up and drew the curtain aside, just far enough to block the light from the room and enable him to see out. There was nothing but the crazed swirl of white and slashes of lightning, each one a wound in the sky, giant versions of those on Murdoch's chest and abdomen. He could feel the wind beat on the glass, its vibrations thrummed into the hand he pressed against the panel.

"You can't destroy the artifact by simply walking up

to its display case with a sledgehammer. You have to go...*between.* Into the space that separates the breastplate from this world," Murdoch said from behind him. "That space, The Place, is also a shortcut to the museum."

Luke turned from the window. "How do we get there?"

"You have to go through The Place," Murdoch answered. "And by doing so, you'll undermine the breastplate. It will enable you to destroy the thing..."

Murdoch suddenly doubled over, panting for breath. He coughed again. If the light had been blood, he would have bled to death long before now, but, even so, his strength was obviously failing. Luke felt ambivalent about the fact. He barely knew the man, and he wasn't a man anyway. And would he actually die, or simply revert to whatever constituted his natural state? The emotion he did experience, however, was anger at the thought that his actions were manipulated by other forces; gods, The Place. There was fear as well. Once Murdoch was gone, and it wouldn't be long by the look of him, they would be on their own. And he had no idea what he was supposed to do.

"I'll show you the way to the museum," Murdoch said, struggling to his feet.

*

Supported by Alison, Murdoch led the way along the corridor outside Room 240. Luke and Hannah had offered to help, but Alison refused them. Though quickly exhausted, she was sustained by the half-remembered, half-formed story of St Christopher carrying the Christ child. The story gave her certainty that she had to do this alone.

Their progress was slow and awkward. The corridor

seemed longer than it should be. The light was dim and dirty. The lamps in their wall fittings flickered, the glow of their elements worm-like and uncertain. There were too many shadows. The angles were wrong, the walls crooked, the ceilings low, and there were too many doors. Light shifted and played under the jam of each one. The same light, silver white. The same dance, all in perfect synch.

Alison came to understand that it was the light of televisions, on in every room. Each showed an identical programme. A war film, by the sound of it. She heard a ship's siren, aircraft, the heartbeat pulse of guns. Then the hiss and roar of the sea as it was boiled into mountainous white eruptions by bombs and depth charges.

How did she know? There was only sound, and she knew little about the war.

She knew the film, though. She knew it well.

A corvette named *Compass Rose*, Jack Hawkins on the bridge…

"How much further?" she asked, voice breathy from effort.

Murdoch didn't answer. His head hung down. He stumbled. Then he fell to his knees and took Alison with him. The rage of cinematic war grew louder. A hundred rooms, a hundred televisions, a hundred sinking ships and drowning men. Louder, until it filled the corridor with such vivid intensity, she expected to see a rage of sea water crashing between the flock-papered walls towards her.

Someone shouted a warning. Something caught her attention. She looked up. She didn't scream. She couldn't. What she saw made no sense. She heard Luke shouting, telling her to get up, to run. But the words were mere sounds.

It filled the corridor ahead of them, about fifty feet

away. She saw a human torso, male, naked. It had no hair. Its eyes were black pin pricks, its mouth a red slash, which opened to become a dark, howling tunnel. There was another body behind it. Arachnid, too many legs, a tail, curved over its back. It took a moment for her to understand that the other body was part of the human thing. The creature was shadow and angles and blackness and threat.

"Get in a room," Luke said. He sounded dangerously calm. "For fuck's sake, Hannah, get them into a bloody room."

"I'm trying. The door's locked."

Alison dared to look around, frightened to take her eyes off the creature in the corridor but aware that she needed to help. Key, she had the master key. She forced herself up onto her feet, movement made slow by her fear. She drew the card out on its extending chain, the one fixed to the waist of her skirt.

She could hear Hannah, shouting at her to hurry up. She could see the terror in the doctor's eyes. She could feel the weight of the creature's presence bear down on her, could feel the violence within it begin to uncoil. She fumbled the card into the reader. The LED stayed red. She snatched it out and rammed it in again. Green. A click. Audible despite the cacophony of the film.

The door swung open. Luke shoved Hannah inside, then grabbed Alison's arm. She shrugged him off and crouched down beside Murdoch. He looked up. His face was a web of fiery cracks.

"Leave me," he snapped.

"I can't."

"You have to, you have to leave me, and you have to survive. Don't you understand that, Alison? There are times when *you* have to survive."

She shook her head. "I can't..."

"Survive, Alison."

"Christ!"

Luke's cry made her look up. The thing was coming. It hurtled towards her, an explosion of raw hunger and destruction.

"Go!" Murdoch yelled, and she was stung into movement. She threw herself at the open door and stumbled into the room.

The door was slammed shut behind her. The television went dead in that same instant.

And Hannah was shouting now, sobbing. She clawed at the door.

"Luke! Luke! Oh God, no. Luke!"

There was no reply, only the scratch and scrabble of insectile legs like the scrape of a thousand leafless branches against a window. There was the thud of a huge body slammed against the wall.

Then it was gone.

And there was silence.

CHAPTER FIVE: THE PLACE

Some long-shredded part of Tiamat's mind recoiled from the obscenity of what remained in her womb. It was a mere passing thread, blown by the winds of her needs. Yet it troubled her. That tiny voice, that spark of something that should have been crushed. But there was no time to concern herself over it now.

Crina's body was changing, a metamorphosis wrought with unspeakable agonies as joints wrenched into new configurations, as bones stretched and twisted, as tissue was pulled taut, torn, repaired, as flesh was peeled to reveal organic machineries created from the raw gristle and meat of the stolen carcase.

When it was done, Tiamat's rage and pain were terrible. They drove her against the walls of the room, which shattered and gave her exit into the howling white chaos outside.

*

Luke ran. Every breath, a sob. He must not fall or trip or slow down or look back. He could hear the scorpion man. He could hear it getting closer.

Ahead, the light changed. The borderline between The Place and the hotel. What he needed would be there. In his own world.

He could barely breathe, the panic was back, a roar of blood and voices and images. There was heat and carpet and dim light and the scrabbling of the scorpion's legs and the screams for help and then mercy from Greene and the light, the light, the fucking light.

He all but fell into the hotel proper, across the line between ochre dullness and a brighter, electric glow. His chest burned, pain speared into his heart.

It was close now, so close. Raw violence, raw hatred.

There. What he needed. He grabbed at the fire extinguisher as he blundered past, crashed against a wall to stop himself and spun around.

Nothing else. Only the thing's face and open mouth and its howl of rage and soulless, formless eyes and the sting and invertebrate horror of its body and the speed of its approach, and imminent terrible death.

Luke fumbled at the extinguisher's safety pin. It wouldn't budge, wouldn't fucking budge. He tore his finger, saw blood. Yanked again, again. The pin slid free. He hoisted the tank, aimed it, waited.

The scorpion man exploded out of the darkness it brought with it. And there was nothing else he could see or hear or feel.

He jammed his fingers up against the extinguisher's trigger.

The creature hit him. The collision knocked him back. Shock and pain and a blast of icy, blinding vapour. The scorpion squealed and reared and clawed at its face.

When the extinguisher was spent, Luke lifted it and smashed it against the creature's head, again, again and again. The thing's flesh split, but there was no blood. The skull fractured like an eggshell, and beneath was a fibrous pulp, like the meat of some foul fruit. The thing squealed and grabbed at him, but it was dying. Twitching. Gasping for air. A collapsed, angular, mass of limbs and bloated, quivering abdomen. The tail waved, flopped against the wall. The creature grew still.

There wasn't much room to get past the thing. Luke crushed himself tight into the gap. Then he was through.

He ran down the corridor, back into The Place, where there were now junctions and corners. He couldn't remember the way. Christ, it was like being in a maze.

Then someone called his name.

*

Hannah pushed herself back from the door. She wanted to stay there, forever. She wanted to shout out Luke's name until she was hoarse. But she had a job to do. She had to destroy the breastplate. She turned and saw Alison, who looked pale and drawn. Her eyes were red-rimmed from crying.

"It's you and me," Hannah said.

Alison nodded.

"Are you okay? Ready?"

"Yes," Alison said.

Hannah hesitated at the door. There were no sounds. She could only presume that the scorpion was gone.

Luke was gone.

She opened the door, quickly, tensing as she did so. Outside, there was nothing but the dull-lit corridor, the worn, decayed wallpaper. And the maddening angles and low ceiling. There was no sign of what she feared. No blood. No torn remains, nothing to weep over. Luke and Murdoch had both vanished.

Alison beside her, she set off down the corridor. Its

curve, which she didn't remember from before, restricted their view to a few metres. If there were any monsters waiting for them, they wouldn't see them until it was too late. Hannah experienced an odd resignation. It numbed her fear. It made her tired. She stopped believing that they would make it to the museum alive.

The floor was soft. She wondered why she hadn't noticed it before. It bowed under her feet.

The light grew worse. It flickered and buzzed. It left splashes of shadow and turned everything a dirty shade of ochre. Hannah felt her foot sink into the carpet, as if the floor had turned to mud. She wrenched her foot free and fell against the wall. Which was also soft. It breathed, it moved. There was something, under the wallpaper, under the plaster. Hannah was reminded of the sudden, pre-birth movements of the scorpion men as they scuttered about the inside of Crina's womb.

The two women resumed walking. Whatever moved under the wallpaper reached towards them now; hands trapped under membranous plaster and flocked paper.

Then the floor gave way.

Hannah fell, sucked down. She threw herself forward and clawed at the carpet, but there was nothing to grip. Alison shouted, dropped to her knees and reached out to her.

There was a warmth about Hannah's legs, her waist, as if she was sliding into a bath of some glutinous fluid. She could see Alison's mouth work, the panic in the woman's eyes. But Hannah couldn't hear what she was saying. Other voices filled her head; whispers, familiar, familial, soothing. The warmth flooded up into her body. She didn't have to fight this. She had come from a womb, and now it was time to return to it. She lay her cheek against the carpet and let her body slide slowly into the softness. She wanted the voices, the singing and whispering. They took away her fear. She was weary and in need of the sleep they offered.

*

Every turn Luke made led him deeper into a maze of identical corridors. It didn't matter, not at that moment. Nothing mattered but the voice. Hannah. She was shouting for help. She sounded frightened, as if she too was lost. Her cries led him on down corridor after corridor, each one decorated with that same bloody wallpaper and carpeted with the same threadbare carpet.

And somewhere, moving in, were the scorpion men. He glimpsed them, crammed into side corridors; tangles of legs, misshapen geometries of human torsos and curved stings.

"Luke!"

It was Hannah.

"Help me!"

He plunged into yet another corridor. It twisted and turned and grew smaller and dank. The paper was mouldy, splashed with stain, blistered and peeling from the rotten plaster beneath. Something breathed wetly ahead of him in the darkness. Hannah's voice echoed from an entrance to his right. He followed it.

"Help me, Luke, please, God, help me!"

Darkness folded itself about him, covered his face, seeped into his mouth, and he tasted it. The taste was sour. Dusty. He spat it out, saw light and ran for it. Another passage, this one lined with roots.

He was going deeper into the Place. He had to get out, go back. Things were coming.

Scorpions, perhaps, or worse. But Hannah still called to him. From behind, from the right, the left, ahead, her voice bounced, rebounded and echoed from the walls and through his head.

"Hannah!"

"Luke!"

He called, she answered, but never from directly ahead, always from another turn. Always just out of reach. Each corridor was more grotesque than the one before. Walls that thrummed with a heartbeat of their own, walls covered in flesh through which blue and red veins could be seen, walls of faces.

"Hannah!"

"Luke, I'm here. Luke, please help me. Please. I love you, please help me!"

He stopped. The voice was close now.

"Luke? Can you hear me? Jesus, where are you?"

He ran, drawn by her voice. He ran, out of breath, repeating her name over and over again.

Until.

He saw a figure, ahead of him, silhouetted against a bright, reddish light. The figure's arms were splayed, and it struggled with trapped-animal desperation. It was Hannah, naked, caught in some sort of web. Dark things moved in, a slow crawl of liquid shadow that closed about her. Hannah screamed, and his name formed the foundation of her screams.

She screamed until it seemed as if her sanity would be torn apart. He took a step forward. Then hesitated. This wasn't right.

Her scream was an accusation.

And he knew.

She shrieked his name, but he knew he had to run. He knew he had to leave her. He knew that trying to save her would be madness.

So he ran.

Corners, junctions, trusting to instinct, half-mad with grief and self-loathing but knowing that he had to run.

Until he found the way up ahead blocked by a familiar tangle of legs and squat, dark body. It hissed and broke into a charge.

*

"Hannah, Hannah, grab my hand."

The voice was an irritation that jarred against her peace. She was going home. She needed to go home. She could feel her mother's hands on her waist. She could hear her father, laughing. She wanted to go back to them. She needed to go back.

Someone grabbed her wrist. She opened her eyes, angry now, about to hurl a rebuke at whoever was mauling at her. Then she understood that she was dying. She understood that she had to get away. She clutched at Alison's outstretched hand. The woman's face was contorted with effort. Hannah kicked against the thickness that sucked at her. The voices turned malevolent, threats she couldn't understand, delivered in a language of gibbering, hisses and snarls.

"Let go!" she shouted at Alison. "You can't...you won't pull me out."

"I must," Alison yelled back. She slid towards the softness, scrabbled at the carpet with her heels. "I have to..."

"It's not working. Let go. For Christ's sake, Alison, let fucking go!"

Alison flinched, as if stung by the violence of Hannah's language. She fell back and landed on her bottom. Hannah slapped both palms on the solid floor in front of her, arms apart, in line with her shoulders. Then she pressed down and slowly, painfully lifted herself out of the mire. Enraged, the voices grew louder and their threats more vicious. Hannah's arms shook with effort, she felt her strength ebb. But she was moving, rising slowly from the ooze. Up, until her arms were straight and she pitched forward onto the floor. Alison was back, helping her as she hauled her right knee onto the carpet and used it to lever her left leg free.

"Hannah…"

She looked back, startled by her mother's voice. She saw her rise from the mire, head, neck, shoulder. She threw herself onto Hannah's back, sobbed into the borrowed parka she wore. Hannah wanted to turn, twist around so that she could hold the woman who had given her life and sacrificed everything for her.

Then Alison's fist closed about her hair and jerked her head back and she was shouting into Hannah's face to get away. Sobbing with effort and grief, Hannah wrenched herself free, scrambled clear on her hands and knees, then crushed herself against the wall and cried.

Her mother, father, Luke. Too much loss.

When she able to, Hannah sat up and saw Alison, crouched beside her. "You okay?"

Hannah nodded. "Thank you," she said.

"It wasn't your time. I couldn't let you die." Alison stood abruptly, as if cutting the conversation. "Come on, we have to keep moving."

Alison helped Hannah to her feet. They walked, inured now to the strangeness of the corridors, the distortions of scale and perspective, the movements that rippled through the walls. Distance and time were hard to judge, but after a while the light ahead changed, and a few moments later they entered the museum.

*

The museum was located in the dining room and library of a large Georgian house. The wall between the two rooms had been demolished in the first years of the twentieth century by its Edwardian owner, an adventurer who had given them up to show off his collection of curios and loot.

The place was silent but for the howl of the storm

that battered at its windows and pressed against its walls.

Hannah and Alison stood on the landing at the top of a double staircase that curved down to the ground floor like the mandibles of a giant insect. The landing narrowed into a gallery that stretched away on either side and was lined with glass cases. Each case, Hannah knew from previous visits, was filled with pinned butterflies and other insects. She had always been more affected by the cruelty of killing for display than impressed by the breadth of the collection.

The main floor below was a maze of larger cabinets and exhibits, mostly statues and weaponry, including two sets of medieval armour.

The Babylonian artifact, donated by Luke, was in a new-looking case in the centre of the ground floor. A position of honour and unveiled by the mayor of Eastlee eight years ago. There were photographs of the ceremony on the walls down there, including two featuring Luke, his smile forced as he shook hands with the mayor.

More poignant still was the sight of Luke's ladder and tools, tucked away neatly in the far corner. He had been in the middle of redecorating the museum, an annual winter event. The ordinary was always the worst. Hannah had discovered that when clearing the few possessions her parents owned; a comb, a pair of socks, a sewing box. A Bible.

She was glad they hadn't known the truth about the God they worshipped and trusted so devoutly. She wondered if they knew the truth now.

But all this was irrelevant, because they were not alone in the museum. There were three scorpion men crammed into the spaces between the exhibits, motionless, facing the locked and barred front doors. Presumably, they believed that this was where their prey would enter the museum, which meant that it was just possible that they hadn't seen Hannah or Alison.

Hannah backed slowly away. Alison already stood by the doorway through which they had come. The museum lights were on, though they cast the same dismal, dirty light that had illuminated the corridors of The Place. Did that mean that the museum existed there, rather than in the familiar world?

"There's no way we go downstairs," Hannah said.

"Yes, there is," Alison answered. She was pale. Her voice was hoarse, thick, as if she could barely speak.

"What are you going to do? Alison -"

"I'll distract them, lead them back into the hotel, the Place, whatever it is."

"No, that's insane. They'll catch you…Alison, you can't."

"What's your plan, then, Hannah?" There was no malice in the question. In fact, Alison's hand was on her arm as she asked it. Hannah could see the raw fear in the woman's eyes. "You have to destroy that armour. I'll try to give you as much time as I can."

Hannah had no answer.

"I know the hotel, there are back stairs, unused corridors and rooms…" She shrugged. "I'll think of something. And…it feels right, as if it is what I'm supposed to do." Alison took a deep breath. "You need to hide. Under one of those." She pointed to the cabinets on the gallery to the right. "It's not ideal, but…"

"I'll come for you, Alison, when it's done."

"I know."

Hannah moved slowly. She chose the largest of the nearby display cabinets. She lowered herself to her hands and knees and crawled under it. Her body was stiff and unresponsive, every movement required effort, willpower. The reality of what Alison intended to do was too terrible for thought. Instead, Hannah concentrated on folding herself into the shadow at the back of the cabinet. The floor was cold and gritty. She curled up, on her side, like a sleeping dog. The world became a narrow horizontal band. All she could see were the ornate railings that separated the gallery from the open space above the museum.

There was a moment of quiet. When only the storm could be heard. And the heavy rhythm of her own heartbeat. She was trapped. If one of the scorpion men found her, she was finished. Her death would be terrible.

Then Alison screamed, "Come on, you fucking bastards!"

Hannah whimpered in fear as she heard the scramble of the scorpions' legs. She hugged herself more tightly. She willed herself to disappear. She saw the insect legs of a scorpion. Close, scrabbling at the polished floor, bony, chitinous, steel-smooth. Close, so close she could touch them. Another. The cabinet rocked and bucked as a scorpion blundered into it. She drew in a shallow, tremulous breath as the case teetered, then settled.

Alison's screeched taunts faded. The wind howled, and the great windows rattled. Thunder growled, and lightning blazed electric white.

Hannah crawled from her hiding place.

There would be a scorpion man, one that had stayed behind. Waiting for her. She would see it, clearly and terrifyingly for one single moment, the most vivid moment of her life. Then it would explode into movement and there would be violence and pain beyond anything she could imagine -

Remaining on her hands and knees, she scuttled, almost an insect herself, to the railings and peered down. She clutched the posts like a child looking through the bars of its cot. The museum appeared to be empty. Alison...she forced the thought down. She had to complete the task. She had to save the world. The thought made her chuckle.

She got to her feet and walked carefully down the stairs. She crossed to the display case. The breastplate was an unprepossessing scrap of corroded, rust-coloured metal. Its edges were ragged, its surface pockmarked and in places holed all the way through. There was something else. The surface was webbed with a network of tiny fractures, from which thread-like filaments of light shone. Did that mean that the metal had weakened? Murdoch had told them that to destroy it, they had to get between it and the world.

Hannah remembered the mire, the quick sand, and then dragging herself from the grip of her mother and father, and Alison, walking away from Murdoch because trying to save him would have been suicide. Had each of those acts somehow undermined the fabric of the breastplate?

No time to ponder this, or anything else. Hannah looked around and saw what she needed. A case full of ancient weapons. Among them, a mace, short wooden handle, heavy-looking, spiked metal ball attached to one end.

First, she needed to break the case. She noticed that one of the suits of armour held a long-handled weapon tipped with a combination blade and spike at its business end. She grabbed at it and tried to wrench it out of the suit's gauntleted fist. The armour swayed. Then fell in a deafening metallic waterfall of noise. Hannah jumped back and froze. Surely, the scorpions must have heard that. She wondered how far Alison had got. Whether the creatures had caught her.

Hannah stared up at the landing, at the entrance to The Place. Nothing. Perhaps she had got away with this. She retrieved the weapon from the wreckage of the armour and returned to the display cabinet. She took a steadying breath, then rammed the long wooden handle into the glass.

Which broke. Easily. Everything was easy now. Did that mean that the worst part of this was over? She reached into the case, carefully, fearful of tearing her arm on the jagged teeth of glass that still clung to the frame. She grasped the handle of the mace with both hands and hauled it out. Jesus, how did people wield things like this in the heat of a battle?

Cradling the mace awkwardly in her arms, Hannah crossed to the breastplate's display case. She didn't hesitate. Every second's delay could mean that the scorpion men were on their way back.

Which would mean that Alison had lost them. Or…

She smashed the case. Then dropped the mace, reached in and grabbed the breastplate. She pulled it forward and the breastplate, and its stand toppled out and onto the floor. Hannah crouched down to pick up the mace. Only a few more seconds, and it would be done –

There was a roar, an explosion, and she was thrown forward. She collided with the case and stumbled back. She coughed on dust, shivered as the wind burrowed through the parka and her sweater. She saw snow and light.

A thing of awful beauty had entered the museum. A woman – a giant, her body a graceful, yet incomprehensible thing of impossible geometry. In part, a flayed horror of raw muscle and tendons, in part a confusion of the mechanical and organic, of vessels and flesh and tubes and meshed cogs. It glowed, it sang. It regarded Hannah with the contempt of a man regarding a rat, and she recognised, in its features, the remnants of the woman who had once been Crina.

Her abdomen was a transparent sac, and floating inside, suspended, naked, in clear fluid was the most beautiful man Hannah had ever seen.

*

With no thought or plan, driven by a madness of fear and anger, Luke ran at the scorpion man. Then dived at its legs. He felt the shockwave of the tail whip over his back and smack against the wall. A dull thud, a puff of plaster. Then he was on the floor. Under the creature. Caged by its legs. Its segmented abdomen close and pulsing and dark. He heard it hiss and squeal. He rolled over onto his back and saw the body slide over him. Now. It had to be now!

He wrenched the Stanley knife from his jeans pocket and stabbed upwards as hard as he was able. The blade tore through the creature's thin exoskeleton. Luke ripped the knife back towards himself. Vitals looped out in a shower of thick, mucus-like fluid. It reared up and crashed down, and its legs gave way. Luke struggled under the heaving torn body of the thing, deafened by its squeals and shrieks. The weight of it dropped onto him, then lifted. He thrust himself forward, yelling with effort and raw terror. He passed under the curl of its tail and scrambled to his feet. He danced around to watch, knife still in his hand. The thing convulsed, twisted back on itself, the tail waved wildly. It couldn't turn around, not easily. It collapsed, and the human torso swayed, head thrown back. More of the dark mucus spilled from between its lips.

Luke ran. He saw a glimmer of light. He forced himself on, a final effort.

He heard a voice. Hannah. Another illusion -

She shouted one word that rebounded, shattering and fading with distance, leaving a final shred for him to hear. It was not a cry for help this time. It was:

"Bitch!"

*

"Bitch!"

Crina saw, through Tiamat's eyes, the woman she recognised as the doctor who had tried to help her. The woman had shouted that single word of defiance, surely all that remained to her. She saw her and felt Tiamat raise her hand to destroy her. Crina fought against the restraints, against the bonds that held her. Tiamat was weak, wracked with pain, all strength given up to the vehicle she had formed around her womb that contained her beloved. Distorted and ruined as it was, this was still Crina's body, and it welcomed her. She felt herself flow outwards through familiar pathways. It brought pain. The fabric of her body was stretched, twisted, torn and changed. Tautened nerves gave their agonies to her. The thing was too big and cumbersome, alien and infected by poisons that rushed in to force her back. Crina pressed on, assailed now by a madness of hate and joy and fear as she passed from darkness into blinding white light. From cold into a furnace. The invader, the thief of her flesh, was vast. Tiamat's being, her *self*, was flung outwards across impossible distances. The core of her, her soul, was a bloated, rotten spider at the centre of an infinite web. But like all spiders, while their snares and their poisons were deadly, their soft, pulsing bodies were fragile.

Tiamat was distracted, her attention on the doctor. Crina pushed outwards, spread thin, her strength reduced. The drumming rhythm of her heart, for too long the soundtrack of her captivity, was suddenly her own. It too brought pain, and suffocation, as it tried but failed to service Tiamat's huge frame.

Tiamat felt her, swatted at her weakly, a passing itch, a sting. Nothing.

Then Tiamat's thoughts were Crina's thoughts, and

Crina's hers. Crina howled silently as Tiamat turned on her and tore at the last shreds of her coherence.

Hannah saw it, the moment of weakness and distraction, saw Tiamat rear back and falter, even as she opened her mouth to laugh, revealing the light-drenched machineries and pulsing tissue within. The child-thing danced, puppet-like in its glass-walled womb as Tiamat beat at her invisible enemy. Hannah forced herself up onto her feet. She scrambled to where the mace lay on the floor. She fell and rolled clumsily as Tiamat's hand carved a furrow of destruction through display cases and exhibits. She felt the shock wave of its passing as it swept over her head and lay, stunned, disoriented.

A thud, more wood and glass splintered as Tiamat crashed to her knees, clutching at her own head.

She spoke. Her voice so loud the floor thrummed and the air itself seemed to bend under the impact of her words. But Hannah recognised the voice.

"NOW DOCTOR, YOU GET HAMMER NOW -"

The last word stretched into a jet engine shriek of rage, which slammed Hannah's scattered senses together and drove her across the floor to the discarded mace.

The weapon was in her hands. Heavy, brutal.

She struggled to her feet and stood over the breastplate. She hoisted the mace up and over her head. Out of the corner of her eye, she saw Tiamat tear at herself, saw the structures collapse. Hannah wavered, unbalanced by the weight of the weapon.

A final world-fracturing roar from Tiamat caused Hannah to look around. The creature beat at the womb sac in its belly, then ripped it apart even as she disintegrated into a million fragments of flesh and machinery and flame. The child-man rolled free in a torrent of fluid. It mewled, whimpered, then its head snapped up and it hissed, forked tongue flickering from between its sawblade teeth. He was no longer beautiful.

Panicked now, Hannah brought the mace down towards the breastplate.

The child-man, the thing Murdoch had called Kingu, the Anti-Christ, the Great Beast, exploded into motion, fast, too fast to see.

An impact hurled Hannah sideways, and the floor slammed into her arm and shoulder. She couldn't breathe. Even as she rolled onto her back, clawing for air, the thing was on her. It hands were pressed against either side of her head. She stared up, saw its white, formless eyes, its glistening wet flesh. And knew real fear.

Even as it twisted her head violently, and too far, to her left, she heard Luke's cry of bleak rage. Then the sound of his grief and anger was cut off by a loud snap, which filled her head and was illuminated by an electric flash of blue-white light. There was an instant of pain. Then a tidal wave of darkness swept in. And she fell.

*

Alison ran. Her body was giving up, her heart felt as if it was about to stop. She could barely breathe. But raw fear drove her on, the fear of the hunted animal.

They were behind her, scrabbling along the walls, blundering round the corners, the spaces too tight for them to run as fast as she knew they could.

She also knew they would catch up with her soon, and when they did, they would tear her apart. The reality of this, her last night on Earth, was a dark thing that filled her head and made her cry. She wanted her mother and father, she wanted the grandfather she had killed (freed), she wanted Laura. She wanted Murdoch to be here with her. She wanted to live.

But she ran on, crashed through fire doors and onto the back fire escape. She ran up the narrow stairway towards the abandoned rooms on the top floor. She forced every last spark of energy into the task. Toward the place where she would die. She had already chosen the means. An open window. A moment of flight through the storm.

*

Luke launched himself into the ruined museum. He crashed through the broken display cases and barged into the child-man with every ounce of strength he had left. The creature flew from atop Hannah's body and onto the floor. Luke stopped dead and stared down at her. Hannah's head was twisted to her left. Her eyes wide open but sightless. A thin trail of blood spilled from the corner of her mouth. He wanted to wipe it away. He wanted to hold her and care for her.

He heard a snatch of laughter and looked up to see the child-man spin back up onto his feet with a balletic grace that seemed more terrible than graceful. In defiance of gravity, the thing whirled about, opened its mouth to deliver a stream of incoherent mewling and went for the breastplate.

Once again, Luke threw himself at the creature and their bodies collided. But it was ready this time, and Luke was thrown back into the wreckage of a display cabinet. He felt his clothes and flesh torn by splintered wood and broken glass as he fell heavily onto his belly. Too late. He had failed. Again. He couldn't move, and neither did he want to. He was bleeding. He could feel it, seeping into his shirt and sweater, each heartbeat brought a fresh wash of it. Warm, comforting almost. His strength and will seemed to flow out of him with the blood.

Slowly, painfully he raised his head to see the child-man return to the breastplate. At the same time, he saw the mace, just beyond the reach of Hannah's dead fingers.

Hannah...

The rage came back.

He wrenched himself from the floor, dizzy, in pain. He grabbed at the mace, and it weighed a thousand tons as he hauled it up and above his head. The action brought fresh bleeding. He saw a triangle of glass, embedded in his wet, red sweater, just below his ribs. Something important had been severed. The already dim light in the museum was fading towards darkness.

Hannah...

"Fucker!" The oath gave him what he needed. His last surge of anger and energy. The child-man paused and turned.

Luke threw himself into the blow, swung the mace around with his entire body. The impact was brutal, a moment of unutterable violence and destruction as he whirled past and down towards the floor.

The child-man's head exploded, puffed out of existence in a spray of bone-shrapnel and blood. Its body remained standing for a moment, then collapsed, clouding to dust long before it hit the ground.

Luke came to rest beside the breastplate. He had to destroy the thing, but too much of his life had already bled away.

No, he had to finish the job. For Hannah. For Greene and all the others. He rolled over and grabbed the rusting fragment. He felt its coarse, ruined surface, saw filigrees of liquid light.

And the bleeding stopped.

He was on his knees, no memory of the action. Strength surged through him, from the points of contact between his fingers and the metal. He laughed, unable to stop himself. The fucking thing had healed him. The thing had brought him back to life. Carefully, he pulled the glass fragment from his chest. There was a sharp pain but no blood.

He looked up and saw Hannah.

And he was on his feet, breastplate clutched against his chest.

*

Alison leaned against the wall of the corridor on the top floor. It was damp and dank up here. The air, thick and dusty. The light worked, but it was as dirty and dull as that in The Place.

She had outrun them, for now. The stairs had been narrow enough to slow the scorpion men down, but they were coming, inexorably, relentless in their need for her destruction.

She went to the nearest of the doors and dragged it open. The room inside was empty and mouldering. She stood a moment, afraid, unsure. She grasped at threads of wild hope; the scorpion men had given up, they were lost…

She went to the room's big sash window. To her surprise, it slid upwards. But not far enough. Cold air blasted in through the gap. She pulled it down, then took off her jacket and balled it around her fist. She pounded at the glass with all her might.

There wasn't much time. The scorpions were coming, she could feel their approach. Closer and closer.

Alison resumed her battering. The glass seemed as strong as iron. Something scrabbled and skittered on the other side of the door. Panicked now, she hammered her fist at the window. It shook in its frame. She panted and swore, then shouted and drove her fist through the glass, which erupted outwards, its fragments instantly lost in the snow. She clambered awkwardly up onto the windowsill and knelt there, cramped in the small

242

opening she had made. The cold and the wind were like the icy suburbs of Hell.

The door behind her shuddered under a series of impacts.

Alison closed her eyes. She couldn't. She couldn't...

*

Luke kneeled across Hannah, each knee on either side of her body. Her utter stillness mocked what he was about to do. Despite his own recovery, the act seemed like an outrageous folly, a black joke. The dead were dead. God knew, he had seen enough of them – been the cause of too many of them. This was like a desecration. He should let her rest, in peace.

He could barely see for his tears. But he had to try, he owed her that.

Shaking, clumsy, he laid the rusty, broken artifact on her chest, then took her right hand in his. A little warmth remained there, but it was fading fast. He squeezed it, brought it to his lips and kissed it, then laid it on the breastplate. Her beautiful, smooth, sweet skin against its corroded metal.

Wrong. Nothing happened. And why should it –

She gasped, a sudden intake of air. Luke heard a sharp crack. Hannah

blinked. *Blinked.* Then she turned her head to stare up at him. For a moment, it seemed as if she didn't know who he was. Luke saw the same terror he had seen in Crina's eyes when she first awoke and found herself in his bed.

Then Hannah whispered his name.

Luke climbed away from her and sat clutching the breastplate as he watched her sit up. She covered her face with her hands, then looked at him. "I thought...I thought I was..."

"You were," Luke said. "It was this thing…it brought you back."

"You have to break it now, Luke."

He shook his head. "It healed me, it brought you back to life, Hannah. We can't destroy it. You're a doctor, a healer, with this you could…Christ, Hannah, just think what you could do."

Hannah struggled to her feet. She looked weak, she wavered, as if dizzy. She crouched down and pushed the mace across the floor towards Luke.

"You must. Please."

*

The first of the scorpion men burst into the room in a cloud of dust and broken wood. Alison twisted her head to watch its approach. She was paralysed. The wind tugged at her, the cold stabbed through her blouse and raked at her skin. She turned away and sobbed Laura's name and pushed herself forward into the freezing empty dark.

And stopped, because suddenly there was.

Nothing.

She leaned precariously out of the broken window. Aware that the wind had dropped, that the blizzard was spent. That the room behind her was empty.

She remained where she was, now oblivious to the cold.

Now that the storm had eased, she could hear the sea, loud and restless. She wavered; almost fell, grabbed at the window frame and jumped awkwardly back in the room.

She crossed to gaping hole in the wall, where the door had been. She clambered over the slabs of plaster and broken wood and peered, fearfully, into the corridor.

Which was empty.

EPILOGUE

They stood by the sea's edge; Luke, Hannah, Alison. The wind was icy, but the snow had stopped, and it was no longer blowing a gale. The sea was calm. Static flashed, lightning-like over the troubled surface of the water into which Luke emptied a plastic bag full of rust-red, metallic dust.

"Done," he said.

"Up there," Hannah said, and Luke looked upward to see stars shine through the wounds in the dissolving cloud. He reached out and felt Hannah's hand in his.

"Home," she said.

Which would be her house, of course. Luke's bungalow was a ruin. Contaminated. It was repairable though. Whether they (they?) could ever live there was another matter. Of no concern tonight.

A fourth figure appeared. A woman, bundled into a coat, stumbling a little on the sand.

"Alison?" she said. "You phoned me, what the hell is wrong? It's three in the morning."

"Laura," Alison said and went to her.

As Luke led Hannah up off the beach, he turned and saw the two women embrace.

Ahead, the promenade streetlamps suddenly glowed softly back into life. Other lights came on.

And more stars broke through the dying shreds of the storm.

ENDS

Former electrician, college lecturer (I'd rather teach electrical installation than do it anymore), musician (never been booed off stage - so far), actor (ham), Director (drama queen), Terry Grimwood also squeezes in a little writing now and then.

His short fiction has appeared in a wide range of genre of magazines and anthologies and he has two collections under his belt. The latest being *There is a Way to Live Forever*, published by Black Shuck Books. He is the author of three novels, three plays and the co-author of a number of electrical and engineering text books for Pearson Educational.

He writes because he has no choice but to write.

BIBLIOGRAPHY
Short fiction in magazines including:
Nemonymous
Bare Bone
Peeping Tom
Midnight Street
Legend
HorrorZine

Collections

The Exaggerated Man (theEXAGGERATEDpress)
There is a Way to Live Forever (Black Shuck Books)

Anthology Appearances Include:
Darkness Rising 7 (Prime)
Paraspheres (Omnidawn press)
PunkPunk (Dog Horn)
We Are We Going (Eibonvale)
Blind Swimmer (Eibonvale)
Sensorama (Eibonvale)
Creeping Crawlers (Shadow)
Ghost Highways (Midnight street)
Night Light (Midnight Street)
Aliens (Tickety Boo)
Space (Tickety Boo)
Something Remains (Alchemy)
Tales from the Vatican Vaults (Robinson)
Hanging by Our Fingertips (Kristall Ink)

Editor and Publisher
The Monster Book for Girls
(theEXAGGERATEDpress)
The Dark Heart of Peeping
Tom (theEXAGGERATEDpress)
Wordland Magazine
theEXAGGERATEDpress

Novels
Axe (Double Dragon)
Bloody War (Eibonvale)
Deadside Revolution (Horrific Tales)

Novellas
The Places Between (Pendragon then re-issued by theEXAGGERATEDpress as eBook)
Soul Masque (Spectral Press)
Enuma Elis (HellBound Books)
Joe*

Plays
The Bayonet (first performed in 1994)
Tattletale Mary (first performed in 1996)*
Tales from the Nightside (first performed in 2005)*
All – the EXAGGERATED press
 *forthcoming

LINKS

Facebook -
https://www.facebook.com/terry.grimwood.9
Amazon -
https://www.amazon.co.uk/s/ref=nb_sb_noss?url=searc
h-alias%3Dstripbooks&field-
keywords=Terry+Grimwood
LinkedIn - https://www.linkedin.com/in/terry-
grimwood-8bb09750/
theEXAGGERATEDpress -
https://exaggeratedpress.weebly.com/
Wordland - https://wordlandhome.weebly.com/

Alice In Horrorland

By

Vanessa Hawkins

Dedication

To Everyone who's fallen down the rabbit hole...

255

Chapter 1
Down The Manhole

The moonlight caught in her blue eyes. Just moments before, as she had been walking home, the glowing orb had been shrouded beneath a froth of cloud. She was surprised to see the nude moon, and deemed herself fortunate. It wasn't always possible for it to shine through the dismal fog of London's polluted skyline. It was a lovely white, pearlescent, resembling a hole in the sky.

Alice wondered what it would be like to live on the moon, to crawl through the darkness surrounding the world and sit upon its creamy surface. She could gawk aimlessly at the strange fellows wandering the globe below and marvel in their day-to-day lives. *But wasn't there a man on the moon,* she thought, her brows knitting together as she stood in the lonely streets of London. *If so, was he a cruel man? The world below was already rife with cruel, heartless men,* she mused.

Alice looked back down, rubbing her cold hands together as she continued to walk back to the orphanage.

Perhaps it wasn't a man in the moon at all, she thought to herself, wrinkling her nose as the foul scent of the Thames began blowing through the ramshackle houses with the wind. *Maybe the face in the moon was a young girl? A sister? A mother? Who could really tell?* Alice couldn't remember her own mother. Maybe her lost mum was the face in the moon, watching over her, scrutinizing all the dirt left on Alice's apron, the loose threads dangling from the hem of a once blue dress.

Alice sighed. Her arms were still heavily soiled from the chimney sweep she had been forced to do. Though the other match girls of the factory had been allowed to leave their work after six, Alice had been required to stay and sweep chimneys after accidently dropping a match. It had been that, or take a beating. Alice figured she had already missed supper; no food would have been saved for her at the orphanage, *but that was alright*, she thought, rubbing her jaw. She had an awful toothache anyway.

The damp, sooty brick of the buildings crowding the street were made blurry not only by the thick blanket of industry, but by a subtle mist. It was a humid summer's night, and it had rained all day, making the city of London sweat much like a rotund rich man. Despite this, the denizens of London continued to walk the streets, dark clothes making them apparitions, walking shades wandering to their allotted hosts. They paid Alice no mind, splashing their footsteps hurriedly alongside her as they passed. Alice in turn did the same, watching her feet, the soft reflection of the moon in the mud puddles. She hadn't realized that she had almost stepped on the creature until it was underfoot.

"Oh!" she shrieked, causing a few of the London nightwalkers to pay her a glance and a scowl before continuing on. A white rabbit, coat as pure as ivory, skittered away. It stopped at the mouth of an ally, its nose wiggling in the air as it stood on its back legs to regard her. Alice stared in wonder, thinking how odd and reproachful its oily black eyes were.

"I'm sorr—"

But, before she had the chance to continue, the creature bounded away into the alley.

Alice frowned, suddenly aware of the blackening sky and retreating moon. At once the world fell dark, and the blackness hid the city. Disoriented, Alice looked to and fro, watching for a light. Peering back down into the alleyway she thought she saw the white rabbit.

"Wait," she called, hearing the splash of water beneath her feet as she ran. "Mister Rabbit! Please, I'm terribly sorry." She stretched both hands out as she went and felt for the alley walls that she couldn't otherwise see. The rabbit was out of sight and she stumbled, falling forward. Alice thought she would tumble into the inky cobbles, but before her knees could buckle, something pulled at her apron strings. Mystified, Alice found herself righted again.

The odd phenomenon was unable to hold any distraction for the young girl, however. Instead of peering behind, Alice bounded forward again, hoping to espy that wonderful white rabbit. Her youth granting privilege to queer wonders.

The moon, as though willing to grant her wish, peeked out from the clouds again, and the alley brightened into gray. Alice skidded to a halt just short of colliding into a young gentleman. He was awash in an alabaster tailcoat and long top hat with blue feathers. He had a myriad of other complexities attached to his wardrobe. Decorated buttons, a long flowing cravat and beaded bracelets hung from his suit and around his arms. Alice felt her throat close at the sight of him. How beautiful he looked embraced by the moonlight. He had soft features, a young, smooth face and pointed chin, with large black eyes and a sly grin. He regarded her with a pocket watch in his hand. Alice thought he looked wildly out of place.

"Evening Miss," he said, his voice much deeper than his face implied it would be. Alice gulped in a breath like a drowning man. She wasn't sure why, but her knees were shaking. "I think my watch may be broken. Do you know where I could find the Prince of Timekeepers?"

He turned on his heel towards her and half of him was swallowed by the darkness. Alice felt mesmerized by his face, so much so that she didn't notice the rather odd shadow he was casting upon the cobbles.

"You mean Big Ben?" she managed to say, wringing her hands together. She thought it odd that he hadn't referred to it by its nickname like most of the other Londoners did. Though he did look from away, his accent was relatively local sounding.

The gentleman paused a moment, struck by her use of the name. "Ben?" Turning his head, he chuckled up into the sky, his eyes thoughtful black spheres. Alice was silenced by the calm recognition on his face, which in turn seemed to steady her legs and keep her knees from wobbling.

"Yes," he said at last, turning his head downward to regard her, "I'm looking for *your* Ben."

Alice opened her mouth to speak but could only manage an awkward smile. He was observing her with more alacrity now, searching her face, scrutinizing the dirt and soot upon her clothes with amused fascination. "I can show you," she said, her words clumsy as they stumbled from between her lips.

"Please do," he shivered. Once again he looked down at his pocket watch. "I am dreadfully worried I may be late." He didn't *seem* concerned, Alice thought as she moved around him. She hadn't noticed before, but as she walked forward she noticed a large glassy eye right in the middle of his watch lid. It was cerulean with a dark rift in the center. It reminded her of a cat's eye, but it was far clearer, with veins of icy blue waving at the edges. Swirling, gothic designs framed the eye, coiling like bronze whirlpools. Beneath the odd watch lid, numbers were just barely visible.

"After you?" the man prompted, taking note of Alice's bizarre pause. The girl snapped to attention like a branch breaking in reverse. With a nod she jumped forward on the balls of her feet.

The clock tower wasn't very far; you could see it from most open roads. With the full moon shining upon it, Alice figured Big Ben's large round face would be visible if they came up George Street towards the Thames. She hoped the wind would have changed by then. The stench of the river was nauseating.

Alice didn't look back to regard the gentleman as she led the way. She could *feel* him behind her and it unsettled her. The few denizens that continued to wander the city streets would not notice the small, filthy girl in a blue dress, but they did look back, curious to confirm that a small white rabbit was hopping behind her.

"I must be going mad," one gentleman said to himself, feeling muddled as he stepped into his personal apartments to forget the entire spectacle.

When Alice looked back to signal that they had arrived, she was surprised to find the young, white clad gentleman's eyes round as saucers.

"We're here," she said, confused as to why he suddenly looked so concerned.

"Is that really the time?" he asked, peering back down into the face of his watch with alarm.

"Big Ben is always correct," Alice said with a nod. "They say the first strike for each hour is accurate to within one second of time." She had heard that exact phrase described by the cantankerous old barber on Fleet Street. To confirm what she had said, Alice turned, hoping to see the face of the clock tower for herself.

"I'm late!" the man exclaimed. Alice balked.

She couldn't believe her eyes. It was ten minutes to midnight! She had to be up in five hours for work tomorrow! Where had the time gone? Alice was sure she'd feel the switch if she was slow at the factory tomorrow morning.

"I'm late! Utterly, utterly late!" Her attention diverted, Alice turned towards the gentleman. She could see the face of his pocket watch now. It read twelve o'clock. The worry conveyed upon his features compelled her to forget her own for the moment as she stepped forward to assuage his alarm.

"Only by ten minutes, Mister—"

He was stuffing the watch into the inner pocket of his tailcoat. Beads hanging from his wrists clicked together. The pretty buttons adorning his coat seemed to swirl and contort into cogs and toothed gears. Alice's eyes widened. "Don't worry," she began, pausing as he drew a metal mask from his pocket. *That mask is much too big to have fit into his trouser pocket*, she thought, but the design was so captivating that Alice felt her brain ignore reason. It was a white rabbit mask, and covered only the top half of his face. There was a red heart in the outer corner of the right eye; the left was covered by a monocle with a clock in the center. The long inner ears were decorated with swirling gears, completely framed in brass.

"Where are—" but Alice was interrupted again, this time by an unexplainable marvel. The young man, with his white suit and plethora of trinkets, immediately collapsed. He folded together much like a handkerchief at the hands of a ghostly butler. The twin points of his tailcoat went straight as a board and transformed into long white *furry* ears.

"Mister *Rabbit?*" Alice held both hands to her mouth, capturing her gasp of horror and slight curiosity within dirty, calloused palms. The white creature wriggled its nose and blinked at her with its large pitch-colored eyes, the—now plausible?—lady of the moon hid her face behind the smog of London. Alice took a step forward as the white rabbit bounded down the road and disappeared. She leapt forward in an attempt to catch up to it.

"Wait!" she called, running through the darkness. Inside of her young body, logic and childlike innocence wrestled to know more. At eleven Alice was old enough to know that young gentlemen didn't turn into rabbits, but she was young enough to hope that they did. She ran after him, hardly able to see without the moon, hearing "I'm late!" being shouted in front of her even though there were no audible footsteps.

"Mister Rabbit, wait please! What are you late for?"

"No time, young one! No time!"

Alice panted, splashing through the puddles, seeing the faint outline of buildings and sodden walkways blur by as she went. She could taste sulfur in the air despite the damp curtain of humidity. Her tongue felt dry and cracked.

"Where did you go?" she called, stopping as her chest began to hurt. She could feel a stitch in her side, and her tooth began to ache again. Slouching over, grasping at her ribs as strands of her grimy yellow hair fell in front of her face, Alice gulped in a large breath of wet air and continued to walk, searching as she went.

"No time to say, you know the way. Be gone before another day," he said.

"I can't see you!"

DONG Dong! Ding DONG! Dong Dung Ding

DONG!

Big Ben was resounding throughout London in a deep, throaty melody, a harbinger for the midnight hour. Alice could feel tears welling in her eyes as she tried without success to locate the white rabbit. The donging of the bell somehow added a sick sense of urgency to it all that infuriated her heartbeat. She *had* to find him. It was as though, if not, all would be lost.

". . . can't be late. . ."

DONG!

There he was! A glint from something polished drew her to him. His black eyes shined like gemstones from beneath a broken goods wagon. Tall buildings on either side framed the small road he had tucked himself into and walled in the darkness like a windowless room.

DONG!

Alice was delighted. "Wait, please!" she demanded, running and stumbling. A furious excitement washed over her in her haste to sate her blind curiosity. A white rabbit? What could a creature like that *possibly* be late *for*?

DONG!

"Curiosity killed the cat, my dear," he said, chuckling.

She hit her head. Or at least, Alice had the sensation of something tremendous splitting apart her forehead. Her dress inhaled, gasping in the empty space suddenly attempting to swallow her. Her shoes slipped from both feet as she fell. Something sticky and warm rushed between her eyes.

Alice fell into the open manhole, clawing at the cobbles like a mad thing and splitting apart her fingernails as she went. The last thing she remembered seeing was the young gentleman, back in his white suit, looking down at her from the London streetway. His pocket watch with the cerulean eye winked in one hand.

His rabbit mask sat askew upon his face. The clock tower gonged out the time behind him.

"Welcome to Horrorland, Alice. *HeeHEEHee!*" Something chuckled all around her.

Alice screamed. From the darkness, long floppy limbs reached out, grabbing at her legs, her ankles, her feet, hauling her down away from London.

From above, the White Rabbit grinned, his face framed in the round manhole like a man in the moon.

Chapter 2
Pillars And Hacksaws

No.

To Alice, it was one of those words that hadn't any meaning. A sound, like a subtle exhalation of breath that put sentiment to the feelings of the individual, without conveying the immensity of what you wanted to ensue. No, meant nothing, especially now as she was drug down beneath the Earth. No didn't make the worms wiggling out the dirt disappear, nor the skeletons with their white skulls and graying teeth smile any less as she fell farther and farther into the ground.

Was she dying? As Alice dropped deeper into the dirt she had the grisly thought that perhaps she was dead. Was she a corpse reluctant to accept its grave?

Everything was spinning, even when the spongy appendages let go and she drifted downwards with the aid of gravity alone. The dirt and cobbles of London descended into the city sewers. Rats and human waste bobbed in the throwaway, along with human bodies forgotten: both alive and dead. Alice screamed again as she fell through the watery surface of raw sewage, but when her mouth wasn't filled with all the terrible things that floated in the underbelly of London city, she realized that she was still falling. This time much more slowly.

Alice was somewhere else. The dirt walls around her were transformed into thick, red curtains, like something a theatre would use to keep the audience from seeing the show prematurely. But, there were porcelain dolls poking out from the folds, eyes as wide as moons, watching as she fell.

"H-hello?" Alice called, feeling her skin prickling beneath their stare.

"Come for tea, Alice," one called, its voice shrill.

"You've come for tea at last!" another exclaimed. There was laughter all around her. Something sinister and conspiratorial echoed within the chuckles of the dolls.

"Can you tell me where I am?" Alice asked, feeling disoriented as she watched all the nude dollies begin to slide down the curtains to keep at eye level with her. She could see each darkened cleft between the joints in their limbs. Some were filled with spiders that danced along the glass and disappeared back within their bodies. Others were only filled with darkness. Although the dolls spoke, their pouted little lips never seemed to move.

"You're in Horrorland, Alice," one doll with a bald head said.

"You're just in time for tea!" another with no head continued.

"Tea? With who?" A swinging seat, much like the ones Alice had seen in children's books, swept down to catch her. Alice grasped the two ropes on either side as her backside slid across the board of the swing, gasping in a moment of shock. She looked up and bit her lip. She realized that the ropes were not in fact attached to anything, and that she was still falling.

The dolls continued to climb down after her, but there were more now. Some were without eyes, some with an article of clothing and most without. Some of the dolls had mismatched limbs. One had the head of a horse, another, a head of a rabbit. Once, Alice saw one with lobster claws. Sometimes the dolls didn't climb down, but just disappeared into the folds of the curtain and reappeared farther down. Alice didn't like their large glassy eyes. They were cold, with irises like empty wounds.

"Maybe the mad one," one said. It had buttons for eyes.

"The mad one?" Alice heard them whispering, talking to each other more than addressing her questions. "Why would he be angry?"

"Angry," they all whispered, similar to a chorus of locusts

"If not the mad one, hopefully not the Queen."

"The Queen!" The word was drawn out. It moaned from all the dolls like a violent wind, causing them to scuttle back inside the curtain. Who was this queen, Alice thought. She had been about to ask when the seat of the swing moved beneath her and butted her off.

"Get off my face, petulant girl!"

Alice held her hands to her mouth, muffling her shriek of surprise as she watched the ropes of the swing turn into snakes and slither into the mouth of the now sentient board. She could still hear the whispers of the dolls echoing behind the living swing's mumbles of admonition.

"Where is the White Rabbit?" she probed, filled with wonder at the curiosities unravelling before her. But there was no answer as the curtains began to wriggle, stiffening into hard wooden boards as tables, chairs and all manner of furniture began to float up around her. Skeletons sat within the otherwise empty seating, some holding tea cups, others holding playing cards. Their bones were bleached a wonderfully stark white, like rich ladies lace. The skeletons had all their teeth as well! Alice leaned away as she fell past them, a twang of pain developing in her mouth as she recalled her toothache. She noticed how the rib cages of each skeleton had been shattered on the left side.

"Take heart, Alice!" She heard the dolls cry again, sobbing in whispers now.

"Take heart!"

"Take heart!|

"I don't understand!" Alice felt tears welling in her eyes. She lurched forward, grabbing at the tablecloth of a passing dining set. Dolls tumbled over, all around her, spinning head downwards with limbs straight at their side like dead things. One doll with a heart shaped hole missing from its chest, red thread sewn around it, frowned.

"Take heart, Alice..." it said, passing her a silver needle that it had taken from inside its heart.

Alice, hands shaking, lip trembling, took the silver needle, but before she could answer the doll she was swept up in a tide of red, sliding down something hard and smooth as the sewing gift was lost in the scarlet water. *I'm drowning!* she thought, opening her eyes as she let out all her air in a moment of terror. Trying to swim, Alice kicked her legs, flailing her arms in a wild attempt to gain purchase on something that would help hoist her head above water.

A rope! Alice grabbed onto the thin wet cord and pulled. It was becoming harder and harder to see. The translucent red liquid all around her was becoming more viscous, rising from below in a torrent resembling an opening sluice gate. Alice glanced downward, still hauling at the braided rope. A rather lumpy bag was at the bottom, red fluid blooming from between its coarse knitting.

It looks like a teabag. . .

She was in an enormous teacup! Alice pulled at the cord, one bare foot touching the pouch of tea. She pulled, feeling the syrup-like fluid rising around her. Closing her eyes, Alice felt panic dance in her chest, squeezing at her lungs until they hurt.

I'm going to die!

There was light above! She scrambled harder, kicking, pulling, screaming as she hurried to the top. There were things in the water around her, large things. Something sharp and painful jabbed in her leg. Alice felt the heavy weight of darkness begin to pull her under. Letting go of the rope, her arms clawed for the surface. She touched one of the floating things in the water and waved it down in an effort to go up.

It worked! Alice gasped, heart mad within her chest. The surface of the teacup rippled out in bloody rings all around her. As she waded for the edge, Alice noticed tiny hearts floating on the surface, pumping and beating as though still within some living creature. She threw one she had taken in a moment of panic, and it plopped on the floor, blood spurting from severed arteries and pooling around it like a shadow.

Alice retched over the edge of the teacup, face and arms drenched in blood. It ran through her hair, in thick warm fingers over her neck and torso as she attempted to pull herself up over the edge.

What? She glanced from left to right, overhead. The teacup, which had seemed bottomless, was perhaps of a height to her own. Alice pressed her bare feet to the porcelain curve of the teacup and felt the weight of the dense gore around her. As she pulled a leg forward to straddle the macabre cup, she noticed the silver needle embedded into her left leg.

"What is going on?" she winced as she let herself down, pulling the needle from her leg as tears welled up on her cheeks. The dolls that had fallen with her were no longer animate, but lying broken on the floor. Their faces were chipped; their mismatched limbs all askew left her trembling.

"Alice!" Alice turned, fists clutched at her chest. The room was spinning. Dirt, wood and furniture churned in an arch around her, funnelling away into a large open corridor. The dolls, the blood, the teacup, all transformed into heavy stone and moss, trees and grass, the curtain into a vibrant blue. Now before her was a yawning hole framed in flora, leading from her trembling location into a blue sky.

"Don't be afraid!" It was the rabbit! Alice called to him, waving an arm as he stopped and glanced backwards. Long white ears twitched in recognition, but a moment later he was hopping swiftly down the open tunnel towards the roiling blue sky at the end, paying her no further mind.

"Please wait, Mr. Rabbit!" She reached forward, needle in hand, meaning to run after him when something stopped her. Verdant trees arching from the mossy ground overhead, the emerald grass and soft cloud spinning slowly at the end, all looking like it were a field caught up in a whirlwind, was not real. Alice tried to walk forward. It was nothing but a painting on the wall, marred now by a protruding silver needle embedded in the canvass.

"You can't go that way!" a muffled voice cried from behind her.

Alice turned. There was nothing but a single room. The floors were black-and-white tiles, the walls a red-and-ivory wallpaper: bisected colors that led downwards into black-and- gold baseboards. In the heart of the room was a slab of white marble. Red veins curled around the surface of the stone like broken blood vessels. In the center of it was what appeared to be a man, but with the head of a boar.

"Excuse me?" Alice stammered. She thought the boar man was another doll. Glassy eyes stared forward towards the ceiling and dead leaves burst out a large hole in its abdomen. It looked like some kind of scarecrow a farmer would use. Alice hoped that indeed, that was all it was.

"If you use me I bet you could go, but you'd have to pull me out first."

Alice was scanning the room, trying to locate the voice, sure that it hadn't come from the man with a boar's head. "Where are you?"

"Silly girl, I'm the pain in the neck!" The voice, which seemed rather high, did not come from the creature's mouth, but from the side of its neck. In fact, it didn't come from the boar at all. Instead, embedded in the throat of the beast, right where the head of the boar shifted into the pink flesh of a man was a bloodied hacksaw.

Alice grit her teeth together, taking a tentative step forward as her hands curled about the ends of her hair, wringing it nervously.

"A-are you alright?" she asked, a bit lost for words. The empty space between the Hacksaw's blade and handle moved like a mouth. There were large wooden pegs in the grip as well that twitched as it spoke. Alice thought they may have been eyes. They were gritty around the edges with a clean sphere in the middle that resembled a pupil.

"I've bit off more than I can chew," it said, lurching back and forth in an attempt to remove its teeth from the creature's neck. "I hadn't expected it to be quite so tough! Give me a hand? It's really quite lodged in my teeth at the moment."

Alice chewed at her bottom lip, but meandered forward. "Should I—" she began, reaching out, reluctant to touch it.

"You can grab my handle, yes. I'll close my eyes so you won't poke me."

Alice did as she was told, noticing the congealed blood bubbling at the wound where the Hacksaw met flesh.

"Now just give me a good wiggle," it continued, "back and forth, a bit up and a bit down." Alice did as instructed, clenching her teeth together and grimacing as the large boar head continued to spurt out blood despite its open, leaf-filled belly. She recoiled as it splattered across her face and fell backwards. Where the blood from the teacup had been watery and diluted, this was like the stiff paste she used to make the fuel for the matchsticks.

Alice wiped at the sticky goo and watched it turn to droopy, red strings at the end of her fingertips.

"You've done it!" She heard the Hacksaw say. It sat in the scoop of fabric where her —now bloody—blue dress bowed between her legs. Alice licked her lips, tasting a bitter flavor in her mouth. The flavor prompted her to recall her toothache, and so she sucked at her inner cheek as the saw continued to speak.

"Now you can hack apart that portrait," it said, its gritty wooden eyes pointing towards the mural upon the wall.

Alice pressed her lips into a thin line, picking up the talking hacksaw gingerly in her fingers so not to accidentally touch it inappropriately.

"Do you really think it's alright to do so?" she asked, regarding the wall. From the floor the mural looked like someone had carefully painted a lush forest landscape then rolled up the canvass for transport. From her point of view, it was as though Alice was looking down the tube from one side.

"Well there's no one here to get irate," it replied. Alice looked past its mouth and imagined the still dolls that had been lying on the floor.

"I-I suppose you're right," she said, pushing herself up from the floor.

"Careful now, Alice," it sang in a high pitched tune.

"How did you know my name?" she asked.

It seemed to shrug, if a hacksaw could shrug, that was. "A heart beats its name, my dear."

Alice frowned, wondering how her heart sounded to a talking saw. She carefully gripped the handle in both hands, trying to discern where first she should begin to cut. It all looked so magnificently crafted that she felt quite terrible to have to spoil it. She searched for some plain space in which to begin before Alice noticed the silver needle still sticking out of the canvass, right in the center of the orbish blue sky.

She slowly plucked it out. Alice wasn't entirely sure why—though Horrorland did seem the place for uncertainties—but as the thin needle rubbed between her fingertips still sticky with the boar man's blood, Alice thought to place the small instrument within a pocket of her dress, weaving it through the fabric to keep it in place. A souvenir? Or perhaps a tool for later? Alice wasn't entirely sure, but she did it nevertheless.

"I'm sorry," she said to the painting, angling the front tooth of the Hacksaw in place against the pinhole. It didn't take much for the paper to rip, as it did so the Hacksaw sang with glee, seemingly overwhelmed by its taste.

"There's only a keyhole," she said when the painting hung in tatters along the wall. It was a large keyhole, perhaps as tall as her calves and twice as wide. It was bordered in brass, with a crown etched into the design at the top.

"The gate to Horrorland. But, you are far too big to enter, my dear."

Alice backed up a step. There was a gray light emitting from the keyhole. It shone across the floor like the splayed hand of an old woman, but Alice was careful not to let it touch her.

"I've got to find the White Rabbit." She looked up, back into the gaping hole that she had fallen from. "Or back home to London, at least." She wasn't sure why. London was an awful, terrible place. Her parents were dead or gone, her friends nothing more than familiar faces she slept and worked with. Was London better than Horrorland? Alice wasn't sure.

"Well," crooned the Hacksaw, "you could always hack off your own arms."

Alice looked down, startled. "What?" she cried.

"Probably your legs too if you wanted to fit," it continued. "I could help you, you know. I'm awfully sharp!"

Alice was incredulous. "H-how would I get through without any arms or legs?" she asked.

"You could roll?" the thing suggested, the toothy blade moving like a bottom lip. "It won't hurt very much. Let me try it."

Alice shook her head. "No!"

But the Hacksaw would hear none of it. "How do you expect to leave, then," it screamed, wobbling in her grasp as it attempted to jerk its blade towards her, "you want to stay here with me? You'll starve, Alice!" She grimaced. The thing continued, "you'll *starve* and then I'll eat you *anyway!*"

She threw it from her, and the Hacksaw spun away on the checkered black and white floor towards the marble slab, just at the feet of the dead—inanimate? — boar man. The saw shrieked madly.

"Hickery, dickery DOCK! You can't get through the LOCK! So hack off your HEAD and you'll be DEAD, HICKERY DICKERY DOCK!"

Alice trembled, covering her mouth and backing away as the Hacksaw erupted in laughter.

"Oh Alice! You should have simply met my friend, Sir Manfred Pigsnout!" it cackled, regarding the drooping, half severed head of the half man. "He died yesterday! I chopped him up myself. He was such a *bore!*"

"This is madness," Alice muttered. Worse than the old man who muttered to himself on Sundays, she thought. Walking backwards and not surprised when she ran into the wall, Alice jumped again when a sound whispered through the keyhole.

"Ya havin' a bit o' a yap? A row of sorts?" the voice called, prompting Alice to turn and stoop upon hands and knees.

"Please help me," she replied, looking back towards the cackling Hacksaw, "there's a saw that wants to cut off my arms!" And legs, she would have added, had she thought the extra bit of information would have hastened a reply.

"A saw ya say." Alice knelt down lower upon her forearms, trying to get a look at the creature speaking on the other side. "I saw a saw once, I did. I saw a saw who saw another saw who was seein' a sea saw. It didn't work out, I saw to that, seein' as I saw the problems from day one." Alice felt her head grow fuzzy.

"Please sir," she begged, looking back again, "can't you help me?"

There was a shuffle from the other side, a long silence, then a crackle of something knocking together. "I'm supposin' I can give it a go. Like to 'elp out when I can, I do."

Alice bit her lip, watching as a tiny glass bottle rolled

through to the other side of the keyhole. It was stoppered with a glass cork that resembled a crying infant's head, and had a brightly colored tag on the end that read in bold black letters: **DIMINUT PILLS.**

"Dooon't be takin' too much of them pills now," the voice warned, "they're bound to make ya too small minded if ya do, and those kinds of people just can't make a go of it here in Horrorland."

"Small minded?"

"Aye."

Alice started, hearing the metallic scrape of something from behind her. Looking back again, her heart began to thud louder as she saw that looney hacksaw wiggling its jaw in an attempt to move itself closer to her.

"You don't want to be small minded in Horrorland, Alice. Oh no!" the Hacksaw said, its saw blades that made up its face almost maniacal. Alice unstoppered the cork. The saw continued to haul itself forward, mostly by the teeth of its lower jawblade. "The Queen is sure to find you then. Let me have your limbs. She's sure to leave a young girl like you alone if you don't have any arms or legs."

Taking two in hand, Alice swallowed the pills. They were chalky, and left her mouth feeling dry, but they went down well without water.

"No! You won't taste as well if you do that!"

But, as the Hacksaw spoke, Alice felt her head grow fuzzy again. She thought the room must be spinning and so tucked her head until it touched the floor, arms reaching overtop as though to keep her in place. The metallic shush of the murderous saw seemed to grow louder around her, and her limbs felt odd and wobbly as she dropped the bottle and heard it clink on the ground.

"Oiy? Ya there, Miss? I told ya not to be takin' too much."

Alice groaned. "My head feels a bit topsy turvy."

"Ya best be gettin' through the hole, then."

Alice agreed, especially when she noticed that the keyhole had since grown to the size of a church door. It looked majestic, the brass gleaming in the light of the room, the crown on top decorated with engraved hearts and chips of colorful stone that she hadn't noticed before. The gray light that flooded from the opening looked less sinister now too, pooling on the floor from a winding corridor beyond.

"Wow!" she exclaimed, her voice solemn.

"SEE-SAW MARGERY DAW! A PISKY CAME AND ATE HER JAW!"

Alice screamed. The Hacksaw was enormous now, its gritty wooden eyes riddled with holes where small worms had burrowed through the wood. Rust corroded the toothy grin of its blade, and the blood from before looked like jelly between the grooves.

And it was right behind her.

Everything's not gotten larger! I've gotten smaller! Her mind hollered as her feet slipped upon the glassy floor. Alice sprung towards the keyhole, fleeing down the inner corridor as she went. The inside was filled with all sorts of portraits that she was sure were all quite wonderful if she had the chance to look. But like her heartbeat, Alice raced through, not noticing the regal faces that stared back and sometimes gasped at the vulgar way in which she ran past without so much as a hello.

In fact, if the homicidal hacksaw had not forced her to forget her manners, Alice might not have caught her bare foot on the welcome mat to Horrorland and tumbled head over heels outside.

"Oiy! Watch out now!"

Flat on her back, looking up at the bright gray sky, Alice watched as dark jagged tree branches shifted in the wind, resembling stone black lightning bolts perpetually suspended in the air. They seemed to grow out of the cliff that housed whatever sort of chamber she had just exited. Perched upon them was some kind of extraordinary bird with a cloud for a body and ice for a beak.

She sat on her backside for a moment or two, arms spread out to either side. There was something foul in the air here, damp and musty, with a bit of smoke.

"Thank you so much," she said at last, bending at the middle to sit up and address the goodfellow who had given her the pill bottle, "I was terribly afra-AAAH!"

The man, if indeed he was one, stood almost as tall as Big Ben itself! His face—a thin, gaunt looking thing with a nose so flat it was more like two holes upon his face than an olfactory organ—was half obscured by his scruffy, blue green hair and brown flat cap: pulled over his brow to tame his wild mane.

What startled Alice the most was the fact that his face was currently a foot or two away from her. His mouth— hanging open in a rather obtuse expression of boredom and decorated on one side by a smoking pipe—was filled with large, square teeth with gaps in between, and seemed to be emitting the foul smell that currently engulfed her.

He pursed his lips when she screamed, his head— currently held within his palm—cocking to the side. He sat quite strange in the grass, with one forearm held out in front of him with his chest lying on the dirt. His back was arched up and around so that his bare feet and knobbly toes were held above his head, almost resting upon his cap. He held a cigar between his first largest and second biggest toe.

"What ya screamin' fer, love?" he asked, obviously perplexed.

Alice held her hands to her mouth, feeling her breath

on the back of her palms. "I'm sorry," she began, words muffled. "You just startled me. I'm not used to being so small."

He smiled, teeth gray like tombstones. "'Ere! Take ya a drag of me cigar. It'll cure what ails ya." His back arched even more. *Is he made of clay?* Alice thought until his left foot was right in front of her face, proffering the smoking juggernaut of rolled up tobacco to her.

Alice stalled, couldn't help when a scowl crossed her face. "N-no thank you," she tried.

"Can't be big minded again without takin' a huff o' dryweed," he explained.

Big minded. He must mean it will return me to size. "But..." she hesitated. "It's currently between your toes."

He pulled back, his smile disappearing into a thin line as he contemplated her assertion. "Ya?" he said, looking up at the tightly wound smoke. He smiled again, this time his toothy grin practically devouring his face.

"Oiy! Miss Prissy Pants can't take a toke off me ol' toe cigar, eh?" He chuckled, and like a coiled worm slowly unwinding, set himself upright with both feet on the ground, transferring his cigar from foot to hand in a perfect fluid movement. At full height, he was really all arms and legs. There were thick black spines poking out along his sides. What Alice had thought was the long fork of his blue tailcoat, was in fact something prehensile that resembled the legs on a spider. He had antennae as well, and his eyes—which Alice was sure were nothing but gaping black caverns—remained hidden beneath his mop of mossy, blue hair.

"'Ere then. Take a puff of me pipe." He handed her a long calabash pipe. Winding threads of white, black and red smoke curled at the end, smelling a bit like pepper. "It'll make ya big minded, but don't be takin' too long a draught or you'll be bound to be seein' stars."

Alice wrinkled her nose, walking up to the pipe as he stooped so she could reach it. The end reminded her a bit of a mushroom, and she thought of the poisonous ones she sometimes saw growing on the darker streets of London, usually tucked between the corners of roads and buildings where workers couldn't lay stone.

"O-okay," she mumbled, reaching forward to take hold of the shaft. Though she wasn't small enough to find it cumbersome to use, he held it steady for her as she inhaled through the stem. There was a familiar taste to it that she couldn't quite place, but as she felt her limbs begin to lengthen her toothache came back again, this time with much more force.

"That's probably enough anyways," he said, placing it back in his mouth and giving it a few hearty puffs, "ya alright?"

Alice held her cheek, but nodded when she was addressed. "Yes, thank you." He was still taller than her, but seemed thinner and much less intimidating now. She could also see behind him, and better feel the pall of mist settling on her skin.

"Is this Horrorland?" she asked, shifting on her right leg to see past him. Rolling brown hills that looked like old rye bread dough fumbled past the horizon, sprouting long, black trees. Alice remembered the same gray sky from London, only instead of being filled by the smog of factories, Horrorland was swollen with gloomy rain clouds that lent body to the fog.

"Aye." He removed the cigar, snubbed the end on the brass border of the keyhole door and placed it into his jacket pocket. Alice watched him, marvelling over the fluidity of his movements and how smooth they appeared to be.

"I-I'm sorry." She shifted from one foot to the other. "My name is Alice. Thank you so much for helping me out back there. I—" she paused, the scent of pepper still in the air.

"I'm the Caterpillar," he said, thumping his chest with a wide smile. "Pillar they call me. I'm more a pill than a cat, I'd say, and most agree too, so the name's fittin'!"

Alice nodded, though wasn't sure she understood. "Well thank you, Pillar."

"Ain't nothin', Alice." He pulled at his lapels, tipping his chin up with his back straight. A few blackflies zoomed around his head, but kept away from the thin snakes pouring out his pipe. "Ain't often anybody be comin' to Horrorland."

"The White Rabbit!" she exclaimed, prompting him to lose the rigidness of his backbone. "Can you tell me where the White Rabbit is?"

"The Rabbit? Why you want a know somethin' like that?"

Alice screwed up her face, the wrinkles in her nose making it appear like there was a worm on her face. "He brought me here; I'm quite certain! I'd very much like to know why." She still wasn't sure if she wanted to go home yet, but Alice *was* certain she'd like to ask him a few questions.

The Caterpillar—he did look a bit like one, what with all the tiny appendages sticking out every which way— took a long draught on his pipe, pulling his right leg up to rest his bare foot on his left leg like a ballerina. "I don't know where the Rabbit is. Ya can check down the path. Usually he works for the Queen so we Horror folk don't much like talkin' to him."

"Who is the Queen?"

He smacked his lips, sucking at his large tombstone teeth. For a moment, Alice thought she saw something bright shine down from the sifting, gray clouds. Not a moon, but it resembled a cat's eye.

Pillar laughed. "Maybe you ought ta ask her. No doubt you'll be meetin' her someday."

"Someday?" Alice wasn't so sure she'd like to meet the Queen.

Pillar sang. "Someday, someday, a young girl lost her bleedin' way. And so astray, she made her way, down to Horrorland to pay!" He somersaulted, the red, white and black smoke looking like translucent streamers.

"Pay what?" Alice stomped her foot, thinking the grass was rather pokey.

"An eye for an eye, but she's not called the Queen of eyes!" Pillar stopped, grabbing himself by the chest. "If only she were!" He pulled up his bangs, hat almost tipping off from his head as he showed her the large open holes of his eye sockets.

Alice felt her heart shudder as she stepped away from him.

"They're in there," he said, letting his blue, green mane drop down again, "no need to be afraid!"

"I think I ought to go," Alice smiled, trying to make the expression reach her eyes. "I really need to find the White Rabbit." She started around him, taking note of a small path camouflaged between the short brown growth of grass. Mushrooms popped up along it, some with caps that looked like a clock face, where others were plain and some the colors of red and pink.

It was certainly uncanny, but as Alice meandered towards the concealed roadway, Pillar cartwheeled right in her way, holding out his hand.

"Fine enough then, mam," he said, "but I'll be needin' that pill bottle back before ya be headin' on ya way."

Alice looked at the back of his hand. It was turned towards the ground. She wondered if he'd expect her to place it upon his knuckles, and if he'd be able to catch it in time before it fell off.

"Oh, well, certainly," she said, fishing into her apron pocket to retrieve it. There was only a needle inside however, weaved through the fabric of her dress so it wouldn't come dislodged and poke her. She must have left the pill bottle back in the room, in fact, she was certain she had. The bottle hadn't shrunk with her.

"I'm sorry," she said, biting her lip, "I must have left it back in the room with the Hacksaw."

Pillar frowned, jerking himself just enough to quickly correct his posture and stand upright again.

"Ya left it in the other room?" he said, looking past her and walking towards the keyhole. Popping his head inside, when he spoke again his voice was muffled. "'Ey you! Give me back me bottle!" he yelled.

Though Alice assumed he was talking to the Hacksaw, she apologized again. "You ought not to go in there. That hacksaw is quite mad! Who knows what it'll try and do."

Pillar gave a grunt in response, but was quick to realize that no amount of grunting or pushing was going to allow himself into the corridor leading to his pill bottle. Hauling himself out and almost losing antennae in the process, he looked back at Alice and huffed.

"I helped you out, I did! And you left me bleedin' pill bottle in the room with a crazed hacksaw with no arms in which to pitch it back!"

Alice stepped back, careful not to tread on the mushrooms. "Maybe you could shrink yourself?"

"'Ow am I supposed to do that without me pills? A pipe only makes you big minded. Pills make ya small minded! I need to be small minded." He turned again, peering into the keyhole, his frown growing deeper upon his face.

He pulled at his hair. "The Duchess is gonna have me rump in a stew, she is! The Tweeds will wrap me up in bacon and feed me to a Jollywag! They'll bury me in jelly," he cried, "then, when I think alls said 'n done, they'll bury me in the Midwife tree and make a real pill out a me!"

He turned on his heel, grabbed the young girl by the frock and gave her a shake. "All because you didn't bring the blasted pill bottle back here!"

Alice gave a shout, wincing as he took hold of her bloody clothes. "I'm sorry," she sobbed, head bobbing back and forth like a ball on a stick, "I didn't mean to!"

The Caterpillar sobered, antennae weaving about his head, probing at her soiled hair.

"*You* will have to explain to the Duchess," he said, biting at his bottom lip with his teeth.

Alice paused, opening her eyes and blinking at him. "What?"

"Aye," he seemed to be agreeing with himself. "You can tell her what happened. You'll be the one in trouble, not I."

Alice trembled, thinking of what the Duchess may be like. She imagined her Headmistress back at the orphanage in London. Gritting her teeth, Alice shook her head. "I don't want to be in trouble. I really didn't mean to."

But the Caterpillar nodded, looking down at her chest. "You have a heart, don't ya?"

"I—" she wasn't completely sure she understood his question. Alice thought she was a good person. Even if that wasn't what he meant, if the Duchess was a cruel woman it wasn't right that he should take the blame.

"A-alright," she continued, "I'll explain it."

Pillar pursed his lips, giving his cap an appreciative tuck. "Good on ya, love!" he said, straight-faced. Then, grabbing her by the hand, he began pulling her along, trampling over the mushrooms and squashing their odd looking caps all over the brown grass.

"We'll go to 'er House of Cards. You tell 'er what

happened. *You* lost the pills." He stopped, holding her hand firmly as he turned to stare at her. The little spines on his sides seemed to quiver while his tombstone teeth poked out his face, making him look quite grave. "You understand?"

Alice, again, nodded. "Y-yes," she said, quiet as a dormouse.

His grin almost consumed the entirety of his face. "Fantastic!" he hollered, smoking his pipe as the serpents of smoke slithered past.

Chapter 3
Pigs And A Pepper Mill

Horrorland was a tumult of odd objects all slightly dour and gruesome. As they walked along the backs of the brown, rye-dough colored hills, in the valleys Alice could see red ponds the shade of fresh scabs. Purple flowers made homes around the banks, and sometimes puffy, white jellyfish floated to the surface then up into the iron sky to join the clouds and fog.

The Caterpillar drug her along, but did let go of her wrist after a time. Sometimes he walked on all fours along the path, using his spines for balance, and other times he somersaulted. If she fell behind, caught in the sullen whimsy of her surroundings, he'd do the worm, calling for her to catch up as he pumped up and down upon his chest and knees like a wave.

"What is that?" Alice asked

"A graveyard nook to read a book."

"And that right there?"

"A Hollow Bear!"

"That thing flying?"

He laughed, paying her silly questions very little mind. "Everyone knows that pigs can fly. Don't be daft, they live up high!"

Alice huffed. "Pigs don't fly in London."

"What a boring place it must be."

To that, Alice had to agree. Though she wasn't entirely sure that it was a nicer place, London was far less interesting and far more likely to just stay the same. Horrorland was terrible! But, it was also very lively and spellbinding.

From the rye-dough hills the pathway broadened. Square stone blocks the color of cherry and eggshell swept along the brown grass and welcomed the odd patterned mushroom caps to its border. The black tree trunks with spindly branches grasped at fat fleshy fronds that looked like boney fingers holding up a gelatinous pink balloon. Alice was both thrilled and horrified when she approached one. Fish swam from within. Some fish had a human torso, like a mermaid or merman, but others were reversed. Some of the creatures even looked as though they had been turned inside out.

"Pillar?"

"We call 'em Brain Stems! If ya don't mind killing a few dreams, ya can drink what's inside the fronds." He smacked his lips. "Tasty, tasty! They make ya loopy though. If ya drink too much, you'll CRRCK!" He made a death noise, slicing a finger across his throat. "Then before ya know it, yer fertilizer! Pushin' up daisies." He laughed. "Daisies bein' another Brain Stem, that is."

Alice walked past, but couldn't help but peer into the branches of another. "This one has food inside! Lollies, chocolate and mince pies with pudding!"

Pillar turned to join her, poking at the rather gummy surface of the rose colored brain bush.

"The bloke who died must've dreamt up a feast!" He

slurped his tongue over his lips. "I could go for a hog hoof blood sausage right about now. Give me some fat for dippin' and a bit a weed for sippin'!" Pillar cackled.

Alice hadn't realized how hungry she was. Her stomach however, seemed inclined to remind her as it rumbled out its protest.

"Come on now! Pitch forward! I'm sure the Duchess will give ya a bean or two to eat." He pirouetted, almost catching her on one of his spines.

"I thought I'd be in trouble."

"You think she's heartless?" The Caterpillar roared with mirth, waving her off when Alice shrugged her shoulders. Tickled, he lit his pipe anew. "Hurry along, Alice! Her House of Cards is along the way." He took a dram. "Just beyond the Carol Groves!"

The Carol Groves was an awful place that split apart the hills until they looked like upturned cracked eggs. Long bald, white trunks that looked like bleached human femurs rose into the sky, ending in nobs in which the Carolling Hobgobs burrowed and lived.

Fat birds with fat bottoms and long fleshy wattles that hung to their breastbones all yammered out deep, anguished moans. Each of a varying pitch and speed, there were so many of them that it was impossible to hear anything else.

Gray fields with bone white trees and moaning Hobgobs filled Alice with dread. Some of the Hobgobs were missing their feathers, some had waves of crust around each eye. As they walked along the path—littered with quills and ticks and bird dung—Alice kept her limbs tucked in close.

"It's awful. Why do you call it the Carol Groves when it's less a song and more an agony?"

"Trash to one is treasure to two." Pillar didn't look back, but the smoke from his pipe waved after him, blowing against her face.

They continued on. Alice had cupped both hands over her ears as they went, but the sound of the birds continued to rave on and on. Once, when she wasn't paying close enough attention to the road, she had almost stepped on a dead one. Its eye had popped out from its head, dangling like a billiard from the eye socket. Alice screamed, jumping forward and running into the back of the Caterpillar.

"Oiy," he said, eyes sparkling. "Ya must keep yer rowdiness under control here, Alice. The Duchess won't approve of overlooked manners."

He swung one arm out in an arc. Alice could see the House of Cards as it teetered on one side of two hills, held up in the center by a long rickety ladder of playing cards.

"Has it ever fallen?" she asked, amazed that such a large house could survive any amount of wind or weather.

Pillar sucked the inside of his cheek then shrugged, continuing on his way without another word. Alice followed after, mimicking his silence, eyes consumed by the large manor wobbling between the two hills.

Up closer it was plain to see the spades, diamonds and clubs of the cards. There were so many of them propped together. Their backsides were black, with the crest of a pig in the center. Wings sprouted off the swine's back, and Alice thought that perhaps flying pigs would make London more interesting after all.

A few Hobgobs pecked at the grass outside as they approached along the path. They moaned as the couple walked by, and again Alice clapped her hands over her ears to avoid hearing their incessant *carolling*.

An arched bridge, also made from large playing cards, ran the space between the two hills and served as a pathway to the inside of the manor. Alice was curious why there were no heart cards, but when she asked the

Caterpillar he would only say:

"Horrorland is heartless."

Which prompted her to shut her mouth.

Inside wasn't very decorative, and due to the placement of the cards it looked like a circus of flying swine had been let loose upon the walls. There hadn't been a courtyard outside due to the precarious placing of the house upon twin slopes, however, inside seemed to make up for it. What would otherwise be a grand foyer was instead a garden. A marbled fountain, seemingly made from the same red veined stone that the Hacksaw had been found upon, spurted out some kind of black liquid, and all about it were a menagerie of odd birds.

Some had beaks that looked like sheers; others had bladed wings that shushed when they were opened. Some of the avian creatures were too fat to fly so they perched in the graying shrubbery haphazardly growing here and there, while a myriad of otherworldly plants made their home along the railings of a large staircase just beyond the fountain, in the middle of grand room.

Pillar let himself in with neither a thought nor care to the strange things living around him. As Alice followed after, watching with cautious delight, she was careful not to step or get in the way of anything.

"Hurry, hurry! Up the stairs! We can't be late. 'Ave a care!"

"You sound like the White Rabbit," Alice mumbled.

At the top there was a set of double doors. On the left, embedded into the wood, was a crank, much like one on a pepper mill. Pillar laughed, pointing to it with his finger as he somersaulted backwards and rested on his arms with legs in the air.

"Open it, won't you?"

Alice regarded him. "How?"

"Turn it, turn it, turn it around!" He took another deep inhale from his pipe, spinning his index finger round in circle to emphasise his point.

Biting her lip, Alice walked forward. The crank was large, much larger than an arm or a leg. It had a wooden grip but the mechanism itself was made from copper. Alice was quite certain she wasn't going to be able to make the thing budge at all, but as she leaned into it, the mill moved smoothly. The sound of pepper grinding from within the door was quiet and somehow satisfying.

"ACHOO!"

She jumped back. "Someone sneezed!" she said.

But Pillar was already on his feet, beating at the door in a fury. "Let us in!" he snapped, pummeling with both fists. "Don't make us beat ya harder!"

The doors opened towards them. The sniffle of something living on the other side worried Alice, but her heart stopped when she saw the face of a baby living within the wood.

"Don't be so mean to me!" it cried, wiggling its nose, trying to rid its face of the tiny ground pepper pieces that had fallen from the grinder just above its head.

The Caterpillar grinned, shaking his head and long antennae. Though the pipe-loving bug-man had a surplus of arms, the baby was just a big round brown face in the wood, unable to swat the pepper from its chubby, round nose.

"He only sneezes to annoy," he explained to Alice. "Open up when we please! Else beatings, beatings you'll enjoy! Ya know I never tease!" Pillar bopped the wood on the noggin again, causing the door child to wince as he walked away.

Alice however, feeling mortified, apologized before following after. "I didn't mean to make you sneeze," she said, wiping the pepper from his face as the babe continued to whine. "I'm so terribly sorry."

"It's alright, Alice," it snuffled, wrinkling its nose as large alligator tears ran down the wood onto the floor. "I do enjoy the pepper mill," he said, large eyes widening to the size of dinner plates. "I just don't like when people beat on me."

"Maybe you ought to stay open?"

"Don't tell me how to be a door. I don't tell you how to be daft!"

To which Alice promptly walked away.

The room inside was made of mirrors and shaped like a donut with a table in the middle. Each pane of glass showed a different kind of reflection. Alice glanced at a few as she went. She saw herself as large and small, fat and wide, as a boy and as a hen, but as they drew closer to the table, Alice found that the two men reclining at it better contended for her attention.

They were large, as though made of rounded melons. Thick brown hair curled beneath black bowler caps, and they were both wearing black tweed overcoats atop white and red striped shirts. The both of them were playing chess as Pillar approached, scratching at rounded chins, pinching thin, wrinkled lips. Alice could tell right away that they were brothers because they both perfectly resembled one another. In fact, if she hadn't been sure they were in the center of the room, she may have thought there was only one man, feigning interest in a game of chess with his reflection.

"'Ey! It's the Tweeds! It's nice seein' ya two blokes! Still battling on?" Pillar raised his arms as though expecting one of them to rise and meet him in an embrace, though didn't look sullen when the pair of them paid him no mind.

"Lookee, lookee, it's the Caterpillar."

"You've chewed off one too many leaves, Pillhead." The two men didn't look up, seemed quite entranced within their game. Next to Pillar, they looked like pumpkins beside a long green onion.

"What do you mean, fellers?"

"The Duchess says you took too many Diminuts. Right Dum?"

The other man nodded, leaning forward to position his knight. "Right, Dee. The Caterpillar took 'em all. Only supposed to take half."

"I only took me share, I did!" Pillar's antennae bobbed on top of his head, as though in agreement. He took a suck of his pipe. "I'd a shown you too, but this here girl lost the bottle. All of it. You can ask 'er if ya like." He turned around, spinning on the heel of his left foot. "Alice, please! Tell the Tweedles what happened. Dum and Dee are dying to know."

Together, the large round men nodded, then looked in their coat pockets to draw out a cigar. Popping it into their mouths, Tweedle Dee lit Dum's cigar, while Dee returned the favor. When they stood to face her, Alice felt her entire face turn white. They were as big and tall as boulders.

"I—" she stammered, feeling like her voice was forever caught in her throat.

"A cat has got her tongue, Dee."

"Or did Pillar cut it off to suit his needs?"

Their voices were woolly and deep, like the sound of a breath across the nozzle of a bottle. They regarded her oddly, squinting their eyes.

"I'm so very sorry. I lost the bottle quite by accident. A hacksaw was—"

"A hacksaw?" One brother looked to the other.

"A saw that hacks," one Tweed explained.

"Ah!"

Alice continued, picking at her fingernails, ushered encouragingly by the Caterpillar from behind the brothers. "Anyway, when I ran away I left the pills behind. Then I got too big to go back and fetch them."

"Big minded!" Pillar corrected, smiling with graying tombstone teeth.

Alice nodded, chewing on her bottom lip. "And it's really not Pillar's fault. He gave them to me out of the kindness of his heart."

Again the brothers regarded one another.

"Heart?" one asked the other.

"Heart," the other agreed.

Again, from behind, Alice saw Pillar fidget on his feet.

"The Duchess will want to hear of this heart, Dee." The brother smiled, large crooked teeth sticking out from his gums like rounded stones from the mud.

"You're right, Dum!" They both laughed, and Alice paled as one of them took a giant step towards her.

"I'm telling you the truth," she cried, kicking her legs as Tweedle Dum threw her over his shoulder. "I didn't mean to lose it, I didn't!"

"Hear that?" Tweedle Dee said, grabbing the Caterpillar by the antennae, calloused against Pillar's cowardly pleas of mercy. "Bu-Bump, bu-Bump, bu-Bump!"

"Getting faster, too," Dum replied, squeezing Alice as she screamed.

"I just wanted to find the White Rabbit!" Alice sobbed. Pillar tried to fight, but even his spines were fruitless against the thick Tweed overcoat each brother wore. The frustrated Caterpillar tried pleading first, then cussing, then pleading again, but Alice only sobbed as they were both carted away through a maze of mirrors that eventually yawned into a large kitchen. Pots and pans and cupboards made from playing cards, bodies of birds, of pigs, of baby rats, hung from the ceiling. Steam pooled along the floor. It looked like fog but smelled of pepper and wafted apart as the brothers stomped in, their footsteps almost as loud as the heart beating within Alice's chest.

"What do you ninny's want now?" The Duchess was

a short woman, long beaked nose with one thick brow across her never-ending forehead. It was white and bald, like an impossibly brilliant cue ball, but her face tapered down into a pointed chin that was rivaled in sharpness only by her long slender nose. She was swatting herself with a dishrag when the Tweeds arrived, trying to keep her pale skin from perspiring from the heat that permeated the kitchen.

However, before the Tweedles had even deigned to answer, the Duchess frowned, the right side of her mouth wrinkling downwards as she caught a glimpse of Pillar riding on the shoulder of one of her two massive henchmen.

"Pillar," she began, her voice almost the same cadence as the Hobgob birds from the Carol Groves. "What have you got up to this time?" She turned with her question, moving towards a rather large cook stove. Stationed beside it was another woman, long and lean, dressed in a white apron with her hair held together in a bonnet. Alice thought she must have been a cook, though she looked rather muddled as she fiddled through the large library of spices held in cabinets along the wall, throwing those she had no use for on the floor to spin away.

"Nothin' yer Grace! I was mindin' me own business, ya see! Just thought to stop and 'elp out a poor soul, and now I'm being prosecuted!"

Picking up a spoon, the Duchess stirred the cloudy blue soup in the pot on the stove. Though much smaller than the cook, she was very round in the hips, and reminded Alice of a gourd.

"He lost the Diminut Pills," Tweedle Dee explained.

Dum agreed, "He gave them to Alice."

The Duchess looked up, spoon at her lips as she sipped at the blue soup.

"Needs more pepper," she complained, throwing it

back to the cook.

"Please Ma'am, I didn't mean to lose them." Alice was facing away from it all, her feet crossed against the chest of the rotund Dum's chest, but when she lifted her legs just a bit, she could see through to the other side, and at the upside down woman. "Please don't be cross with me."

The Duchess, frowning again, spat at the large bowler-wearing twin. "Turn her around, now! How am I supposed to have a conversation with a girl's backside?" There was a clatter on the floor, the smell of coriander, and without much else for notice, Alice was dropped from the hulking man's shoulder onto the ground.

"Better," the Duchess concluded as Alice lamented the sudden soreness in her rump.

Bending down, the older woman squinted her eyes, her one large brow furrowing as she took in the features of the young girl. From up close, it was plain to see that despite the smoothness of the older woman's face, the Duchess was quite old. Wrinkled dugs, pushed together like old potatoes, framed the top of her corset. Though she had a slim waist, it was quite obvious that the legs beneath her skirts were tremendous by the small glance Alice had gleaned from her ankles.

"You are awfully filthy." The Duchess straightened, grabbing at her washcloth and fanning herself once again. "How dare you think to come into my House of Cards dressed the way you are! Did you not think to have a wash?"

Alice flushed. "I—"

"She's not from Horrorland, ya Grace," Pillar exclaimed overtop Alice's stuttering. "She fell in through one o' the Rabbit's holes, she did. 'Ave a listen! 'Ave a listen! It's sure a sound ya won't be missin'!"

The Duchess' frown deepened as she regarded the flailing Caterpillar, but as he continued to sing, curiosity began to meander into her features until she turned back to Alice with an inquiring look.

She turned her ear to the young girl, leaning forward at the waist. Alice bit her lip, growing nervous as the woman steadily seemed more and more intrigued. "Is it—do I hear—"

"Yes!" Pillar hollered again.

Alice started, leaning back on her palms as the woman pressed her face to the young girl's chest and grabbed her about the waist. "A heartbeat!" the Duchess cried, holding Alice still despite the young match girl's subtle protests.

"What's that?" Dum asked Dee.

"Bu-Bump, Bu-Bump, Bu-Bump!" the other replied.

"Oh."

"Child," the Duchess pulled back, hands still wrapped around Alice's hips, "did you *know* you had a heart?" Behind her the white cook paused, looking over her shoulder. She licked her lips, her squat features scrunched up in thought.

"I thought everyone did," Alice admitted, not sure how she felt about being the center of attention.

The Duchess pulled away, thumb and finger on her chin as she paced back and forth from one end of the kitchen to the other. Her massive hips swayed so much that everyone had stepped back, giving her a wide girth. Alice made sure that when she stood, she did so as well.

"I've never cooked a heart before," the cook muttered, turning away from the cook stove to regard the girl. "I wonder what kind of things we could make with a heartbeat."

Alice paled, but before she had the chance to do anything the Duchess grabbed the spoon from the table, knocking the taller woman on the skull so hard that the cook stumbled back against the wall.

"Are you mad?" the Duchess screamed, hitting the

cook again as blood seeped through the back of the cook's white bonnet. "Do you want the Queen of Hearts coming down on us all?"

The cook paled, grabbing the back of her head, nodding as she cowed before the Duchess' wrath. "Thinking aloud is all, your Grace. Thinking aloud."

"The *help* doesn't *think*!" she screamed again, wagging the spoon in the tall woman's face, turning on her heel to face the young girl. "Please, ignore my cook. She's a bit of a dullard, you see. Not very smart."

"I—" Alice couldn't help but stare at the blood on the spoon.

"Come. Let's get you washed and dressed appropriately. Then we can discuss what is to happen." Alice tried not to shrink away from the Duchess' touch, but as the woman linked her arm through hers, Alice couldn't help but shiver.

"What about me, your Grace?" Pillar was still held fast by both antennae, but he smiled despite himself, showing off every one of his graying tombstone teeth.

The Duchess paused, making a rosebud with her tiny Cupid's bow red lips. "I think you both are in need of a good washing," she said, turning again to lead her guest from the kitchens. "Make sure our lovely Caterpillar is cleansed well, Dum. Dee."

The brothers laughed. "Yes, Duchess," they said in unison, turning back towards their hall of mirrors.

Chapter 4
A Bath, A Tale, And A Beating Heart

How in the world could you be so dirty?" Alice felt her teeth chatter as the Duchess poured another pitcher of cold water atop her head. They were both sitting in the bathroom, the Duchess on a plush velvet chair, Alice in a brass basin. She could hear the echo of their voices bouncing off the walls. Though the tub was directly in the center of the room, it was easy to see the red diamond face card watching them beside the doorway.

"I fell into a teacup of blood," Alice tried to reason. It seemed absurd, like it most certainly merited more explanation, but the Duchess' nod of complete comprehension stalled her from continuing.

"Well, a bit more soap and water and you'll be clean as an infant's insides."

Alice wasn't sure what that meant, or if she thought an infant's insides would indeed be very clean, but she certainly didn't argue. The Duchess—who acted so sweet now—scared Alice, and not just because the match girl found her to be so terribly ugly.

"Please don't be mad at Pillar. He did help me," Alice said, lifting one arm when instructed so that the Duchess could scrub beneath her armpit.

"The Caterpillar will be fine. He's been big minded for far too long. The Tweedles are just going to return him back to normal." Alice wasn't sure that Horrorland *had* a normal.

"Can you tell me about the White Rabbit?"

"He's the Prince of Timekeepers," the Duchess replied simply, bending to retrieve a towel from the floor. "He works for the Queen."

Alice stepped from the tub when instructed, allowing for the squat Duchess to dry her off. Alice glared at the King of Diamonds in the corner, could swear his eyes had moved to regard her, but continued on nevertheless.

"Who is the Queen of Hearts?" Alice asked, wincing only a little as the woman shook at the snarls in her long yellow hair.

The Duchess hesitated, her face a blank slate. Instead of answering, the older woman held up a white dress with a yellow sash across the middle, and tugged it over Alice's head. It was perhaps the softest, most wonderful looking dress ever. *In London, no one wore white, especially poor little match girls,* Alice thought.

"Open your mouth," she ordered the girl, fingering something in her lap. Alice again obeyed, was surprised when something sweet was placed upon her tongue. "That will help with that toothache of yours." Alice chewed, had actually forgotten about the dull ache in the back of her jaw, but as the candy began to melt, she was pleased to find the pain ebbing away.

"Thank you," she said, finding the candy sweet and chewy. It stuck to the roof of her mouth, disintegrated at the back of her throat. "But the Queen—"

"Is the ruler of Horrorland, of course." The Duchess

held up a brush from a small basket at her feet and instructed Alice to sit as she ran the bristles through her long, golden hair. As the woman pulled gently at the snarls, Alice could smell pepper from the Duchess' dress overpowering the scent of soap and oil from the bath. She sat back against the older woman, feeling the girth of the Duchess' enormous legs. They reminded Alice of old cooked yams: hard and yet vaguely pliable.

"Why doesn't anyone want to speak about her?" Again Alice looked towards the King in the corner. She hadn't noticed before, but he was holding an axe one hand. He was wearing a tabard full of diamonds and adorned with gems. Every now and then, from the corner of his eye, Alice was sure that he was looking at them.

The Duchess sighed, pulling at the brush, struggling through the knots in the young girl's hair. "You ought to stay far, far away from the Queen, Alice. Though her name is deceiving, the Queen of Hearts is undoubtedly heartless."

"So she is unkind?"

The Duchess let out a dry laugh. "That too, I suppose. But no, she is really, really without a heart."

How could someone be without a heart? Alice winced beneath the brush, regarding the black backsides of the card house. Flying pigs—the crest of the Duchess' household—adorned many spaces along the walls, looking like a whimsical farmland constellation. The only pigs Alice ever really remembered seeing were the ones butchered at the market, or squeezed tightly into crates. The pigs on the wall looked far happier.

"Which is why you must be careful," the Duchess tapped her on the head, signalling for her to stand. "No one else in Horrorland has a heart. And you," she gestured, "tromping around with that noisy thump, thump, thumping is going to cause all sorts of trouble."

"No one in Horrorland has a heart?" *Didn't a person need one in order to live?*

The Duchess frowned, setting the brush on the table and folding her hands in her lap. "Some of us used to. But, the Queen took them all."

"Took?" Alice was aghast.

"Every one." The Duchess nodded. "In many manners, many ways, the Queen of Hearts will have her way." The older woman's eyes narrowed, drawing her brow down lower across her forehead. "So you'll have to excuse some of the lesser plebs in the Queendom. They've not all adapted properly since their extraction." The Duchess stood, grabbing her dishrag to fan herself. "Like the Caterpillar," she spat.

Alice turned with her as the Duchess began to leave, once more eyeing the King in the corner. "Well, I suppose I don't need to see her. I just want to find—"

"The White Rabbit, I know." The pair exited the bathroom into a long corridor. It was lit by the daylight pouring through many of the open windows. Alice saw on the wall many of the other face cards: the Jack of Spades, King of Clubs, but there were no other queens, nor any heart cards.

"You ought to be careful of the Rabbit, you know. In all likelihood, the Prince of Timekeepers brought you here to harvest."

"Harvest?"

"Like a pumpkin."

Alice was quite sure she didn't want her heart harvested by the Queen of Hearts, and the thought that the White Rabbit had only lured her here as prey made her considerably sad. She could recall him vividly in her mind, standing in the gray pall of London in a suit the color of moonlight. His smooth, pale features, mysterious eyes and curling smile had made her heart beat louder.

"Hmph," the Duchess sneered, "that thing makes more commotion than the Tweedles!"

Alice looked from side to side, not sure as to what the Duchess had been referring, but didn't reply. Instead, she followed down the hall until the two of them entered into another room filled with bottles and tubes, several stoves and an assortment of drying herbs and tonics.

"Where are we?" Alice asked, tasting something foul in the air and wishing she had savored her candy more.

"This is where all my medicines, stimulants, downers, pills and smokables are made."

The room was crowded with tables, so much so that as the Duchess walked among them she was forced to walk sideways in order to fit her sizeable hips through. "The Diminut Pills—the ones you lost—" she said curling her lip, "were all made here."

Flitting here and there Alice saw the cook again, tossing ingredients into pots and cauldrons, mumbling and fretting as she went. The red stain on her bonnet was still there, but the woman seemed disinclined to care.

"Now." The Duchess turned, waving the dishrag in front of her face and almost swatting Alice in the process. "Since you lost my precious pills, you will go and fetch me the ingredients to make more."

Alice nodded, eyes darting from a glass jar on the table—filled with what looked like pickled nuts and bolts—back to the Duchess. "What kind of ingredients?" she asked.

"Cook!"

From the back, the taller woman in a white apron began to shout. "We need sap from the Midwife Tree!"

"Is that all there is to it?" the Duchess replied, looking back with doubt in her eyes.

The cook nodded, waving an arm without looking up. "We've everything else. Worm blood, cricket brains, beard from a shrew and the hopes from a dead dog."

Alice paled.

"Get just the sap! But get a lot! Better more than getting naught." The cook frowned. "Take the Caterpillar. He knows the way."

The Duchess smiled, showing off long crooked teeth. "He'll be waiting in the hall of mirrors," she said, and despite her earlier kindness, there was something sinister sparking behind her eyes. "I'm sure he'll be feeling much transformed after spending his time with the Tweedles."

"I hope you didn't hurt him," Alice ventured. But the Duchess placed a reassuring hand on her shoulder, ushering her out into the hall.

"Habit hurt him, my dear. You ought to be careful of it. Too much of one thing is bound to make your mind a muddle."

"I see."

"Candy?"

Alice clapped her hands together. "Oh, yes please!"

Chapter 5
A Much Ado About Nobody

Alice returned to the hall of mirrors with a lantern filled with black, wriggling leeches. The fat, shiny worms were small, but smeared against the glass. Alice wasn't sure exactly what she was supposed to do with them, but the Duchess had instructed her that they were necessary in harvesting the sap of the Midwife Tree.

"Pillar?" she called, looking around at the polished looking glasses. The table in the center was all set up to play a fresh game of chess, but the Tweedle brothers were nowhere in sight. Pursing her lips, Alice sincerely hoped she wouldn't have to go off to find the tree herself. She had no idea of what it may look like, and in Horrorland, Alice figured it could really be akin to anything.

"He's comin' Miss," a familiar voice said from behind her.

"He's a bit slower these days." The brother's laughed, holding onto their large bellies as Alice turned around. The bowlers on their heads jostled from their chuckling, and the bridge of their bulbous noses wrinkled, making their nostrils appear enormous.

He really was a caterpillar, Alice thought, watching as the once young man slid into the room. His blue suit, once slim and baggy, strained against his abdomen. His legs, forelegs, mid legs and back legs were all bare, and the bits of clothing he was able to wear disappeared into his segments as he ambled forward. He still had a somewhat human face, with his graying tomb-like teeth, but otherwise Pillar was utterly transformed.

He still had a pipe dangling out of his mouth however, but the lines of smoke were just plain gray now, without any hints of black or red.

"Alice."

"Mr. Caterpillar," Alice cried, walking towards him as quickly as she was able while carting around the worm filled lantern. "What did they do to you?"

Pillar frowned, his large blue face and black eyes looking like a wax bag filled with goo. "They took away me medication, they did. The Duchess says I can't have no more 'till I help ya bring back some o' the ingredients to be makin' Diminuts." He turned sidelong, scowling at the chortling Tweedles.

"Don't worry, Miss. He shouldn't *bug* ya too much!"

Yeah," the other agreed, "he should be able to hold his own; after all he is a cater-*pillar!*"

They roared again, holding each other up, stumbling back towards the table and their chess game. "If he fails, maybe we can skin him and put him in the *cater-combs!*"

Tweedle Dum nodded. "Or chop him into bits and stuff him in our cater-*pillows!*"

"Hopefully he turns over a new leaf!"

Pillar snorted, antennae folding back behind his long, angular head. Alice bit her lip, sensing his annoyance and feeling a bit awkward. "Shall we go?" she asked, shrugging, trying to appear nonchalant amid the bellows of incessant laughter so that Pillar would not feel too embarrassed.

"Aye! It's gotten much too fat headed in 'ere!" He sat up, using one set of legs as a pair of arms as he grabbed a hold of his pipe. He was an awfully large caterpillar, probably at least the length of three of her. When he sat up, looking almost like a half man, half bug-like thing, he was less long but only a tad bit taller than she was.

"Will you lead the way?" she said, keeping her voice high and sweet.

Pillar removed the calabash pipe from his mouth, making round circles of smoke as he began to crawl away. "With pleasure, mam," he said, sparing only one cursory glance backward before making his way out the hall of mirrors.

"It was nice meeting you," Alice had said before she left, but the two twins were so much absorbed in their fun that she was quite certain that they hadn't heard her.

"How long until we get to the tree?" Alice asked once they were outside, hoping that Pillar's sour mood may improve when he was away from the presence of the brothers.

The Caterpillar smoked, making odd shapes as he went. "I'd say the length of three mimsy yadders, the dance of a horse fly and three lifetimes of the left leg of a mayfly."

Alice paused. "I'm afraid I don't understand."

Pillar shook his head. "That's how *long* it will take," he spat. Alice was silent, looking down to regard the lantern stuffed with leeches. She decided very quickly not to talk to him anymore, unless he addressed her first. She hoped his temperament would improve quickly, at least, and not last as long as a mimsy yadder.

They had departed through the same way as they had

entered the House of Cards, through the front, but the duo didn't have to traverse back along the Carol Groves. In fact, they had wandered around to the back, discovering another card bridge that sloped downward between the twin slopes of the hills. Alice was very relieved to not have to go back through the Hobgobs and even more delighted when they entered the forests beyond.

Witchwood forest was a tangle of color. Unlike the graying fields that she had first encountered beyond the keyhole door, the woodlands were awash in bright, fluorescent flora and fauna. The same clock capped mushrooms from before grew in clusters against the tall, long limbed Bone Trees, and other fungi with toothy gills smiled back at her as she went, blue bottle flies flitting from their undersides, bums really looking like bottles.

Curling vines thick as a human's torso grew up past the treetops. Some had winding heads, reminding Alice of the sticky buns she sometimes saw at market, while others were unwound and looked like sickles. All around her was wonder, and queer little creatures, the stuff of nightmares and dreams.

"Careful of the Butcher Brier," the Caterpillar warned, puffing out a cloud of smoke that balled itself up and tumbled away into the likeness of a kitten, "its thorns can be deadly."

Her eyes widened. In the brier, stuck through the chest with a butcher knife, was a duckling, half hatched with a hat upon his head.

"Oh my gosh!" she exclaimed, placing the lantern on the path. The briar's thorns: large, shining butcher knives, were bloody now as they stuck the bird who was half alive.

"Let us help you," she said, moving towards it, unsure of how she could aid him.

But the duckling coughed, looking at Alice with eyes the color of pond scum.

"I am Nobody, fear me not. Death and torment, Nobody sought. Nobody remembers, Nobody knows, Nobody's friends with Nobody's foes." Blood began to leak out the duckling's bill. Alice reached forward to touch him, to perhaps help him from the brier, but the knives resisted, growing up around the duckling, turning their blades towards her and cracking his shell till it fell away.

"Nobody dies without a friend, Nobody truly loves the end." The duckling smiled, and Alice found herself pulled away, back into the path as the knife pierced into the duckling's belly, killing him.

"We could have helped him," Alice cried, watching incredulously as the Caterpillar sighed, breathing out a peal of three bells.

"Nobody can help himself. Let's go."

His many feet tapped along the cobbled path. Alice watched him go, looking back at the skewered young duckling trapped in the Butcher Brier. "*I* could have helped him," she said, quiet in her own gloom.

"You're wrong." The Caterpillar's antennae bobbed. Alice picked up the leeches, inhaling through her nose as she looked back at the now dead duckling in the brier.

"I'm sorry, Mr. Duck."

"Ya ought not to be."

Alice followed after him, careful of the other briers, thinking that perhaps the Caterpillar was more calloused as a bug than he had been as a man, wondering if Horrorland was named for all its horrible things, or if horrible things just happened in Horrorland.

Chapter 6
Cats, Pillars And Vorpal Swords

The Midwife Tree is named for the dead babes that were buried and consumed beneath it."

It was perhaps, horrifyingly, the largest, most knotted tree Alice had ever seen.

Roots tangled on the ground like snarled stone ropes, burrowing into the upturned dirt that looked as though it had been freshly tilled. It didn't rise straight up like the Bone Trees or long limbed birches, but grew off to the side, bare branches clawing at the sky as large tumor-like growths grew beneath its bark.

Beside her the Caterpillar puffed, looking thoughtful as he blew smoke through his large tomb-like teeth. "Sometimes when a child dies, someone will carve an 'ole in the tree and cover it with mud. Those bumps on its side are where the bark grows over."

Alice's knuckles whitened on the handle of the lantern. "Why do people do that?"

Pillar looked sidelong at her, raising an eyebrow. Alice thought him to be much friendlier looking as a man, as well as much more mannerly. "All sorts do it so that the trees can absorb them, return them to life, I suppose." He smacked his lips, tiny spines upon his back twitching. "The tree's alive, ain't it? Guess all sorts think the babes are too. Like little 'earts they help it grow and live on." He inhaled again, this time blowing out a smoky beating heart. It was wobbled and malformed, made of cogs and pipes and skin. It was a heart, yet not a heart at all.

"Alright then, place the leeches. More the merrier and more the medication." Turning his backside around cumbersomely, the Caterpillar took the lantern from her, opening its top and fingering the small black worms within.

"You gotta squash their heads almost; else they won't latch on and suck the sap."

Alice felt her heart sink into her bowels. "We can't use the leeches!" she said. "They'll take the life from the tree. What about the children?"

"Dead as doornails." He squeezed one of the worms against the bark, pressing too hard and popping its head into goo.

"But you said—"

"I don't want to be like this." Faster than she imagined he could, Pillar turned, his blue face red. "I gave you those pills and you *lost* them! Lost, lost with a cost!" His voice boomed, making her tremble. "So squash those bleedin' 'eads on the tree and 'elp me get some sap, else I'll stick em onto you and see what a bloody 'eartbeat tastes like!"

Alice stepped back.

The Caterpillar slinked forward, a struggling black worm in one of his many hands. "Al-ice! Al-ice! Al-ice!" he snarled, mimicking her heartbeat.

"Please, I don't want to—"

"*AL-ICE! AL-ICE! AL-ICE! AL-ICE! AL-ICE!*" He

laughed, tombstone teeth grinning at her as he lunged, grabbing her in all his arms.

"Get a 'eartbeat, yes I will! Better than a wee ol' pill!"

Alice screamed, kicking her feet, arms held to her sides as he hugged her to his torso. She could see all the way into his gullet as he opened his mouth. Could see the sores, the scabs, the tar within, a library of medication chronicling his habits.

"Help! Please, no!" she cried, trying to kick at him, only knocking the buttons from his coat. As she flailed and kicked and spat, her hair fell into her face, blinding her.

"Eat you up, one whole swallow! In my belly you shall wallow!"

"That's enough of that, now."

Alice fell, rolling backward heels over head as Pillar screamed. Something vile and warm ran down her front, splashing on her legs. Scrambling backwards, hauled by her instinct to get away, Alice watched with horror as his severed arms writhed upon the ground, still in their sleeves, scrambling to get her.

"Snicker-snack." The White Rabbit smiled, turning his sword sidelong as the Caterpillar snarled, blood running from his eyes, between his tombstone teeth. "One bad habit is a waste, two or more you're disgraced!" the Rabbit said.

Without any arms, Pillar hurled his body at him, weight alone carrying enough strength to knock the Rabbit down. In his suit and hat, still white as the moon, the White Rabbit dodged, his blade a bolt of light, his wry smile encouraging madness, stupidity, and rage.

"Pillar, stop!" Alice said, blood upon her clothes as she scrambled from the severed, still-crawling arms.

But the Caterpillar wailed, spittle flying from his open maw as he hurled himself from left to right. The

Rabbit dove, avoid and leapt, much too quick, and too adept.

"One, two! One, two! And through and through!" The White Rabbit lunged, the sword flashing like a sunspot. "You slig slug with your avid habit! Be undone by me, the Rabbit!"

The sword pierced Pillar through the middle. Like a blade through hot butter the Caterpillar's insides yawned away, accommodating the sword like a devoted doorman. Alice felt the blood drain from her face. The severed arms flopped like lifeless dolls. As the Rabbit backed away, the blade drew upwards, halving Pillar down the middle until he was two, and wondrous wings hidden in his body slopped out around him like a shroud.

Alice covered her mouth. "Pillar." The lantern of leeches was but a splatter of guts and glass upon the ground. The wings: majestic and soft and covered in the slime of Pillar's insides, were attached to his back, but the man, like the Caterpillar, was cut in twain. Teeth were scattered like tombstones upon the ground.

"Frabjous day," the Rabbit muttered, looking down at the bisected body with a smug grin. "Are you quite alright?"

Her eyes flitted from the body of the Caterpillar to the White Rabbit. He looked resplendent in his white suit, and not a droplet of blood had splashed upon him. He was wearing a cape buttoned at his shoulders the color of midnight blue, and as he reached down to help her to her feet, Alice could see the bronze chain of his pocket watch.

"I… You didn't need to kill him." She blushed as her hand touched his.

"He was quite far gone in madness, my dear." The White Rabbit still had the sword in hand. It gleamed like an ember though it didn't feel warm to stand beside it.

"I'm certain he would have devoured you, and I simply couldn't have that."

Alice bit her lip, thinking about what the Duchess had said about him harvesting her, being in the employ of the Queen.

Well, thank you," she said, feeling unsure as she watched the pool of Pillar's blood grow beneath him.

The Rabbit nodded, reaching into his jacket to withdraw his watch. The cerulean eye with its black pupil like a rift within the sea winked back at her as he opened it, revealing the clock face with a missing minute hand.

"You're quite welcome, Alice." The sword shone vibrantly as he pressed the tip into the center of the watch. It disappeared like a ray a light into bag of complete darkness. The hilt, looking oddly like a clock tower, also vanished, until the minute hand appeared again on the face of the pocket watch, revealing the time to be a moment before midnight.

"I'm glad you managed to find me."

Alice, suddenly remembering all the trouble and toil she had gone through to get here, stomped her foot. "You left me! Alone! I was almost hacked apart with a saw, beaten by Tweedles and accosted by a Caterpillar! I demand you take me back to London."

He clicked his watched closed, depositing it back into his pocket. The beads around his wrists ticked against each other. His cape fluttered. "You really want to go back to London, Alice?"

Alice frowned, hesitating. "I—"

"Wouldn't you rather attend a ball with me?" He turned, standing up straight and gesturing with the crook of his arm. Though it had been daylight when she left to find the Midwife Tree, and despite the time it said on his watch, Alice was certain that it was still daylight. Splashes of light fell through the treetops, resembling missing jigsaw pieces on the path.

He could see her trepidation, could see her nervous glances towards the dead Caterpillar at the foot of the Midwife Tree.

Springing on the back of his heels, the White Rabbit hopped forward, taking her arm in his as he led her away from the carnage. "It's a tea party ball, you know. So many wonderful creatures of Horrorland shall attend. Quite safe."

Alice watched her feet, noticing the red footprints she was leaving behind.

"What were you late for?" she asked, blue eyes sparkling. He was a lot taller than her, with oaky brown hair short and well-trimmed. His beads ticked and his clock tocked, he stood proud with a sharp jaw and wonderfully beautiful features.

"Why, the ball of course."

"HeeHEeHHEeeeHEEE!"

It sounded like a child's laugh: quick and fleeting, curious in the way it started without cause yet also peculiar for that very reason. Alice looked up, watching as the jigsaw pieces shining through the trees were swallowed in night and the treetops whispered as their leaves were brushed by wind.

"Poor, little Cat. A Pillar fallen. What sorrow burrows in Horrorland? *HeeheeHEe!*"

The voice was from behind them, though the laugher's echo was a dome encompassing. Alice turned, arm still taken by the Rabbit as she looked upon an odd backed cat, lapping at the dead man's blood.

"Tasty! Who knew he was who he wanted to be, all along?" The cat laughed again. It was like a hiss, like a hiccup at the same time. "Trapped within a habit. *Tsk, tsk!*" He began to turn, faded into mist before Alice saw its face.

"Go away, Cheshire." The Rabbit frowned, rolling

his eyes. Alice wondered why he looked so exacerbated.

"Horrorland is our heart; we all would die if we depart." She felt something between her legs, like a breeze. Pushing at her skirts, Alice turned, unlinking her arm with the White Rabbit as she felt soft paws upon her back.

"Who are you?" Alice asked, feeling something on her shoulders jump away.

It fled in the space around her like a ghost. "A smile in the darkest dark, a funeral and amusement park." Again the treetops whistled as the wind blew upwards. Alice saw the canopy open, revealing the midnight sky and crescent, yellow moon.

"Quit hiding, Cat, and show her who you are!"

"*HeheHEheheHE!* Alice, Alice, made of mice. Will you always be so nice?"

The moon teetered, turning awry. Overtop, blinking open, two holes appeared. One was a cerulean blue with a rift in the middle. The other was a gaping bloody hole.

"Oh my gosh…" Alice whispered, biting at her nail.

"Pish, posh, oh my gosh!" The cat appeared, its tail like a long rope that curled at the end. It was gray, like mist, but with four slashes across its back which looked to have been broken, or run over by a wagon wheel. "Alice," it hissed again, "so nice to meet you." The Cat smiled, sharp, unnaturally long teeth devouring its face and almost reaching the corners of its eyes.

"This is the Cheshire Cat," the White Rabbit explained, looking quite displeased. The cat rolled over, floating lackadaisically in the space before her. Its body faded and reappeared as its head continued to roll around, regarding her from different angles.

"Alice, Alice full of malice?" it asked. It drug out its hiss, prolonging the steaming consonant to reveal more of its sinister smile.

"N-no." Alice was worried. The Cheshire Cat

reminded her Dinah, and the memory picked at the back of her mind like it were a scab. "Can I help you?"

"Would you help if you could? Helpings what all people should."

The Rabbit vaulted forward, swinging his hand through the misty body of the topsy turvy feline. Smoke darted away, ambling through the darken space but began to reform, albeit a bit farther from the Rabbit's reach this time.

"Naughty, naughty little Rabbit. Why can't we all just cohabit?"

"Alice," the Rabbit gripped her by the shoulder, leaning down to regard her, "why are you crying?"

Alice darted away, hiding her eyes as the forest blurred around her. Jagged thorn bushes ripped at her clothing, red eyes blazed in the darkness, but as she ran all Alice could think of was her poor little kitten with a rut down its back.

London was a nasty place: a city of gutters, smoke, human waste. She remembered coming back from the factory, how the small gray kitten had mewed at her, hugged her legs and licked at her ankles. Alice had taken the small thing home, back to the orphanage. She had fed the thing, pet and cared for it until the Headmistress saw her, and threw it in the road.

"We've no food for gutter cats!" she had shrieked.

The moon was taken by the smog of factories, and though Alice had snuck out to look for the kitten, she hadn't a light to find it. She had promised to look in the morning before work and dropped a scrap of dried pork in the road in hopes the creature would find it.

Dinah. She dreamt of its name. Alice couldn't wait to suggest the name to her, hoped she would mew and insist it was a good one. But in the morning she found it in the road. A wagon tread down its back. Its sides split open and its insides out.

London crept on uncaring. Alice went to work.

She cried that day and was given a beating.

No time to cry in London.

Alice sat. Her heart was heaving in her chest; her face was red and spotty. She wiped her nose and licked her lips, wondering what Horrorland was.

"Am I dreaming?" she sobbed, the birch trees a cage around her. "Have I gone mad?"

"We're all mad here, my dear." The same lithe giggle echoed around her. Though the Cheshire Cat was invisible, Alice somehow knew exactly where it was. Its form appeared, foggy and light, and wrapped about her neck before wafting backwards with the wind.

"I don't understand what Horrorland is." She balled up her fists, pressing them against her thighs.

"It used to be quite wonderful," the Cheshire Cat mused, its floating head turning upside down, "but, then the Queen lost her heart."

"How?"

The Cat smiled again, his needle-like grin menacing and wry. "I heard she gave her heart away, and it was never returned. So sad, so sad, and now we all have gone quite mad."

"You look like Dinah." At least, parts of him did. The coat, the blue eye, the broken spot across his back.

"*HeehEEHEe,*" it giggled, "some would say that *you* look like dinner!"

"That's not—"

"Be careful Alice, don't be too nice. You'll lose your heart. Take my advice."

Its head began to fade, leaving only the bright curve of its smile. Alice could hear something running through the woods after her.

"Please! Tell me more!" she called, standing to her feet.

"The Rabbit comes. He won't be late. The Hatter's

ball, we'll congregate! *HEEheEHEE!*"

"Alice!" She turned, surprised. He was before her, legs of a rabbit, torso of a man. Removing his mask he transformed back, but the Cat was gone. His laugh a leftover from cryptic reflections.

"Are you alright?" The White Rabbit watched the darkness, peering past the ivory trunks of Birchwood trees. "The Cheshire Cat is crazed. A thing of death and madness."

"May I call you Ben?" She looked up, her blue eyes brimming with thought, with sunny reflections. The White Rabbit paled, if such could be so, the moonlight of his skin was already polished alabaster, but something dulled the brightness of his features, turning it to paste.

"What—"

"Ben," she suggested. "I don't want to call you Rabbit." Alice turned, rubbing her arms, feeling the angry, red trenches where the branches had scratched her skin. "You are the Prince of Timekeepers after all." She stepped forward, hoping to see a ribbon of fog, a rope of mist. "May I call you Ben?"

The Rabbit pondered, his smile overturned. "Sure," he said, "but only when we are alone."

Alice looked back at him. "Thank you, Ben," she smiled. "Shall we go attend the ball?"

But the Rabbit wasn't sure. Something strange was happening, and it warped before his eyes. Alice, Alice full of malice? Alice, Alice made of mice, will you always be so nice?

'Ben' looked up into the sky. Stars made roads in the cosmos and sometimes at the corner of his eyes they converged to tell a story he hadn't heard before. What did that Cheshire Cat know? Who was this girl he had meant to harvest?

Alice took him by the arm, and the Rabbit followed.

"What will the ball be like?" she asked, and for the first time the White Rabbit noticed how blue her eyes were.

"Wonderful," he said.

Chapter 7
The Space Between A Heartbeat

The Mad Hatter's castle was crooked. Dozens of smokestacks rose like minarets, topped with chimney caps like looked like witch's hats. They pointed into the star studded sky like broken, twisted fingers, and fat clouds converged upon them with lightning flashing in their bellies.

The Hatter's castle sat on a hill that looked like a broken canine. Skinny buttresses held up the top floor and turrets, while the bottom merged into the earth like a growth. Tall windows that looked like an upside-down wine glass without a stem were colored beautifully in stained glass, and as the two walked arm in arm up the path, the windows shone with light, beckoning the outside in.

The Rabbit smiled. Alice felt his arm tense, whether from excitement or from trepidation, she wasn't sure. He seemed changed after her encounter with the Cheshire Cat. Perhaps it was herself, however, that had been warped. Perhaps Alice was beginning to understand

Horrorland.

"Is this where the ball is, Ben?" she asked, a cool wind fingering down her spine and making her shiver.

The Rabbit regarded her, raising a finger to his lips. "Yes," he said with barely a noise. "Everyone comes to the Tea Party Ball. But you wouldn't want them to grow curious of you."

Alice frowned. "Curious?"

He straightened, his blue cloak waving like the sea at night. "Curiosity killed the cat." He grinned, looking at her with not the manner of a rabbit, but the mien of a wolf. "We can't go there yet, anyway," he continued, looking away. "You are not dressed for a ball, my sweet."

Alice felt her heart pounding in her chest as her breath misted from between her lips. He looked so lovely in the night. Though there was no moon, he was forever shining like a canine on obsidian, or candle wax on a pitch black shroud.

It was true however. Her dress was quite soiled. The Caterpillar's blood had spotted the white lace the Duchess had gifted to her. Alice wondered how angry the Duchess would be to know how the Caterpillar had died. Would she care? Would she be irate that Alice had not returned with the leeches filled with Midwife Sap? Were the babes buried in the tree truly safe? Were they dead? If so, who cared?

"What do we do?" Alice asked. All the questions in her mind were like oblong shards of glass, all cut and broken from different *ruined* objects, yet trying to fit together in an effort to keep her sane. They nicked at her brain, and Alice winced to keep them calm inside her mind.

The Rabbit returned his eyes to the castle, reaching into his pocket where she knew he kept his watch. "The night is young. Look and see." He opened the decorated instrument. It still read a moment to midnight. "We'll return again to this tea party."

The beads at his wrists ticked as he removed his mask. The brass border gleamed as he donned it, the red heart at the corner of one eye shining like saffron. He began his gradual transformation. His knees buckled, thighs expanding into thick meaty hips while his biceps enlarged and flanks pushed outward. His top hat ripped in twain and formed upwards into long, white ears, while his suit clung to his body until it was only fur: white as snow.

He wasn't the small creature she had seen in London, but a massive beast with ruby eyes and blue in his ears. She had stepped away when his body began to form, but as he stood before her now, nose wiggling curiously, Alice felt her breath hitch and her eyes grow glassy.

"We shall be late if you don't hurry," he said, his voice unchanged. Alice stepped forward, placing a hand on his shoulder, feeling the softness of his fur. It reminded her of nothing, for Alice had never felt anything so soft.

He grinned at her marvel, his red eyes winking back her reflection. "Alice, take heed. We must increase our speed," he whispered. "Get on my back, my dear."

"A-are," the thought was baffling, "are you sure?" She felt like it would be a terrible trespass, like giggling while at work, or how terrible dropping a match would be.

But the White Rabbit inclined his head, nodding patiently as she obliged. He felt warm between her knees, like she was astride something that had sat long in the sun. As he ran his body moved beneath her gently.

The Hatter's castle was swept away, capped chimneys blending into the forest treetops until they disappeared entirely. Alice crouched between the Rabbit's shoulders, smelling the earthy scent of his white coat and warm skin. The wind fingered at her hair as he ran swiftly through the trees, dodging briers and glowing mushrooms. She had thought she saw a carriage along the path, but as Alice had lifted her head to see better, the Rabbit had bounded from the path, and together they found themselves lost within the forest.

"Where are we going?" Alice enquired, holding on tightly as he weaved and ducked beneath the forest foliage.

"A place to change," he replied, ears bouncing back and forth.

It was hard to see. Shadows blanketed the forest, and without a moon to see, there was nothing to highlight the abstract shapes that converged in the darkness. Alice ducked her head, pressing a temple to his back as she wondered about the Cat.

Dinah. Alice was surprised she had so easily forgotten her. She hadn't known the kitten long, but she had fallen in love with it fast. Was her heart so contrary as to leave behind the first real love she had felt? Alice didn't remember her parents, had been told nothing about her mother or father. For the entirety of her life she had lived in the embrace of the orphanage, surrounded by girls who came and went but mostly came and stayed. Even then they were detached girls, most remembering the families that had abandoned them or decayed into the next world.

Alice hadn't any friends; she had girls she made matches with. Alice lived with ghosts and worked with automated humans. Was she to be the same? A heartless factory instrument?

Why had she so quickly forgotten Dinah?

Alice promised she wouldn't again. She promised she would honor Dinah, and while swiftly riding through the forests of Horrorland, Alice vowed that the poor little kitten that had broken its back would exist forever in her mind.

"We are here."

Alice looked up as the Rabbit stopped. High on a cliff side they both stood, a curling tree with roots in its branches standing stark and alone before them. Alice climbed down from the Rabbit's back as he removed his mask. She walked ahead, curious about the queer sight before her.

There was a door at the peak of the cliff. Large and uneven. It was taller on one side than the other. At the ground it was perhaps two feet in width, but at the top it was three at least. There was nothing beyond the door itself, but empty space and the promise of falling.

"There is only a door," she said looking back.

The Rabbit approached, a man once again. He didn't seem inclined to answer as he tucked his mask away, the beads on his wrists ticking.

Alice rubbed her hands together, walking to the edge. There was no way to stand behind the door; it was much too close to the threshold. Below she could see the forest, and beyond the bald hills of Horrorland. She saw the Hatter's castle as well, a bright star in the darkness. But there was one more thing, up in the sky. It was so far distant, beyond the hills and forests. It looked like a black cloud but it was darker still. It was an absence of light, a tear in the sky. It was like a jet black dress in a dark room with a hole missing.

"There only *needs* to be a door, my dear."

She wanted to ask about it. What was the nothing in the sky?

"Can something come from nothing? *HeeHEehee.*"

Alice started at the sound of the Cat, but jumped when the Rabbit took her by the hand. Almost stumbling from the cliff side, he pulled her back, and she fell towards him. He hadn't heard the voice, only she had, and of this Alice was sure when she looked up and saw him.

"Are you alright?" he asked with a grin, and though she looked around her and saw nothing, Alice was sure the Cheshire Cat had been there, cackling into her mind.

"Yes," she said, standing straight, feeling her heart alive within her chest.

"Then come."

He held her hand, his fingers long and chill as they guided her to the front of the door. The brass knob was tarnished. There were webs beneath it, but when the door was opened the inside was clean, a warmly lit room with a fire.

"Is this your home?" Alice asked, lingering on the doorstep, afraid of falling from a dream.

The Rabbit smiled again. Alice thought him a library of secrets the way he always regarded her. "No," he admitted, walking inside, "this has never been a home but a storage of theories long abandoned and vastly unexplored."

"I don't understand." Reluctantly she followed after.

"No one does. Not even the Queen who created it."

Holding the door ajar for her, the Rabbit watched as Alice gingerly stepped inside. She was afraid the floor would fall. He closed it after, saying not a word as he left to explore a wardrobe.

"This place is strange," she muttered, watching the walls and studying the décor.

The house was small, but not cramped or uncomfortable. It was only one room and lit by a large fireplace. Two beds were on either side of the room, sectioned off by privacy screens. Two large, high backed chairs sat before the fire, subtle green in color.

The house was unlike anything Alice had seen in Horrorland. It looked normal, untainted by madness or ludicrous, upside down logic. The fire burned brightly and emanated a warmth that was as familiar as her own bed at the orphanage. Though there were picture frames upon the wall, there were no portraits inside. A carpet on the floor was soiled.

"A dress, a dress to address a party!" the White Rabbit sung. Though the wardrobe he rifled through was old and plain, the gowns inside were much the opposite, glittering with gemstones and elegant with lace. Alice was drawn to the chairs by the fire.

It seemed to her so strange how they were placed side by side. Big plush cushions lining the back made them the loveliest pieces in the room, besides that of the dresses in the closet. Alice walked between the chairs, running her hand along the upholstery. As she passed she saw there were people sitting in the chairs, and standing before the fire she regarded them, her eyes worried and sad.

They were marionettes: dolls with ropes about their wrists, and strings attached at the tops of their heads. They had no face, which was the most disturbing, and one was dressed as a woman where the other was a man.

"They are puppets?" Alice whispered, bending to inspect their hands. Each one held their own pull string in the palm of their hands, almost as though entreating someone to come and bring them to life. "Rabbit! What is this?"

Alice looked up as he drew close, a dress held up within his hand. "I told you I shall never know."

"Then how did you *know* it existed?"

He narrowed his eyes, wiggling a finger at her with a smirk. "Logic, logic, pedagogic, in Horrorland it's quite exotic!" Turning, he hooked the gown on the screen by the bed, the white tails of his jacket flourishing behind him as he spun back around to address her.

"I helped her once, the Queen." He paused, then walking forward slowly the Rabbit too ran a hand on the back of one plush, verdant chair. "She had me play the puppeteer for her." He fingered the strings attached to the marionette dressed as a man in suit and trousers. Alice hadn't noticed before, but there were hearts stitched on the breasts of both puppets, precisely like the dolls at the entrance to Horrorland.

"Why?"

His expression changed, and though the Rabbit continued to smile it was rueful now, more a mask than the one he held in his pocket. "Us heartless creatures of Horrorland weren't always so," he said. "The Queen, she tried to find her heart. She tried to create one." He swept his hands around the room. "Secrets like these were the fruits of her labour, and locked away when they failed to work. Alice," his eyes were hard, "the Queen of Hearts was always heartless, but we in Horrorland were not. We were but her last resort."

"Are you heartless too, Rabbit?"

He paused. Looking down his nose at her, the wry smile returned to his lips as his eyes glinted wickedly in the firelight. "My heart was stolen long ago, dear girl."

She looked away, unable to face the darkness in his eyes. *Who had stolen the White Rabbit's heart?* She thought. Had it been the Queen? Did the malevolence in his eyes mean she had ripped it from him unwillingly? Why did he help her still, if so?

"I'm sorry to ask. It was rude of me to do so," she said, feeling very uncomfortable.

He cocked his head to the side, noticing the flush upon her cheeks. Running his fingers against the side of her face the White Rabbit marvelled at the warmth she emanated and listened to the beating of her heart.

"You ought to dress, little Alice," he said, feeling her shiver. "The Tea Party Ball will grow cold without your warmth." Moving away he grasped the door handle, his mind a flurry of unexpected curiosities.

Regarding his pocket watch, trying to ignore the

hidden library unveiling itself in his mind, the White Rabbit tsked. "A minute to midnight. We're late, I'm afraid." And walking out the door he lectured her to be quick once more before closing it. "The night is young but ages fast, time always moves, it never lasts."

Except for your pocket watch, Alice thought, donning the dress he had given her.

Chapter 8
The Mad Tea Ball

They walked into the Hatter's castle arm in arm, but when they converged within the crowd of people, the White Rabbit vanished from sight. Alice was alone amid the decorated denizens of Horrorland, of who were dressed in a myriad of odd accoutrements. Women in full-length gowns with glittering beads and shiny lace aired themselves with fans of sandalwood, but on their shoulders they wore gruesome heads. Some wore horses, some wore wolves, some wore turtles, birds or bears, but that they weren't their own was plain to see.

Along their necks or at their shoulders Alice could see the bloody rim where the head of the beast met the shoulders of the person within. Sometimes thick, black stitches stuck out along their skin, threading the two parts together, other times there was just a macabre lip that hung around the neck and produced a shadow.

The inside of the castle itself was cavernous. Voices big and small bounced throughout the ballroom, getting lost within the high ceiling where stony beasts kept their wake upon granite perches.

They had been led into the ballroom area by a tortoise wearing a bowtie. There hadn't been much of a foyer, rather the large threshold of the entryway exploded into the vast entertaining space. Therefore, as Alice watched the odd sight of the tortoise, wondering how he could in fact stand with such an enormous shell upon his back, the Rabbit had taken his chance to escape, leaving her by herself.

"Sorry! Excuse me!" She wasn't sure why, but Alice was convinced that she must have been the smallest person at the party. Everyone towered over her. If they weren't a good head and shoulders bigger in height, they were almost twice as wide it seemed. Alice wondered if everyone was sampling from the Duchess' Big Minded pills, and if so, where on earth were they available to try. She did noticed however, that almost everyone was holding a teacup in their hand. Perhaps that was the reason they were the size they were.

"Alice! Oh! Where is the little heart beater!"

Alice turned, hearing her name shrieked through the crowd. It was greeting guests as it went, saying hellos, how to dos, and exclaiming at ball gowns before appearing in front of her.

The Mad Hatter was a spectacle in a dress of thin, vertically striped black and white. Her smile, which curled at the end in the shape of a bold square lollipop, expanded past her lips in a stitched up scar that looked like it couldn't quite contain the mirth she usually expressed upon her face. She tipped the brim of her black top hat in greeting, clicking the heels of her oversized shoes together as she tossed her long, straight, fire tossed hair behind her shoulders.

"Alice!" the Hatter called again, reaching forward and taking both hands in hers. "I'm hearing *so* much about you! Come! Welcome to my tea party ball!" Her eyes were wide. The whites were exposed all around her pupils and made her look quite looney. She was wearing a rather bold leather corset overtop a black waistcoat with tails.

"Are you the Hatter?" Alice asked, mindful when the woman enlaced their fingers together and began to lead her away.

"The *Mad* Hatter!" The woman smiled again, looking back. The stitches strained to hold her face together. "And I haven't heard a heart like yours in a very long time." She stopped, all of a sudden horrified. "Why, you haven't yourself a cup of tea!" she shrieked.

Alice held up both hands as the Hatter let her go. "It's quite alright. I only just got here."

"DORMOUSE!" The guests froze, the idle chatter and white noise of the ballroom halted as quickly as a heart attack. Alice looked all around her, her face a prodigy of embarrassment.

"It's really alright, I don't need—"

But before she could finish a mouse ran up, scurrying between her knees, hardly larger than a small balloon. "Yes, Hatter?" it said.

"She has no tea."

"Yes Hatter."

The woman's face reddened, a card in the ribbon on her hat quivering on the brim.

"Were you sleeping again?" the Mad Hatter asked.

The Dormouse yawned, as though confirming the suspicion. Alice thought he looked quite cute in a small mouse-sized coat and trousers, though three whiskers were bent on one side, as though he had been laying on them.

"I sleep when I breathe, Hatter. It is how I am. I am what I am and I'm all that I am." The mouse smiled, large bags under his eyes warping the shape of his face.

Still, the patrons of the tea party were silent, enrapt

with the confrontation.

"Do you breathe when you sleep?" The Hatter folded her arms behind her back, her lollipop grin subtle despite the scars upon her face.

The Dormouse agreed, looking about the room as though it were quite an obvious answer. "I do, Hatter," he said in his high soprano, squeaky voice.

The Hatter began to pace about, thinking, pondering, as though trying to solve a riddle presented in the air before her eyes.

"So you breathe when you sleep and you sleep when you breathe?"

Again, the Dormouse nodded.

"Then!" The Hatter raised a finger, her smile a monster upon her face. "To wake up you must stop!" She looked down, eyes manic. "Correct?"

The Dormouse yawned. "Stop what?"

Alice stepped back, her black dress whooshing against the skirts of a lady headed-hippopotamus.

"BREATHING!" The Hatter smashed her foot down, her large clunky shoes splattering the small Dormouse against the black and white diamond floor. He seemed to pop like a balloon, and an eye rolled out and bounded between the guests as the Hatter ground her foot into to the floor, laughing with eyes wide as dinner plates.

"Tea, Miss?" Another creature asked Alice. He had a head like a hare. Though he had a cravat tied beneath his chin, Alice was certain he was not wearing a mask. His mouth moved when he spoke, and his ears bobbed back and forth at the slightest change in noise.

The Mad Hatter picked up her foot, grimacing at the foul smell of the stringy guts stuck to the bottom of her shoe. Then, like a glass quickly shattering and popping back together, she stood up straight, rushing towards the serving Hare and throwing herself beneath its arm.

"Marsh Hare!" she crooned, her long top hat bopping

him in the nose. "Always a charmer, he is." The Hare passed Alice a cup of tea, his long front teeth folding over his bottom lip to his chin.

"The entertainment is here," the Hare explained. His pupils grew and shrunk within his irises like thrumming vortexes. Sometimes they were but pinpricks, and at other times they were inky black pits in his eye sockets.

The Hatter nodded, and gradually the volume about them began to rise. "Alice! Drink and stay and watch the play!" she sang, bouncing about each foot. "I promise you will LOVE my entertainment! They're a circus, you see. A Circus of Glee!" A stitch upon her face snapped as she twirled in a flourish, bounding away.

"I think I've stepped in someone's gum," she muttered as she went.

Alice didn't drink her tea as she was ushered to the back of the ballroom. Cupping it in her hand, she stood amongst the others in the front, careful not to let the tea spill on the dress the Rabbit had chosen for her.

There was a stage up front, hidden by a red and black curtain. The Mad Hatter herself was on the stage, smiling wickedly as she watched her guests congregate in front. Alice waved unsurely as the Hatter smiled at her, noticing the splash of red gore still present upon her shoe.

"Ladies and Gentlemen, creatures of Horrorland, I'm so wickedly pleased to introduce to you the delectable darlings of death and destruction, the sinister sweetipies of slaughter and sorrow, The Mad Caps of Horrorland!"

A great applause rose up from the antechamber as the disguised guests cheered and clapped their mirth. The curtain was drug from the floor, and several hundred red crystals at the bottom fluttered up like ruby raindrops as the menagerie beneath was revealed to their audience.

The Mad Hatter beamed, chuckling maniacally as women and men dressed in feather boas and furs, in tights and jester caps and garishly painted makeup began to cavort on stage, kicking up their legs as small fish men in trousers flopped upright on their tails, blowing into trumpets.

"Welcome esteemed guests, to my freak show," the Mad Hatter shrieked.

Alice bit her lip as the Mad Hatter flourished about the stage. She noticed stitches on the dancer's limbs. They bled and seeped each time they kicked their legs up. There were hooks in the gills of the fish, and their eyes were vacant as they blew into their tarnished brown horns.

"This is terrible!" Alice wailed. But as she looked around, the young match girl marvelled at how transfixed everyone was.

"Drink the tea, my dear," the Marsh Hare directed, appearing beside her. Alice started, hearing the music growing louder from the stage.

"I don't know if I should," she said, scared at the way his eyes continued to feverishly dilate.

"You can't come to the Hatter's Tea Party Ball and not drink her tea."

Alice shouted, pushing back as the Hare took hold of her. His large brown paws wrapped about her shoulders and pulled her in closer to him. He took the cup from her other hand.

"I don't want to drink it!" she yelled, listening to the laughter growing around her. But the Hare insisted, his large tooth brown at the gums as he tipped the tea cup into her mouth, prying apart her teeth with ragged, sharp fingernails. Alice felt the tea slide down her throat, thick and full of grit. It poured over her chin, into her nostrils until the Marsh Hare began to throb in her vision, his grand white tooth a doorway into madness.

"We're all mad here, Alice!" she heard someone say, and turning, finally released from the Marsh Hare's grip,

Alice could see that the people of the ball were no longer wearing masks, but were indeed creatures of two bodies. Horse women wearing dresses, Birdmen in tuxedos, and Cats in hats, snapping their suspenders, all enjoying the Hatter's circus of beautiful ladies and gentlemen who swung on trapeze and somersaulted as a school of fish played fervently upon polished trombones and trumpets.

"I—" Alice felt transfixed. High along the ceiling the gargoyles on their perches carried fire sparking wands in their talons, and upon the floor the white diamonds spun like dancing stars.

"I will show you, my lovely, WONDERFUL guests! Something most feared, more horrid, most foul."

Alice pushed her way up towards the stage, feeling her heart shuddering against her rib cage.

"What is it?" she hollered with the others, noticing now how the Hatter's smile seemed to lift off the sides of her face.

"The Jabberwocky is the spawn of all your nightmares! And here! At *my* tea party, for your birthday present," the Hatter cackled again, flipping back upon her palms. "I will show the creature to you!"

There was a cheer from the crowd. Beside her a Pig lady with purple lipstick laughed. Alice smiled and joined along.

"Show us!" she cried with the crowd.

The Hatter squealed in delight. "Are you certain, my lovely little lumplings? With jaws that bite and claws that catch? Your life today it may dispatch!"

They cheered again. Beside her the Marsh Hare opened his large maw and screamed in mirth and terrible delight. Alice watched in wonder how his black gums bled into his teeth, running in a river down the groove bisecting the door-like pane of his protruding front tooth. Globes of red spittle flew from his mouth as he hollered, down the front of his white shirt and blending into the lapels of his scarlet top coat.

The Hatter hissed, her black lollipop smile twisting upon her cheeks, pulling at the stitches until the swirling ends of her grin were higher than her nose. She pulled her top hat down to shroud her eyes. She turned with a flourish, the tails of her coat spinning away behind her.

"Bring out the Jabberwocky!" she commanded.

It came from the floor, rising from the stage like a body would rise from the dead. Wrapped in a birthday present, white paper was pearlescent in the candlelight while the red ribbon tying it together glowed from the tiny gold designs of roaring monsters and hell beasts. Alice's eyes were like boiled eggs as she again stepped forward, attempting to garner the best spot in which to see the reveal. All around her the scent of squeezed bodies and farm animals sweating profusely was attempting to wrestle the attention away from the box on stage, but holding her nose, Alice pressed her lips in a thin line, too overwhelmed with curiosity to care.

The Hatter laughed again as a long band of crimson silk was lowered towards her like a slash. Kicking off her blood stained shoes, the Mad Hatter split the silk into two long ropes, and wrapped her feet about the ends until she could be held aloft.

Made aerial by the silk, the Hatter twirled and bent, weaving in and out as she whirled up higher into the air.

"Does anyone have a pair of scissors?" she called, suspended upside down, her body so knotted within the silken snakes that it held her in place just above the ribbon. When no one seemed to move, the Hatter laughed again. "You knuckleheads! Dolts! Bad brains all filled with nuts and bolts!" She cackled, removing the top hat from her head to reveal a pair of scissors embedded into the top of her skull.

"At least some of us pay mind to use our noggins!"

the Hatter laughed, a chorus of animal headed patrons joining her in her wake. Alice winced as the Hatter hauled on the pair of silver shears, feeling an ache in her own head from the sight of it. Clipped red hair fell down like twirling tapeworms as the Hatter removed the cutters, a font of blood welling at the top of her head before she replaced her hat.

"Now, my darlings," she hissed, turning so that her belly was perfectly perpendicular to the ribbon. "May all your nightmares come true." Blood ran down the Hatter's forehead. As she clipped the ribbon and the panels of the gift box began to fall away, the Mad Hatter rolled upwards, away from the contents as fast as she could, chortling with closed eyes.

"What is so horrib—" Alice began.

People screamed. Beside her the pig woman had been so afraid she had urinated herself, slipping on the spot on the floor as she had tried to run away from the now open box. Some guests could only balk at the Jabberwocky; others held their faces in terror while some coiled up like a ball of string and wept like infants.

Alice was confused. Stepping towards the stage, now able to climb up as so many had fled, she approached the open box as it lay sprawled like a picnic cloth across the floor.

"I don't understand," she said, turning on her heel. "There is nothing here." She studied the box, the left over paper, even the monstrous designs decorating the ribbon with gold lines. "Where is the Jabberwocky, Hatter?" Alice looked up, watching as the woman unwound herself from the ribbon. She was wearing a blindfold around her head and now carried a large sword in her left hand like an anchor.

"Can't you not hear it? The screaming? The flaying it does?" The Hatter held onto her ears, shaking her head. "It's too horrible to bear."

"Why do you have a blindfold on?" Alice felt her heart skip, afraid that the Hatter's inability to see the anything meant something would suddenly step out to hurt her. "What is everyone running away from?"

But the Hatter shook her head.

"Ohh! You can't see anything," she smiled. "The Jabberwocky changes you know. It *is* everyone's greatest fear. All. At. The same. Time." She pointed her fingers, twirling them in a circle before pressing them to the young match girl's temples. "Could it be that Alice has no fear? Hmm?"

Beyond the stage, Alice heard a bloodletting scream and stood horrified as the Marsh Hare ripped off his own ears. Nubby stumps pumped blood over his head as he fell to his knees, fear-struck from the thing he was seeing.

"You've poisoned the tea!" Alice accused.

The Hatter cried. "Did I?" she asked, waving the sword about like a wizard's wand, more precccupied with her position on stage.

"You must have! Look at these people. They're terrified."

"Did you drink the tea?"

Alice paused. "Y-yes," she replied, looking about the room again, silent when the Hatter's smile twisted inward, becoming a knot upon her face.

"Well then! Apparently the beast must be slain to be conquered." She turned, the sash over her eyes waving behind her. Holding the sword in front of her like a knight, the Mad Hatter hollered to the empty box. Tipping her hat like a knight's helm and running forward as though galloping upon the horse, the Hatter held an awesome duel, fighting the Jabberwocky to the ground until the sword pierced its belly and its entrails slopped upon the floor.

There were times in which Alice thought she really

was fighting off something. Something unknown seemed to throw her off her feet, pick her up until she was hanging in the air. Sometimes the Hatter screamed, the fright she projected being hauled up from the very bowels of her belly. Despite the blindfold Alice knew that whatever it was the Hatter was fighting, it was indeed something she was horrified of.

"Why?" Alice whispered, backing away as the Hatter pled on her back with her sword raised.

"Please!" The blindfold had slipped from her eyes; her hat was on the ground behind her. "No more chair! NO MORE CHAIR!" But still she laughed. The smile raped her features until she was able to wrestle free and stab the sword all the way to the hilt into the center of the box.

"I don't understand."

"And you won't."

Alice looked behind, seeing the White Rabbit before her below the stage. He was holding out a hand, watching the Hatter with mistrust.

"I—"

"The creatures of Horrorland must live in madness. It is madness that conquers our fears here. Without madness we would be swept away by what haunts us the most."

Alice regarded him. He was wearing his rabbit's mask, though his human features remained unchanged.

"But why the Jabberwocky?"

He regarded her. Through the slits in his mask where she knew his eyes to be, there were only wide black holes staring back.

"Forced to see our worst fear keeps us mad. The Hatter protects us all with her tea parties." He sighed, inclining his head in a gesture that demanded her to look back to the stage. Alice did, and watched as the Hatter continued to stab at the nothingness with—not a sword—but a cane of candy.

She wondered what the Hatter feared most.

"Probably the Queen," the Rabbit replied, as though able to read her thoughts. Alice felt her eyes water.

"This is just foolish," she whispered, "it's a revolution. You're all mad to face the horror, but you horrify yourself to stay that way."

The White Rabbit licked his lips. "I've long thought that perhaps Horrorland is the perfect revolution." By instinct, he dug into his pocket, withdrawing his watch. Still, it remained at a minute to midnight. "Horrorland was bred on the face of a broken clock. It shall forever remain in time and yet time does not exist. Horrorland was once something, but it is nothing at the same time: which does not exist. Horrorland is a paradox."

Alice narrowed her eyes. Her head hurt. "Why can't I see anything? Why can't I see a Jabberwocky?"

The Rabbit frowned. "Perhaps because your heart beats, and despite being in Horrorland you are still apart of time." He snapped the lid of his watch closed, pressing his thumb into the cerulean eye almost spitefully. "Or perhaps because you fear nothing most of all." He looked down at her.

"Alice, Alice full of malice," his eyes were piercing, cold, like blue stones set upon white granite. "Do you fear nothing? Having nothing? Being nothing? Knowing nothing?"

Alice drew back, unsure of what to say. "I don't know. I fear a lot of things." She clasped her hands together, looking at the frightened guests cowering on the floor in terror, digging at their own skin, wetting themselves. "Right now, I'm afraid of not being afraid."

The Rabbit cocked his brow. "Why? Do you *want* to see the Jabberwocky?"

"If I could, perhaps I could tell them all it will be ok."

The Rabbit laughed. "You can't see everyone's Jabberwocky," he mocked.

"But if I could, maybe Horrorland wouldn't be so horrible."

The Rabbit paused. Had been about to say something but stopped short, caught amidst his own thoughts. When he finally did look like he would reply, something had changed. The Hatter jumped up, raising her pretend sword into the air as the lights dimmed.

"The Jabberwocky is banished again," she screamed, "for another year." The guests uncurled, jumping to their feet, surreal in their ability to so quickly forget their own greatest fears. The few of them that had shredded their skin, or torn their ears, seemed dumb to the pain or consequences of the Jabberwocky. They cheered all the same, even with blood dripping down the sides of their face, matting their fur.

"To Dwell in Hell or furbelow in lunacy?" the Hatter snorted, popping the candied cane into her mouth. "Well Ladies, Gentlemen. Things. We furbelow!" Tea was brought out almost immediately, though this time Alice adamantly refused, noticing how the bloody lips of the hollowed out head-masks once again appeared against the throats of each guest.

"Rabbit?" She turned. He had been looking up as the lights changed. The fish musicians on stage, floundering to regain their purchase, took out their instruments again, and a woman in a long slate gray gown, choke marks about her neck, came out behind the Hatter, smiling before she began to sing.

The atmosphere was transformed. Alice watched as the ballroom turned from something grisly and terrifying into the majestic space it had been when she had first entered. Ladies and their partners began to dance, oblivious to any blood or soil upon their clothes. High in the airy rafters of the castle the gargoyles turned into angels and the torchlight popped off the wooden handles and danced in the air like windborne dandelion seeds.

"Alice," the Rabbit turned to her, smile as sharp as a razor blade. "Would you care to dance?"

When she didn't respond he grasped her hand, pulling her towards him as the school of fish produced living music notes to flutter like birds around the ballroom. The Hatter herself sat transfixed by the band, admiring the lovely songstress as she sat on the stage in her black and white striped dress and black coat.

Alice watched, studying the face of his mask as the Rabbit whirled her around the dance floor. He still looked like moonlight, his skin shining and polished. She was wearing black—the dress he had chosen for her from the house on the cliff—but it sparkled like starlight, flaring out in pleats along the skirt as the lace beneath spun in tandem to their dancing. Alice thought her heart would jump out of her chest, pound through the delicate embroidered heart sewn into the left breast of her dress, but it didn't.

He spun her outwards and caught her when he pulled her back, despite her feet feeling tangled and clumsy. Alice had never danced before, but as he swooped and pressed her to his chest, she found that she wanted to dance, that her greatest fear may have been the song ending and he never wanting to dance with her again.

The Rabbit was magnificent. The way he moved, ushered her where she needed to be, took each stride in confidence, sent her emotions away on a zephyr. But, even as her heart danced, sang and endeavoured to lead her astray, her mind intervened like a knife, piercing through her ribs.

"Rabbit..." she said his name, but even as she did tears rolled down her face. His expression turned grave, but still he continued to dance, hands grasping her hand and waist.

"Alice, Alice small and nice—"

"Did you bring me here to harvest my heart for the Queen?"

He stopped, as though struck, and the fear upon his face was more an answer than she imagined.

"I—" Never before had Alice heard him fail to find a reply. She tore her hand away from him...

... When the ballroom doors opened and out stepped the Queen of Hearts.

Chapter 9
The Queen's Cemetery

Y our Majesty!" The Hatter jumped from the stage and despite her grin, the sweat shining on her brow, and the grit of her teeth, expressed an emotion entirely different than the one stitched into her skin.

The Queen had entered through the main door and was unaccompanied by any kind of retinue or hand servants; however the guests formed a path to the stage regardless, struck quiet by her sudden appearance at the Tea Party Ball.

The Queen of Hearts was a tall woman, thin and waif-like with round spectacles upon her nose. She certainly did not look like a queen in her gray/blue dress with apron. She had the air of a scientist, certainly not royalty. Long thin hair hung lank behind her shoulders, and durable gloves adorned each arm all the way to the elbow. The Queen had small, pursed lips and an upturned nose, but she was not ugly. Her intimidating air of power and influence reached across the entire room, commanding absolute obedience and servitude as the guests watched her, all with wide, worrisome eyes.

Alice had craned her neck to see her, but as the Queen walked onto the dance floor the White Rabbit pushed the match girl harshly behind him, his grip upon her wrist shaking.

"Hatter." The Queen looked down at the decorated woman. She was at least a foot taller than the castle master. The Queen of Hearts was like a blade dangling over everyone's head all at once, and they watched her, waiting for the inevitable drop. "You look surprised to see me." She looked around, narrowed her eyes as though spotting something distasteful, then looked back.

"No, no! You are always welcome to my ballroom, your Majesty!" The Hatter's bottom lip trembled and she wrung her hands together. Though she was trying to appear earnest, the Hatter's right eye twitched in the Queen's presence.

"I'd hope so." The Queen turned again. Alice, from behind the Rabbit's back, was confused, but as the match girl peeked from behind Ben's cape to take a look, the Rabbit forced her back, shushing her.

"I've been hearing tell of a heart in Horrorland. One that beats and quivers and pumps." The Queen turned around, hands clasped behind her back. The long hemline of her skirt was tattered and stained in a green and black liquid. "I sincerely hope my faithful subjects have not been hiding a heart in their midst!" She looked about the room, smiling at the mask donned guests. She fingered their chins and flicked their ears as she walked among them.

Then the Queen twisted, hearing something again, and the candlelight reflected upon her glasses.

Unlike the Jabberwocky where the guests trembled and wet themselves, the Queen of Hearts froze the guests with fear. It was as though the Queen had reached into the chest of every one and gripped their insides in her palm. Alice was sure that if any of them were to run, or cower, or scream, they would find themselves hollow, staring at their own gore upon the ballroom floor.

"We would never!" the Mad Hatter replied, and taking her by the chin the Queen smiled.

"Wouldn't you," she asked, bending low, her lips almost brushing the Hatter's, "but then why do I hear it? The flutter of a heart!" She stood straight, "I'd hate to have to bring you all back to my laboratory one by one. Open you up and check your empty cavities." Again, clasping her arms behind her back the Queen of Hearts began to walk about the crowd, looking to and fro like a buyer at a butcher shop. "Perhaps you regrew one," she asked a horse-headed gentleman, "or, I merely didn't take them all as I had intended."

The pig-headed women in the large skirted gown hid her face behind her fan. She was holding a teacup in the other. The Queen took it, sipped, then threw the cup to shatter on the floor. "Which one of you slipped beneath my watchful eye?" she asked.

Alice bit her lip, wondering why the White Rabbit had not spoken up. Alice knew that he had meant to harvest her, but now, as the Queen drew nearer and nearer still, he began to push his mask into her hand, ushering her to put it on.

"There is no one here with a beating heart, my Queen," the Hatter pled.

"Nonsense," she yelled, "I can hear it. Beating, beating, beating its name!" She turned again, raised her ear.

"It is only the music, Majesty."

"Is it?" She looked away, espying something in the crowd. "It has been a long time since I've heard a beating heart... maybe you are right, Hatter." The Queen walked away from her, drawing nearer to the

Rabbit with a sharp grin upon her face.

"My precious Rabbit. Prince of Timekeepers." She caressed his face. "My Ben. Have you brought me a present? Will you prove to me there are liars among us?"

The Rabbit steeled his resolve, straightening up and pressing his arms to his side. "I'm sorry, my Queen," he said, "I was unable to procure you a heart."

Her face was stoic, her eyes cold and thoughtful. "I am disappointed in you, Ben." There was blood upon her apron. "Have you betrayed me as well?"

"Never, my Queen."

She stepped forward, taller by two heads than the White Rabbit. In fact the Queen of Hearts towered above them all. "Yours is the only heart I never knew," she said, pressing a palm to his chest thoughtfully.

"That is untrue. You stole it long ago," he replied.

She inhaled through her nose. "Oh?" Though her face resembled a stone, she acted curious. "Did I lose it?" But he didn't reply.

The Queen began to walk around him, her footsteps ticking like a clock as she regarded every inch of her Prince of Timekeepers. "I know there is a heart in Horrorland," she said, her face a prodigy of calm. "I can feel it. It pounds in my mind like a fist!" The Queen stopped. "If I find my loyal subjects have hidden it," her face was grave, "then I suppose I will be forced to create better ones with the pieces they leave behind." Her steps were the only noise in the chamber.

In a corner, far from the Queen of Hearts, Alice shivered. She had almost been stepped on twice, but as a white rabbit she had managed to run as fast as she could away from the Queen. Alice hoped she was far enough away that the Queen could no longer hear her heart beating.

"Remember that, subjects. Betray me and I shall

remodel your remains into more loyal serfs," she said, moving to leave.

"Thank you so much for coming, my gracious, wonderful Queen!" the Hatter said, grovelling at the woman's heels as she walked back to the door. "Come back anytime, *anytime*!"

The Queen paused again, turning so that she could cup the Hatter's chin. The Queen tsked.

"Do you really mean that, Hatter? After all I've done to you?"

"Absolutely!"

"I know how you fear me. I know who your Jabberwocky resembles." She withdrew from her apron a needle with black thread.

"I like being mad, my Queen. Mad, mad better than sad. A loony is glad when the mind has gone bad!"

Drawing the Hatter closer, the Queen of Hearts re-stitched the broken thread upon her face, grasping her like she was a lump of clay. "Don't betray me, Hatter. Fear without madness is a terrible thing."

"I know that too well, Majesty."

The Queen nodded, spinning on her heel she left the Tea Party Ball in silence, her absence like great swift wound in the flesh that took a moment to bleed.

Even after the front door closed shut, and the inhabitants of Horrorland began to relax, it was a great many minutes before anyone had dared to utter a word. When they did, out poured a melody of unrest.

"We are dead," a tortoise yelled. "The Queen will slaughter us all!"

"Hatter! Why protect the girl? We all heard her heart beating!" another wearing a head of a lion shrieked.

"Take her to the Queen now! We can still be saved!"

"This is madness!"

"Foolery!"

"We will all be tortured and turned into mad dolls!"

"Alice." The White Rabbit stooped towards her, looking over his shoulder, offering a hand so that she could climb into his arms. "We need to leave before they discover what I've done." Alice wanted to ask him why, to know what had made him hide her from the Queen, but instead she did as she was instructed, keeping quiet as he tucked her beneath his coat.

"You're all lambs," the Hatter shouted, trying to maintain order. "You wear those masks but only to hide your fear of the Queen! Why didn't any of you speak up?" she yelled. "Because you remember what the Queen of Hearts did to you when she ripped out your hearts! Do you want to give that pain to Alice?"

"Better her than us!" the Pig woman said, to which the others agreed.

"She'll dissect us."

"Fill us with worms!"

"Give the girl to her! Let the Queen tear out her heart and become one of us!"

"A little pain for one, and a lot less for many!" the Marsh Hare snickered, playing with the stumps where his ears used to be.

The Hatter was quiet, her voice stifled over the sounds of angry protests. From along the wall however, the Rabbit skulked, watching carefully as the guests bickered and fought, resolved to give up the girl.

But Alice quivered upon his breast as she listened within her guise as a rabbit. The Queen of Hearts was chilling, her very presence reaching in to freeze the hearts of those around her. Had she been so cruel to all these creatures? Did the Queen of Hearts so desire a heart that she'd dissect each being of Horrorland to find one? Did she have their hearts still?

"Rabbit…" she said, pulling his mask from her face. "I cannot run away and leave these people to suffer." She began to transform back. Letting go of her the

White Rabbit whispered his disapproval, begging her to re-don the mask before anyone could see her.

"Alice, you don't know what she'll do to you."

"You would have given me to her. Why not now?"

He took her by the hands, pressing them to his chest. "Please, before they hear your heart beating. Put it back on. I can take you back to London; I can take you away from Horrorland."

Alice shook her head. "No. I won't leave you all here to suffer."

"It's her!" Alice turned, her black dress shimmering in the candlelight as a frog in a tuxedo dangled out his tongue at her.

"Alice, Alice! Take her to the Queen!" someone shouted.

"Put the mask on!" the Rabbit pled.

But Alice shook her head. "I'll go!" she shouted at the mob as they rushed to take hold of her. "Take me to your Queen."

From the back the Hatter screamed, admonishing her guests, beating some bloody with a cane she had picked up from upon the floor.

"Stop, you bloody animals!" The Rabbit pushed himself in front of her, trying to fend them off as they wrenched at Alice's arms, tearing at her dress in an effort to claim her. "You'll kill her at this rate!"

But no one could hear anyone from over the shouting. The chaos was terrifying. Men and women and frogs and wolves all tumbled and fell over top each other, hoping to drag the girl away and humble themselves at the foot of the Queen.

"Oh Horrorland used to be sooOOoO Wonderful! *HEEheehee!* What happened, I wonder?"

The candlelight was snuffed out. The wisps that had been floating about the room extinguished as a shifting grey and purple cloud consumed the light, wafting about the room like a mad ghost.

"The Cheshire Cat!" Alice called.

"*HeheheHEhe!* What mad devotion the Queen inspires in her subjects!" His face appeared like the moon from behind a cloud. Large, needle-like teeth glowed in the darkness. The denizens of Horrorland shied away as the Cheshire Cat curled his long, smoky tail about Alice's waist, appearing like a hat atop her head.

"Can you take me to the Queen, Cheshire?" Alice asked, rubbing at her arms where she had been scratched.

The Cat purred, his tail flicking at the end. "You want to go to the Queen?" he echoed loudly so that the entirety of the Tea Party guests could hear. "*HEehee!* Whatever for, my dear?"

Alice pressed her teeth together, looking at the floor. "I don't want anyone else to die," she said.

"Else? You mean like the Caterpillar?" The Cat laughed. "Was that your fault, my dear?"

"I don't know." She looked at the people. Their masks were soiled, bloody; some so torn up darkened red holes marred the features. "But I don't want people to suffer because of me."

"You can't go to the Queen!" the Rabbit shouted, pushing through the now hushed crowd to stand before her. "She may not just remove your heart. She may… she could do so many horrible things to you."

The Cat cackled, hopping from Alice's head to float about the suited White Rabbit. "You were the one who brought her here, Rabbit. *HeehEEHEE!* Did you have a change of *heart*?" The Cat spun round, this time perching on Alice's shoulder.

"I'm late, I'm late: the Rabbit yells. To drag a girl straight down to hell! *HEE!*"

"Cat!" Alice stomped her foot. "Please! I must go to

the Queen."

The Cheshire Cat took to the air again, floating hither and thither as his one good eye regarded her and the other stared like an open wound was apt to. "The Queen's laboratory is in the clouds. Only floating things aloud."

"Then help me to float." The cat rolled over, exposing its belly, fading in and out of existence.

"Hmm…" it purred, brushing at its whiskers, picking at the gaps between its teeth with a claw. "I know a way," the Cat proclaimed, swaying from side to side.

"How?"

It smiled. Looking up at the ceiling of the ballroom it began to pull, as though hauling down an invisible rope. Alice and the guests stared into the high rafters, their mouths parting when a noose began to lower from one of the supports.

"I—" Alice grasped her throat, swallowing as the rope was lowered before her, dangling just low enough that she'd have to stand on the tops of her toes to reach it.

But the cat laughed, stretching his arms wide as the loop in the rope expanded. In an instant it was as large as a door. From the braids flowers bloomed in sooty black.

"Step inside," the Cat goaded, swimming in the area around her, "do you dare? Float on a noose up in the air?" Thorns grew along the rope, sharp as stilettos. Alice pressed her lips together, ignoring the protests of the Rabbit as she carefully placed her feet upon the bottom of the looping rope, hanging onto the sides carefully like a swing.

"Alice wait!" Turning, she watched as the Hatter pushed her way through the crowd, beating off guests with her cane. "If you go, take this," she removed her hat, the playing card shaking in its brim as she passed it off. "It will help you!"

Alice paused, almost cutting her palm upon the thorns. "But—"

"Madness is a great thing, my dear. When I was in the Queen's chair suffering beneath her hand, it helped me to survive."

Gingerly, Alice took it, watching as it unravelled like a spool of thread and reformed itself upon her head. It was smaller than before, and sat clipped into her hair like a barrette. The card was still in its brim. Curiously, Alice noticed that it was Ace of Hearts.

"I promise to return it," she said, smiling as she took hold of the large noose once more.

"Be careful, sweet Alice, and forgive these monsters of Horrorland." The Mad Hatter swept her arm out, scowling at the decorated guests. "They've been so long without a heart that they have forgotten how to be human."

"Alice." The Rabbit clenched his hands together, but Alice turned, watching as the Cheshire Cat laughed from the other side.

"Are you ready my dear?" the Cat said as the rope began to rise higher into the air. "I'm sure if you wanted you could return to London. The Rabbit would take you. *HeEhEHe!*"

"No. Take me to her, please."

"How chivalrous! My hero!" The Cat cackled. As the noose rose to its greatest height in the ballroom, the Cheshire Cat's grin devoured its face as it evaporated, and a milky film covered the gap in the rope.

"Time to take a tumble through the looking glass, my dear. *HeeHEe!*"

Appearing farther away, in the arms of a gargoyle, the Cat rushed forward, slamming into the small of the match girl's back and pushing her through the reflection in the rope. Like a bubble being blown, the shifting oily substance consumed her, and Alice fell, not to the ballroom floor like she had expected, but into darkness, straight into the belly of a boat.

There was a pain in her leg as she turned, half aware of a buzzing in her ears.

"It's not broken."

Alice rubbed at her forehead, moaning as she sat up. The boat was small, nothing but a rowboat, but at the helm, reclining on the prow was the Cheshire Cat, one eye close while the other one remained eternally open.

"Where are we?" she asked, looking around to see where the buzzing was coming from.

"Floating on Karen." His long, rope-like tail playfully hung from the prow, moving from side to side.

"Karen?"

"The name of the boat."

Alice looked over the side, momentarily in awe of the spectacle before her. They were both upon a boat being carried into the sky on a swarm of buzzing locusts. Some flew into her hair as she looked over the side, and Alice screamed, swatting at them.

"They're locusts!" She said, falling on her back and crouching within the seats of the small vessel.

"Aye, Aye Alice! *Hee!* You should be thankful they've agreed to take us. Not many things in Horrorland will willfully fly into the Floating Lab. Oops!" It had begun to rain. The Cheshire Cat propped up his tail, forming a squat umbrella at the end to keep him from becoming wet.

Alice blinked. It didn't just start as a drizzle, but poured down like a floodgate opening all at once. She rubbed at her face, only the light of the moon and stars offering enough illumination so she could see. But it wasn't just a normal rain, no. It was raining large, oblong drops of blood, some with a thin film that left a residue on the wooden boards of the rowboat.

"It's blood!" Alice cried, rubbing her hands on her dress to try and remove the color of it.

The Cat laughed, shaking his head as his smile once again consumed his face. "Of course. We must be below the Cemetery of Scares."

"What is that?" It was hard to hear over the sound of rainfall and the buzzing of locusts beneath them.

"A metaphor, probably." The Cat chortled, blood running in rivulets down the peaks of his umbrella. "Whoever walks through it usually finds themselves within it. These locusts are cruel."

The bottom of the boat was filling with blood. Dead bugs floundered in the red pools and crawled up her legs for reprieve as she swatted them away.

"Why?" she screamed again, tucking her arms and legs into her stomach.

"They are going to deposit you there, in the Cemetery." The Cat exploded, a cloud of purple and gray shifted in its wake, disappearing beneath the Hatter's hat upon her head.

"Where are you going?"

"To get a better look," he chuckled, "to see what things come out and jump, and get your heart to really pump."

Alice fell back as the boat landed, covering her head with her hands as the locusts separated and flew up along the sides of the boat to disperse. The bloody rain in the boat sloshed about her legs, leaving her skin pink like a cooked ham.

"I'm scared," she said, picking herself out of the boat, scratching at her head, sure there were still bugs crawling within.

"The Cemetery of Scares earns its name," the Cat mused, its voice echoing in her head.

Alice was standing on the edge, could see the moon bright and angry in front of her, watching her like a swollen, glowing face. Below, the clouds roiled, the shush of rain beneath almost as loud as the retreating locusts. Alice couldn't see the Hatter's castle or anything else through the cloud and fog, but somehow she knew they were there. Beyond, tall tiered hills loomed before her, filled with jagged tombstones like candles on a multilayered birthday cake. Nude, black trees poked up through the graying grass, hosting long, splintered signposts pointing here and there.

But, far in the distance Alice could see it. The Queen's laboratory was large, reminded her of the factories back in London. Steam, smog and smoke frothed from long pipes and chimneys. Like the Hatter's castle which boasted many spewing minarets, the Queen's lab was similar, but with far more. It rose up like a browning slab of metal.

"I would say it wasn't too late to turn back, but it is. *HeheHEheHEhe!*" Alice breathed in through her nose, took a step forward and began to walk towards the Queen's lab.

The cemetery was choked with trees and winding pathways. She could see odd, crooked backed creatures bent over the graves, digging up corpses. At one interval, she noticed an open gravesite. When she had bent to inspect it, she shrieked as a small fist sized creature held up a severed arm and waved it at her.

"Five shillings for a wave," it yelled, "never be bothered to use your own again!" Alice quickly moved away, frightened by the long pointed teeth and orb-like eyes of the creature.

"I don't like this place," she said, hearing only a muffled laugh in response.

The signposts were jumbled. Some were blank, mouldering boards of wood that said nothing, while some pointed to long dead denizens of Horrorland. Climbing over the unkempt paths that meandered across the hillside, Alice paused when she was sure she saw another Midwife Tree. It was bent sideways like the last, roots splitting the earth like large pipes. Alice thought of the Caterpillar and his addiction to big and small minded Diminut Pills as she passed, feeling sad.

"I feel bad that he died," she said.

"The owl says whoOoo? *Hee!*"

"The Caterpillar."

"The dead cat asks why?"

Alice looked up, as though able to see him on the brim of the Hatter's hat. "I didn't want Pillar to die," she said, "he wouldn't have if I hadn't forgotten his pills in the room with the Hacksaw."

She could feel the Cheshire Cat upon her head, turning in a circle and settling in a nest of her hair. "The pills would have killed him eventually," he demanded. "The Diminuts turned him into something he was not." Alice began to move away, "Small minded, big minded. Just have a mind is what I say. Let it grow on its own."

There was a fork in the road after. Rusted with two bent prongs, the utensil stuck out from the dirt with a body held aloft in its remaining, upright spines. Alice regarded it, a chill wind fingering her spine as she drew closer. It was surrounded by tombstones, some with names, but most without. The damp air made her feel heavy as she walked forward to read the name on the handle.

"Here lies Ginger Ward," Alice looked towards another stone. "Dean and Dumas Tweed, brothers," she shook her head. "What is this?"

"Dead names," the Cat replied.

"It's Tweedle Dum and Tweedle Dee. Is the girl upon the fork the cook?" Alice took another step, wanting to read another grave marker but found the rest were blank.

"A heart beats its name, my dear. *HeHEhehEHE!*"

Alice ran forward along the path. There were other

graves as well, some large and intricate, others mere blocks of stone with a name on top.

"Is everyone in Horrorland here," she asked, "is the Queen here?" The Cemetery of Scares was too big. Every time she wandered over a hill another took its place in the distance.

"Oh yesss," The Cheshire Cat hissed, peaking out her hat and grinning. Turning corporeal again, he stretched within the open space, his broken back twisting horribly as it sloped beneath the curve of its belly.

"Cat?" Alice paused, folding her arms together.

"Girl."

"What is your name?" The Cat turned, its four paws smoking in the air as it appeared to climb a set of stairs towards her.

"I wouldn't know my dear." It licked at its chest, rubbing a paw over its face as its tail flicked at her chin. "I'm afraid I've lost it." He smiled, his head twisting to the side as his body evaporated. "Careful not to misplace yours too, Alice."

She continued to walk the cemetery, glancing at the gravestones, careful not to disturb the myriad of creatures decorating open graves, digging up new ones and devouring decomposed waste. She wondered if she looked long enough if she could find the Duchess here, or the Mad Hatter's name, or perhaps even the White Rabbit's. What would they be called? What names would be given to such queer creatures of Horrorland? Alice wanted to know, but she needed to get to the Queen.

Every step Alice took weighed at her heart. Every hill: a tumor eating away at her resolve. Alice began to fear the tombstones that jutted up like fragments of bone and skull. Even the ground beneath her was frightful. The more she walked the more malleable it appeared, until Alice was quite certain she was walking on graying flesh rather than soil.

She began to cry, pulling at the skin beneath her eyes, trying to focus on the laboratory in the distance. The creatures in the graves had started to follow after her, spades in their hands.

"Careful my dear. *HEeHeEHee!* Else the Cemetery of Scares will find a new body."

"Leave me alone," but they sniffed at her heels, licking at the imprints her soles left in the dirt. "Stop!"

"Alice, did you break a match?"

Alice turned, seeing her Headmistress before her. Her crown of gray hair fell into the old woman's sagging, scowling features. "The foreman said he can't keep girls who can't do their jobs." Alice trembled. "Come here now. You're to have another beating."

"But I've already—"

"Two will ensure you don't do it again!"

Alice screamed, tearing at her hair. The beatings! Too many beatings!

"I hope someday I get adopted."

"You won't."

Alice stared. She was sitting in the room they all shared at the orphanage. She remembered one girl had the bear. There was only one. They took turns sleeping with it at night. There was still a week and half until Alice would have the bear again.

"The Headmistress said there is no hope for us. If our own mums and dads didn't want us why would anyone else."

Alice cried, sitting in the dirt, hitting herself in the head with both fists.

"I'm in Horrorland!"

"Where?" The girls looked confused.

"Alice has gone mad!"

"No! I *am* in Horrorland!"

"Dinah?" Alice wept, picking up the dead kitten in

her hands, seeing the bones poking out its belly. Why had this happened? Why was the world so cruel?

"It is a cruel world, Alice. But so too is Horrorland." Alice opened her eyes; saw the needle-like teeth of the Cheshire Cat as he bobbed in front of her face.

"What is happening?" she asked, still seeing London beneath her eyelids.

"The Cemetery wants to bury you. Run." The Cat laughed. "Run, run as fast as you can, or it will CATCH YOU! *HEHEHEHEhehehehEHehe!*"

Alice sprinted away through the Cheshire Cat. His smoke departed around her and she felt her legs ache. The small creatures that had been at her heels ran after her, throwing the spades in their hands, slicing at her calves with razor sharp trowels as their jaws opened and snapped shut, exhaling a deep hissing roar.

Alice could see the gates leaving the cemetery. Briers and bushes grew to either side and something stooped beyond the gates, paying her no mind as she screamed for help and ran with all the strength her legs could afford.

"Leave me alone!" she hollered, hearing the Cat inside her head, laughing and telling her to go faster.

"A foot ahead and foot behind, fast and quick: a rabbit's mind. Be sure to go, your bones they'll grind and dine, dine, dine upon your meat."

Alice jumped, feeling something slice into the muscle on her leg as she leapt over the threshold, arms about her head when she feared she hadn't quite made it. But when a moment had passed, and a warm sensation poured over her calf, Alice looked up, hearing the sneers of the grave creatures behind her as they began to depart.

"I'm alive," she said, turning on her back, wincing at the pain in her leg. A spade as sharp as a sword was stuck into the flesh, poking out the other side. Just in front of her was a man, painting what appeared to be a rose bush. Behind her was the cemetery gate.

"Excuse me," Alice called, grimacing as she tried to sit up. The man was square, a living card with a heart shaped hole through his abdomen. He was leaned over the bush, slopping what appeared to be red paint over flower bulbs, a hood covering his shoulders and the back of his head.

Alice pulled the spade from her calf, clenching her teeth together and whining from the pain. Throwing it to the side, she forced herself upright, hobbling on her good leg to garner the card man's attention.

"Hello?" she said again. There was what appeared to be a large sack in front of him. It was zipped open, and the paint inside looked congealed, as though incredibly old and unstirred.

"Must paint them red, keep them alive, one heart, two hearts, on blood they thrive!" His voice was shaky, as though he shivered from the cold as he worked. Alice cocked her brow, flexing her fingers as she hopped forward, trying to keep her weight from her injured leg. The wind was cool, but hardly frosty enough to make one quiver, she thought.

"Would you—" she stopped, eliciting a sharp cry as she accidently stepped back upon her bleeding leg. It wasn't a bag of paint before him, but a walrus wearing a tie. It had been cut open, white blobs of fat framing a bloody endometrium. The singing man was stooped before the body, slapping a paintbrush into the folds of the creature's gore and painting the flowers upon the brier.

Only it wasn't flowers in the bush, but human-sized hearts. The valves of each organ reached into the branches, pumping in the blood that was soaking upon their membranes. They were all differing sizes, some as large as a fist, others as big as an infant's head.

"*HEeheeHEe!* The Queen's experiments, no doubt! Grow your own when without!" Alice staggered. "I'm sure they're probably quite good pan fried with butter, too! Especially the small ones! *HEE!*"

Alice turned, wanting to run, but when her leg collapsed she felt the dirt spray in her teeth as she fell. The man behind her hissed, his concentration broken as Alice began to claw away from him.

"More paint, more paint to ease my plaint, the Queen of I shall not attaint!"

His mouth opened into a grin, long threads of saliva stretching from the top of his gums to the bottom. Alice kicked, screaming at the pain in her leg as she tried to back away upon her elbows, digging grooves into the pathway.

The Cheshire Cat bolted from her hat like swift cough of exhaust and appeared before her, his one cerulean eye wide and searching.

"Alice!" There was no chuckle in his voice now, but bitter fear. "She hears it beating, thumping, bleating!"

"Help me, Cat!" the match girl wailed, unable to tear her eyes from the bloody armed man. His face was gaunt, the skin stretched across his skull like a drum. He had no teeth, only a cavernous maw slick with yellow spittle.

The Cheshire Cat moved one way then the other, his movements frantic and quick. "Get up! Get up! She comes. SHE COMES!" He curled around her like a whirlwind as she tried desperately to pick herself up. The creature in front of her was waving the paint brush. Flecks of wet blood sprayed the ground and the white plane of his body, some going through the heart shaped hole in his middle and flattening into coin shaped blobs on the ground.

"I can't!" Her hair fell into her face, and she felt sweat stinging at her eyes as she tried to pick herself up.

Every time Alice used her leg she felt the flesh yawn open and split into unbearable pain. Tears fell down her cheeks, down her neck and into the collar of her dress. Her palms were sticky, and the grit from the dirt path stuck into the calloused base of her fingers and bled.

"I'm going to die!" she cried.

"I'm sorry Alice! She's here, she's here, I must not be near!" The Cat sped off, his tail a bright slash in the dark sky. The man with the paint brush was standing over top of her. Drool hung down from his bottom lip, dangling like a translucent pendulum over her torso. Back and forth, back and forth.

"So, a heart does beat in my kingdom." Alice couldn't see her until she tipped her head back. The Queen of Hearts was a long blade of a woman still, both hands crossed behind her back. "Perhaps once I'm through with you I'll ensure my subjects all get a good dousing in fire. They've earned it, don't you think?"

Alice couldn't think through the pain. Black spots floated in her vision, crowding at the edge of her consciousness. Though she was sure the Queen was stoic and unmoving behind her, she swayed in Alice's vision. "I'm scared," the match girl said, falling backwards, something sharp spearing the back of her head.

Alice was aware of the Queen kneeling before her, of the monster card/man breathing loudly as though right next to her ear.

"You should be. Horrorland is a frightful place," the Queen of Hearts said, removing a syringe from her apron pocket. Testing the needle, Alice blinked when the fluid spat out the top, spraying her across the face.

"Help me," she cried, sobbing.

The Queen's eyes narrowed, and pausing for the moment she regarded the girl thoughtfully, brushing a hand through her yellow hair and pulling it away from the young girl's face.

"Perhaps," she said, her voice deep like a chasm, "but first you must help me." The Queen stuck the needle into the young girl's neck, and Alice had an astute feeling of falling through the ground as the medicine took effect and drowned her in complete and utter darkness.

Chapter 10
A Battle For Stolen Hearts

She woke up, curiously, to light pouring through a window. It wasn't the gray, polluted light of London, overflowing with angry particles or dust motes from the orphanage, but pure light, falling like a clean blade through a clear window.

Alice's vision was foggy as she began to wake, and there was a sharp pain emanating from the small of her back. As the blurry film covering her eyes began to fade, Alice was shrewdly aware that she was bound by her arms, and that her wounded leg was slightly elevated in the air upon a sling. There was a lantern above her head, and the hood around the unlit bulb gave the impression of an open eye watching her. As the details of her surroundings began to become finer, Alice noticed a spider's web hanging from the bulb, dangling over her face with a small dead insect attached at the end. She gasped, realizing her small exhalations were causing it to teeter and loosen above her. She did not want it to fall upon her face.

"You're awake, good." Alice looked to the side, her eyes roaming across the room to the Queen of Hearts. The Queen's glasses hung impotently from her nose, reflecting the light from the window perpendicular to her current location. "Don't move."

Of course, Alice immediately defied the suggestion, shifting her weight to become more comfortable on the metal table in which she had been placed. She winced as a searing shock of pain bolted up from her calf and ignited in her brain. Her face was sticky from sweat, and pieces of hair fell into her eyes as she tried to look down.

Her leg within the sling had been completely sliced open to the bone. Flaps of skin and muscle were pulled away like a banana peel, pinned down to either side.

"I told you not to move. I haven't finished with your leg," the Queen sighed. "Petulant girl."

The young match girl held her breath as the Queen removed her needle from her apron and set it on the table beside her. Alice couldn't help but think it looked the same as the silver one still tucked away in the pocket of her black dress. She had remembered to remove it from her soiled clothes at the Duchess' House of Cards, and again when she had attended the house on the cliff. It was in the hemline of her gown, woven within the lace that decorated the edges.

Alice had tried to watch closely as the Queen went to work, but as the older woman began to stir a poultice made from glowing mushrooms, Alice tipped her head back, crying out as the Queen administered the concoction and sewed up her leg. After, and without allowing a rest, the Queen of Hearts equipped Alice with a brace, screwing it tightly against her skin.

She worked without talking and with great concentration. Alice noticed however that every now and then the Queen would look towards her with frustration, not at her face, but at her chest, and demand she be quiet.

"You're interrupting my work!" the Queen snapped. Alice was almost entirely certain that the Queen was referring to her heartbeat, which palpitated within her chest like a spooked animal within a cage.

Alice fell asleep, waking hours later to candlelight in exchange of the sunshine. The Queen was still there with her, only this time she was slicing apart a large, cleaned brain. Alice had been sitting up, wrists bound to a chair, her one leg still extended upon a sling. She watched with tears in her eyes as the Queen cut into the brain like it were a sausage. Blood spurted from between the snarled tubes, but congealed like jam upon each segment.

"What are you doing?" Alice whispered, still feeling rather weak.

"Ingredients," the Queen replied, placing the pieces into a bowl before carefully lifting one portion of the cut brain and throwing it into a metal bin.

"For what?"

"Madness. Go to sleep. I want you to heal before I extract your heart." She licked her fingers, again withdrawing a syringe from her apron. Alice had tried to protest but as the sting of medicine infiltrated her system, she closed her eyes, hoping to see the sunlight again when she awoke.

There was never anyone else that came. Over the next several days Alice wandered in a daze, strapped down by leather bonds, chains and ropes. The Queen was a fixture in her lab, never leaving, always attending to experiments and ghoulish trials. In one corner another brier of human hearts flourished, and with blood she watered them twice a day, though from where she had obtained the blood, Alice didn't know.

"Queen," Alice beckoned one day, perhaps weeks,

months, hours after her capture.

The Queen was sewing an arm onto a corpse when the young girl called out. Wiggling leeches wagged like tails along the two halves of the arm, getting in the way of her needle. Every now and then, irritated, the Queen would poke one and fling it across the room, resuming her task as the black worm writhed in its final moments before death.

"Please," Alice said again, her throat tight and parched.

The Queen of Hearts sighed, pressing her teeth together as she snapped her body towards the bound girl.

"I'm very hungry. Thirsty. May I have a bit of water, please?"

The Queen stared at her, dull blue eyes momentarily dazed. "Ah," she said at last, "I forgot you need to eat." She stabbed the needle into the flesh of the arm she had been working on and left the lab, returning a few moments later with a black stoneware bowl and spoon.

"Come," she addressed, waiting for the mechanical device in the corner to respond. What had looked like a heap of sharp metal immediately animated at the command. Joints of brass and steel, resembling the spawn of an enormous spider and a human hand with sharpened claws at the end, scuttled across the stone floor, settling as a chair beneath her as the Queen of Hearts sat. Alice wasn't able to ask the Queen whether she had created the strange contraption herself until the soup was half gone and her throat had relaxed enough for her to speak comfortably.

"I make many things. Sometimes I must destroy some to make others." The older woman carefully scooped up another spoonful, fetching a cube of meat into the wooden utensil to feed to her.

Alice closed her eyes as she opened her mouth to receive the spoon. The soup tasted alright, though the meat was a bit tough and filled with gristle and pieces of cartilage that crunched between her teeth. Round, oily globes of fat floated on the top of the broth, but it smelled like rosemary and thyme.

There were many questions that Alice wished to ask her, but the one that came out was: "Why do you want my heart?"

Though she had thought perhaps the Queen would be irate at her frank trespass, the woman instead was quiet, taking another spoon to feed her. "That should be a simple conclusion to reach, even for you," she waited for Alice to take the bite, "because I don't have one."

Alice swallowed. "Why?"

The Queen sat back, removed her glasses and gloves and wiped at her brow. She seemed exasperated, like a woman trying to teach a dumb dog tricks but to no avail.

"I gave it away a long time ago, I think," she regarded the girl, her stony face erased of any kind of expression, "I don't remember why. Perhaps someone took it. But," she paused, again fishing out some meat within the broth, "I wish not to be heartless anymore."

Alice couldn't imagine what it meant to be without a heart. The Queen was so despondent, cold like snow. She was a phantom of a woman, and though she sat before her now, feeding her with her own two hands, Alice couldn't help but feel like she was very, very far away.

"I see the Hatter gave you her hat. That is good. When I remove your heart you can escape the pain."

"Will I go mad?" Alice asked, biting her lip to keep it from trembling.

"Maybe. People tolerate pain differently than others. A long time ago when I extracted the Hatter's heart I gave that hat to her. It made her smile so much that she split her face almost in half. I had to sew it shut."

"I thought…"

The Queen laughed. "You thought I ripped her smile? No." She stirred the bowl, setting it upon the floor beside the young girl's chair. "Horrorland and all the creatures inside of it are mine. I may have demanded their hearts but I don't wish them to suffer cruelty." Her eyes narrowed, and Alice flinched.

"I know you came here to spare them. I respect that. But they still lied and tried to hide you," she stood, the contraption beneath her readjusting and skittering to her side. "They will have to pay for their insolence."

"Please! Don't hurt them."

The Queen laughed. "Find your head," she said to her machine as it clattered away to comply. "You are in Horrorland, little girl. What is Horrorland without horror?"

"But... I heard it used to be quite wonderful."

To that the Queen chuckled, staring down at her like a cat regarding a mouse. "It was never wonderful here," she said, "open your eyes, child." The Queen turned, watching as the metal joined machine clattered to a halt in front of her. Atop it, resting on the back of his palm was the severed head of the Marsh Hare. Alice palled, knowing it was him by the bloody nubs where he had ripped off his own ears.

"Once I remove your heart you will see how horrible it all is." The Queen looked down, quickly examining her leg. "One more day," she mused, "then the procedure will begin."

Alice looked away, black spots crowding her vision as the Queen returned to her sewing. Alice felt a pain in her head, and as she squeezed her eyes shut, the black spots solidified into balloons with clown faces painted on their surface.

Am I going mad already? She thought as she tried to grasp them, wanting to float away. But her arms were pinned and she couldn't. Alice had to watch as they filled the room and the window and blocked out the sun until she was certain she had fallen asleep.

The Queen of Hearts had removed her bonds the next day, then attended to her leg. The brace was removed, and though the limb felt rather floppy as she tried to stand, Alice was told it would get better and heal with time.

It was hard to gauge the Queen. Her callousness and taciturn demeanor was framed within impassive gestures of kindness. As much as Alice feared the Queen, she couldn't come to hate her. It was as though she were a product of her experiments herself, a machine well-oiled that went about her chores with the impression of being aloof but who in reality didn't know any better.

The Queen was heartless, but contrary to the claims of the Cheshire Cat, she was not mad. Alice believed her when she said she created Horrorland. She *was* the heart of it all. But she was a heart without a heart.

Horrorland used to be quite wonderful, the Cat and the White Rabbit had said. Alice thought they must have been right.

"Did you take the hearts of your subjects in an attempt to replace your own?" Alice had asked, rubbing at her sore wrists. They were rubbed raw over the several days of confinement.

The Queen of Hearts towered over her. She had incredibly long legs, and though her dress was cinched at the waist by her apron, she was so thin and board-like Alice thought she must have never eaten a large meal all her life. To which the young girl could miserably relate.

"I took them looking for my own," the Queen replied, sitting down upon a wooden chair.

"Your own?"

She sighed. "You would do good to retain the information people give to you." The Queen untied the back of her apron and placed it to the side. "A long time ago I gave my heart away. I think I gave it to someone I loved." Alice was certain that for a brief moment sadness had crossed the Queen's eyes. "But the person never returned it." She swept her hair to the side, unzipping the back of her dress just enough to bare her shoulder. "I looked for my heart in all the creatures of Horrorland. I wanted it back, I felt lost without it. But no one had mine, and if they had they had thrown it away." She paused, regarding the girl in front of her.

"If I haven't a heart then no one will have one. Theirs will belong to me until mine is returned."

She pulled down her dress. Alice frowned. Above the older woman's breast, stitched in red thread, was a loose scrap of skin covering what appeared to be a hole in the Queen's chest. She picked at the seams, pulling it apart. Alice watched her wince and fumble as her hair fell from her shoulders into the covered wound.

"Please," Alice begged, removing the needle from the hem of her own dress, "let me help you."

The Queen sat back, surprised as the girl bent to help. Using the silver needle the dolls had gifted her at the start of her journey in Horrorland, Alice carefully picked at the stitches until the hole was exposed. It burrowed right through the Queen's chest cavity, past several broken ribs and ran deep into her body. Alice peeled the skin away, setting it aside for her as the Queen watched.

"Is this what it is like to have a heart?" The Queen asked, noticing the concern on the girl's features.

"I don't understand." Alice had blood on her fingertips. The Queen removed her apron from the armrest, began to wipe the blood from girl's hands.

"You care so much. For everyone. For people like me who would harm you." It was strange to her, a paradox for a creature to help its predator.

"No," Alice said, "not everyone with a heart cares." She pressed her lips into a thin line. "There are plenty of people who do terrible things and have hearts."

"So, it is just you, then," the Queen nodded, "you are young…"

Alice removed her hand from the Queen's, stepping back. "Horrorland may be a terrible place, full of misery and madness and death, but it is filled with kindness too, deep down. Your people—without their hearts—tried to save me. Many wanted to give me up." Alice stooped, grasping the Queen's hands again.

"People are the same." Alice shook her head. "They can be cruel and kind. I think that though you've lost your heart you know what you do is wrong. That's why you want to claim it back. You want to make Horrorland wonderful again."

"It was never wonderful," the Queen insisted.

"But it could be," Alice trembled, her face wet. "I'm only a girl from an orphanage. I'm a nobody, a match girl who drops too many matches and must be beaten." She blinked, her vision wavering beneath her tears. "I will give you my heart, your Majesty. You don't have to take it."

The Queen was quiet, silently studying the girl's face. "Why?"

"Because the Queen of Hearts, of Horrorland, ought to have a heart more than I, and because," she wiped her face, "if I give it to you perhaps you won't be a cruel person. Maybe you'll become the Queen who cares for her people."

There was silence in the room, save for the rhythmic thrumming of a heartbeat. The Queen sat still before Alice, glassy eyes staring at the girl sat at her feet. She wondered if perhaps she had been like this: so full of emotion and compassion for others. The Queen wondered how her own heart had influenced her, if it had.

The Queen of Hearts leaned forward, reaching an arm

out to touch the young girl's face. She was warm, like a corpse sitting in the sun, and her eyes were full of earnest hope and tears.

Being earnest, hope, sadness, the Queen understood the words but couldn't remember how they felt. However, seeing Alice before her, entreating her to take her heart, she felt something within her wraith-like body that tugged at her memories and made her uncomfortable.

"Thank you," she said, though not because she felt thankful, but because she knew it was what she was supposed to say. "It will make it easier if you are compliant."

Alice shook her head, struck by the coldness of the Queen's tone as the woman removed her hand from her face.

Alice had been certain something had occurred within the psychology of the Queen. She had seen her thoughts, her mind trying to comprehend Alice's generosity, her kindness. But as the Queen stood up, replacing her gown upon her shoulder and covering the hole in her chest, Alice despaired to think that perhaps the Queen of Hearts had gone far too long without a heart to remember what those feelings were.

"Come now, child. Let us start the extraction." She had moved towards the metal slab. There were four tanned leather straps with steel buckles on top. Alice moved as she was told, thinking of the boar man she had seen beyond the keyhole door. She wondered if the Queen would use a hacksaw to remove her heart, or would she be more precise.

Standing beside the slab, Alice bit her lip, this time drawing blood. She was standing next to the Queen, still in the sparkling black dress the White Rabbit had picked out for her in the house. She wondered why the Queen had built it, but she was certain, like the Rabbit had said, that she no longer remembered why.

"I'm sorry," Alice said, turning to face the Queen. Alice embraced her waist, pressing her nose into the Queen's stomach as tears welled at the corners of her eyes. "I'm sorry that no one ever returned your heart," she said. The Queen had stilled at the touch, but slowly, relaxing into the child, touched her head, smoothing down the golden mane of the girl from London.

Alice was warm, and pressed against her the Queen could hear her heartbeat from within the girl's body. It was fast, honest, but the Queen could not hear it properly. She had forgotten how to understand it. But still, feeling the girl against her brought warmth to her face.

Alice retreated, moving to sit then lay upon the operating table. She had begun to remove her dress but the Queen had held up a hand.

"I'll cut through it," she said, her voice quiet, a bit different than it was before. "It looked pretty on you. You should leave it on." Alice nodded, feeling unsure about the compliment. She sat her head back as her hair haloed around her head and shoulders. She could see the hesitation on the Queen's face as she had moved to retrieve her knife. Alice had wanted to ask, but before she could the Queen offered her a red pill.

"It will help you go numb."

Alice took the pill, thinking it resembled the head on a match.

When the Queen cut into her it didn't hurt. She could feel the edge of the knife drawing away flesh and peeling through skin and tissue, but the pain was absent. Alice stared into the window until the blades of sunlight were gone, sheathed in darkness and replaced with the subtle hint of moonlight. Alice thought of the night where she had seen the fullness of the moon in London, and the White Rabbit gazing upon Big Ben. It had been so rare to see the moon, but perhaps it had been all the more beautiful because.

"Does it hurt? I can give you another pill," the Queen asked. But Alice smiled, shaking her head.

"I don't feel anything," she replied. The Queen of Hearts frowned.

Alice thought she had fallen asleep, but when she opened her eyes the Queen was there still, a mask shielding her face, goggles about her eyes. The older woman was holding the bloody knife in her hand, but she had stopped cutting, was staring down into Alice's open chest cavity.

"There it is," she said. Alice looked, lowering her chin in an attempt to glance at her own heart. It thumped quietly, swelling and deflating in a quick rhythm. The slick, slimy membrane popped with purple veins and clouds of blood vessels. Though she couldn't see the valves, Alice could see how it thrived within her body, never skipping a beat.

"It's only small. But you can have it," Alice said, her face pale. She had dark circles bruising around her eyes, and as the Queen regarded her, she couldn't help but think how sickly the young girl suddenly looked.

"I—" The Queen stammered, removing her mask and goggles. She had been searching all her life for a heart to be hers, but looking at it now, she felt wrong, like she hadn't any right to it.

"I give it to you," Alice said. "Just don't lose it. Cherish it, please."

The Queen hovered over her, the knife trembling in her hand. She could hear the name beating as it pumped.

"Alice? Your heart speaks its name." She licked her lips. "It's very beautiful." The Queen stood, the chair beneath her clattering against the floor. "I can't take it," she said, "I know what it's like to give your heart away. I won't allow it."

Alice cried, laughing incredulously amid her tears as the Queen began to unbind her. She ripped away the leather straps and cut at the buckles. "You need to go!" the Queen yelled, her eyes wide and sincere. "I'll sew it back first!"

"But I want you to have it."

"You're too young to give your heart away. Alice…" The Queen took the girl's face in her hands, and Alice was amazed to see her so sincere. "Share it."

"*HEEHeehee!*" Alice glanced up, watching as the haze of purple cloud began to descend. "The creatures of Horrorland are here, my Queen."

The Queen of Hearts turned, anger flaring in her eyes. "What?"

The Cat somersaulted, his long smile tearing through the blackness. "The White Rabbit's come, bringing all the land, in search of a heart, he makes a bold stand."

"He stands against me?" the Queen roared, throwing the knife upon the ground. "He stands against the Queen of Hearts?"

Again the Cat laughed. "He stands for Alice I would think, a tad too late, not quite in sync."

"And you, Cheshire? Do you stand with him?"

He grinned, his tail a trail of cloud and dust. "I hate to stand, I like to float. Between the siege lies the mote."

The Queen snarled, swatting the Cat away until he dispersed like a swarm. Going to the window her dress flared out behind her as she leant forward, interrupting the moonbeams that slivered through the glass and leant light to the darkened laboratory they had been standing in.

Alice sat up, pressing her fingers around the hole in her heart like a cage, worried that it may slip out if she jostled too much.

"Queen?" she called, her voice faint.

"They're here." Alice could hear the exasperation in

the Queen's tone, but there was something else there too, something boarding defeat and exhaustion.

"Let me talk to—"

"No!" She spun on her heel, her hair curtaining her face as she removed her glasses. "I am the Queen of Horrorland!" she yelled. "I will address my subjects, not you!" She removed her gloves, small delicate hands pale and oddly fragile in the candlelight. Alice remembered a time when she was younger, how a woman had told her that she had the hands of a pianist.

"I'm coming with you," Alice replied, jumping from the slab and walking after her as the Queen of Hearts began to leave. Though the Queen had paused, she didn't say anything as she wandered down the halls and lonely corridors of her laboratory.

Alice walked with her, sometimes losing pace as her strength waned. Pipes and machines frothing with steam crowded the halls until they became hard to navigate through. Sometimes exposed copper pipes and hot iron cables littered the floor and wires hung like vines, ready to snag neglectful trespassers, but the Queen weaved in and out between them effortlessly, even stopping to help Alice when the girl got too far behind.

"Hurry," she said.

Alice couldn't help but feel touched at her concern.

"I'm sorry," Alice replied, keeping her hand over the hole in her heart. She felt it pump faster against her palm.

The throne room was the last chamber they had entered. Large and hollow like an inhaling lung, what had once probably been a majestic room of frescos and silk tapestries had been transformed. Giant gears turned in sync with one another, vomiting out clouds of smoke and steam. A large mural behind a golden throne decorated with ruby hearts, was dull with dust and cobwebs, and enormous glass vials filled with the fetal remains of past experiments took the place of splendorous statues and gargoyles.

Alice had collapsed, pressing her palm firmly to her chest as she bent double. She thought she would retch, she was so exhausted. But, when she looked up into the vials she felt wonder close around her throat until she felt like she could no longer breathe.

A cat, curled up with its head in its paws was in one of the vials. Feeding into it was some kind of purple liquid.

"Dinah?" Alice murmured, her eyes drawn to the next vial. An old woman, ugly with a large forehead, stewed within. Without her clothes or perpetual scowl, it was hard to recognize her. But Alice saw the Duchess and someone else within her. The next body in the vial was not a body at all, but the moon, large and bright. Inside that was a man—though perhaps it could have been a woman who could know. A mother? A father? The White Rabbit?

"What are these?" Alice called, staring at the Queen's back as she went towards the large chamber doors at the end of the room.

"*HeEhEE!* They are memories, dear Alice."

"Of what?" She heard the Queen throw open the doors, the sound of shrill cries and screams echoed beyond.

The Cheshire Cat giggled, hiccupping in mirth. Alice didn't understand. "The Queen had tried to remember, but she couldn't. *HEHEHE!*" The Cat spun around them, its grin growing longer and wider until both ends touched, resembling a toothy heart upon his face. Tail whipping and snapping, the vials began to crack as he struck them. Water drained and pooled about the floor. The pressure in the vials became too much until they all began to burst, the contents turning to a shapeless slop along the cobbled floor.

"Cat!" Alice screamed. Horrified as he began to whirl away and disappear.

"You'll understand one day, my dear. *Heeheehee!"* And like a bolt of lightning he snapped away, disappearing into the darkness of the rafters, his voice echoing like a ghost in her mind.

"Beware the revolution!"

Alice, looking back to the door, ran after the Queen, frightened of the screaming and protests from the other side.

"Stop!" she yelled.

Chapter 11
The Jabberwocky

The Queen's laboratory was situated upon a knoll. Though it wasn't as large as the Hatter's castle, it was much, much taller. The entirety of the structure was made up of steel, iron and stone. Pipes snaked like veins along the outside, and large metal rivets dimpled the exposed surface like open pores.

The crowd was an undulating mass of ignited roars and bellows. All sorts of creatures Alice had never seen before congregated before the Queen's lab, pumping fists, forks, spoons, swords, dead fish and jagged metal hooks. *Perhaps they had been the real creatures beneath the masks at the Tea Party Ball,* she thought, but Alice wasn't sure. She did however recognise the Rabbit, looking resplendent in his white suit and top hat despite the scowl on his face.

"You've some nerve," the Queen spoke, her voice loud and commanding as she stood outside the door. Her dress inhaled the wind, exhaling violently out behind her. "My Prince of Timekeepers, holding a coup?"

The crowd was at the bottom of the hill like a spill. There was a long path constructed into the hillock, burrowing into the ground and framed with metal and iron. The pieces were soldered together like an ill-fitting jigsaw made to fit, and though the crowd beneath was angry and large, the Queen was magnificent, made so by her pride and resolve.

"Unhand Alice! We will not allow you to take her heart!"

Alice walked out from the doors, holding her chest as the wind threw her hair into her face. When the White Rabbit saw her he called out to her, pulling a sword from the face of his watch. It shone brilliantly like a snap of lightning, "Alice. We are here to save you!" he yelled.

Though she hadn't moved towards him, the Queen held out her hand as though to block the young girl's path. "You dare raise the Vorpal Sword to me," she hissed, "after I gave you the ability to travel through time? After I tore out the Cheshire Cat's eye so that you would have the power of time?"

Alice pressed her lips together, watching as the Queen's shadow grew darker and longer. From her back, drawing out the hole where her heart used to be, crimson muck poured like a font, congealing on the ground. Alice stepped away, but looked up when the Rabbit called to her again.

"Alice please! I know I've broken your heart dear one, but unlike the Queen's it shall mend." Around her the wind began to pick up, and though she couldn't see anything, Alice felt like something was drawing nearer, approaching.

"Please leave, Ben," she said. "You don't understand!"

Beside him, the Hatter tore at her hair. "The Queen is summoning the Jabberwocky! Rabbit! We can't fight the

Jabberwocky!"

"Face your fears!" the Rabbit roared, pushing the woman away when she grabbed at his lapels.

"I've not my hat!" The Hatter's eyes grew wide like medallions. Ripping the skin at her throat, she turned into the crowd. "My tongue as a sponge to clean her floor, fed hair until I die! I'll live in pain in fear in death my soul she'll petrify!" She ran back along the crowd, her skirts fluttering like raven wings.

"Run! The jabberwocky comes! Fools we were to challenge the Queen of Hearts who knows our fears!"

Though the Rabbit roared out in protest, the crowd turned into madness. Creatures turned to run and hide, some were pushed back in the fray, accused of cowardice. The Rabbit had tried to regroup them, but as the Queen's shadow began to pool down the sloped path towards them, a creature surfaced from within the bloody muck. Large teeth dripping in ichor screamed as oily wings swept to either side, large like helium balloons.

Alice had rushed forward, stunned when she saw the Queen grinning madly at the deranged crowd of people trying to get away from the Jabberwocky. Thick lines of blood ran from her eye sockets, her nostrils and from both ears, wrapping like ribbons along the column of her throat to add to the animated sludge composing the Jabberwocky. The shoulder of her gown had fallen away as well, and the large gaping hole in the Queen's chest was exposed, pouring out black and blood like a burst sluice gate.

"Queen!" Alice cried, holding the Queen's arms and trying to shake her, but she snarled instead to the crowd, her voice as loud as thunder.

"Wallow in my Horrorland!" She laughed. And Alice saw they did.

People were upon the ground, tearing at their clothes

as their fingertips bled and their nails ripped from nail beds. The bloody Jabberwocky wailed and devoured the creatures. The ichor poured over them, drenching them all in nightmares. Alice saw a frog in trousers ram the hook he had been carrying into his own skull, watched a girl with spots tear her own throat out with a curtain rod. Another one beside her choked on her long dark curls as she stuffed them into her own mouth.

"Please, Queen! Stop this!" Alice cried again, shutting her eyes so she would not have to see the mayhem of the people's greatest fears.

"They took my heart and destroyed it, yet they wish to salvage yours? They can all die. I am their Queen!"

"No!" Alice turned, watching as the Rabbit transformed behind them, long ears folding back together to frame his top hat as the blue from his inner ears warped into cerulean feathers.

"No one took your heart!" he said. "You gave it away willingly, out of love and devotion. You told me once, a long time ago! You told me that very story! Only… you've forgotten who you gifted it to!"

Alice stumbled away, was pushed behind the Queen of Hearts as the manic woman slid through the muck at her feet to regard him. She held out a hand so that Alice could not join the Rabbit at his side, but also, Alice saw, to keep the Jabberwocky's bloody ichor from touching the young girl.

"Who then?" the Queen screamed, blond hair drenched in blood as it ran from out her ears and turned her eyes into gory red spheres.

The Rabbit paused, sword held out to the side, blue cape waving like the sea behind him.

"I don't know," he whispered, his voice barely audible above the wind, "a long time ago, before you became the mad scientist of Horrorland you are now, you stole my heart. Not like the others… I gave it to you." He stood up straight, a beam of light in the darkness. "But the heartless Queen that you became could not comprehend the gift I wanted to give and it broke." He snarled. "Like everything else you touch! I won't let you ruin Alice as well!"

He leapt forward, sword blazing. Still behind her the creatures of Horrorland were confronting the Jabberwocky, suffering beneath the agonies of their fears, tortured by terror. Alice saw the Hatter screaming into the crowd, a torch of fire in her hand as she lit creatures on fire.

"I'm not astray, your servant pray, who lights the enemies in your way! Queen of Hearts of fears of dust, I'll kill them all if you say I must!" Cackling, the Mad Hatter watched as hapless creatures struck helpless by fright melted beneath the flame of her torch, skin slipping from bone like hot wax.

The Queen laughed as the Rabbit leapt. Raising a hand to protect the hole in her chest, the sword flashed for her neck.

Blackened blood squirted through her fingertips. It transformed into small winged bats, flying towards him and spraying on his suit, into his face and eyes as she stepped back, away from the Vorpal blade. "What do you fear the most, my precious Ben?" The Queen laughed. He spat, staggering away. The moon above turned red.

But he didn't react. Instead he wiped at his face as the ichor of the Jabberwocky ran down his chin. "I live in my greatest fear every day," and as the Queen stood stunned, the White Rabbit lunged again, sword flashing viciously…

…as it went snicker snack.

Chapter 12
Alice's Revolution

Alice screamed as the Queen of Hearts fell. The Queen's eyes were as wide as full moons. Her open mouth framed an O as her hair curtained her face and she tipped backwards upon the cobbles. Alice had tried to prevent the blow, had tried to push herself into the way, but the Queen of Hearts had held her aside, shoved her back until Alice lay within the muck of the Jabberwocky, watching as the Vorpal Sword slid out the Queen's torso.

"No!" Alice screamed, scrambling through the bloody mess towards the Queen. The enormous winged beast began to collapse as the ichor from her eyes, nose and ears stopped pouring from her orifices and began to cool upon the ground.

"Get away from her!" Alice screamed again, trembling from shock. The Rabbit withdrew, knuckles whitening on the hilt of the blade, his expression hard.

"Can't you see what she did to everyone?" he asked, his voice a violent calm as he gestured to the crowd of people still writhing from fear, some dead because of it.

"Yes!" Alice sobbed, looking up then closing her eyes as she pressed her palms upon the wound in the Queen's stomach. "I know but—" Alice shook her head, shushing her as the Queen coughed and more blood ran down her chin.

"She created this awful place. All the fear and misery," the Rabbit continued.

Alice turned to regard him. She sank to her knees, crawling closer to the Queen's side. "Imagine how much fear and agony she must have experienced to create this place!" Alice yelled, looking back to her. The match girl felt her own heart beating so madly from within her chest that she thought it may fall out. "It's not an excuse for what she did but—" Alice shook her head, shushing the woman as she tried to speak. "What monsters haunted her so that she could create the Jabberwocky in the first place?"

"Alice."

Alice ignored him. "I'm sorry, Queen," she said, "I'm sorry." She could feel the Queen's blood cooling, could hear the screaming of the crowd quieting as the Jabberwocky disappeared.

Plunging her hand into her own chest Alice screamed as she tore out her own heart. Cords and arteries ripped apart, sounding in her ears horribly. Blood squirted between her fingertips. From behind her the White Rabbit dropped his sword, rushing towards her as she shrieked in pain.

"Alice! What are you doing?" he cried, taking her by the back of the shoulders as she threatened to collapse. "You can't do this! She doesn't deserve it!"

Alice could hardly speak. Breathing was hard, but as she looked upon her own heart clasped within her hand, she smiled when she saw it still beating.

"Rabbit," she said, eyes gaunt, blurry from the pain.

"No one can tell another who they can or cannot give their heart to." She smiled and looked at the Queen, removing the silver needle from the hem of her black dress. "I want her to have it," Alice said, her hands shaking as she gingerly placed the heart within the Queen's chest. "I want Horrorland to become wonderful again."

From behind her she could hear the Rabbit breathing. She wasn't sure if the rapid exhalations he exerted were sobs, or breaths of perturbed disbelief, but she listened to the rhythmic beats of her own heartbeat, ticking like a clock as she began to join the arteries together, using strands of her own hair as thread.

In truth, Alice had never been a seamstress. She was a poor match girl who had grown up in an orphanage, surrounded by loneliness and the detritus of London's smog filled streets. But as she worked away at the Queen's heart, threading together long empty valves and stitching veins together, it felt almost natural, like she had always known how to do it.

The creatures of Horrorland gathered around her, bloody and scarred from their own fears unearthed by the Jabberwocky. Though Alice had feared that they would stop her, they instead paid tribute to her work, in awe of the gift she was bestowing upon the Queen of Hearts.

What would the Queen of Hearts be like? As more and more time when on, Alice could hear their doubts whispered from ear to ear. Would a heart really transform the Queen, or give her more purpose to warp the world? Their concerns weighed heavily upon her shoulders as Alice continued to thread the needle time and again.

There had been one moment when the White Rabbit had sought to interject, but was held at bay by the Hatter. "Leave her be and let her go. It is her heart to bestow."

"This is our chance," he swung his sword behind him. "We could end the reign of the Queen right now.

"No." The Hatter smiled, the curly ends of her lollipop grin pushing at her eyes until they resembled crescent moons.

"She's your greatest fear!"

The Mad Hatter nodded. "And I would face her, Rabbit." She turned, looking at Alice's back as she bent to ensure that the heart she had gifted was secure within the Queen's chest. "You loved her once, maybe with Alice's heart inside her you may do so again."

The White Rabbit stepped back, anger deflated.

"And if you kill her now, you'll also kill Alice. Look." The Rabbit knew it was so. The young girl was so bent over the Queen that to thrust the Vorpal Sword into the monarch's chest meant going through Alice's small frame as well. Even if he had the chance to miss, he was sure that Alice would have tried anything to thwart the blow.

The Rabbit wanted to understand why, but as he stood behind the Hatter, collecting in the crowd of semi-silent observers, he couldn't understand. He thought perhaps, if he had gotten closer, was able to watch them both, that he may espy a hint of the comprehension he was looking for. The White Rabbit passed his sword to the Hatter, slowly drawing forward to crouch beside the Queen and regard the resolve upon Alice's face.

He had thought she would protest, or perhaps grow defensive at his position beside the Queen he wished to destroy, but with a flush upon her cheeks, Alice smiled, regarding him with affection.

The Rabbit was silent. When Alice had finished stitching the heart together she began to embroider a web around it. The hole in the Queen's heart was made smaller by the golden hairs sewn into the flesh. Like a jewel within a spider's web it began to beat, exposed for all to see.

The creatures around them gasped. The White Rabbit felt his mouth drop open. The Hatter dropped to a knee beside them both, taking the Queen's wrist in her hand.

"Something is happening!" the Hatter cried.

Slowly, the veins upon the Queen's arms began to bulge. Her face, bloody and pale, began to rose, and her cheeks, once gaunt, became fuller. Alice brushed her fingertips over the Queen's face, feeling tired. She wiped up the blood that had dried upon her skin, around her neck, and looked again to the Rabbit who was transfixed upon the Queen of Horrorland.

"I think she will be ok," Alice said, looking inside his coat and seeing the ears of his rabbit's mask poking out from beyond his pocket.

The Queen then gasped, her eyes giant globes. Her body hitched forward, in rhythm of her heart beat, and the Queen clutched at her chest, feeling the taut strings of Alice's hair protecting the working organ within.

"It works," the Rabbit whispered, his fingers trembling as they struggled to ascertain what it was they should do. He took the Queen's hand in his, was astounded by its warmth. "Alice!" He smiled, and the match girl felt tears well again within her eyes at the hope she found in his.

The crowd around them stepped forward.

"What is—" the Queen had tried to speak, looking down upon herself. Alice sat forward, pressing a finger to her own lips.

"Shh," she cooed, "listen to it."

The Queen sat back, struggling to understand what was happening inside her. To the amazement of all, the Queen of Hearts began to cry. For once her stony expression cracked, revealing relief and hopeful regret. "I can it hear it," she sobbed. "I can hear it beating." The

Queen held out her hands and Alice took them.

"I give it to you." Alice said. "Treat it well. Treat them well."

The Queen sat up and regarded her subjects. She saw them all for what they were and it troubled her. "I'm so sorry," she said, looking at the White Rabbit, the Hatter, the bleeding denizens of Horrorland. "I'm—"

She paused, and a chuckle of sinister mirth echoed in her head.

"HeeHEe!"

"Alice." The Queen turned, shock upon her features. "Look at you."

Though the Queen had flowered and blossomed, Alice had withered. Her face had grown sallow, her eyes sinking into dark sockets. What had once been the face and glow of youth had transformed. Alice was a shade of her former self, gray and terrible.

"I'm fine."

But, the Queen could hear her own heartbeat now. And as it thumped within her chest she heard the name that echoed.

"Alice, Alice full of malice!" the Cat called. Though no one could see it, the Queen of Hearts had. The Cheshire Cat bounded behind them, a cloud of purple smog that hovered about the young girl's head. He disappeared within the hole in her chest.

"Al-ice! Al-ice! AL-ICE! HEeHeE!"

"No!" The Queen rushed forward, arms extended. "You can't! I must return it. You must take it back Alice!"

Alice had fallen backwards as the Rabbit grasped the Queen's shoulders. A look of wonder was on his face as he tried to calm her.

"But she gave it to you, your majesty. So Horrorland may be great again!"

"I don't deserve it!" The Queen of Hearts lunged

forward as Alice crawled backwards. The young girl's eyes were drawn to the Rabbit's mask. "Alice needs it. It's hers. Give it back to her!" Tears were running down the Queen's face. "She can't give it to me! It's too late for me! Too late!"

Alice bit her lip. She could see the anguish on the Queen's face and it gladdened her. It really had worked. The Queen could feel again. She could regret and love, and as she struggled against the White Rabbit's grip upon her shoulders, Alice shook her head, proud to know that she had been the one who had brought back the Queen's compassion.

"I gave it to you," Alice said, standing, like all the others oblivious to the cerulean eye winking wickedly out the hole in her chest. "Please cherish it." And snapping forward like a viper, Alice stole the Rabbit's mask, donning it herself as she transformed into a white rabbit and began to run.

"No!" the Queen wailed behind her. "You don't understand! Horrorland will never change if we don't return her heart! Stop, Alice!"

But Alice was deaf to her calls. Like the wind she maneuvered between the crowd, her eyes as swift as her legs. She heard the people exclaim as she went, could hear the Rabbit calling to her, but Alice knew that in order for her gift to be received she had to quit Horrorland for good.

"I can grant you a boat."

"Cat!" She hadn't expected him to be there, but as she ran she heard him like a bell within her head. "Please help me. It will never be wonderful if the Queen returns my heart."

The Cheshire Cat laughed within her head. "Never, never," he agreed.

Alice ran through the Butcher Briers, past Midwife Trees and the burrowing imps in the Cemetery of

Scares. Her blue eyes danced along the locusts as they swarmed the floating boat and landed it, her rabbit fur wet not with blood but by the cool rain that now poured from the clouds in the sky.

Alice ran through the hills, past the Hatter's castle, the forests, the glowing mushrooms, and the House of Cards where the Duchess and the Tweedle Brothers made their bottles of small and big minded Diminut pills. Only once did she stop, and that was at the corpse of Pillar. Still laying on the forest floor, his wings half eaten by worms and bugs, Alice hopped forward once, then scurried away, afraid that as fast as she was she would still be caught if she loitered too long.

I'm sorry, she thought anyway, remembering his voice and tombstone teeth.

"You've nothing to be sorry for. He tried to kill you."

Yes, but—

"He would have eaten your heart and left Horrorland to suffer beneath the heartless Queen."

Alice felt her feet slow. Brambles and ferns slapped her in the face, making her return slower. But as she went so too did she listen to the Cat whispering in her ear.

"You gave them your heart, Alice. You gave them everything. You will return to London alone."

It's alright.

"Is it?"

Alice wondered what it would be like, after she was gone. As she ran over the gray hillscapes towards the keyhole door, she wondered what color and life the Queen would bring to Horrorland.

But she would never know, and for a moment the thought made her angry.

No, she thought, pausing at the gate and turning. The clouds that had strangled the sky before were gone, and in the distance she was sure she saw the floating laboratory. Her long rabbit ears listened, could hear the howl of the wind. But even now Horrorland had brightened, and as the dawn began to fill the sky Alice felt a chill sweep in her bones, ruffling her fur.

"Will I be alright, Cat?"

She hadn't seen him, but she could feel him all around her, smiling his Cheshire smile.

"Someday, *hee!*"

Alice turned, hopping in through the keyhole door. Though she had expected to see the Hacksaw and the dead boar man, none of them were inside. Instead, she found herself within a sewer.

No longer a rabbit, but a girl wearing a mask, Alice turned on her heel, regarding the wall behind her.

"Cat?" she called, hearing a gong and crack in the distance.

Looking about, she noticed a ladder climbing up towards the city streets. Removing her mask, catching the string on the small top hat upon her head, Alice climbed slowly as the clock made a dreadful noise and stopped.

"Rabbit?" she called, noticing a pair of white rabbit ears poking out in the open space of the manhole. Alice climbed faster, being careful not to fall, but when she reached the surface and climbed out, back into London, all that was there was a dead bunny, run over in the road.

She bent down, taking the corpse in her hands. Its fur was white, though dirty and yellowed by the light of the streetlamps.

Looking up, Alice was calm as she stared into the dreary London night. The moon above that once shined like a pearl seemed like nothing but a void in the sky now. No longer was there any pretence of men or women in the moon. It was only empty, a white rock dangling precariously above the earth like a guillotine.

Alice stood, not knowing where to go. She could see Big Ben in front of her. A minute to midnight, its face read. But something was wrong. Something seemed broken.

Alice touched her chest, feeling the hole where her heart used to be.

Nothing seemed to matter anymore.

She pictured herself in the aftertime, as a grown woman; and how she would keep, through all her riper years, the simple heart of her childhood, now only within her memory.

Alice stared into the dark and dismal London skyline, at the broken face of Big Ben. She thought about how she would gather all her future children, and make their eyes bright and eager with many a strange tale of Horrorland. She would feel all their simple sorrows, their fears, remembering her own adventures, and the sad summer days of childhood.

"They'll remember," she said aloud. She walked down the London street with the Rabbit's mask and Hatter's hat. Above her a one eyed cat chuckled amidst the smog.

"*I'll* remember how sweetly your heart beats your name. *HeeheE!*" It cackled, dissolving into cloud and dust. "Even when *you* cannot recall, your *Majesty*."

END

A life-long lover of horror, Vanessa wrote her first story in the genre when she was only in grade five. It was titled *Mutilated* and it warranted her a trip to the school guidance counselor. A lifetime later, she continues to write about anything gruesome, terrifying, paranormal and erotic, though she has since found herself enthralled in the world of fantasy steampunk. Her first two books *Gloryhill* and *A Sinister Portrait of Cherie Rose* exemplify her fascination with the weird.

Currently she is partying it up in St. George, NB with her husband Brendon and a dog she really wants but hasn't gotten yet.

Bibliography
"A Happy Ending" published by The Bookends Review
"Gloryhill" Self Published by Friesen Press
"Body or Soul: Musings of a Killer" Published in the *"Peripheral Portraits"* Anthology through the Busan Writing Group

"A Sinister Portrait of Cherie Rose" Self Published through Createspace
"The Princess" Published in the "Graveyard Girls"

Anthology through HellBound Books Publishing
To be Released this fall: *"The Curious Case of Simon Todd"* Published through Books We Love Publishing

Facebook:
https://www.facebook.com/vanessa.brown.587

Other HellBound Books Titles
Available at: www.hellboundbookspublishing.com

Road Kill

Everything is bigger in Texas - including the horror!

A Piney woods meth dealer clones Adolph Hitler. A nightmare exorcist meets an inexorable fined. An eyeball collector gets collected. The apparition of a lynching victim tracks down his executioners. A Texas lawman is undone by shades of his past. A Baphomet recruits converts as a local summer camp. The tales of the baker's dozen who appear in this anthology demonstrate why everything is scarier in Texas…

Including tales of terror from

Jeremy Hepler
Madison Estes
Bret McCormick
James H Longmore
ER Bills
Shawana Borman

And many more...

<u>Graveyard Girls</u>

Female authors + Horror = something spectacularly terrifying!

A delicious collection of horrific tales and darkest poetry from the cream of the crop, all lovingly compiled by the incomparable Gerri R Gray! Nestling between the covers of this formidable tome are twenty-five of the very best lady authors writing on the horror scene today!

These tales of terror are guaranteed to chill your very soul and awaken you in the dead of the night with fear-sweat clinging to your every pore and your heart pounding hard and heavy in your labored breast…

Featuring superlative horror from: Xtina Marie, M. W. Brown, Rebecca Kolodziej, Anya Lee, Barbara Jacobson, Gerri R. Gray, Christina Bergling, Julia Benally, Olga Werby, Kelly Glover, Lee Franklin, Linda M. Crate, Vanessa Hawkins, P. Alanna Roethle, J Snow, Evelyn Eve, Serena Daniels, S. E. Davis, Sam Hill, J. C. Raye, Donna J. W. Munro, R. J. Murray, C. Bailey-Bacchus, Varonica Chaney, Marian Finch (Lady Marian).

Schlock! Horror!

An anthology of short stories based upon/inspired by and in loving homage to all of those great gorefest movies and books of the 1980's (not necessarily base in that era, although some do ride that wave of nostalgia!), the golden age when horror well and truly came kicking, screaming and spraying blood, gore & body parts out from the shadows...

This exemplary 80's themed/inspired tales of terror has been adjudicated and compiled by one Mr Bret McCormick, himself a writer, producer and director of many a schlock classic, including Bio-Tech Warrior, Time Tracers, The Abomination, Ozone: The Attack of the Redneck Mutants and the inimitable Repligator.

Featuring stories from: Todd Sullivan, Timothy C Hobbs, Mark Thomas, Andrew Post, James B. Pepe, Thomas Vaughn, Edward Karpp, Jaap Boekestein, Lisa Alfano, L.C.Holt, John Adam Gosham, Brandon Cracraft, M. Earl Smith, Sarah Cannavo, James Gardner, Bret McCormick, and James H Longmore.

The Children of Hydesville

"A contemporary ghost story made all the more terrifying for being based upon actual events."

When the terrifying entity that Maggie and Katie Fox unleashed in Hydesville in 1848 returns in 2018, a gallery owner, his wife, a journalist and her boyfriend join forces to battle it.

Manhattanites Derek David and his wife Edith receive an invitation to visit the Keilgarden Colony. Founded in 1948 with funds from Derek's great grandfather, the Colony is a secluded community dedicated to nurturing children with psychic abilities. Located five hours north of the city in the village of Hydesville, the compound was built on land that includes the cottage where Maggie and Katie Fox first heard the ghostly rappings in 1848 which started the Spiritualist movement.

The Southern House

There are some places that lie where the barrier between worlds is thin and growing thinner. These corridors are as old as the Earth itself, hidden in dark and forgotten places, waiting to be found. There is a being who stalks these places and travels between those worlds. He was given the name Mr. Shift by generations of children and madmen.

Just as Hickory Grimble hits rock bottom, he inherits his grandparents' farm and believes his luck is changing. He soon finds he inherited more than money and land.

Haunted by his own inner demons, now he has new problems. He begins to see strange creatures on the dark, sprawling acreage, animals that have no business living in middle Tennessee. He also discovers a decrepit, abandoned house in the forest that never seems to be in the same place twice.

Balanced on a razor's edge between, addiction and fate, Hick is now face to face with an ancient evil that has returned once more to claim more of the town's children.

HellBound Books Publishing

**A HellBound Books LLC
Publication**

http://www.hellboundbookspublishing.com

Printed in the United States of America

www.ingramcontent.com/pod-product-compliance
Lightning Source LLC
Chambersburg PA
CBHW050608170726
48283CB00001B/161